Also by Margot Livesey

Learning by Heart

Homework

Criminals

The Missing World

Eva Moves the Furniture

Additional Acclaim for *Banishing Verona*

"In Livesey's deft hands, their connection is as credible (and incredible) as love itself.... [She] pulls it off effortlessly."

—The Boston Globe

"Remarkable... In *Banishing Verona*, [Livesey] weaves a story that has plenty of heft—and that challenges the reader to rethink their own notions about the power of romantic love."   *—People*

"Livesey's sparkling novel is part oddball love story, part suspense tale, about the wondrous and terrifying ways life can change when fear is no longer the master."

—The Miami Herald

"Livesey's winning new book... captures the magic of an unlikely young romance by never subjecting it to too much analysis.... [Her lovers'] longing for each other, tender, mutual, and inexplicable, is this lovely book's powerful underlying chord."

—Entertainment Weekly

"Livesey's finest achievement yet."   *—The Seattle Times*

"Delightful... Livesey's utter faith in her two main characters makes *Banishing Verona* the coziest love story about alienation ever written."   *—Newsday*

"An enthralling novel of desire, deception, and trust."

—O magazine

"Perhaps because she doesn't adhere to any one genre, Livesey has stayed out of the blockbuster bestseller spotlight.... All that may change with *Banishing Verona,* a suspenseful, satisfying, lovely story.... One of Livesey's greatest gifts is a quiet, lyrical authority that makes it easy for her readers to follow her anywhere, and believe in the journey every step of the way."

—*Elle* magazine

"Anyone who picks up *Banishing Verona* will be dazzled by Livesey's ability to plumb the depths of the terrain she knows best—the inner workings of the human heart."

—*Boston* magazine

"[Livesey's] great gift is for concrete, tactile detail. Characters' appearances are rendered with startling vividness.... And Livesey has a wonderful way with evocations of atmosphere and states of mind."   —*The New York Times Book Review*

Banishing Verona

Margot Livesey

Picador
Henry Holt and Company | New York

www.picadorusa.com

Picador® is a U.S. registered trademark and is used by Henry Holt and Company under license from Pan Books Limited.

For information on Picador Reading Group Guides, as well as ordering, please contact Picador.
Phone: 646-307-5626
Fax: 212-253-9627
E-mail: readinggroupguides@picadorusa.com

A version of Chapter 1 appeared in a slightly different form in *The New Yorker*.

Library of Congress Cataloging-in-Publication Data

Livesey, Margot.
    Banishing Verona : a novel / Margot Livesey.
        p.   cm.
    ISBN 0-312-42520-1
    EAN 978-0-312-42520-3
    1. Women broadcasters—Fiction.   2. Problem families—Fiction.   3. Pregnant women—Fiction.   4. London (England)—Fiction.   5. Boston (Mass.)—Fiction.
    6. Carpenters—Fiction.   I. Title.

PR9199.3.L563B36   2004
813'.54—dc22

                                                                    2004052383

First published in the United States by Henry Holt and Company

First Picador Edition: September 2005

10   9   8   7   6   5   4   3   2   1

For Susan Brison

Banishing Verona

Zeke

1

He had replaced five lightbulbs that day and by late afternoon could not help anticipating the soft *ping* of the filament flying apart whenever he reached for a switch. The third time, the fixture in the hall, the thought zigzagged across his mind that these little explosions were a sign, like the two dogs he had come across in the autumn, greyhound and bulldog, locked together on the grassy slope of the local park. He had given them a wide berth; still, he had felt responsible when on the bus next day a man turned puce and fell to the floor. By the fifth bulb, though, he had relinquished superstition and was blaming London Electricity. Some irregularity in the current, some unexpected surge, was slaughtering the bulbs. He pictured a man at head office filling his idle minutes by pulling a lever. Meanwhile, hour by hour he emptied the upstairs rooms, slipping the bulbs from bedside lights and desk lamps.

He had just replaced the fifth bulb when the doorbell rang. Often, if he were up a ladder, Zeke didn't bother to answer the knocks and rings of late afternoon; the owners of the house, the Barrows, were away and the callers were never for him. But now the pallor of the sky, the flashes of light and dark, the weariness of working alone, all conspired to make even the prospect of rebuffing a smartly dressed double-glazing salesman, or a disheveled collector for Oxfam, a pleasure. Last Friday, in a similar mood, he had found a boy on the doorstep, thin as a junkie, pretending to be blind. He had the dark glasses, the cane, the fluttery stuff with the hands. You're a painter, he had said, sniffing slightly. Zeke had given him fifty pence. Later he had looked out of the window and seen the boy sitting on a wall, reading a newspaper.

He set aside the wallpaper steamer and went to open the front door. On the doorstep a woman, minus collecting tin or clipboard, filled his vision. He hadn't replaced the hall bulb yet, and in the dim light her features took a moment to assemble. He made out abrupt dark eyebrows above a substantial nose and plump, glistening lips—the opposite of pretty.

Briefly, Zeke was baffled. Then he went through the steps he'd learned from the poster he'd been given at the clinic. Eyes wide, a glimpse of teeth, corners of the mouth turning up rather than down—usually these indicated a smile, which could, he knew, mean anger but often meant the opposite. Yes, she was smiling, although not necessarily for him. Her expression had clearly been prepared in advance, but he admired the way she held her face steady at the sight of him, and of his work clothes. His jeans and shirt were so paint-spattered as to be almost a separate entity.

"Good afternoon." She stretched out a hand and, seeing his, white with plaster, faltered, neither withdrawing nor completing the gesture.

"Hi," he said, hating the single stupid syllable. She was tall for a woman, his height save for the step, and dimly familiar, though not as herself. As she began to speak, he realized who she reminded him of: the bust of Beethoven on his father's piano, something about the expansiveness of her features, the way her tawny hair sprang back from her forehead.

"I'm the Barrows' niece," she said.

In the cold air her breath streamed toward him, feathery plumes, carrying more words, perhaps an entire sentence, which Zeke lost as he took in the little beads of moisture on her upper lip.

When her mouth stopped moving he said, "I'm Zeke, the painter. The Barrows are away."

"But they told you I was coming," she said, with no hint of a question. He was still wondering—had they or hadn't they?—when she stooped, and he saw that she was not alone. Before he could offer to help she swept past him, a suitcase in each hand. He turned from closing the door to find she had set the cases at the foot of the stairs and was standing in the doorway, surveying the living room. Under the influence of her attention, Zeke saw again what his work had revealed: the ragged plaster painted not a single color but in pale bands of blue and brown, gray and yellow, the work of some artist he couldn't name. In the middle of the floor, like an ungainly prehistoric animal, squatted the furniture, piled up and draped in dust sheets.

"Cool," she said. "You could do a mural, hunting and fishing, golfing and shopping."

"I don't think your aunt and uncle—" Then he caught himself: humor. That had always been tricky for him. Even a question about a hen crossing the road could make him pause. "I told them it was a big job. You never know what you'll find underneath the paper. And Emmanuel, the guy who helps me, did his back in."

"How?" she said.

"What?"

"How"—she patted the small of her own back—"did he hurt his back?"

"Reaching for a corner, he claims. Snooker, not painting." In the bare space their voices emerged as if they were on a stage. Hers was unusually deep, warm, and melodious. It made him think of the chiming of his favorite clock. As for his, Zeke wasn't sure. He had read that humans hear their own voices through the jaw rather than the air; every time a tooth is lost or filled, the timbre changes.

"When are my aunt and uncle due back?"

"This Saturday, they told me."

She moved her head up and down and finally took off her coat.

He had noticed earlier, returning from even a quick trip to the corner shop, how the emptiness of the room made it seem as if the cold had followed him indoors; in fact, the heating was on full blast (not his bill), and the house was snug as a tea cozy. She retreated to sling her coat over the banister and advanced into the room in the same greedy way she'd entered the house, her dark-green dress swaying as she walked. In the bay she turned, and he saw, silhouetted against the window, her belly.

"Don't," she said, "let me interrupt your work."

A sentence appeared in Zeke's head: I'd like to tie you to the bed. How did that get there, inside his brain, about this woman? He had never done, or even considered doing, such a thing. "I won't," he said.

He was no longer certain she was ugly, only that he wanted to keep looking to make sure. But in the empty room he did not dare. This must be why people had furniture, not just for comfort but, like clothing, for camouflage. While he stood rooted beside his worktable, puzzling over these aberrant thoughts, she wandered from one spot to the next, talking about the time she had painted her room.

"I was fifteen," she said, circling the fireplace, "when my parents agreed to let me do it. First I wrote on the wall the names of everyone I wanted to get rid of—mother, father, brother, the boy at school who didn't like me—then I slapped on the paint, unfortunately deep purple."

"Did it work?" he asked, imagining all the things he could write.

Her head, her eyes, swung toward him and he had the sense of being seen at last. "Well, it worked for the boy at school, but not"—her eyebrows dashed together—"for my brother."

She walked over to examine the little tower of empty takeaway containers he had made, precariously balanced beside his worktable. Was he collecting them, she asked and, without waiting for an answer, launched into another story. Years ago, when she'd been hitchhiking outside Oxford, a man who sold these containers had picked her up. "I remember it started to pour. The windscreen wipers were going full tilt and suddenly he said do you ever think of killing yourself? His voice was so casual, I thought I'd misunderstood."

Zeke's skin prickled.

"Then he asked if I'd read *Steppenwolf.* I said yes, though to be honest I wasn't sure. It's one of those books that for a while was in the ether. I looked over at this stout middle-aged man, and his eyes were full of tears. I think of it every day, he said. There's always the razor and the knife."

Was she trying to tell him she was upset, he wondered. If so, he needed to confess that he was no good at metaphors and subtexts and other people's problems. But already she was examining a roll of lining paper and asking its purpose. He explained about the old houses of London, how the walls were held up by wood-chip paper. When you removed it, which he'd spent the last three days doing, the only way to get a smooth finish was to put on new paper and paint over that.

"Let me make some tea," he concluded, backing out of the room. In the kitchen, he hovered beside the dormant kettle and, to his own stupefaction, imagined telling her the story of his breakdown. Surely she would listen to him like she had the container salesman. Don't, he admonished. You only met her fifteen minutes ago. Even people he had known for years tended to back away when he mentioned his difficulties. As the kettle rumbled to a boil he heard a thud from the hall, followed by another. Her stockinged feet appeared in the doorway, and he understood not only the noises he'd just heard but those that came most nights through his bedroom ceiling: one shoe, two shoe.

"Which side are you on?" he said, offering a mug of tea.

"Roundheads or cavaliers? Arsenal or Chelsea? Flat earth or solar system?"

"Mr. or Mrs. Barrow. Whose niece are you?"

"Mister's, can't you tell?" She turned and, heels striking the floor, carried her tea upstairs.

Alone with his own tea, Zeke thought, I am profoundly boring. He searched high and low in the rooms of his brain, checking the long front hall, the living room, the dining room, the narrow stairs, and couldn't find a trace of disagreement.

Normally he quit at five, but today he kept pressing spackle into even the smallest cracks until close to six-thirty. Then, in the face of an unbroken silence from above, he admitted defeat. He tidied his tools, washed his hands, and called the news of his departure, wanly, up the stairs.

"Wait." There she was on the landing. "Are you coming to-morrow? When?"

Her tawny hair was sticking up like a cockatoo's crest. "I aim for eight," he told her. "Not to worry. I can let myself in."

"I need keys." She swam down the stairs into the light, stopping on the last one, hand outstretched. He should have guessed then from the way her hazel eyes fastened on his that something was awry, either she wasn't on good terms with her aunt and uncle or Ms. F—weren't all fetuses female at first?—was a problematic guest, but the warmth of her breath, the lilt of her perfume, expunged rational thought. Helpless, he laid the keys in her palm.

"Will you be up to let me in?" he said. One cheek, her left, bore the crease of a pillow.

"Up with the lark, up with the milkman."

"Are you all right?" he found himself asking.

"Probably," she said. And then—surely all the buses of London rose an inch into the air—she leaned forward and pressed her lips, gently, to his.

The next morning Zeke rang the bell, knocked, tried the knob. The door stayed shut, the windows dark. Feeling like a dolt, he even bent down and called through the letter box. By the end of five minutes, he was holding on to himself, a kite on a gusty day. He fished around in his pockets, his bag, and was rewarded with a vision of his mobile phone in the pocket of his other jacket. As he walked around the corner, he counted the cigarette butts in the gutter—some crushed, some not—to keep himself from floating away. Seven, eight, eleven. Twice he had to stop and retrace his steps to make sure he hadn't missed one. Look down, he thought, not up. In the forecourt of the underground station, he saw a free phone and, trying not to think of all the hands, the mouths, that had passed this way, dialed the Barrows' number. The answering machine clicked on with a brief nasal message. She's stepped out for a paper, he told himself; she's taking a bath. Walking back, he forgot about the cigarettes and placed his feet securely in the middle of each paving stone.

At the house, nothing had changed. He knocked, rang, shouted again, before climbing in through the living room window. He had opened it the day before while using the steamer and, in the excitement of her arrival, neglected his usual security measures. Now the ease with which the sash slid up made him feel stricken. He had left her at the mercy of any passing vandal.

Inside he began to tiptoe toward the hall; then, reconsidering, attempted his normal stride. "Hello. Anyone home?"

He switched things on: kettle, radio, lights. Even the man at London Electricity had forgotten him. Everything worked perfectly. He made the obligatory cup of tea and set to work, but after ten minutes of sanding he couldn't stand it. The awful possibility—she was gone—leaped into his head and ricocheted around. He laid the sandpaper aside and, wiping his powdery hands on his jeans, climbed the stairs.

He had reconnoitered the first day he had the house to himself, as he always did, flitting through bedrooms, checking wardrobes and cupboards and the dark spaces beneath desks and tables. He wasn't snooping for kinky underwear or exotic substances but rather—it was the way he coped with strange houses—looking for a hiding place. Sometimes, when he felt particularly shaky, he even stored provisions there: a bottle of water, a packet of biscuits. Here at the Barrows', he'd chosen the pedestal desk in the study. With his knees drawn up, the wooden U was an almost perfect fit. Now he moved from one lightbulbless room to another. In the master bedroom the tattered floral wallpaper made his teeth ache. Then the study, his hiding place, surrounded by machines: computer, printer, fax, even a photocopier. Last, the spare room, distinguished by the boxes stacked along the wall and the miscellaneous furniture.

Had he ever been so glad to see a suitcase? The larger of the two lay open at the foot of the bed, revealing a tumble of garments, red, purple, white, blue; the smaller, still closed, stood by the window with a red sticker proclaiming FRAGILE. Neither, unfortunately, had a label with her name. He stepped over to the bed and knelt to bury his face in the pillow. Here she was, and here.

The scrape of a door hurled him to his feet. The last thing he wanted was to be caught mooning over a pillow. "Hello," he called, starting down the stairs.

She was in the hall, her cheeks glowing, her hair darker than the day before, bearing the marks of a comb. "I went to get us fried-egg sandwiches." She flourished a paper bag.

Us, he thought. "Thank you," he said, and explained, though she didn't seem concerned, that he had broken in. In the kitchen he set out plates, salt and pepper, sheets of paper towel. He had had his usual bowl of cereal only an hour ago; now, following her example, he ate ravenously. She was wearing a faded blue sweatshirt, the sleeves rolled up as if it had once belonged to someone else, the hem stretched tight over her belly. How far along was she, he wondered, trying to recall various friends. Six months, maybe seven. Watching her raise the bread to pepper the egg, he realized he had dreamed about her the night before.

Only a fragment remained, her winching a metal bucket, brimming with water, out of a well. But before he could tell her, she was talking again. One spring, apparently, she had worked as a cleaner in an office building and had eaten a fried-egg sandwich every day. From the way she spoke, he understood that this was not her present occupation.

"So what are we doing today?" she said, wiping her hands on the paper towel. "Putting up lining paper?"

He began to stammer. He was making good progress. Besides, her aunt and uncle were paying him a fair wage.

"But you must need help," she said, "and I need something to take my mind off things."

At the time he assumed a covert reference to her pregnancy. Later, when he scrutinized her every utterance, it became one of those mysterious manhole covers, briefly raised over the dark river of secrecy. Meanwhile, before he could urge further objections—the dust, the fumes—she had spotted a pair of coveralls hanging on the back door, and the next thing he knew she had scrambled into them and was demonstrating how well they fit; her belly split the front like a chestnut its shell. "Come on," she said. "I bet you're paid by the job, not the hour."

At first he was embarrassed telling a woman, older he guessed by perhaps a decade, what to do, but she turned out to be much more biddable than Emmanuel. As they finished the sanding, he on the ladder, she on foot, she lobbed questions in his direction. Despite her careless manner, he sensed that she was in fact listening to whatever he chose to answer. Whereas the doctors, without exception, as soon as he opened his mouth, had focused on pencil sharpeners, radiators, doorknobs. They were paid—not enough, not by him—to barely feign attention, scribble a couple of notes, and finally write a prescription that would propel him, thank God, out of their offices. But this woman with her fierce brow, her chapped knuckles, for whatever reason actually seemed interested.

"So." She folded sandpaper onto the sanding block. "How did you become a painter? Is it the family business, or your heart's desire?"

"Neither." In the hope of asking about her, he offered himself. "My father was a greengrocer in Brighton. He got up at four every day except Sunday to go to market. Then he worked until seven at night, keeping the shop stocked, dealing with customers."

"Brighton is nice. Did you live near the sea?"

"If I stood on my bed on tiptoe, there was a little triangle of water." He had done this precisely once, dismayed at what his maneuver had revealed. Now he climbed down the ladder, moved it four feet, climbed back up, and started on the next stretch of cornice.

"I used to think," she said, "life would make sense if I could see the sea every day."

"Not for me." He brushed away a cobweb. "A street makes sense, a house makes sense, but the sea just goes on and on: wave, wave, wave. I couldn't wait to get away. We moved when I was ten." In London, Highbury, his parents had a new shop, bigger and busier. "I used to help in the evenings, on Saturdays, stocking the bins, fetching and carrying. Then one day one of our regulars, Mrs. Oma, said when you're the boss and suddenly I realized what my father was preparing me for. I started to pay attention in school, do my homework. It drove him mad. 'Do you want to be a dreamer all your life,' he used to say, 'head stuck in a book?'"

"Careful," she said.

Beneath his savage gestures the ladder swayed like a sapling.

Over fresh sandpaper he admitted he had studied accounting at university. "I wanted to do anthropology—I'd read this book about the rain-forest tribes of Papua, New Guinea—but I didn't have the nerve. I needed to know I was heading toward a job." She didn't ask the obvious question, and, as he finished the upper half of the wall, this enabled him to venture into that territory he'd imagined while making tea the previous afternoon. "The day after my final exams I couldn't leave the house. The people I shared with had all gone away, and I'd been looking forward to having the place to myself. But as soon as I stepped outside I worried that I'd left the gas on or the iron or the lights or I hadn't locked the door or I hadn't locked the window or I hadn't flushed the toilet or my mother was trying to phone. It didn't matter how often I checked, it didn't matter if I wrote down that I'd checked, I'd reach the street and have to go back. Remember in *Gulliver's*

Travels when the Lilliputians tie him down? It was like that. Hundreds of strands of anxiety tugging at me. Soon it was easier not to try to get away."

"That sounds horrid," she said.

He set the ladder aside and began to cut the lining paper. She was still listening, he could tell from the angle of her head, and to the accompaniment of the scissors' muttering blades he finished his story. "When I got better I knew I couldn't be an accountant. I like numbers, the way they can't be two things at once, but I couldn't cope with the people on the other end of them. One of our neighbors did odd jobs and I started helping him. Phil is different. Not like me," he added hastily. A strip of paper released from the roll fell to the floor. "Words take longer to get from one part of his brain to another, like running in sand, but they always arrive. I felt okay with him and gradually—he wanted to be a piano tuner—I took over the business."

"Your dad must have gone nuts."

A hot, dry wind blew through the room. Zeke dropped the scissors. "Break," he said.

He started to ask her questions, the same ones she'd asked him, where she grew up, what her mum and dad did. After all these hours it was too late to ask her name. Other topics too, he sensed—her presence here, Ms. F's father—would be unwelcome. She told him she'd grown up near York. Her father had managed a golf course and then bluffed his way into teaching at a private school. His only qualification was being able to talk the hind legs off a donkey. Her mother, after years as a bored housewife, had opened a junk shop. "She'd invent the most amazing histories for her goods: this was Marie Antoinette's hot water bottle, this was Hitler's fountain pen. I take after both of them."

"Do you mean that?" Zeke said.

She looked up from the paper she was spreading with paste, her eyes narrowing as if to distinguish some distant landmark. "Yes and no. I grew up determined to be as different from them as possible, but since they died a few years ago sometimes I'll catch myself tying my shoelaces in the same fussy way my mother did. Or overtipping in a restaurant just so no one will think I'm my father's daughter."

"I'm sorry they're dead," he said.

She dipped the brush in the paste and drew it steadily across the paper. "I studied English at university. That's almost as useless as anthropology."

At lunchtime she opened a tin of tomato soup and he shared the ham sandwiches he'd brought. They worked on through the darkening afternoon. Oughtn't she to take a rest, he wondered, but now that they were putting up the lining paper she seemed determined to finish. She shrugged off his suggestion that they wait until tomorrow. The streetlights came on, buzzy amber splodges; in the houses opposite, curtains were drawn. He bungled the last piece of paper, a tricky corner, then bungled it again. "If at first you don't succeed," she chanted from the foot of the ladder, "try, try, and try again. My English teacher used to say that all the time."

While he mounted the ladder once more she described Robert the Bruce, a rebel leader hiding in a cave on some Scottish mountain, drawing inspiration from the arachnid's repeated efforts to anchor its web. Zeke smoothed the top of the paper into place and, slowly descending, pressed the seams together.

Now what, he thought, glancing around the bare room. Dismissal?

"Maybe you could make a fire," she said, "while I see if there's anything for supper?"

"A fire?" For a moment he saw himself soaking the dust sheets with petrol, the flames leaping at the pile of furniture, but then she pointed at the fireplace, the grate messy with cinders. She left the room and he knelt to roll newspapers, add kindling, firelighters, and coal, tasks he hadn't performed since leaving his drafty house at university. When he came into the kitchen, she was at the stove, stirring a saucepan. "Frozen lasagna," she announced. "Tinned spinach, fresh carrots. There's beer in the cupboard under the stairs."

"Thanks. I think I'll have some juice."

"Don't you drink?"

"Not often. It makes me..." He hesitated between *weird* and *stupid*.

Presumably he chose the latter, because she said, "Not so stupid you don't know it." She reached for a glass and he saw the golden-brown liquid topped with froth. Stop, he wanted to say. Ms. F doesn't deserve to start life with a hangover. But before he could think of a polite way, or indeed any way, to voice his concern she was shouting, "Christ!"

He watched, bewildered, as she grabbed the saucepan and began to bang it against the stove.

And then he was in the hall. He had seen her full mouth stretched wide, her eyes glinting, not gestures that had appeared on his poster but, combined with the shouting, fairly unequivocal. In the living room he bent to tend the fire, fighting the desire to climb out of the window and never come back. The first flare of the firelighter had died down and the coals were glowing dully when he heard her footsteps. Fourteen steps carried her into his presence.

"Sorry. I got a little carried away."

He could feel her standing behind him. Don't touch me, he thought.

Do.

"I take my cooking seriously," she said, "even when it is just tins. What makes you angry?"

You drinking beer, Emmanuel being a wanker, my life. Using the tongs, he moved a knob of coal an inch to the right, an inch to the left.

"If I promise to be quiet will you come back and keep me company?"

She walked away, not waiting for an answer, and he thought of all the tiny motions, the vertebrae sliding against each other, the hip joints swiveling in their sockets, the tarsals and metatarsals flexing and straightening, that make up departure. Yet the most essential motion, the one that couldn't be named or diagrammed, was what spilled a mood into a room. How he knew, with absolute certainty, that she wasn't taking his answer for granted, in either direction, but leaving him alone to figure it out.

Follow, said the fire, and he did.

As he sat back down at the kitchen table, she was peering into the oven. "Is there a reason," she said, directing her words to the lasagna, "for upstairs to be plunged in Stygian gloom?"

He told her about the five lightbulbs of the day before.

"Interesting." She closed the oven door and turned to face him. "I'm usually all right with appliances, but I can't wear a watch for more than a few days before it goes haywire. It's happened four times now."

"Why?" he said, fascinated.

She moved her shoulders up and down. "Who knows? The watchmaker I went to had some mad theory about personal electricity."

They ate off a card table in front of the fire in the freshly papered room. In the light of the candles the ladder cast a hangman's shadow and the pile of furniture loomed. They talked about computers, and whether a person could ever really disappear, and if life was better in Papua, New Guinea. She told a story about her grandfather, who had fought in the First World War and come home to start a railway. As she finished, the phone began to ring in the kitchen and upstairs. They both sat silently until it stopped. At last she spoke about herself but almost, Zeke noticed, as if she were talking about another person. Well, that was something he understood. He often felt as if the events in his life, the things people claimed he'd said and done, were really part of a stranger's story.

"Once, years ago, I had a friend called Marian. She was the opposite of me: tiny, ferocious, funny, incredibly well-organized.

We shared an office at my first real job, and four or five nights a week after work we'd go out for a drink. We couldn't get enough of each other's company."

But when she'd been promoted and Marian hadn't their friendship had dwindled. "She would phone and write, but I was always too busy to get together. We'd meet every two or three months. Then one night she phoned around eleven. She said she had the flu. She kept talking about a cat she'd had as a child. 'I'm worried about Pushkin,' she kept saying. 'I'm worried I forgot to feed him.' I promised to come round first thing in the morning. When I got there at nine-thirty, the ambulance was already parked outside."

He watched her lips, her eyes, her cheeks, the muscles of her throat and forehead, and fewer and fewer of her words reached him. But when her story was done, the candles guttering, the fire dying, her face wore an expression he understood. He reached across the table and took her hand in his. "You did what you could. You don't expect people to die of the flu, not young healthy people." As he squeezed her palm against his own, her face changed, the light in her eyes leaping and fading. Had he been too bold? No, the candles were the culprits. Together they snuffed the flames.

She led him up the stairs. "Help me," she said, presenting the coveralls. Soon she was naked, ample and unabashed. Can this be happening, Zeke thought. Then she was pulling back the covers and he was lost.

When he found himself again, minutes or hours later, basking in the warmth of her proximity, he began to talk about his clocks. "I buy them from jumble sales and junk shops and repair them. I have nine up and ticking, though two are still erratic."

"Do you know about the clock in Prague, in the Old Town Square?"

"Tell me."

A famous clockmaker had made it for the king. When it was finished and everyone had agreed it was a masterpiece, the king ordered his soldiers to blind the clockmaker so that his clock could never be surpassed. For years the blind man lived on the king's charity in a cottage below the castle. At last, on his deathbed, he asked to be carried into the presence of his masterpiece. He passed his hands over the mechanism, and the clock was silent for two hundred years.

"You mean"—Zeke stared up into the darkness—"he did something to the springs?"

"I suppose."

"But how could he bear to?"

She kissed his shoulder. "Revenge," she said. "How else can we rewrite the past?"

He kissed her back. "I can't answer that right now, but I will eventually."

As her breathing grew louder and slower, he felt his anxieties gathering. He tried to calm himself by counting the parts of their bodies that were touching, the parts he still had to touch. He counted her breaths, his own, the cars passing in the street outside until at last he realized the situation was hopeless. "I have to go home," he said.

"Must you?"

No, he thought, not if you'll talk to me all night long in that drowsy voice. "I'm sorry. It's not you. I just can't handle strange houses, strange beds." He touched her cheek. "But I can learn."

The next morning Zeke knocked only once before setting aside the fried-egg sandwiches—he'd chosen brown bread in an effort to offset last night's beer—and sliding the blade of his penknife under the catch of the side window. He left the bag of sandwiches on the kitchen table and climbed the stairs, hoping to find her still in bed, warm and sleepy, hoping to slip in beside her. And this time, he thought, however stupid, however embarrassing, he would ask her name.

The bed was unmade, empty and cold to the touch, the suitcases gone. At the foot of the bed the rug was rolled up, and spread-eagled on the bare wooden boards lay the coveralls, neatly buttoned, arms and legs stretched wide, like an empty person. Only when he knelt to pick them up did Zeke discover the three-inch nails that skewered the collar, pinned the cuffs and ankles to the floor.

2

His first thought was that she had been taken by force, kidnapped, stolen, but when he returned downstairs he saw the keys lying on the kitchen table. In his distraction he had not noticed them as he set down the sandwiches, nor the sheet of paper with a single line written in pencil: *Thursday, 7 A.M. Thanks for everything. I'll be in touch soon.* So then he had to consider the other dreadful possibility: he had driven her to flight. Somehow he had misunderstood when she led him upstairs. His attentions—such a cool word for the exquisite shock of flesh on flesh—had been unwelcome. If that were the case, though, why had she reached into her suitcase and, after some searching, produced a pack of condoms? Well, not his attentions but something in the aftermath, some inadvertent comment or gesture. He went over and over what he recalled of their exchanges as they lay side by side, touching at ankle, thigh, elbow, shoulder. Still nothing came to mind. She had kissed him when he got up to leave and said see you tomorrow. Perhaps there was a third alternative: an emergency had arisen not for her but demanding her immediate presence—a friend or family member in trouble—which had made her rush off without so much as a proper note. Even as he labored over the explanation, meticulously fitting the cogs and springs together, oiling the movement and tightening the tiny screws, the image of the coveralls, nailed to the floor, hovered on the edge of his vision.

He could not have said how long he sat at the table before he had his first truly consoling thought. She was the Barrows' niece. When they returned from Latvia, all would become clear. With this in mind he was able, at last, to open the paper bag and eat one of the sandwiches, now cold and limp. The other he kept, just in case. Soon, she had said.

He didn't turn on the radio, he didn't go out for lunch, he left the bathroom door ajar and refrained from using power tools, but no one rang the doorbell and the only phone call, on either his answering machine at home or his mobile, came from his mother, who had already left several brief imperious messages. He worked until his usual time and left a note fastened to the stepladder: *Thursday, 5 P.M. I'll be back first thing tomorrow.* After some hesitation he used both locks on the front door; he still had responsibilities to her aunt and uncle. He was loading the wallpaper steamer into his van when he heard a distinctive tapping sound. The fake blind boy was making his way along the sidewalk. Forgetting his fraud, Zeke stared openly.

"Alms, give me alms for the love of God," croaked the boy, stopping right beside the van and aiming his black sunglasses at Zeke. "How about a pound, man?"

Zeke fished a coin from his pocket. "Do you know where she is?"

"Who?" The boy rapped his cane twice, hard, on the sidewalk as if he were the one demanding answers. Beneath the jagged strands of brown hair, his right ear, Zeke noticed, was missing a V-shaped piece from the lobe.

"The Barrows' niece. She came to the house and helped me and now she's gone."

"How the fuck," said the blind boy, "would I know where anyone is? I don't even know where I am myself." He seized the pound and continued tapping down the street.

———

Zeke could have finished the living room the day she left, he had already painted the woodwork, but he lingered hopefully through the following day, postponing his next job. The Barrows—as he retouched an awkward corner, applied an extra coat to the skirting boards—were the winners. At last, when all his tools were packed, the floors swept, the kitchen cleaned, he gave in and climbed the stairs one more time. He stopped first in the master bedroom and then in the study, delaying as long as possible the moment when he must confront her absence. If only he had stayed here, he would know why she had carried away her suitcases and Ms. F. The coveralls, he felt sure, were a message, but not in any language he could understand. Were they a promise or a threat? Was she saying: wait, I will return? Or help, I am in danger? He had removed them the day before when he couldn't stand the sight of them any longer.

Finally, he entered her room. He had not touched a thing, besides the coveralls, since he found her gone. Now he stood just inside the door, taking in the desolate space. Who could believe that furnishings and objects were inanimate when you saw how, ownerless, they lost their luster? And what of us, he thought, turning on the bedside light where she had reinstalled a bulb. Aren't we too diminished when nothing reflects our spirits? That was how he felt about his clocks; their presence amplified his own. He looked at the chest of drawers, the wardrobe, the chairs, and, last of all, the unmade bed whose wrinkled sheets still held, barely, the shape of her. They miss her, he thought.

He pulled his sweater over his head, unbuttoned his shirt, unzipped his jeans. He folded his clothes neatly on the foot of the bed, and naked, almost shivering, climbed between the sheets. I don't want to rewrite the past, he thought, gazing up at the ceiling. I want to rewrite the present. He rolled over and buried his face in the pillow, breathing in the smells of cold and loneliness. Beneath the pillow, his fingers encountered something unexpected. He drew the book into the light. It was of modest size, maybe nine inches by seven, and bound in soft brown leather, like the books he'd seen in cases at the British Museum. With a little encouragement, it fell open to reveal a page of handwriting.

He stared in surprise. Not a book she was reading but one she was writing. And then, a second surprise, the writing itself. He had expected her script to explode across the page, comparable to the bold manner in which she entered rooms. Instead, the letters marched in small, neat rows from left to right.

He raised his glass. "To Edith, who didn't change." He tipped his head back and drank until the glass was empty. "Did I mention the farmer's daughter," he said, "as sweet a piece of crumpet as ever I squeezed? She made such a racket, I had to put my hand over her mouth."

Quickly he closed the book. None of his business, but all the rooms, all the nooks and corners of his brain, were suddenly filled with sunlight. Her aunt and uncle returned tomorrow, and he had the perfect excuse to see her again. With this thought he slid from the bed, dressed, and straightened the sheets. Let the next guest enjoy the oceanic smudges of their lovemaking. Carrying the book, he made his way downstairs.

He had been home barely long enough to take a shower and change when the doorbell rang. It buzzed, stopped, and buzzed again. He dropped the dish towel he was holding and ran. Absurd, but she had found him once, why not again? He flung wide the hall door, spun down the stairs, opened the front door. For one second, perhaps two, hope persisted. On the doorstep stood a woman wearing a dark jacket, black-and-white checked skirt, sleek boots, and—this seemed crucial—carrying two plastic shopping bags.

"Zeke, I was worried you weren't back yet."

"Mum."

"Gwen," she corrected, as she did over and over.

Deflated, he stared at her china-blue eyes, her pink cheeks. Familiarity, as he'd tried to explain to the most intelligent of the doctors, didn't necessarily make recognition easier, in fact, sometimes the reverse. Whereas a stranger, an elderly man with bushy eyebrows and high coloring, seen once during a freak hailstorm at a bus stop, was instantly recognizable six months later in the queue at the post office.

"No, no," she said, as he reached for the groceries, "I'm balanced."

She was past him and up the stairs in a flash. He stepped out to the curb and, just in case, scanned the dusky street. Only the usual parked cars, dustbins, lampposts, and leafless elms greeted his gaze. Walking among them were those at one end of a lead, on two legs, and those at the other, on four, panting, pulling, peeing. The hour of the dog.

He reached the kitchen in time for Gwen's first volley. When truly aggravated, she sometimes launched her attack before the target was in range, heedless that her missiles fell on empty chairs and tables. "You always did keep the place like a laboratory," she said, flinging a reproachful red-tipped hand toward his shining sink, his unblemished stove. She herself, working all day in the shop, made a virtue out of unwiped counters, unswept floors. "Don't get me wrong," she added. "Nothing the matter with some spit and polish, but at your age you should have better things to do."

"Why didn't you let me know you were coming?"

"Why should I phone when you never answer? I've left all these messages, asking you to call."

Never was an exaggeration, else he wouldn't stay in business, but it was true that his mother's voice emerging from the answering machine seldom prompted him to pick up the receiver. The machine was among his treasured possessions. If only there were a comparable invention to deal with actual people that you could carry around to intercede between you and them, he'd give a year's pay.

He watched as she bent to put a pint of milk in the fridge, her skirt riding up her black-stockinged thighs. Not the sort of thing you ought to notice about your mother, but these days everything was in disarray. Besides, Gwen wanted to be noticed. With her swinging blond hair, her vivid lipstick, she could almost pass for one of the schoolgirls he saw most mornings on his way to work. He had been sixteen before he understood, not through any special insight but a comment of the boy next door—your mum's a knockout—that what he was watching in the shop, day after day, right under his father's nose, was flirtation.

Lovely ripe melons, Gwen would say with a wink. Nice firm cucumber. Everyone, she insisted, can always buy one more thing than they've thought of at home. She would go all out, especially with Roger, the dark-eyed waiter from the local Italian restaurant. She would offer him oranges to sample, mushrooms to inspect. Sorry, he'd say, flaunting a sheet of paper, not on the chef's list. One afternoon when she'd been pushing the pears—Don't you use them in your poofy salads?—and Roger was offering his usual denials, Zeke happened to catch sight of the list. *Cress,* he read, *garlic, fennel, 3 lb. pears.* But before he could remind him, Roger had announced, as if granting a huge favor, that he would take some pears. Later when Zeke told Gwen what he'd seen, she had laughed and said Roger liked making her work.

Now, he knew, she had her own list, which, when it suited her, she would reveal. The last time she'd dropped in like this unexpectedly, with groceries, she had wanted him to do a job, at cost, for her sister. He watched her produce a bunch of parsley, too limp to sell. What if he said he had a prior engagement, or simply bolted? But she rolled over him like fog: inescapable. Sit down, she told him, and he did, a prisoner in his own flat.

"Jersey toms, carrots, onions, a couple of beetroot, a nice cauliflower—they aren't selling, I don't know why—some grannies for your lunch, a lemon."

The other bag held provisions from the supermarket next door, oil, butter, flour—she wasn't taking any chances on his larder—and from the fishmonger across the street. Zeke had to look away when she unwrapped two speckled trout and dangled one toward him.

"Ray recommended them. Straight from the fish farm this morning. He said to let you know he'll be calling soon about his front hall."

"No hurry." With his bulging eyes and minimal chin, Ray bore a strong resemblance to his watery wares; he had always been among Zeke's favorite neighbors.

While she peeled the potatoes, Gwen asked about his customers, the ones who were refusing to pay. "Was there something they wanted you to do over?"

"No, they kept saying how pleased they were."

"So?" Nails flashing, she quartered the potatoes. "What's the problem?"

Zeke described the various stages of nonpayment: they didn't have the cash, they were out when he went round at the agreed time, they claimed the check was in the post. Then he had gone back with Emmanuel. Mrs. Patterson had cracked the door, still on its chain, and at the sight of them tried to close it but Emmanuel, a veteran of such greetings, had already jammed his foot in the gap. He had pounded on the door, screaming, until Zeke finally managed to drag him away. Two days later he had pretended the check had come and paid Emmanuel his share.

"Bastards," said his mother now. "You gave them a written estimate, didn't you?"

He nodded.

She slammed the cauliflower down on the stove. Like the niece, he thought happily. "We'll fix them," Gwen said. "How much do they owe?"

"Four thirty."

"And do they have it?"

"He's a teacher and she works at a hotel. But Mum, we can't just barge in."

She gave him a look that long experience allowed him to recognize as withering. "We won't need to."

A memory, far from reassuring, of his mother marching into his history classroom surfaced. Do you know how many spelling errors there are on this page alone? she had said to Mr. Hoffman, holding out Zeke's essay on the Corn Laws. And your only comment is "good research." More recently, at various clinics, she had let fly at the vague diagnosis: dysfunctional, Asperger's syndrome. He never should have mentioned the Pattersons, but often when Gwen phoned, he found himself casting around for safe topics and, one beleaguered day last week, had offered them up.

Only when they were seated and eating did she say, "You must be wondering to what you owe the honor. Your dad had a little attack last Monday."

Discussing the Pattersons, he had momentarily forgotten the cause of her visit. Now her words conjured midget muggers, schoolboys barely up to his father's waist, rifling his pockets for chewing gum and change. "Did he lose much?"

"Zeke"—her voice spiraled—"your father had a heart attack."

He was on his feet. "Christ, where is he? Is he all right? What are we doing, eating, leaving him alone?"

Gwen took his arm and guided him back to the table. "Sit down. I didn't mean to scare you. I wouldn't be here if he weren't okay. He's in the hospital. You can come and see him when he gets home tomorrow."

"Why didn't you tell me straightaway?" Not the question he meant to ask and one to which, anyway, he guessed the answer: his mother regarded her only son as broken beyond fixing.

"I'm sorry," she said. "As soon as we got him to the hospital it was clear he was going to be fine and I didn't want to leave a message. That's why I came round. Then I got distracted by the Pattersons."

"But how is he? Is he all right?"

"The doctor says there's every reason to expect he'll make a full recovery, but he's scared. You know what his first words were when he came round? 'I've been waiting for this.' His father died of a heart attack at fifty-two. And his brother Stephen, of course. That's why he's always been so fussy about food, used to go bonkers when he caught you having a fag. Remember that time you figured out he'd lied about his age? It was the same thing, not vanity but some mad notion he could cheat death."

She stabbed her fork into a piece of cauliflower.

"And me," she added.

"You?"

"The younger wife, marrying late. He kept saying it was wrong for him to have a family, that he'd only end up letting us down. We were courting for two years before I talked him round."

Which meant, he knew, getting knocked up. They'd made no secret of the fact that his birth, six months after the wedding, was not premature. Gwen had been sixteen. "I didn't know," he said. "I mean, I knew about Grandpa and Uncle Steve but I just thought Dad was a health nut."

She sat back, eyes flat on him. For a moment he pictured the poor trout's head, staring blindly in the dustbin. "You don't get it, do you?"

He didn't. "I wish you'd told me sooner," he said cautiously. "I could have come to the hospital, helped cheer him up."

"Your strong suit." Her teeth appeared in bewildering fashion and, equally bewildering, disappeared. "Zeke, your father is fifty-seven. He can't go on working twelve hours a day, and I can't run the shop alone."

"But you're not alone," he managed.

"Right." She began to tick them off on her fingers. "Rani, Jerome, Tom, Subhas, Jack, and now 'no problem' Kevin. Each a disaster, in different ways."

He felt as if he were in the presence of a champion bricklayer; the wall was rising around him with astonishing speed. He did his best to slow her down, steal a few bricks, let a batch of cement harden. "Mum, I'll do whatever you need, you know that. But maybe if you can't cope with the shop, it's time to talk about selling. After all, Dad will be retiring soon."

"And then what? He'll sit around enjoying his hobbies. You'll support him?" She planted her elbows on the table. "I probably shouldn't tell you this, but unfortunately I know how you feel. I'm fed up with the shop too, and I was planning to leave your father. Well, that's on the back burner now. I've no idea if Maurice will wait. It's not as if I can promise anything."

"Maurice?" She had said the name as if he were already acquainted with its owner. Then, seeing the way her eyes shone, he understood. This was the phenomenon he had read about so often: meeting someone else. In the waiting rooms of various doctors and clinics, he'd taken to studying women's magazines and discovered, amid the many articles about weight loss and hair management, the problem pages. He found the desperate little narratives both baffling and consoling. Who were these people who offered up the intimate details of their lives for any reader's cold-hearted gaze? And then someone else, a stranger in an office, wrote back claiming to know more about the letter writer's situation than they did themselves. Get rid of Dave; tell Nick no sex until he proves he loves you; your friend needs professional help. But this was his mother, his parents, and none of the advice seemed remotely useful. He held on to the edge of the table. "Maurice?" he said again. "But what about Roger, all those blokes?"

Gwen made a barking sound. "Roger? He's very happy with Nathan. Oh, I must tell him you thought we were an item. He'll be thrilled."

She was still talking as he let go of the table, stood up, and carried the dishes to the sink. He washed the plates, the cutlery, the pots and pans, the grill, everything there was to wash. When at last he turned around, she was sitting, arms folded, legs crossed, waiting.

"Zeke, this is nuts. It would be different if you had gone into accounting, but basically you're a glorified handyman. What do you have to lose by managing the shop? You'll get a decent salary, and your father will be over the moon. He won't be breathing down your neck, I promise. The world's going to fall apart if we all start treating each other like dirt."

Finally—he had lost count of how often he used the word *no*—he pried her out of his kitchen. Gwen had her own indestructible carapace, the one she took everywhere, but for a moment, when he'd asked, for the third time, if he could walk her to her car, he had wondered whether she was reluctant to go home; he pictured the empty rooms spelling out his father's illness more clearly than any doctor, her lover banished to some dingy pub. She had even suggested calling on his recalcitrant customers, but he'd persuaded her that showing up at nine on a Friday night was a bad idea. Tomorrow after work—he was putting in one of his rare Saturdays—he'd come round to see his father, then he and Gwen could make a plan about visiting the Pattersons and escorting them to the bank machine. "We'll phone first," she said, "to make sure they're home."

"But maybe," he said unthinkingly, "they're like me."

Got you, said Gwen's china-blue eyes, but she let it pass for now. "Don't worry. I'll tell them they won the lottery or their MP wants to chat."

He walked her down the street, dodged her kiss, and loped back to the flat. She wrung him out, emptied him, and what was he left with? Scraps and shadows. As he reached for the light switch in the hall he recalled the five lightbulbs. They had been a sign after all, not about her but about his father. In the living room he took refuge with his clocks. Scanning their neat faces, he saw that the forties traveling clock had lost eleven minutes since yesterday. As he pressed it to his ear, he recalled the rest of the story she had told about Robert the Bruce. After he died, his body was buried in the usual way but his heart was sealed into a lead canister, which the

Black Douglas had carried on the Crusades and, at the height of the fighting, hurled into battle. But here's the truly amazing thing, she had said. Later the heart was found and brought back to Scotland to be buried.

The clock sounded fine, as far as Zeke could tell. One afternoon in Brighton his Uncle Stephen had told him that clocks make only one sound, *tick-tick*, which the human ear splits into two: *tick-tock*. A few months later he had dropped dead, planting an apple tree. Zeke reset the clock, giving it another chance, and put it back on the table. Both his parents, he thought, had heart trouble: his father's no longer tick-tocking steadily but faltering; his mother's a gift given twice over. Through the ceiling came a thud and, just when he was beginning to get impatient, another.

3

The next morning, on the fifth attempt, he managed to close the door behind him and, by dint of counting each crack in the paving stones, make his way to his van, parked at the end of the street. Once he was seated behind the steering wheel, with the familiar knobs and levers, matters grew a little easier. I mustn't let this happen again, he thought. She needs me. Dad needs me. To his relief his new employer, a chef, was out for the day and he had the house to himself. He found the perfect hiding place, an alcove off the hall, and set to work without further delay. As he removed the old kitchen cabinets, he kept picturing his father, not the angry man who had strode into doctors' offices when Zeke fell ill but the one who had spent Sundays with him on the beach at Brighton, building castles out of pebbles, creating moats and waterways, and who later, in London, had taken him kite-flying on Parliament Hill and done with him the things a normal boy would have done with friends. As soon as the last of the cabinets was stacked in the chef's front garden, Zeke put away his tools and set off to visit him.

But when he opened the door of his parents' house it was as if a large hand were pressing against his sternum. The very air was altered, and the temptation to flee was so strong that he had to seize hold of the doorknob. Gone was the nose-tickling embrace of fruit and Gwen's perfume and in its place was something synthetic and slightly tangy which, after a few cautious breaths, Zeke identified as approximating the smell of a freshly opened bag of elastic bands. Everything is changing, he thought. Slowly, reluctantly, he edged along the hall and, in the few inches between the door and the jamb, discovered his father.

Or whoever the hospital had sent home in his place. There were always stories in the newspapers about babies being switched; why not fathers? He had last seen Don in late December, when they had gone to a performance of *Iolanthe*. He had been dressed to the nines in the shirt Gwen had given him for Christmas and the new suit he had bought himself in the Boxing Day sales. Give me a nudge, he had told Zeke, if I start singing along. He had joined his first Gilbert and Sullivan Society at the age of sixteen and been a robust member ever since. Now, a man with hair the color of dishwater, wearing pale blue pajamas and a tartan dressing-gown, sat in his father's chair, staring blankly in the direction of the television. Beside the chair stood an odd metal contraption, like half a cage.

"Cat got your tongue?"

Even the voice was different. Zeke glanced uncertainly over his shoulder. Was it possible that somehow he had come into the wrong house? But there was his father's piano with the bust of Beethoven. While he continued to hesitate in the doorway, the man levered himself out of the chair, seized the metal contraption, and began to push his slippered feet across the floor. Six inches, six inches, six inches. Just past the sofa he stalled, clinging to the frame.

"So, you've come to see your future," the man said. "The doctors couldn't find one thing to tell me to do differently: exercise—yes; low salt—yes; low fat—yes; smoking—no; drinking—moderate; reasons to live—plenty. Not one thing, except take the pills, take the pills."

He shuffled backward, plucked a bottle from among the phalanx on the table, and rattled it in Zeke's direction. And with that gesture Zeke finally, unmistakably, recognized his father.

"Dad, I'm sorry I didn't come sooner. Mum—" He was about to explain that he hadn't known about the attack when he caught sight of a bandage bisecting his father's neck. Rusty spots, blood perhaps, were seeping through the folds. This was worse, much worse than he'd imagined. "How are you?" he said lamely.

"Weren't you listening? I feel like shit warmed over. I feel like Lazarus before Christ hauled him out of his coffin. I've worked all my life, winter, summer, rain, shine, a fortnight's holiday a year, I looked after my mum and dad, I've never been in debt, owed no man favors, and here I am, at fifty-two, a wreck."

Fifty-seven, Zeke wanted to say.

"And"—his father glared—"here you'll be one day."

He sensed his own heart pumping in steady contradiction, the valves deftly opening and closing. "You're bound to feel rotten at the moment. You'll soon be back on your feet."

"For fucking what? For how fucking long?"

The words followed Zeke through the door. In the hall he rested his forehead against the wall, seeking comfort in the cool pressure of the plaster. I wish you were dead, he thought, swinging his fists against the wall. What's the use of not being dead if you're going to be like this? Then, between one fist fall and the next, he understood that, yet again, he had things back to front. Life had failed his father in several significant respects—his struggling shop, his pathetic son, his unreliable health—but that did not mean he was ready to die. In fact, the reverse. Christ, if he ever found out about Maurice.

He straightened and let himself out of the house. All day, while he wasn't reminiscing about his father, he had wrestled with the question of an appropriate gift. When he had had his breakdown, people had brought flowers and grapes, grapes and flowers. The flowers, for the most part, he didn't mind. The grapes, however a fruit he'd always enjoyed filching in the shop, he had come to hate, rotting little spheres of sweetness, their slippery seeds poised to take root in stomach and intestine. Neither had seemed suitable for his father. Books, except for ones about Italy, he despised; he already had all of Gilbert and Sullivan. Zeke was still agonizing as, leaving the chef's house, he spotted a pet shop with a parking space in front. Now, opening the back of the van, he thought, I hope this isn't another of my blunders. He lifted out the cage from where he'd wedged it, between two buckets of emulsion paint, and hurried toward the house. Drafts, the salesman at Fur, Fin and Feathers had said, were, along with cats, the big danger.

"Dad, I brought you this, for company."

His father was back in his chair. Without looking at Zeke, he shook a little cup and dropped two dice on the table. He picked them up, shook them again, dropped them again. Zeke set the cage on the floor. For a moment, as he reached to remove the towel, he pictured the parrot magically flown, but there it was, its plumage a mix of mango and avocado, a red blaze on each wing, blinking on its perch. In the shop it had seemed the ideal gift, clean, companiable, possibly conversational: what could be better? My health, his father's posture declared. Your obedience.

"Good boy," said Zeke. Best not even to consider this from the parrot's point of view. Happily, however, the bird seemed oblivious to its chilly reception; it hopped from foot to foot and clicked its remarkable beak. The clicking, at last, roused his father.

"What the hell is that?"

"A parrot." He began to explain the advantages, including that he could return it at any time during the next three days.

"Not enough," his father interrupted, "that *you're* sure to outlive me. You got me the one pet that will too. Twenty years from now"—he spat the words faster and faster—"you and Gwen will be having your tea and the parrot will start yammering, and one of you will look up from your baked beans and say doesn't it remind you of someone? And the other will say, maybe that old geezer—Ron, John, used to be your husband, used to be your father."

"You don't have to keep it."

The parrot unfurled a long purple tongue and flicked up a sunflower seed. Zeke lifted a pile of newspapers off a small table and set the cage there. Then he backed out of the room again, muttering that he was going to give a hand at the shop.

His father made some unintelligible sound.

In Tibetan temples, the niece had told him, they placed gargoyles at the entrances to scare worshippers out of their mundane concerns. He closed the door of the house and, hoping that the chilly air would do the same for him, opened his jacket, rolled up his sleeves, and set off down the street. Where had she gone in such haste that she could leave only a one-line note? Tomorrow the Barrows would give him the answer.

His mother, hair shining, face pale beneath the fluorescent lights, was tipping potatoes into a canvas bag held by a skinny androgynous figure dressed in flared jeans and a duffel coat.

"Carrots, onions, parsnips?" Gwen asked. "Lovely cabbage?"

As soon as she spoke, he guessed the shopper's gender, a hypothesis that was confirmed when the figure said, "Just a bit of salad. A cucumber. Lettuce," and, from beneath long dark lashes, shot him a sideways glance. Did he know her from somewhere? He turned determinedly to study the beetroot.

"Well?" said Gwen, as soon as the wraithlike girl had paid and left the shop.

"You didn't tell me he was in such a state. He called me a coward, said I'd been running away all my life. If he ever finds out—"

"It'll kill him?" she suggested, with what he called an antilaugh, a sound that approximated normal laughter while signaling its opposite. "I do have that in mind. But it's odd that you should. If Don had to choose between a faithful wife and a son to take over the business, I bet a pint of blood—"

Saved by a woman with a French accent asking if she was too late for a pound of mushrooms. At once Gwen was urging aubergines, offering half price on the peppers. He had witnessed this phenomenon before, on thousands of occasions; still, he couldn't understand how a person could be grimly belligerent one minute, praising vegetables the next. Feelings don't stay constant, his nurse had said. Mine do, he had insisted, constant as cathedrals. He began to carry in the crates of apples and oranges from the sidewalk, a job he had done so often that his body needed no instructions. Now, with every crate, he felt the weight of a possible future. It was one thing to help out for a few days or a few weeks, another to see himself here year in, year out. Two more late customers appeared, one asking for okra, and then Gwen had the till emptied and the deposit organized, and he had everything stowed for the night and the grill down.

As they walked home, she resorted to another of her old tricks, talking not about what concerned them both most closely, his father or the shop, but Zeke's recalcitrant customers.

"Any kids?" she said.

"None that I noticed."

"Burglar alarms? Weight-lifting equipment?"

"Why are you asking this stuff?" he said. "You're not going to make a scene, are you?"

"A scene may occur," his mother said, opening their front door, "but I won't be making it." In her presence the new rubbery smell of the house was less noticeable. His father's voice could be heard from the living room. "Oh, God," she said, "now he's off with the fairies."

"No, I forgot to tell you. I did something daft." He explained about the bird.

To his surprise, she was nodding. "You say we've got three days, so let's wait and see. Don can't say thanks for anything these days. A parrot may be just the ticket."

Priscilla, the nervous divorcée next door, was asked to keep an ear out for Don and they were off. Sitting beside Gwen in her car as she darted through the local streets, Zeke realized that she was not merely unafraid of the Pattersons but looking forward to this encounter. She had changed into a tight red top and put on fresh makeup. How can I be her child, he thought, knowing that she often asked the same question.

"Here we go." She tucked the car into a space as deftly as a pie into the oven. "Leave the talking to me, and whatever you do don't apologize."

He began to propose alternatives: a letter, the small claims court, those rabbis in the East End who solved people's quarrels using the Talmud.

"Shush. Stand out of sight, and when they open the door follow me inside."

Feeling worse by the second, he lurked in the shadow of the wall. Gwen knocked once, then stood waiting, shoulders straight, heels together, the model of a demure library campaigner. "Mrs. Patterson?" she said, when the door opened. "I phoned about the library. If I could come in, just for a moment, to explain our petition."

The affirmative noises were still sounding, when, with a quick glance in Zeke's direction, she stepped smartly over the threshold. He followed. In the dreary hallway he resisted the temptation to crouch behind her. The light oozing from the overhead bulb was the color of weak tea, and everything but Gwen seemed diminished. Certainly the woman backing down the hall offered no particular threat. With her white hair and plump cheeks, she reminded Zeke of a sheep in a children's story.

The smell of paint was gone, and briefly he wondered if the whole thing were a dream. Perhaps, after giving them an estimate, he had never actually done the work. Then he saw the barometer in its wooden case, hanging on the wall beside the coat stand, and remembered tapping it, day after day, as he came and went, waiting for its pronouncements: dry, fair, unsettled, rain, stormy.

"Let me start again," Gwen said. She was holding out a piece of paper, not the promised petition but a copy of Zeke's bill. "Is there some problem with my son's work?"

Mrs. Patterson's cheeks filled with color as if someone had pumped dye into them. "What are you doing?" she said in a small voice. "You can't just barge in."

"You can't just not pay your bills. Is there a problem? Something in the estimate Zeke failed to do?"

"William, William."

"What is it, dear? I'm busy."

Zeke had forgotten how much he hated that plummy schoolmaster's baritone. The rest of William, when he appeared at the top of the stairs, pen in hand, was equally obnoxious. Several of Zeke's lecturers at university had perfected this air of self-importance; whenever he dared to appear at their office hours, one glance had been enough to make him swallow his questions and scurry away. Halfway down the stairs, William's pace slowed. His gaze had fallen on Gwen.

"Mr. Patterson? I'm Zeke's mother. As you know, my son spent a week painting two of your bedrooms, including replacing one of the ceilings. The agreed work was done at the agreed time, but for some reason ever since you've been unable to find your checkbook."

She had noticed, Zeke saw at once, the direction of Mr. Patterson's eyeballs. Her chest in its low-cut red top rose visibly, and she delivered her speech with cutting firmness. Bad boy, naughty boy.

"Delighted to meet you." Mr. Patterson came forward with outstretched hand. "Ethel"—she could have been an entire form of fifth-year boys—"I'll take care of this."

Ethel, not so sheeplike after all, held her ground. Her feet, clad in rather smart slippers, dug almost visibly into the wooden floor. Something to be learned here, Zeke noted. You may not have the gumption to rush into combat, but you can still prevent the other person from sweeping to victory. Her obstinacy was rewarded by a brief scowl from Mr. Patterson before he set to work on Gwen.

"I'm so sorry you've had this aggravation. We've had trouble in the past, tradesmen billing us twice. I'm afraid I thought your son was on the fiddle. It was only when I looked at our bank statement the other day that I realized he'd failed to cash the check."

On the couple of occasions when Emmanuel had tried to collect unpaid bills, he'd gone in guns blazing; if that didn't work, nowhere to go but down. In contrast Zeke admired his mother's deployment of steely politeness and veiled threats and her acceptance of face-saving surrender. Within a matter of minutes she was graciously agreeing to take a check and allowing Mr. Patterson to stand quite close while he wrote it.

"So sorry," he said, "for any inconvenience."

Driving home, she was exuberant. "Sometimes I think if I had my life over again, I'd be a bailiff. I love that moment when people realize you're not going to disappear, that it's their money or their kneecaps. Do you know what I mean?"

"I do," he said. Although he didn't share her enthusiasm, not a speck of it, he could see that Gwen had felt as if her skin fit perfectly while she chided the Pattersons. Which was just how he had felt with the Barrows' niece.

4

"Such an improvement," said Mrs. Barrow, Ariel. Arms outspread, she jerked around in a circle like a mechanical ballerina before climbing onto the sofa, where her feet, Zeke could not help noticing, dangled childishly several inches above the floor. He'd read a book once about an emperor in Africa who had a servant whose only job was to place the appropriate pillow beneath his feet whenever he sat down. "I'm glad you suggested white for the moldings," she added.

"And you were right about the lining paper," said Gerald. "You wouldn't even know it was there."

The room, with its bright rugs and immaculate walls, was almost unrecognizable. So too were its owners. Not just his usual failure, though. The Barrows really did look different, cheeks plumper, hair glossier, as if ten days of Latvian cuisine—smoked fish? dumplings?—had rejuvenated them. Gerald had even attempted a mustache, a flimsy fringe on his upper lip that surely had not been present a fortnight ago.

"We'll certainly get in touch the next time we need work done," he said.

As he spoke, Gerald edged forward in his seat—a sign, Zeke

knew, that it was time for him, well paid, well praised, to depart. He shifted forward in his own seat. "About your niece," he said, and heard his voice sag unconvincingly. "I borrowed a book of hers. I was wondering, can you give me her address to send it back?"

He had worked hard on the phrasing, searching for the tone that, in this matter of utmost urgency, would convey humdrum duty. Now on the faces of the Barrows, he watched his words produce an identical expression, one he couldn't begin to categorize.

"We don't have a niece," Gerald said. "Neither of us."

"Perhaps you misunderstood one of our neighbors," said Ariel.

Really, thought Zeke, do I seem the kind of moron who doesn't know a neighbor from a niece? "Maybe," he persisted, inching even closer to the edge of his seat, "she's not exactly a niece. A friend, the daughter of friends, someone you think of as a niece?"

In their presence he could see that she did not, remotely, resemble either of them. Certainly not Ariel, with her oddly pointed nose and chin and those leaf-colored eyes so deep-set that she seemed to be peering out at the world. As for Gerald, his features were so regular as to look almost artificial; only his awkwardly angled ears were authentic. What must Zeke say to jog their memories? For the billionth time he wished he could retrieve her first words on the doorstep, when surely she had said her name, but those had flown—indeed, never landed.

"Neither of us has a niece," Gerald repeated. "No one calls us aunt or uncle."

Zeke had worried they might try to fob him off, insist on returning the book themselves, go all prim and say we don't give the address of our beloved niece to strange men. That they would deny her very existence was bewildering. "She said you were expecting her," he said, relishing, in spite of his distress, the secret meanings of the word.

"Expecting?" queried Ariel, heels drumming against the sofa.

Suddenly Gerald was no longer on the edge of his seat but

looming over Zeke. "Are you saying"—the mustache wriggled—"that you let this person into our house?"

Later Zeke would remember his first reaction: not dismay, not chagrin, but a shout of admiration. All along he had known there was something off about her, something not quite legitimate. A black sheep, he had assumed. An unmarried mother. That she was not the Barrows' niece, not even a friend or acquaintance, was fantastic.

Of course they pounced, spewing out questions, so agitated they barely heard his answers. He offered only the dull facts; how she'd arrived one afternoon, spent two nights and one day under their roof. He did not mention the five lightbulbs nor that they'd painted, eaten, lain together. "The next day," he concluded, "I got here soon after eight and she was gone."

"And you're sure you didn't know her?" they kept saying.

"Why would I be asking you," Zeke said crossly, "if I did?"

Gerald began to flail around the room. He bumped into a chair, grazed a table. "So while we were away and you were decorating our living room, a young woman claiming to be related to us was staying here and had the run of our house?"

"Not espccially young." That was one of the things he had liked about her.

"This is completely weird," said Ariel, her deep-set eyes darting from her husband to Zeke and back again. "What I don't understand is why you let her in? Surely you knew we'd have told you if anyone were coming."

"People have relatives who show up out of the blue," he protested. "I was trying to be helpful."

Echoing his own earlier thoughts, Ariel asked if the woman took after either of them. He pretended to consider. "Not really. She said she was Gerald's side of the family. She was tall and she looked a little like Beethoven." There, that would have to do. No Ms. F for them, no glimpse of how she swung across the room, or blew out her cheeks, or bit her nails, or went berserk cooking, or made a sound when they made love like a clock poised to strike the hour.

"Your side of the family, Gerald," said Ariel. "That suggests various possibilities."

Crikey, thought Zeke. A few drops of her anger spattered him as she drove, full steam ahead, toward her husband. But Gerald seemed unaware. "The police," he announced, rocking the standard lamp. "We should call the police. This is breaking and entering."

"I don't see how," said Zeke. "Nothing was broken. And I asked her in."

"Perhaps someone you know," Ariel continued, bright and relentless as a plumber's snake. "One of your hangers-on, your groupies?"

But even as she spoke, Gerald was gone, pounding up the stairs. After a moment, Ariel slipped off the sofa and followed. Alone, Zeke stood up and, in an effort to calm himself, walked over to the bay window. He peered at one of the sills, checking his handiwork. Except for a small pucker in the paint where a fly had met its demise, the surface was immaculate. From overhead came the scuffle of footsteps—searching, he presumed, for clues—but nothing remained save the nail holes, which were once again hidden by a rug. The day she left, he had returned upstairs hour after hour, tiptoeing into the room as if the coveralls were alive and might, if properly approached, confide in him. But however quietly he moved, however patiently he waited, they said nothing. Finally, just before he packed up for the day, he had fetched his claw-head hammer and levered out the nails. He had put them in an envelope and tucked them, along with the coveralls, into a shopping bag that he set beside his bed. What had sustained him since then was the belief that the Barrows would tell him what the garment had failed to do. Now he fingered the fly's grave and grappled with the confounding turn of events.

Upstairs the Barrows' voices rose. Usually Zeke did his utmost to avoid eavesdropping. For years, during his parents' stormiest rows, he had covered his ears and recited the instructions for school evacuation. Today, anxious not to miss a syllable, he hastened to the door.

"Maybe she's a friend of Seth's," said Gerald.

"Maybe," said Ariel, "she's the Empress of Siam."

"You're being ridiculous. She could just as easily be one of your friends. In fact"—there was a loud thud—"she must know one of us. It's too many coincidences—our holiday, the painter being here—to be a total stranger."

Doglike, Zeke shivered. What a dolt he was. Of course she knew the Barrows, though not as their niece. He wanted to run upstairs at once to offer a full description, but Ariel was still hurling gibes and Gerald was shouting, and interrupting either activity was unthinkable. He retreated to the living room and, carefully emptying the pockets, folded his jacket and laid it on the floor beside his chair. Then, he couldn't have said quite why, he walked over to the bay and slid open the side window. He was astride the sill, listening one last time to hear if the Barrows were calming down, when another bulb detonated. The room flashed to darkness.

Outside, forgetting about his van, he wandered from one gray city street to the next. The cold afternoon closed in around him. She was gone, vanished, and he was no closer to finding her than he had been when he rang the Barrows' bell an hour ago. The sidewalks, the passing cars, were filled with women, old, young, tall, short, fat, thin, black, white, but none of them were her. A police car drove sedately by and for a moment he thought of waving it down, but he could hear already the hopeless conversation. A woman, whose name he didn't know, had abruptly left a house she was visiting. So what? The coveralls and five nails were his only proof of her existence. There were machines, he knew, capable of identifying a person from a fleck of skin, a single hair, but how a civilian, not a scientist or a spy, got access to them he had no idea.

The exhilaration he had felt when he first grasped that she was not the Barrows' niece was entirely gone. How was he ever going to find her again?

Crossing yet another street without paying attention, he heard a horn and looked up to see a blue van, like the one Phil drove, swerving to avoid him. At once, for reasons stretching back over a decade, his old friend seemed like the perfect destination. Still studying every woman he passed, Zeke made his way through the side streets to Phil's house and was rewarded by a familiar figure answering the door almost immediately.

"Zeke, is something wrong? Is your dad okay?"

"Yes, it's me. Dad is terrible. How did—"

A sharp cry echoed down the hall and Phil was hurrying toward it. "Come in," he called over his shoulder. "Close the door."

One thing the two men had always shared was a habit of neatness. They put tools away, used masking tape and drop cloths, washed up meticulously. Once, after a particularly trying discussion with a customer, Phil had announced he was going home to clean the windows; Zeke had understood perfectly. Now the kitchen sink overflowed with dishes, the table and floor were strewn with toys and garments. Lying in a cot near the counter was the source of both cry and chaos: Brenda. Phil picked her up and began to walk back and forth. Zeke cleared a chair of clothes, dirty or clean he couldn't tell, and sat down. It was, he realized, almost exactly a year since the evening Phil had appeared at his door, standing very upright—a sure sign, in his case, of drunkenness—to announce that Mavis had said yes.

Yes to what? Zeke had asked.

Yes to getting hitched, tying the knot, marrying your humble friend. He swept his hand over his head and made a deep bow.

Zeke had felt his mouth open. For as long as they had known each other Phil had been courting Mavis. In winter they went dancing twice a week; in summer they shared a garden. Phil referred to her without irony, both in her presence and absence, as the love of his life. Whether Mavis, with her shapely arms and rippling hair, reciprocated had never been clear. She did seem fond of Phil, but Zeke had met her several times in the company of other men. He was still adrift in amazement, each second taking him farther from the appropriate response, when Phil had straightened and—another of his tricks—was quite sober. You're thinking, he had said slowly, why would Mavis, who walks on air, settle for a chap like me.

I was, confessed Zeke.

Phil pulled out a chair, sat down, and placed his hands in his lap. Mavis is pregnant, he said. The three of us plan to live happily ever after.

So you do sleep together, Zeke thought. (He and Emmanuel had often debated the question.) And then immediately revised his thought: not necessarily.

Of course, Phil went on, this doesn't mean she'll settle down. Mavis can't help roaming, but I'll be the house she returns to, and if I choose to keep the door always open, whose business is it but mine?

Why Mavis, Zeke had wanted to say, when there are so many girls who would treat you well? He was torn four-square between envy, anger, exasperation, and bewilderment. Then, looking at Phil's straight back, his crisp jeans, his shining shoes, he recognized the truth: it was no one else's business. Belatedly, he had stepped around the table to embrace his old friend.

Now Brenda continued to cry at full volume, ignoring Phil's comic faces, his offer of a bottle, his soothing remarks. Then quite suddenly, as if a switch had turned, she stopped. Phil sat down. "It's not her fault," he said. "Mavis has gone off and Brenda misses her."

"How old is she?" said Zeke.

"Thirty-four."

"I meant Brenda, actually."

"Five months and eleven days."

He was watching the baby, an expression on his face that Zeke had seen only once or twice before when Phil and Mavis were working side by side in their garden. He ought to say something, something about Mavis and how he was sure she really did love Phil, but in fact he was sure of nothing. Instead, he stepped over to the sink. As he filled the dish rack, he talked about his father. "When I went round, I didn't even recognize him. I know for me that's not saying much, but everything about him was different: his voice, the way he held his head, his wrist bones. And he was angry in the worst way."

"Poor sod," said Phil, gently bouncing Brenda. "He was always so careful. I remember him at the pub, never having crisps or peanuts. Who's minding the shop?"

"My mother, but she can't manage alone." He scrubbed a particularly stubborn smear of red. "I'm afraid that once I start working there, they'll never let me go." He did not add his other, newly acquired fear. If he were stuck in the shop, how could he find the non-niece?

In the early days, when his parents had begged Phil to fire their son so that he would come back to the shop, Phil had staunchly refused. But this afternoon, still bouncing Brenda, he said, "I don't see what choice you have. Of course they'll want you to stay. You'll have to fight that battle later." As if the matter were settled, he launched into an account of Brenda's accomplishments. She liked the swings at the park; her favorite song was "Brown-Eyed Girl"; she could suck her toes and her thumbs with equal ease.

Listening to this litany, Zeke found all his own aggravations transferred to his friend. At last he burst out, "But you can't let her do this."

"Do what?" said Phil mildly.

"Saddle you with Brenda. It's not fair."

Phil raised Brenda so that her face was on the same level as his. "I wouldn't change places with the richest man in New Zealand. Why did you come round? Is something wrong besides your father?"

For the first time since he rang the bell, Zeke had Phil's undivided attention, and for a few seconds, as he scoured a saucepan, he couldn't think where to start. Then he began to explain, not about the Barrows and the niece but how, finally, he had met someone he cared for in the way Phil cared for Mavis, how he had lost her, and had to find her. Across the room he sensed Phil's startled satisfaction at his avowal and then, as the story unfolded, mild annoyance.

"Well," said Phil, "people can't vanish. What does she look like?"

This time he wanted to answer but it was surprisingly hard. A woman, five foot nine or ten, springy hair in many shades of brown, a high forehead engraved with three lines, one broken, two continuous, eyes somewhere between green and brown, a nose like a rudder, ears hidden by aforementioned hair but receptive, broad hands with chapped knuckles. Her feet were bony and made Zeke think of the wings of birds. And her voice? Deep, warm, mellifluous. As for what he had seen when he removed her coveralls, the swell of her belly traced by the linea nigra, that was not to be spoken aloud, even to his old friend.

Phil listened patiently and shook his head. "I can't say she sounds like anyone I know. She said she'd be in touch. Maybe all you can do is wait. Would you like to hold Brenda?"

Zeke was about to say something grumpy—waiting worked for you but you knew who Mavis was—but he saw that Phil was offering the most precious remedy he had. He dried his hands and reached for Brenda. Embracing her soft, warm weight, he did feel slightly better.

He arrived home to find his street jammed with cars. He had to circle twice before he squeezed the van in round the corner. As he walked back toward the house, the noise of riotous pleasure intensified with every step; someone was giving a party. He was just sparing a moment from his own troubles to sympathize with whoever had to endure this havoc at close quarters—and on a Sunday—when, reaching his front door, he discovered that person to be himself. The party had spilled out of the downstairs flat into the common hallway, and Zeke had to fight his way past the revelers. On the stairs, two slender youths were urging a plump woman to chug a beer; all three were clad, minimally, in sheets.

His own flat provided the barest illusion of safety. The floor throbbed. The stove rattled. Not even the loudest of his clocks could be heard. He sat in the kitchen, miserably giving himself over to the vibrations. When he left home that afternoon, he had expected to be in her company by nightfall, at least to have a name and address. Now he was back again, and he knew only who she wasn't. For a few evil seconds the notion that he might never see her again raced through his brain. He leaped to his feet and seized a notebook he'd used for estimates last spring. On an empty page, he began a halting list.

FINDING THE NON-NIECE

1. *Search the city.*
Suppose he could do two hundred houses a day. And suppose there were three million houses in London. That made a mere fifteen thousand days of going door-to-door. By which time he'd be close to eighty and Ms. F would have children of her own.
2. *Watch maternity wards.*
More feasible, but even for those he would have to subcontract. Perhaps he could hire homeless men to work in shifts. Or maybe those Irish girls who begged with their babies in the underground. Emmanuel swore they fed the children cough syrup to keep them quiet.
3. *Find her brother.*
Now why would he think of that? As far as he could recall, she had only mentioned him once. And the brother too was nameless. He was about to score out this suggestion but, as he raised his pen, the memory of how she'd frowned stayed his hand.
4. *Put up posters.*
He could follow the example of people who mislaid pets or bicycles: put up notices on lampposts giving a description and offering

a reward. MISSING WOMAN: tall, white, pregnant, last seen wearing nothing. If only he could draw. She was so vivid inside his head, and yet he was utterly unable to convey her to anyone else.

He couldn't think of a number five. In his agitation, he rose from the table and went over to the window. This was an impossible list, the labors of Hercules with no goddess to lend a hand. That night in the Barrows' living room, while the fire burned and their plates emptied, they had talked about whether a person could ever disappear. People used to be able to, she had said, but not anymore. Everyone is in a computer, even the homeless. That's not true, he had argued. When I couldn't leave my house no one noticed for a week. People don't care about their neighbors, at least not in London.

Below, in the light from the streetlamp, several partygoers were holding cigarettes and cans of beer. "I hope I'm wrong," Zeke said, "and you're right." The words misted against the glass. Then he recalled his jacket lying on the floor. The Barrows were still the only key he had to finding her, though so much harder to turn than he'd imagined. Gerald was too irascible, but Ariel, if he could just get the appropriate pillow under her feet, might be more forthcoming.

Someone was knocking at his door. "Coming," he shouted, and rushed to answer.

The plump girl, her sheet even more precarious, looked at him wild-eyed. "I'm going to be sick," she said, and, before Zeke could intervene, promptly fulfilled her prediction.

5

"Long John Silver. Say Long John Silver."

Zeke had let himself into the house as stealthily as a teenager. Now he lingered beside the coatrack, trying to place his father's words in the appropriate Gilbert and Sullivan. *The Pirates of Penzance* perhaps? Or *H.M.S. Pinafore*? Then he remembered the parrot. He walked briskly down the hall and, knocking once, stepped into the living room. Neither his father in his armchair nor the parrot in its cage looked up as he came in.

"Good bird," said Don. "Say Long John Silver."

The parrot squawked and raised a claw to its beak with a dexterity that reminded Zeke of Brenda. Standing a few feet away, he felt an emotion that it took him several seconds to identify: not pleasure in his father's improvement, not satisfaction at having for once chosen the right gift, but envy. All his life he had been disappointing his father—one might even call it his main occupation—and here was this antediluvian bunch of feathers, in a matter of days, securely lodged in his affections. As the exchange continued, he registered that, barring the bandage on his neck, Don, clean-shaven, clear-eyed, was looking markedly better than he had on Saturday; indeed, better than in several months. His cheeks no longer had a purplish tinge, and even his hair seemed to have regained its color.

"What are you doing here?" he said, at last acknowledging Zeke's presence. "Shouldn't you be messing around with a paintbrush?"

"Dad," he pleaded, "it's five-thirty. I've finished for the day. How are you feeling? Is there anything I can get for you?"

"The doctor prescribes a walk every day." Don patted his thighs as if to encourage them. "Next week he wants me to start going to a gym. I told him it was nuts, me trotting around like a hamster on a treadmill with all the work at the shop, but he insists. Sit down."

Zeke did, in the chair nearest the door. "I saw Phil the other day," he offered. "Brenda is five months old."

"And you," said his father, turning his knees, his chest, his chin toward Zeke, "are twenty-nine, and for most of those years your mother and I have taken care of you. We helped you go to university, we took you in when you were ill. We've done our honest best for a quarter of a century and how do you repay us?"

If only the parrot would speak, if only the phone would ring.

"Do you have a problem with my arithmetic?"

Zeke managed to move his head from side to side.

"I'll be blunt with you," Don continued, eyeing him unwaveringly. "We need you. We need you to work in the shop, even if it's only half days at first. Gwen does a super job, but she can't manage alone. You know the hours, you know how much heavy lifting there is. When can you start?"

Every part of him felt squeezed. He appreciated, absolutely, the justice of his father's calculations. But if he were in the shop twelve hours a day, how could he hope to find her? "Soon," he said. "When I finish this kitchen."

"Soon," repeated his father, as if it were a swearword. "This loony stuff can only take you so far. You know, one of your doctors suggested it was a way of hiding from us. Well, that's not going to work any longer. I nearly died, and if you can't help now we'll follow your example. You ignore a quarter century of affection and we will too. Our house will be closed to you. And—I can't say this more clearly—you will no longer be our son." He looked at Zeke for one final moment and turned back to the parrot. "Say good morning," he said.

How long he stayed in that chair, how he left the room and made his way home, Zeke would never know. The one thing he could have sworn to, on the pendulum of his grandfather clock, was that his father neither looked at him nor spoke to him again. This is the future, he was saying; this is what you're asking for.

Even before Ariel opened her mouth, Zeke recognized that he was in the presence of someone having a difficult day. He had decided not to phone ahead but had driven over in his lunch hour, hoping for the best, and here she was, standing in the doorway, blinking. Her hair was flattened on one side as if she had been lying down, her sweatshirt had a large stain on the sleeve, and the fly of her jeans was an inch short of closed. Normally he would have backed away from such disorder, fearing contagion; today he hoped it might make her an ally.

"Hello," he said. "I'm Zeke Cafarelli, your painter." Always wise to assume that other people shared his difficulties. "I'm sorry to disturb you, but I think I left my jacket here on Sunday."

Ariel's deep-set eyes receded still farther. Really, she was almost too small to be an adult. "I haven't seen it," she said.

For a moment he didn't know what to say. "I remember," he insisted truthfully, "taking it off in your living room."

"I'm sure I'd have noticed a strange jacket in my own home. Well, maybe not."

"Please, could I take a look? Perhaps you thought it belonged to Gerald."

Ariel stepped back and headed toward the kitchen. After a brief hesitation—surely she did not expect him to check the living room by himself?—Zeke followed. Waiting for the Barrows' return, he had managed, just barely, to keep his anxieties at bay. Now, entering this room where everything, except for the pile of papers on the table, looked the same, whatever tiny layer of fortitude he had developed shattered. He longed to throw himself on the floor and beg for Ariel's help. One glance at her untidy person, however, was sufficient to make him sit down and continue to apologize. "I'm sorry about the other day," he said. "I couldn't seem to stop putting my foot in my mouth."

"None of us were at our best. You can imagine the shock. Coming back from a trip to discover that some—" She paused and Zeke kept his face very still, fending off the insults he could feel her longing to hurl at the non-niece. "Some stranger," she concluded, "has been staying in your house."

"But"—he repeated her husband's speculations—"how would a stranger know that you were away and I was working here? She brought two suitcases."

"Suitcases?"

Too late he realized what these might suggest. "For her clothes," he explained. "That was another reason I never doubted she was a friend."

"Gerald thinks that too." She sat straighter, and Zeke recognized a not unfamiliar moment—himself coming into focus—and with it the danger of Ariel, for all her self-absorption, detecting his true motives. He looked back, trying to keep his features calm and pleasant. "Did you hide the stuff, the water and biscuits, under the desk?" she said.

"Yes."

He could see the syllable making its way through the corridors of her brain. Would she ask why? The possibility of their being allies once again opened before him. But she didn't, and they weren't.

"I can't tell you," she said, stressing the verb, not the pronouns, "how strange all this is. A few years ago, at Whitsun, we were burgled. They only took the CD player and the VCR, but my shoes were all over the floor and I had the same awful feeling of people knowing things about me, even stupid things like my shoe size, and of me knowing nothing about them. Still, at least that made sense. Whereas this woman . . ."

"I think she just needed a place to stay." He was about to add that she hadn't seemed that interested in Ariel, or Gerald either, but maybe that would be insulting. "I have to find her," he said simply. "I hoped you would help."

He began to describe her, trying, as he had with Phil, to capture some part of her in words until Ariel held up her hands. "Please," she said. "Perhaps I'm crazy, but I can't get it out of my head that she's connected with Gerald."

"Do you think"—Zeke reached out to straighten the four pencils lying on the table—"he'd tell me where she is?"

"Tell you?" Ariel stood up, although given her size it made little difference.

"Sometimes people talk to me," he said, "because I'm different."

"I can see that." Ariel nodded. "You also—forgive me for being personal—have the face of a Raphael angel."

Zeke nodded back. Women had made this comment before, though with different artists: Donatello, Leonardo, Botticelli. What they meant was that he had fair skin, blue eyes, hair that approximated the color of lemons, and a full mouth. His misfortune, mostly. At school and in the shop, girls had followed him, and later at university a girl called Rhea had sat outside his room, wrapped in a blanket, for a whole unnerving month. Nothing to do with him, just some notion she had because of the incidental conjunction of flesh and bone.

"You'd better go," said Ariel. "If you do find out anything, please don't tell me. I used to believe knowledge was power. But sometimes it's exactly the opposite, plus all the pain."

Thank goodness, thought Zeke, I didn't tell her about Ms. F. "I think," he said carefully, "when we find this woman, she will turn out to have nothing to do with your husband, at least not in that way. And I think—forgive me, I hardly know you—that you might like her."

"Spare me." Ariel's sharp features grew still sharper. "If you want to find Gerald, try the French Bar in Soho. He usually drops in after work, or whatever it is he does all day."

Zeke stood up. Before he could move, she circled the table and put her arms around him. "Poor Ariel," he whispered, and took the opportunity to rearrange her hair. It did not seem appropriate to mention his jacket again; just as well he had emptied the pockets.

As he worked on the traveling clock that evening—it had gained thirteen minutes since his mother's visit—Zeke felt as if two large figures were standing on either side of him, tugging. To his left was the non-niece whom he needed, desperately, to find. To his right was his father, who had left four messages and who now preferred a parrot to his son. How could he choose between them? But as he puffed compressed air into the tightly coiled movement, he decided that tomorrow, come what may, he must go to the shop. He bowed to the shadowy figure of his father and, at least for the present, his father bowed back and released his hold. And in the evening—he turned to the non-niece—he would visit Soho and find Mr. Barrow. She too retreated, smiling.

The next morning, shortly before seven, he was out of bed and driving toward the shop. As a teenager he had risen even earlier than this to accompany his father to market. He remembered the shock of entering the brightly lit warehouse after the dark streets, the aisles already crowded with vendors calling their wares: freshly picked mushrooms from Kent, Guernsey tomatoes, apples from New Zealand, oranges and avocados from Spain, beans from Kenya. At that age almost everything Zeke knew about the world came from fruits and vegetables.

When he pulled into the parking space at the back of the shop, his mother's car was already there. She answered the door, mouth open, eyebrows arched. "Oh, it's you. What are you doing here?"

"I came to help." Wasn't that obvious? "The tiles for the chef's kitchen aren't in yet."

Her eyebrows dropped. "Well," she said, "your timing couldn't be better. Kevin has a dreadful cold. I had to send him home."

Like Phil's kitchen, the shop was in a state he had never seen before, even after the busiest Saturday. The newly purchased produce lay, haphazardly, in the middle of the floor and the floor itself was filthy; worst of all, the bins of fruits and vegetables—his father's pride and joy—were half empty, their contents shriveled, sprouting, sinister. One rotten apple, Don used to say, can lose you a dozen sales. Taking all this in, Zeke understood again the truth of his father's claim that he had almost died. He counted grapefruit as fast as he could until his mother said, "Let's put this stuff away."

After he'd carried the produce into the cooler and swept the floor, he fetched a rubbish bag and started to go through the vegetables. Sometimes leeks could be saved by peeling off the slimy outer layers, ditto celery and cabbage, but no time for that kind of fiddling today. On the other side of the shop, Gwen was working on the fruit. Her hands moved with their customary speed and her dark trousers and blue sweater were familiar, but something was different. Was he just being his usual obtuse self, Zeke wondered, taking in the set of her shoulders, the curve of her jaw. As they converged on the salad, he figured out what the change was: his mother was not wearing makeup. The effect was the opposite of natural. Put on some foundation, he wanted to say. Where's your eyeliner? But neither of them interrupted the radio until everything was ready, the door of the shop unlocked, the awning unfurled, and the crates of apples and oranges stacked on the table in front.

Then Gwen made second cups of tea. "I don't know what happened when you came round the other day," she said, "but Don's been in a foul mood ever since."

Zeke watched the cars in the street outside speeding back and forth, like a separate species. "He's ill," he said.

"He's convalescing and you're not helping. I mean, you are today, but in general you're not." Her voice shrilled. "He could live for another thirty years. Do you want to be at loggerheads the whole time? You said you'd give a hand in the shop, and now you don't answer our calls. You're driving him mad."

Zeke jerked his head, although he wasn't sure what he meant to convey: Yes? I hear you? No? Even before seeing the shop he had known they needed him. He tilted his tea so that little ripples appeared. "What about—?" Surprisingly Maurice's name was right there, waiting to be used, but he had no intention of doing so. Let him be a blank.

"What about him?" Her earrings swayed: simple gold hoops. "On good days I have a drink with Maurice on the way home." She raised her cup, then paused. "Is that what you think? That I want you to take over the shop so I can bolt with Maurice and not feel like a total bitch?"

He felt her gaze boring into his forehead, trying to find a way inside, and turned his own on a scaly pineapple, once a sign of welcome, as the many stone ones on doorsteps and gateposts testified, now a fruit they sold only occasionally. Had he thought that? He wasn't sure. All he knew was that his father's anger was suddenly there in the shop, a weight across his shoulders, heavier than a sack of potatoes or a box of bananas.

"This is not the rest of your life," said his mother. "This is now, and you can always change your mind." He wanted to protest that that was like asking one of his clocks to run backward, but her mouth kept moving. "Of course I'm going to wait until Don's okay, and I'll tell you right now he won't appreciate my loyalty. He'll think I've cheated on him twice over, once in loving Maurice and a second time in standing by him. Mark my words."

She gave Zeke another hard stare, as if somehow he were to blame for this too and, reaching into her pocket, produced a little black tube; soon her mouth was the familiar glossy pink. Zeke seized their mugs and carried them to the sink, where he set to work washing the disappointingly small pile of dishes. He wanted to run out of the shop and keep running until he reached his father. Then he would explain that, as soon as he finished the chef's kitchen and found the non-niece, he would devote himself to fruit and veg full-time for as long as they needed him. He was scrubbing the tea stains from the last mug when the bell pinged. The first customer was through the door, and he and Gwen were in motion.

Once Zeke had asked Phil why he had taken him on, and Phil had said, I saw you at the shop. It was true that, without thinking, Zeke could keep a running total in his head, while tipping broad beans onto the scales and slipping peaches into a bag, but he had forgotten what hard work it was and how noisy. So many people clamoring: Are the avocados ripe? Any watercress? After only an hour his legs ached and his hands smelled of apples and potatoes and money. When he went to the cooler to fetch another box of mushrooms, he had to fight the urge to close the door and sit down in the chilly dark. As a teenager, when he first started working in the shop, his mother had explained over and over that he couldn't simply ask people what they want. He had to be polite. But they've come in to buy something, he'd argue. Why beat around the bush? This isn't beating around the bush, Gwen said. This is showing that you appreciate their custom. Finally he had written it out on a card—1. *Hello*. 2. *How are you?* 3. *Nice/nasty day*. 4. *How can I help you?*—that he kept in his pocket. Although he seldom referred to it, his social skills did improve. Today, however, he rapidly gave up on 1, 2, and 3 and took refuge in the kind of behavior which used to exasperate his parents, regarding people's ankles rather than their eyes.

From this perspective the boots worn by Mavis were interchangeable with those of many of the younger customers. "Hi, Zeke," she said, in her velvety voice, "Mavis. I'd like a pound of tomatoes."

As he stammered out the prices—so much for the ordinary

tomatoes, more for the fancy ones—he wondered was she back with Phil or did she just happen to be in the neighborhood?

"I'd better have the fancy ones," said Mavis. "Nothing is too good for Brenda."

She offered exact change and accepted the tomatoes. And then, with five customers waiting, she hugged Gwen and told her how well she was looking and that she hoped Don was on the mend. For the first time that day Zeke saw his mother's lips part in a way that suggested something other than anger or despair.

By six o'clock he could barely speak; every muscle and tendon ached as he carried in the crates, put the perishable items in the cooler, and washed the floor. His mother was still thanking him when he announced he was off and let himself out of the shop. The streetlights were on and the streets were busy with people coming home from work or heading out for the evening. Among the crowds, Zeke walked more and more slowly until he came to a stop outside a kebab restaurant. As he stared at the meat, revolving indefatigably on its spit, going to Soho seemed out of the question; he would never manage a tricky conversation with Gerald. Tomorrow, he promised the non-niece. Cross my heart. He headed back to the shop, retrieved his van, and drove thankfully home.

He was locking the door of the van when a man's voice called his name.

"Hey, Zeke, where have you been? I was just calling you."

In the gloom he turned to see Emmanuel hurrying toward him, waving. "What are you doing here?" he said. "Aren't you flat on your back?"

"Obviously not. Let's go inside. I want to talk to you."

Definitely his old friend, and yet he too was different. As he ushered him into the hall and upstairs, Zeke understood at least one part of the change. No longer did Emmanuel reek of sweat faintly masked by his grandmother's Christmas gift of Old Spice.

Instead he smelled as if three hospital nurses had just bathed him from top to toe with sandalwood soap. Inside the flat, other changes became apparent. In fact, if Zeke hadn't met him first in the dark, he might have failed to recognize him. Gone was the silly little Dostoyevsky beard; gone the peculiar haircut, shaved sides, long on top, that Emmanuel had cherished for the last two years; gone the hooded sweatshirts and unraveling scarf. Now, in sleek dark clothes and a leather jacket, he looked as if he worked for an auctioneer or an estate agent, rather than wielding a paintbrush.

"So," he said, "you met my friend."

6

Emmanuel refused to say another word until he had a beer. In spite of Zeke's protests, he rooted around in the fridge, contemptuously pushing aside yogurt, hummus, anchovy paste, and grapefruit juice, until he found a bottle he must have brought with him the last time he came around, six months ago, and, oddly, failed to consume. Both the exercise of power and the immediate prospect of alcohol seemed to calm him, draw him back from that brink of swearing and ranting that he needed to fall over every few weeks, not so much out of anger, Zeke had decided after observing the phenomenon on several occasions, as to remember who he was. For himself, Zeke poured a glass of water and sank down into the nearest chair. His emotions were swirling and scattering like leaves in a playground on a windy day; he glimpsed joy, rage, hope, amazement, jealousy, frustration, and exaltation flashing by.

At the table, Emmanuel sat back down and, with a fussy little gesture, adjusted his trousers. Why, Zeke wondered, was his friend suddenly dressed like a fashion plate? Only two black hairs beneath his nose testified to his former scruffy self. Throughout their acquaintance, Emmanuel had always seemed to take for granted his own innate and infinite attractiveness. Once on a hot summer's day as they drove to a job, Zeke had remarked on a rank odor filling the van—maybe a cat had got into the back and peed?—only to realize when they reached the house and the smell followed them indoors that it emanated from his employee. Both his mother and Phil used to ask, with some frequency, why he kept on Emmanuel. Better the devil you know, Zeke would say, shifting his shoulders up and down in the way he'd seen people do when they wanted to emphasize their helplessness. How could he explain that, within a few weeks of hiring him, he had discovered Emmanuel to be selfish, pettily dishonest, inclined to ferret out the worst in people, boastful, clumsy, and lazy? On the credit side, he showed no sign of noticing that Zeke was different. He never made allowances or offered those little sidestepping evasions by which other people signaled their awareness, but persisted in inviting him to the pub, swearing, lying, telling jokes, all just as if he were dealing with a normal person. In response, Zeke did his level best not to force him to acknowledge his mistake.

Now Emmanuel raised the beer bottle, drank, wiped his mouth, and at last allowed himself to be questioned.

"Your friend?" said Zeke.

"Verona," said Emmanuel. "The big girl."

His hands started to describe a curve and stopped. Later, recalling his tone, Zeke guessed that Emmanuel found her intimidating and was anxious that no one, least of all himself, should be aware of this. But that was hindsight. At the moment everything else was swept away by the huge, wonderful fact: Emmanuel knew her. She was a person with a name, Verona, and a history. She had not simply vanished, with her suitcases, into the endless streets.

"Where is she?" he said. "Have you seen her?"

He had made a mistake. Emmanuel, taking another drink, demanded to know what had happened. On learning that Zeke had let her stay at the Barrows', he gave a whoop.

"I don't understand," said Zeke. "Why pretend to be their niece when she was your friend?"

Emmanuel sprawled back in his seat, laddishly. "I told her what a Goody Two-shoes you are. You'd never have let a pal of mine stay at the Barrows'."

"But didn't she realize they'd go berserk when I asked about her? Even if she didn't want to tell me, she could have left a note." Now that her story was beginning to make sense, he could allow himself to be irritated. His interview with Gerald and Ariel had been severely unpleasant.

"Maybe," said Emmanuel, with a bland stare, "that wasn't her main concern."

Her name was Verona and he had met her in Thailand. Remember, when he went last year? Zeke did indeed. Emmanuel had taken off three whole weeks during the busy spring period. The flight is eleven hours, he had said. I can't just pop over for a fortnight. Zeke had nearly gone mad trying to keep up with work until Phil had agreed to help out. Other painters, Zeke knew, didn't mind falling weeks behind schedule—some even seemed to relish their customers' escalating fury—but he couldn't bear the pleas and insults rampaging around in his brain. Emmanuel had returned heavily tanned and even more careless than usual. Twice he'd used the wrong paint. Zeke had wondered if he might be suffering from sunstroke or drugs. Wasn't Thailand one of those places where a joint cost no more than a bar of chocolate?

"I was gobsmacked when she got in touch," said Emmanuel. "To be honest, I didn't think I'd made much of an impression. Mostly she palled around with a couple of dykes." He shook his head in a way that alerted Zeke simultaneously to the meaning of the word and to Emmanuel's attitude toward such a wasteful proclivity. "Then it turned out she needed a place to stay. I should have phoned you but I wanted her off my back, and you know how it is—you feel less of a prick when you make a suggestion—so I sent her to the Barrows'."

In the midst of his amazement, Zeke completely understood this part. People were always getting themselves out of sticky situations by offering his services. No, I'm afraid I can't help you move house/fix your toilet/paint your living room, but my mate Zeke is ever so handy and has all the time in the world.

"I'm sorry about the last couple of weeks," Emmanuel said, tapping the beer bottle on the table—short, short, long, short, short, long—as if sending a message. "My back really was killing me, but it's on the mend. The physiotherapist says I should be able to start work again next week."

"I still don't understand. Why send Verona to the Barrows'?" The pleasure of saying her name almost lifted him out of his seat.

Emmanuel's mouth turned down, like an open umbrella. "It was all a weird rush. One minute I was watching the telly and the next she was standing in my hall with two suitcases, saying she needed a place to stay. Gina was due in half an hour and you know what she's like." The umbrella flipped over; Zeke had no trouble identifying his smile as smug. "So I said the first thing that came into my head. It never occurred to me that she'd wangle a bed at the Barrows'. Crazy," he concluded.

Not crazy, thought Zeke. Mysterious. And what is the point of mystery if not to lead us into new places? "She's going to have a baby," he said.

"I noticed. She didn't strike me as the type, but you never can tell."

"Does she have a job? Where does she live?"

"You know what holidays are like," said Emmanuel, which of course Zeke didn't. Life was hard enough at home, where at least he knew roughly the number of dustbins in the street, without venturing to a place where they might not even have bins or streets. "A group of us came out on the same flight and we hung around together. There was a couple—Trevor and Sara—and the rest of us mixed and matched." He raised his beer bottle and drank.

What does this have to do with anything, thought Zeke, but experience had taught him that Emmanuel often grew sullen if interrupted. He did his best to listen patiently to an account of how one day Trevor had got into trouble in the water. Everyone else thought he was joking, but Verona had swum over and hauled him out. "When they got to the beach, we all ran up to see if Trev was okay. He coughed and spluttered for a couple of minutes. His face was that ghastly green we painted the Padillos' living room. Then he walked off toward his hut without a word. That was the last we saw of him. Next morning the manager told us that he and Sara had left to look at temples."

What was Emmanuel telling him, that Verona was courageous and observant? That Trevor was the father of Ms. F? "And?" Zeke said, keeping firm hold of the table.

"And," said Emmanuel, "that's how I became friends with her. The chick I had a crush on left for Tokyo. Trev and Sara headed for the hills. The dykes went home. Verona started to hang out with me."

"You?" As soon as the syllable left his mouth, he heard how it sounded. Quickly, he asked the question that Emmanuel regarded as his due whenever a woman aged between sixteen and sixty came up in conversation: did she fancy him?

"Who can say? We went on a couple of expeditions, ruins she wanted to see."

How many hours, how many days of her company lay behind that sentence? "Do you know where she lives?" he asked again. "Does she have a job?"

"I think her parents are dead. She has a brother who's some sort of businessman. That's all I know."

"Does she have a job?"

"What is this, the Spanish Inquisition? There was a kind of rule that we didn't pester each other about life back home. Still, with most people you found out what they did pretty quickly. Not Verona. One day she was talking about being a cleaner, the next she was chatting about market research. After she rescued Trevor, someone told me she worked in radio, not famous but well enough known not to want to spread it around."

Zeke nodded. This made sense. If he closed his eyes he could hear her distinctive voice, deep and warm and a little hoarse, as if even late in the day you were the first person she'd spoken to and what she most wanted to do was invite you to a splendid party. "Why did she suddenly need a place to stay?"

"Boyfriend trouble? Landlord trouble? I'm not exactly Mr. Sensitivity, but the way she showed up out of the blue, why wasn't really in order. Didn't you ask?"

For a moment Zeke was taken aback. Had he really failed to pose such an obvious question? Then he remembered. "I thought she was the Barrows' niece," he said, and described her advent on the doorstep with the suitcases.

Emmanuel bobbed his head. "She said you were cool."

The five words took up residence a few inches above the table. Zeke stared at them. "You've spoken to her."

He didn't realize he was standing until Emmanuel rose too and put a hand on his arm. "Hey, take it easy. You look like you've seen a ghost. She phoned."

The light above the table was swinging—one of them must have knocked it—and Emmanuel's face was going in and out of shadow as if he were two different people. "She phoned," Zeke repeated. "When?"

For a few seconds he understood why one might want to pry open the plates of another person's skull, not to harm them but to retrieve essential information. Emmanuel sat down, making the same fussy gesture with his trousers, and began to tap his empty beer bottle again, though no longer rhythmically. "A few days ago," he said. "She said you'd been very kind and she was worried you would worry about her."

"Where is she? How I can reach her?"

"She was calling from a pay phone. We kept having to shout over the announcements, like in a station or an airport. She said to tell you she'd be in touch. I gave her your phone number—home, not mobile. Sounds like you two got something going."

One of Emmanuel's eyelids drooped in a way that Zeke recognized as both comment and invitation. Trying to fend off either, he asked the first question that came to mind. "Why are you looking so posh?"

Instead of telling him to get lost, Emmanuel shifted from side to side in his chair. Gina, he mumbled, had won him a makeover. He had spent a whole day getting his hair cut and learning how to coordinate his wardrobe. "A Saturday," he added, as if Zeke might think this was why he hadn't been at work.

Zeke nodded, trying to imagine his obdurate employee spending a day choosing shirts and trousers; then he thought of the women involved and the scene made sense. "It was really interesting," Emmanuel went on. "We leap to all these conclusions about people based on their appearance, without even knowing that we're doing it. Take shoes, for instance. You can always tell a homeless person by their shoes, even if they've got everything else together. Expensive shoes are the same, they send a message: Here's a person who won't bounce a check."

Zeke pictured Verona's shoes: the suede boots she wore when she arrived and the next day's trainers, nice blue ones he'd warned her might easily get messed up.

"You should try it," Emmanuel was saying. "It doesn't cost that much. Gina says you're okay looking."

Very slowly and very clearly, Zeke said, "Do you know her last name? Do you know how to find her?"

Emmanuel faltered, stopped, peered at Zeke, and sat back in his chair. "You've got a crush on her," he announced. "Who'd have thought it? After all the chicks I try to set you up with, you fall for a woman ten years older who's in some sort of major trouble."

Zeke stood up and took a step toward him.

"MacIntyre. And no, the phone number she gave me is wrong."

She had a name, two names, she was not just a ghost of the system. Forgetting about Emmanuel he gave a little jump, and at that very moment his clocks began to strike, all nine of them, almost in unison.

"Well," said Emmanuel, pushing back his chair, "ask not for whom the bell tolls."

"You can't just leave. What do you mean by trouble? Why is everything so confusing?"

"Christ if I know," said Emmanuel. "I came round to give you the message and let you know I'll be back at work soon. Verona isn't my problem. Yours either."

As Emmanuel's footsteps receded down the stairs, Zeke looked around his familiar kitchen and saw that his possessions had heard the news. The stove gleamed, the fridge purred, the cupboards kept their orderly secrets, the saucepans shone, even the grout between the tiles was lustrous.

"Verona MacIntyre," he said. He could not imagine six more perfect syllables.

Verona

7

Until that Monday afternoon, a damp, drab day in early February remarkable only for fulfilling all expectations of the season, Verona would have claimed herself to be among those few, those happy few, who see themselves clearly. It was a point of obscure and prickly pride that she, unlike her hapless parents, both dead now for several years, or her ne'er-do-well brother, alive and well in Kentish Town, did not harbor illusions, flattering or otherwise, about her own person or nature. She knew she was tall, ambitious, hot-tempered, stubborn, eloquent, an excellent cook, attractive to a fairly small number of men, and, as she'd been slower to realize, a significant number of women. If pressed, she would also have said that she believed herself perfectly capable of following in the footsteps of her grandfather, who had fought in the First World War, of pointing a gun at the enemy, and pulling the trigger. She had ridden a motorcycle at university, tried parachuting and rock climbing, and had twice consumed drugs rashly purchased in public places; she was not afraid of arguments, or dogs, or fast cars, or bad water, or foreign travel.

She had come home that Monday after a production meeting of exasperating length and inconclusiveness, carrying two bags: one containing milk, bread, and muesli, the other orange juice, apples, beetroot, and bananas. Later she was to think of her banter with Lionel at the corner shop—so you're going to call the baby after me? Leonie if it's a girl, promise—as the last exchange of her old life. At the house, she had to juggle the bags in order to fit her keys in the locks: first the outside door; then, upstairs, her own door. When she stepped inside, she switched on the hall light, an ugly fifties fixture that cast a nice rosy glow over the pale walls, and, without stopping to take off her coat, headed to the kitchen. Only after she had set the bags on the counter did she turn on that light. And only then, as the light spilled through the kitchen door into the living room, did she see, seated on the calico-covered sofa she had purchased last autumn after the results of the amniocentesis, two men watching her. For a fraction of a second, such was their dress and demeanor, she was convinced she knew them: that she had asked over some friends from work, lent them a set of keys, and somehow forgotten the whole arrangement.

"Miss MacIntyre," said the man nearer the kitchen, the paler, plumper one, rising to his feet, "don't be upset. My name is Nigel, and this is George. We're friends of Henry's and we just need a word with you. Here, take a seat." He turned on the standard lamp and motioned for her to sit in the wicker armchair, before returning to the sofa.

She could have run for the door, she could have screamed, but she did neither. She did exactly what he asked. Her fear was still tinged with confusion and indignation. Besides, the man had invoked her brother. But as she sat down, the wicker creaked beneath her weight and the small sound brought home what was happening: two strange men had broken into her flat and she was alone with them. Was this a burglary? A kidnapping? A rape? The men seemed so calm, so respectable, more like policemen than thieves.

The other man, the one who'd remained seated, took over. "You must be wondering why we're here," he said. "Your brother is one of our clients. Or perhaps I should say was. He gives every sign of wanting to quit the relationship." His voice had a hint of a West Country accent and his lips moved in a slightly exaggerated way, as if he had grown up in the company of deaf people. Now that she was looking at him, Verona could see that he was older than she'd first thought. In his forties, perhaps. "We were meant to meet last Thursday," he went on. "Henry didn't show up, and since Saturday we've found neither hide nor hair of him. Which, you'll agree, is a little odd for a man who has a pager, two cell phones, an answering machine, and a secretary." Even in the midst of her terror, Verona was briefly comforted by his mild sarcasm. "So," he concluded, "we were hoping you might know his whereabouts."

"Isn't he at home?" Seldom had she struggled harder to produce an audible sentence.

"He hasn't been there in forty-eight hours. And"—the man grimaced—"he phoned his office to say he had the flu. He told a couple of friends he'd gone to Paris. Apparently he didn't phone you."

Involuntarily Verona glanced toward her answering machine.

"We checked," he said.

The plumper, younger man weighed in again. "He's only making things worse by trying to avoid us. If you speak to him, tell him that. Right now, no harm done. Pay us what he owes and we'll forget the whole shenanigans." He flung his arms wide, indicating the extent of the shenanigans and forcing his companion to lean back into the sofa. The pinky on his left hand, Verona saw, stuck out at an odd angle. "But pretty soon it will be too late. No way he'll get away with this unless he's prepared to live in a frigging cave"—his arms flew again—"in frigging Patagonia."

He stood up, came over, and held something out toward her. Automatically her hand rose to accept the small cardboard rectangle: a business card.

"What Nigel's trying to tell you," said the older man, shifting to a more comfortable position now that he had the sofa to himself, "is that as Henry's sister it's in both your and his best interests to get a message to him. Are you all right?" he added.

Yet again her body had betrayed her. Her heart, which she had thought was already pumping to capacity, leaped to some entirely unsuspected level of activity. At the same time, almost in an instant, her hands grew icy as if the blood were seeking safety deep inside her body. Nigel fetched a glass of water, and she made her fingers open and close around it. He stood beside her while she took a few shaky sips. She could smell cinnamon, faintly, on his hands or breath.

Then the two of them let themselves out.

As soon as she heard the outside door close, Verona stood up. The glass fell from her fingers and bounced twice, unbroken, on the rug. And in the time it took to do so she dramatically revised her picture of herself. Just because she was tall and quick-tempered and could clean a sixth-floor window without feeling dizzy did not mean she was brave; she had simply not been tested. She ran to the door and fumbled the mortise lock into place. Then she checked all the windows and drew all the curtains and blinds. As she moved from room to room, it became apparent that listening to her answering machine was only the start; the men had searched the flat meticulously. The novel she was currently reading was at the bottom of the stack of books beside her bed; the CDs she had left out were back in their cases. When she went, unthinkingly, to put away her groceries she noticed that even the boxes of cereal and pasta had been examined.

She seized the phone to call the police, but at the sound of the dial tone the trembling intensified. What on earth would she say? The men had come and gone, doing her no harm, taking nothing. She did not, for an instant, doubt their accusations. She put down the phone, picked it up again, and dialed Toby's number. Thank God, he answered. "Verona, I'm in the middle of cooking supper. Can I call you back?"

"No," she said, but the rest came out jumbled and clotted.

"What is it? Are you on your mobile?"

She put her hand on her belly and, by dint of focusing on the lettering on the phone book, managed to say, "When I came home two strange men were in my living room, looking for Henry."

"Why would they be looking for Henry?" said Toby, clearly still not grasping the enormity of what had occurred—and why should he when Verona, with the men actually in her presence, had taken several minutes to do so? She heard the *ting* of metal on metal, a whisk or fork perhaps. "Isn't he in—" Abruptly the clatter of cookware ceased. "Are you okay? Is something wrong?"

She persuaded him to meet her at Henry's house. Perhaps he had left some clue to his whereabouts. She called a cab, found the keys they'd exchanged in a rare sibling gesture, and turned on every light, two radios, and the television. Stupid to think light and cacophony could protect her, but, closing the door, she felt a little better. And a little better still at the sight of Frazer, who often drove her to the radio station, sitting behind the wheel of the taxi. As usual, he talked incessantly about his five sons, two back in Pakistan, three here, all flourishing. Verona's only task was to say "Really?" or sometimes, for variety, "Great."

Meanwhile her brain seethed. For nearly two decades she had allowed herself to hope that Henry had reformed; at the same time, she now realized, she had also been waiting for the ax to fall. There was a feeling akin to satisfaction in knowing that his true self had, at last, emerged. As the taxi turned into his street, she suddenly wondered if Nigel and George might have followed her. Or, even worse, not needed to because her next move was so obvious. She leaned forward to scan the sidewalks. In the spooky light of the streetlamps she made out a woman pushing a pram, a white car edging into a parking space. Then she saw a dark figure standing on Henry's doorstep.

"Frazer," she said.

"—and Charles is captain of the hospital cricket team—yes?"

The man stepped out of the doorway. As he bent to examine his watch, she recognized Toby. "Stop here," she said, handing

Frazer a ten-pound note. In the midst of his farewells, she extricated herself from the car.

"I thought you were never coming," Toby said. "What's going on?"

Even his irritation was reassuring. She handed him the keys and when they were inside, standing in the kitchen, she told him again about her visitors, starting with the groceries and ending with the business card. As Toby listened, his face grew pale—she could have counted his freckles if there weren't so many—and his topaz-colored eyes widened. "My God, Verona. They could have killed you. Or the baby. Anything could have happened."

"That's what I've been trying to tell you," she said, but when she looked down she saw that her hands were trembling again. This time, though, partly from cold. The house, unlike any place Henry had ever lived, was freezing. Then she remembered that she and Toby had forgotten the burglar alarm. "They were here," she whispered.

"Who?"

"The men who were in my living room. They've been here too." She covered her mouth with her still-icy hands and let the trembling take over.

"Don't, Verona," said Toby. "You've had a shock. I'll make some tea." He turned on the heat, set the oven on high with the door open, and filled the kettle. Then he made her sit down, close to the stove, and knelt before her, rubbing her hands. "That stupid bastard," he said. "What's he got himself into now?"

When they both had cups of tea—he insisted on adding two spoonfuls of sugar to hers—she did her best to tell him what the men had said about Henry. "I wish you'd been there. You'd have understood the implications."

"The implications?" he repeated, his voice shrill. "I think the implications are fairly clear. Henry is involved in something dubious. He owes the men money and he's done a bunk. The question is where to, and can the situation be sorted? When did you last see him?"

"Two or three weeks ago. We had dinner. Maybe you could talk to the men? If we knew what the problem was, perhaps we could fix it." As soon as she'd spoken, she heard how foolish she sounded. This was not some childish scrape she could make better for Henry, some petty wrongdoing to be, at best, apologized for, at worst, concealed.

"Business isn't really my area of expertise." Toby pressed his lips together. "Henry's always led a charmed life, financially and otherwise. I'm sure this is just a temporary setback."

She had forgotten, in spite of repeated evidence, that he was usually on her brother's side. "In general," she said, drinking some tea, "I think a setback or two would be good for Henry, but not in this case. These men don't play by the normal rules. I can picture them shoving him under a bus, throwing him in a ditch."

"Don't." He stood up so quickly that his chair fell over. "Would you like some more tea?" He righted the chair and, not waiting for an answer, went to stand beside the counter.

During the two years Henry had lived in the house, she had been here half a dozen times but only once before, watering the plants while he was on holiday in Italy, without him. Now she looked around the immaculate kitchen as if seeing the sleek granite counters and glittering appliances for the first time. They spoke of something, something essential about her brother, and sitting there in the heat of his pristine oven, she at last understood the syllables they murmured. "The one thing Henry wants," she said, "it isn't fame or love. It's money."

"Doesn't everyone?" Toby said, at last turning around. "Here I am slaving away to write the introduction for a catalog that will earn me three hundred pounds."

"No, that's different." In her impatience to convey her insight, words spilled out. "There are all kinds of things you won't do for money. Basically you're like me; you want to be paid for doing something you'd do anyway. Money is Henry's raison d'être. I used to think he liked making mischief for its own sake. Maybe that was true when he was younger, but nowadays he's much too practical to do something for its own sake. On the other hand, for enough cash, he would literally do almost anything."

Toby stared at her. She thought he was going to contradict her, tell her not to be so cynical about her beloved brother; then his eyes flickered. "I haven't thought about this in years," he said, pulling his chair closer, "but once at university some money went missing from my room—twenty pounds—which was a lot for me then. I reported it to the hall porter and there was quite a fuss, the cleaners taking umbrage and my saying I wasn't accusing them, though of course I was. I remember Henry, lying on my bed, while I ranted on about how I couldn't live this way, suspecting everyone. Finally he said you have to let it go, Tobes, and took me down to the pub. He bought three rounds in a row." Toby shook his head. "Of course I didn't suspect everyone. Henry was in and out of my room all the time."

He set down his tea and tugged at the collar of his shirt as if it had suddenly shrunk. "I thought nothing Henry could do would surprise me."

Verona stood up. "He cares about you," she said, stroking his back. "He really does, but he lacks certain faculties. We're at his mercy when we forget that." On the counter lay her Christmas present to Henry: a book of photographs by a famous French photographer, recommended by her former boyfriend, Jeffrey. She had bought it not so much for the glossy images as for the brief biography of the photographer, which described how, at the age of six, he had resolved never to grow up. Henry was the reverse—he had longed to be an adult—but he shared the same stubborn disregard for natural laws.

Toby squeezed her hand. "That new espresso machine looks like a spaceship. So forgive me for asking, but what are we doing here?"

"I thought we might find some clue as to where Henry's gone."

"You mean like a ticket for Ibiza or a reservation for a hired car in the Orkneys?"

"Probably not, given that they've already searched the place.

But you and I know Henry better than anyone. He might have left something that will speak to us."

He stood up. "Come," he said. He led the way up the two flights of stairs to the top of the house and then—stopping in the doorway of each of the three bedrooms, the study, the video room, and two bathrooms—back down to the kitchen. "I wouldn't have a clue how to search all this, especially when I'm not sure what I'm looking for. Besides, as we've been saying, neither of us does know Henry quite as well as we'd like to think."

She stared at him, beautiful, dependable Toby, less beautiful than when she'd first met him, more dependable. They no longer mentioned the nights they had shared a bed at university, affectionately but ineffectually, or his long-standing and, as far as she knew, unconsummated passion for Henry. Over fifteen years, Toby had been one of her closest and most constant friends and the only one who was in touch with Henry on a regular basis. Everything he said made sense except when she remembered switching on the light and seeing the men.

She was still staring at him when the phone rang. After four rings, Henry's voice came on, urging the caller to leave a message, promising nothing in return.

"Verona, George here. How's it going? We wouldn't have bothered you this afternoon if we hadn't searched Henry's hovel with zero results. But if you do come across anything, please get in touch. You know how to find us."

The block of flats where Toby lived was so solid and decorous, with its wood paneling and leaded windows, that it was almost impossible to imagine any kind of bad behavior occurring within its walls. Nevertheless, Toby wedged a chair under the knob of the front door like people did in films, while Verona locked the windows and drew the curtains. Without consultation, she headed for his bedroom, rather than the futon in the study. They both put their mobile phones on the bedside table, and she added a glass of water and the leather-bound book she had come across in the hasty search of Henry's desk that Toby had permitted after the phone call. For one stunning moment she had thought Henry kept a diary, but a quick glance revealed that this was a much older document, written in faded blue ink by their grandfather. She had flung the book, along with various bank and credit card statements, into a shopping bag.

Now, wearing one of Toby's shirts, she sat up in bed, opened the book to the first page, and read aloud:

This account of my life is for my granddaughter, Verona MacIntyre.

I was born in the town of Kendal in the Lake District in 1898. After several pregnancies that ended badly—one small stone in the churchyard, others too brief even for that—my mother was threatened with dire repercussions for any further attempt. She persisted, for which, I suppose, I ought to be grateful. In the heat of argument she would sometimes remind me of the act of heroism to which I owed my existence; of course it might equally be attributed to another kind of act on my father's part. I was christened Edmund Alfred MacIntyre and, for reasons that remain obscure, known as Jigger.

"Why have I never seen this? How did Henry get his hands on it?"

"I don't know," said Toby wearily. He was lying beside her wearing a pair of dark-blue silk pajamas. "I don't know anything. Would you mind turning out the light?"

It was months since she had shared a bed, and in the darkness she was acutely conscious of his body a few inches away. She lay back, listening to his soft breathing and the grumbling undertone of traffic on the Marylebone Road. Just as she was about to ask if he was all right, he gave a small sigh.

"I'm hopeless in this sort of crisis," he said.

"What I keep thinking is that I should have seen it coming. I had plenty of warning." At school, she told him, the English teacher had found Henry in the cloakroom, going through the pockets of the girls' raincoats. "I remember he made me stay after class. At first I was relieved when it turned out that Henry was the one in trouble, but Mr. Sayers was so serious I was scared. He said he thought Henry had been born without a conscience."

Beside her Toby shifted. "I don't think I'd agree with that," he said slowly. "No, Henry has a conscience. He just does a good job of ignoring it."

Then he asked if he could feel the baby. Gently she placed his hand on her belly.

8

The next morning at the radio station, Verona's first interview was with a young man whose mother had been defrauded by her cleaning woman. "You have to understand," the man insisted— Brian was his name—"Evelyn was like a family friend. She came to all the weddings and christenings and birthday parties. When I used to drop in on Sundays, which was her day off, I'd often find the two of them chatting away over the crossword puzzle. And when Mum went into hospital, Evelyn visited her every day. But the day after she died, Evelyn didn't answer the phone. We never heard from her again. After the funeral it turned out she'd taken over seventy thousand pounds."

"But she loved your mother," Verona suggested.

"I don't know." Brian's protuberant eyes watered alarmingly. On television, tears could be effective; on the radio they were usually disastrous. "Six months ago I would have said yes, absolutely. They were inseparable. They were best friends. I can't believe that was all pretense. At the same time, year after year, Evelyn was steadily emptying my mother's bank accounts, and none of us had a clue."

The next question on her list was, How much did you pay Evelyn? The answer was sure to be incriminating—they had paid the beloved family retainer a pittance—but seeing his brimming eyes, hearing his bewildered tones, she said, "And do you know how Evelyn got the money?"

"That was easy. She paid all the bills, opened all the mail. My mother trusted her completely. She would have signed anything Evelyn asked her to."

"I thought she was your mother's cleaner." Over Brian's shoulder, through the studio window, she could see the producer, spreading her hands. Why wasn't Verona asking the real questions, the hard ones?

"Cleaner and everything else," he said bitterly. "Don't misunderstand me. I wanted my mother to live forever, but we had an agreement that when she died we'd have money to help with our little girl. She's deaf and needs special care. Evelyn used to babysit for us."

"I'm sorry," said Verona. "We have to stop now. Thank you for talking to us today. Before Brian came into the studio, we spoke to a senior officer at the Metropolitan Police. Apparently, incidents of caretakers taking advantage of their charges are on the rise. Be sure to keep an eye on whoever is helping the older members of your family."

She read the news and the weather, and by the time she emerged Brian had gone. Sometimes people lingered after their interviews, misled by her attention at the microphone. Then she had to pretend an urgent appointment and be politely vague about the possibility of future meetings. She made her way past the studios and cluttered cubicles to her boss's office. The angular, incessantly smiling Lois looked up from her desk and smiled even more broadly.

Before she could begin to shred the interview, Verona announced that she needed a few days off. "My blood pressure is a little high. They want to keep me under observation."

"Oh, Verona," said Lois, her smile fading, "why didn't you tell me sooner? Take all the time you need. Casey can do the show. You know, she'll be glad of the experience."

The news flew across the office faster than Verona could retrace her steps, and every other person stopped her with advice and admonitions. Have you tried an aquarium, asked the research assistant. They're meant to be very soothing. Verona promised to investigate. She had intended to go straight to the underground station, but in the street she loitered indecisively beside the newsstand. Contrary to what she had told Toby that morning, she was afraid to go home, and she didn't feel safe at his flat either. At any moment his phone might ring, his door might open, and the men would be there with their questions and demands. Finally—the woman at the newsstand was darting her sharp glances—she crossed the road to the coffee shop.

She ordered a tuna sandwich and, choosing a table near the counter, tried to think what to do next. Instead she found herself remembering a conversation she'd had a couple of months ago with a girl she'd met in her midwife's waiting room. They had exchanged the usual questions about due dates and morning sickness. Then the girl, she could not have been more than seventeen, confided that her mother had died when she was a few months old; she had been brought up by her aunt. She was great, the girl said. I never thought of myself as not having a mother until this. She patted her precise bulge. Now I really, really wish I'd known her.

From her shopping bag she had produced a blue notebook. I'm writing stuff down, she said. So if anything happens the baby will know about me. She had held out the book until Verona realized that she was being invited to read it.

This is a record by me, Cynthia Stenning, of my actions and feelings after I stopped pretending I wasn't pregnant. Even though it's what they call a mistake, I want to say that it's the best thing that ever happened to me. If I was religious I'd say a big thank-you.
Your father, Eddie, says . . .

Before Verona could read further, the receptionist called her name. Your baby's very lucky, she told the girl, and was rewarded with a shy smile. In the midwife's cozy office, she had been over-whelmed by gloomy scenarios. What will happen to the baby, she'd asked, if something happens to me?

You don't mean a good something, like winning the lottery, said the midwife, unfurling her stethoscope, you mean the other kind. Hopefully, your parents or a family member could adopt the baby. That's usually less traumatic for everyone. Or you can ap-point a legal guardian. Tell me what you've been eating.

She had spent several evenings making lists of potential adop-tive parents and eliminating them. Henry was out of the question. Toby, when she asked, said he'd love to be a godfather but he ab-solutely wasn't up to being a father—even for you, darling. The first two couples she picked had also said no, one nicely—they al-ready had a prior commitment—the other less so. In the end she had asked her childhood friend, Lyndsay. She and her husband al-ready had two children who were an excellent advertisement for Lyndsay's humor and creativity and Tom's interest in nature and sport. Besides how could they refuse, given that Tom was a vicar? Verona had intended to begin a notebook for the baby too, but that had never happened.

The door of the coffee shop opened and a woman came in wearing a shiny red macintosh, followed by two older men in suits. "Do you know," the bald one was saying, "which common four-letter girl's name you just add one letter to and you get a completely different name?"

"Tuna sandwich?" said the waitress, and thumped it down.

What she needed, Verona thought as she started to eat, was a place to stay for a few days that had no connection with Henry or, if possible, with her own life. Between bites she got out her ad-dress book and turned the pages. They were filled with the names of people she knew, even some she liked, but as she read them, searching for a refuge, she felt the same futility as she had when considering her friends as prospective parents. Milly Cameron? No, even with the most robust woman, she would not feel safe. Ted and Jane Finch?

"Janet," she called over to the men. They both looked up. "Sorry, I couldn't help eavesdropping," she said. "*Jane* is the four-letter name, and you add a *t* to get *Janet*."

"Well done." The bald man beamed. "You'd be surprised how few people guess."

Which means, thought Verona, that he must go around asking people about girls' names like Diogenes searching for an honest man. But her small success cheered her. And there on the next page were Emmanuel's details transcribed on their last day in Thailand. Of all her friends and acquaintances, he at once seemed the safest, precisely because they hadn't spoken since they parted at Heathrow. And he had a reassuring loutish quality. If he came home to find two strange men in his living room, he would not sit down and politely answer their questions.

"Well done," the bald man cried again, as she left the coffee shop.

Everything conspired to get her swiftly home. In the underground the train was drawing up as she reached the platform; when she emerged from the station, the bus that passed the bottom of her street was waiting. She climbed the stairs at top speed, trying to outstrip her fear. Inside her flat she went cautiously from room to room, turning off the radios and the TV, until she was satisfied that she was alone. Then she put the chain on the door, pulled out two suitcases, and began to pack.

She didn't telephone Emmanuel until the taxi was on its way. If he wasn't at home, she would wait at a nearby pub. Anything was preferable to being here alone, dividing her anxiety between the door and the phone. As she dialed his number, she suddenly remembered how, giving him her own number, she had reversed the first and last digits. Happily he had not stooped to the same duplicity, and he answered on the second ring. "I'm in your neighborhood," she said, trying to sound casual. "I thought I'd come by and say hello."

"When?"

"Now, in twenty minutes, half an hour."

He started to say that this wasn't a good time and she made the standard excuse about losing reception. Again, everything conspired to make the journey easy. The taxi was clean and the driver, save for the small moist sounds of sucking a sweet or a cough drop, silent. From the moment Emmanuel opened the door, however, it was apparent that he was not going to accommodate her. He looked so aghast at the sight of her suitcases that, in spite of everything, she almost laughed.

"You weren't just in the neighborhood," he said.

"No," she agreed. "For reasons I can't go into right now, I need a place to stay for a few days."

"Not here," he said quickly, stepping forward to fill the doorway. "Gina, my girlfriend, will be along any minute. She'd go nuts."

I'm the one who's nuts, thought Verona. Why on earth would a man she hadn't seen in nearly a year, and had scarcely known then, take her in? "I understand," she said, "but can I come in for a minute, while I figure things out? I don't want to stay with friends—I mean," Emmanuel's frown made her add, "people I've known for a long time."

He glanced up and down the street and, perhaps reassured by the empty sidewalks, relented. "Okay, but just for two ticks." He bent to lift her suitcases. "You oughtn't to be carrying these around in your condition."

Leaving the cases in the hall, unambiguously ready for departure, he showed her into a living room riotous with flowery wallpaper. Against the tangled mass of roses, the large-screen television and the posters of Thailand and Spain looked oddly subdued. Emmanuel offered neither a seat nor tea. "So you want to stay with a stranger," he said.

He seemed different: smarter and better-looking than she'd remembered. She nodded, bracing herself to explain even as it dawned on her that he wasn't interested in explanations.

"Let me think," he said. Suddenly exhausted, she sank, uninvited, onto the sofa and watched as he paced back and forth.

"I know," he exclaimed, after half a dozen laps. "You need my mate Zeke. We work together. He's painting a house not far from here. The owners—their name is Barrow—are away on holiday. You can go and talk to him right now."

Verona listened dully. Zeke, Emmanuel, who cared? She let Emmanuel call her another taxi. But when she suggested he phone Zeke, he shook his head and said he'd rather not; he'd taken the last week off work and was dodging his employer's phone calls. "Not that Zeke isn't a nice guy," he said, "but he's a bit of an odd-ball."

"What do you mean, oddball?"

Emmanuel pushed both hands through his shockingly well-cut hair. "He's not slow—I've never seen anyone figure out prices or measurements quicker than Zeke—and he knows every shortcut in north London, but he gets freaked out by things most people wouldn't even notice: like someone parting his hair differently. And he's hopeless at lies. He doesn't tell them himself, and he doesn't—"

Whatever else Zeke didn't was lost in the blare of a car horn. Emmanuel almost ran to pick up the suitcases. By the time Verona reached the street, he had them safely stowed and had given the driver the address. "Great to see you," he said, edging toward the door. "Be sure to tell Zeke my back's wrecked."

As the taxi neared the corner, Verona saw a woman with brightly colored braids falling almost to her waist striding down the sidewalk, but before she could discover if this was the tempestuous Gina, they were in the next street. The taxi was bracingly cold, and as it jerked along she tried to figure out her next move. In no possible world was she going to ask a man she'd never met for a bed for the night, but now it occurred to her that the fact that he didn't know she was coming gave her a certain freedom. Hadn't Emmanuel said the owners of the house were away? Perhaps if she pretended to know the Barrows. No, better still, pretended to be related, nothing too close like a daughter or a sister. After all she had no idea how old they were. But a cousin, or a niece? Yes, that was it. She would announce herself as the niece and act bewildered that they hadn't told him she was coming to stay. "I'm the Barrows' niece," she practiced.

Only after the cab pulled away, leaving her alone with two substantial suitcases in a strange north London street on a cold February afternoon, did Verona realize how completely she was counting on her scenario working out. Emmanuel had been unable to recall the number of the house but it was a short street, he said, and the house was on the left, coming from the main road. The front door is bright blue, he had added, like a swimming pool. Standing at the foot of the street, she spotted an uncurtained bay window, brightly lit and, as she approached, a door of emphatic blueness came into view. A stepladder stood in the middle of the window. She paused, hoping to catch a glimpse of the person on whose good nature and naïveté she planned to impose for the next twenty-four hours.

After seventy seconds the ladder rose into the air and was carried out of sight, but whoever had moved it remained hidden. She took a firmer hold on her suitcases, carried them over to the blue door, and rang the bell.

9

Even as Verona recognized what had woken her—the stubborn song of a blackbird singing its rounds—she realized she had been dreaming. It was the blackbird that reminded her and that, as it continued its song, carried her back, just for an instant. A bird was clutching her wrist. She was holding a hawk, one of her grandfather's, not his pet, Percy, but a smaller, sleeker bird with brindled feathers. No sooner had she looked into its golden eyes than it hurled itself into the air, a tumult of wings, and was gone, as was the rest of the dream. All that remained was the knowledge that, in the midst of so much disarray, her night life had returned; for months after she became pregnant, her sleep had been dull and empty. As for her grandfather's appearance in the dream, that made perfect sense. The previous evening, after Zeke's departure, she had fallen asleep reading the leather-bound book she had found at Henry's. Catching sight of it now, still lying on the duvet beside her, she tucked it under the pillow and climbed out of bed.

She drew the faded curtains to discover the windows streaked with rain. A low mottled sky promised more. Cold air streamed around the ill-fitting sash and she moved closer, offering the taut skin of her belly to the drafts. Below her lay a garden neatly divided into flowerbeds and what looked like rows of leeks, or onions. The blackbird, seemingly oblivious to the weather, was perched on the wall, yellow beak open in lusty song. Oh, Henry, she thought. Where are you?

She pulled on her clothes, not the dress of yesterday, which was also the dress of the day before, but leggings, a T-shirt, and sweatshirt. Downstairs she headed for the kitchen, intending to eat the sensible cereal she had found during her search for food the previous evening, but something about the birdsong made her long to be out on the streets with people heading to work and school. As she slipped on her coat, her fears of the last thirty-six hours seemed vastly exaggerated. The men's visit and their subsequent phone call had been upsetting, but it was Henry they were looking for, not her or Toby. She unlocked all three locks, redid two, and set out to find the row of shops she had seen from the taxi.

She passed a bakery, the window full of plump buns and tarts, and a video shop with a cardboard cutout of a well-known actor dressed as a Roman centurion. Next to that was exactly what she needed: a café with a blackboard outside offering the Builders' Breakfast and the Heart Attack Special. Inside, the windows streamed with condensation; every molecule of air bore its burden of fried food. Behind the counter a pale woman with thick dark braids was talking energetically to a small girl.

Verona waited, listening to the mysterious language full of t's and z's. All the other customers, save for a group of women by the window, were men. At the nearest table, two boys in leather jackets were tucking into bacon and eggs. The boy facing her, she noticed, had lost a piece of his earlobe. Next to them a man with massive cheeks had his napkin tucked into his collar and was eating, with great delicacy, a plate of baked beans.

"Can I help you?" asked the woman in impeccable English.

Verona ordered a fried-egg sandwich and then, an inspiration, "Make that two."

"It'll be three any day now."

"Not for a while," she said, reaching for her purse. After months of being visibly pregnant, she was still taken aback that almost everyone felt free to comment. If you were in Niger, her midwife had told her, people wouldn't just talk; they would touch your belly for luck, yours and theirs. "What language were you speaking?"

"Slovak," said the waitress, seeming neither pleased nor affronted by her curiosity. "The sandwiches will be a couple of minutes."

But the brief exchange had broken Verona's mood. Among a hundred customers, she would be the one the waitress remembered. Oh, yes, the tall pregnant woman. As soon as the sandwiches were ready, she hurried out of the café and down the street, taking no pleasure now in her fellow pedestrians and unexpected leisure. She wanted to be indoors, safe, at the Barrows'. Only when she spotted a dusty white van parked across from the house and recognized the vehicle in which she had watched Zeke drive away the night before, did her pace slow. She remembered his face, the solemn surprise, when she had kissed him.

As she closed the door of the house, Zeke in his paint-stained clothes was coming down the stairs. Apollo descends, she thought. Hermes arrives. Although the Greek gods were surely dark-skinned, more aggressive beings, and why was she thinking such thoughts about a man she scarcely knew, at a time like this? He raised his hand, a gesture halfway between handshake and wave.

"I went to buy us fried-egg sandwiches," she said, holding out the bag.

After a tiny hesitation, his lips parted in a smile. He stepped forward to accept her offering and said he'd broken into the house. A clean, soapy smell wafted from him to her. In the kitchen he laid the table, and offered tea. The sandwich was delicious, sweet with butter, sharp with pepper; she wished she had bought a third. Zeke too ate with gusto. Meanwhile he asked simple, considerate questions: Had she slept well? Was the house warm enough? She told him about a period in her life when she had worked as an office cleaner and eaten a fried-egg sandwich every day. "We were meant to start at six. Instead, we'd come in at eight-thirty and run around with furniture polish. When the manager arrived at nine, he thought we'd been working for hours."

In the face of Zeke's clear-eyed attention, she faltered. It had been an article of faith with her and her friends that cheating large businesses was not a crime, but there was another point of view. Then she pulled herself together. He was a house painter and she was never going to see him again. The night before, after he left, she had sat at the kitchen table and tried to come up with a plan. Her entire list was *Find Henry*. Or, more exactly, *Find Henry before the men do*. As to how to accomplish this, surely someone with the right skills could trace him on the Internet. Toby would know such a person. They could figure it out as soon as she had the house to herself, which would be sooner if she offered to help Zeke.

"So what are we doing today?" she asked. "Putting up the lining paper?"

He reacted as if she had suggested they carry the fridge up and down the street. "Your aunt and uncle," he protested, his hands gripping the table, "are paying me for my work."

"Look, I can wear these." She was already on her feet, moving toward the navy-blue coveralls she had spotted hanging on the back door. Only later did it strike her as odd that, during her sojourn at the Barrows', she had lost all consciousness of stealing from them. Her attitude was like someone in a fairy story who comes across an abandoned well-stocked palace in the woods; everything beneath their roof was hers for the taking. Which must, she thought, be what Henry feels most of the time, everywhere.

As soon as they started work, Zeke's whole manner changed. He was confident, organized, calm. He showed her how to cut the sandpaper and fit it to the sanding block and set her to smoothing the part of the walls that lay within her reach—don't stretch, he urged, don't bend—while he tackled the upper half of the room, using the stepladder. As they worked, he answered her questions with increasing ease and began to ask his own. She tried to answer politely but minimally. Sometimes with strangers she had enjoyed embellishing her life story. Now she was surprised to find herself longing to tell the truth. But the less Zeke knew, the better. She pictured Nigel and George appearing in this room. So you're saying you thought Miss MacIntyre was the Barrows' niece? That seems rather far-fetched.

"Careful." He touched her arm.

Looking down, she discovered she had rubbed the same spot for too long. A hollow was appearing in the wall.

Their hours of sanding made little visible difference, but with each strip of lining paper that Zeke guided into place, another section of the motley-patterned wall disappeared. Verona was torn between satisfaction and dismay. The wildness of the room had made it theirs; now it was becoming the Barrows'. At the same time, she could see that this was the perfect job for Zeke, creating order out of chaos. Her own job, questioning people about minor crimes and novelties, often seemed more like a way of increasing whatever chaos there was around.

He climbed down the ladder and they stood side by side, surveying the room. Just before the silence grew awkward, she asked if they could make a fire and volunteered to see what there was for supper. Once again she searched the Barrows' supplies and found a bunch of carrots in the bottom of the fridge—a little limp, but sautéed they would be fine—some tinned spinach, and, best of all, a frozen lasagna from a good delicatessen. When Zeke came in, she saw him look askance at her foaming glass but a stubborn part of her refused to tell him that it was nonalcoholic beer. Who are you to pass judgment, she thought. And then, suddenly, disaster. The carrots, ignored, were burning.

"Christ." She seized the frying pan and brought it down against the stove. All her anger—at herself, at Henry, at the men—was focused on this convenient juxtaposition of metal on metal. She banged and banged.

When she stopped, she was alone in the kitchen. For one appalled moment she thought she might be alone in the house. Very carefully she set down the frying pan, tiptoed into the living room and there, thank God, he was, kneeling before the fire, holding a pair of tongs toward the still hesitant flames. She apologized. The last of the firelighter flared and died. She apologized some more. "What makes you angry?" she asked. He moved a knob of coal, and another. If only she could stroke his hair, or caress the vertebrae at the top of his spine, two of which were revealed as he bent forward. At last she walked away, trying to demonstrate, with each softly taken step, what a good pacifist she would be.

In the kitchen, she transferred the remaining carrots to a new pan and hid the burned one in the dishwasher, a welcome-home present for the Barrows. She stirred the spinach and found plates and silverware. All the while various factions warred within her. One voice urged her to go back and beg forgiveness. Another suggested she return not to beg but to reason, to lay out the syllogisms that made his staying inevitable. A third wanted to grab the saucepan out of the dishwasher and keep banging until the stove lay in fragments at her feet. A fourth, barely audible, counseled patience.

She was peering at the lasagna, the hot air of the oven gusting against her cheeks, when she heard footsteps in the hall. The steps grew louder. He was in the room, just behind her. Was he here to announce his departure? She remained motionless. Then came the delightful sounds of chair legs scraping on linoleum, followed by others, even more pleasing, of a human body settling onto a chair. She asked some stupid question about why so many lightbulbs were missing—did she actually use the phrase Stygian gloom?— and he explained the extraordinary fatality rate of the last few days.

They ate, they talked, he followed her upstairs. They did things together which both of them had done with others, perhaps with many others, and for a while Verona thought of nothing else.

Only after Zeke left, slipping from the bed and dressing in the dark, did she recall the phone call of a few hours earlier. Perhaps it had been not the phone but a fax. She had discovered the machine yesterday evening and, relieved at not having to explain herself in conversation, sent Toby a note. Now she got up, pulled on her coat—her hasty packing had failed to include a dressing gown— and made her way to the study. She flicked the light switch and was rewarded with a brief flash. Four steps carried her to the little red glow of the machine; a sheet of paper glimmered in the in-tray. The chances of its being for her were minuscule. Still she stood there, hands pressed into the pockets of her coat, refusing to pick it up. Why should Henry intrude even now? She went back to the spare room, flung her coat on a chair, climbed between the sheets, and, picturing that moment when Zeke had helped her out of the coveralls and run his hands over every inch of her belly, fell asleep.

An hour later her eyes opened again. Something had woken her but what? She lay, listening intently to the city silence, trying not to think about Nigel and George. Just as she had decided that the culprit was a passing car or motorbike, a piercing wail erupted from the garden. She couldn't tell if the cats were fighting or mating.

"Knock it off," cried a man's voice.

The only answer was a low, fierce moan eerily like the sound of human lovemaking. Verona climbed out of bed again and walked back across the landing. The red light still glowed. The sheet of paper still lay there. Worse, she supposed, if it hadn't. She picked it up and returned to the bedroom. Sitting up in bed, the duvet snug around her belly, she at last turned it over.

Dearest Verona,

I still don't know what's going on with H. I phoned his office today and the receptionist now says he's convalescing in Normandy for a week. But I did get a visit and this time it was like yours: no warning, the two of them at my kitchen table when I came home. Nothing terrible happened but I was terrified.

They asked where you were and I told them I didn't know. I think they believed me but they are convinced that you're the way to H. and that I'm the way to you.

I'm going to stay with my friends Doug and Simon. They have a burglar alarm, a dog, and a lodger who practices tai chi. If you've heard anything, let me know. Otherwise I'll phone the police tomorrow.

Coward, she thought, crybaby, telltale. With each childish epithet she hurled in Toby's direction, another burst of wailing rose from the garden. Then came a series of oaths followed by the thud of something—a brick, a book—hitting a wall. In the abrupt silence her anger vanished. She remembered how she had felt when she caught sight of the men on her sofa. Terrified didn't begin to describe it.

She let the fax fall to the floor and turned out the light. Again she thought about going to the police. But as she pictured herself talking to some well-meaning sergeant and Henry behind bars, her heart began to race. What could the police do for her and Toby, besides urge them to phone the moment the men reappeared? Round-the-clock bodyguards seemed unlikely.

She thought back to her last meeting with Henry. He had suggested an expensive restaurant overlooking the Thames. At the time she'd assumed he was trying to make amends for their previous encounter, shortly before Christmas, when her refusal, yet again, to name the baby's father had driven him to bribery, increasingly wild guesses, and finally anger. Verona, he'd exhorted, you're my only living family member and you're about to produce my second living family member. I think I have a right to know who I'm going to be related to. He had stalked out of the pub and driven off, gunning the engine by way of rebuke.

She had arrived at the restaurant first and been shown to a table by the window. She had sat, watching the barges and boats come and go, until someone hugged her and she smelled Henry's current cologne. Once, during those early years when she and Toby used to talk endlessly about relationships, he had remarked that Henry was beautiful. Beautiful, she had said. You are besotted. But some facts about her brother were indisputable. He was tall but not awkward about his height like she was, and he chose his clothes with care and wore them well. His ears lay neatly against his close-cropped brown hair. His nose was smaller than hers, though only slightly, and, after he broke it—a car accident, he said on one occasion, a tennis ball on another—a little askew. His eyes were darker than hers, the color of roasted almonds, and only in full sunlight were the green flecks they shared apparent. His most striking feature, as Toby had pointed out, was the groove that ran from his nostrils to his upper lip. Like that pre-Raphaelite model, Toby had said. You know, the one with the mass of hair and a permanent pout. How typical of Henry, Verona had thought, that his best feature has no name.

He had enacted the little drama of arrival, for her, the maître d', and the customers at nearby tables; he made a teasing comment about how radiant she looked, apologized for being late, complained about the traffic, and took his seat. Then there was the turning off of the pager and the mobile phone, a ritual which, even now that these accessories were commonplace, Henry performed in a way that simultaneously feigned modesty and signaled importance. See how I neglect even the most urgent summons for your company. Sometimes Verona found this fuss infuriating, but that evening she had watched with amused tolerance as he pressed various buttons and slipped the machines into the pockets of his jacket, one in each, so as not to spoil the cut. A significant pleasure of pregnancy was that, week by week, she grew less vulnerable to Henry's machinations.

But now, as a car rattled by in the street outside, she remembered herself saying, What's wrong? Is something the matter?

Bad day, he had said. I had one bolshie client after another.

His hands, however, had belied his casual words. Like his ears, they were small and neat; if in some party game they had been the only visible part of him one would have guessed them to belong to a man of much shorter stature, or possibly a woman. They were also the only part of himself that he seemed to forget about. He had sat back in his chair, the picture of good-humored, relaxed attention, and all the while his fingers were testing the blade of the knife, raking the tablecloth with his fork, twitching from plate to napkin to salt dish. He didn't mention the baby except, obliquely, when instead of ordering a bottle of wine he said he'd just have a glass. They had talked about a friend who had finally got a part in a West End play and Henry's new espresso machine, which had arrived from Perugia.

The waiter brought their starters. While she ate her mushroom soup, Henry picked and chose among his whitebait as if some of the small fish were more worthy of being eaten than others. When the plate contained only a few rejects, he excused himself. This too was traditional. After ostentatiously turning off his phone, Henry could seldom get through an hour without looking for messages. Once again she watched the river. Just as she was about to send a waiter to check on him, he reappeared.

Sorry, he said. I've got a lot going on right now.

For years Henry had talked in terms of property deals, each larger and more profitable than its predecessor. Even in the best of circumstances she might not have listened closely to his account of the current one, but just as the waiter brought their entrées and Henry began to speak, a boat rigged with hundreds of tiny white lights sailed into view. All her attention was momentarily captured by this enchanting spectacle. When she turned back to the table, Henry was finishing his explanation.

Everything was in place, he said, taking a mouthful of lamb, the financing, the owners, the buyers. The only problem was we hadn't done our homework.

Looking at his glittering eyes, his ears, which had turned scarlet, she wondered if he had used his trip to the bathroom for other activities besides checking messages. But before she could say anything, he had asked a question of his own.

What's the first thing you remember?

At the time she hadn't thought twice about the abrupt change of topic. The two of them shared a taste for sweeping questions: who's the most interesting person you've met in the last year? What was the worst advertising slogan? I remember, she said, being stuck up a tree. I remember a dress I loved with blue bows. I remember peeling the pebbles off our pebble-dashed house. I remember holding you for the first time and Mum telling me to be careful of your brains. What about you?

The first thing I remember, the very first, is a pillow against my face.

You mean you were sleeping the wrong way?

No, Mum was holding a pillow over my face. It happened more than once. He ate the last mouthful of lamb and mopped his plate.

That's . . . A black hole had opened in her vocabulary. She set down her knife and fork and clenched her fists. Mum would never have done that. Besides, you can't possibly remember that far back.

Wouldn't she? He gave a small, bitter smile. Come on, Verona. You know how my crying drove her mad.

You're saying she tried to kill you?

Well, she probably didn't think of it like that. It would have been a crib death, one of those unfortunate accidents. Coffee, please, he added to the waiter who was clearing their plates. Black.

Now Verona pulled the duvet higher and remembered how, unable to look at Henry, she had stared at the snowy tablecloth. The idea of her mother trying to squeeze the life out of Henry, of Henry waving his puny limbs, was horrifying. Have you ever told me this before? she asked.

No, I'm telling you now. But I've always wondered if you knew. Sometimes you would look after me. I used to think you did it to protect me. And the woman who baby-sat, I'm pretty sure she knew that Mum was off her trolley.

The waiter set down the coffee and Henry asked for a brandy. Here, he said when it came. Have a sip. You look like you've seen a ghost.

He had given her a lift as far as the underground at Green Park.

Their good-byes had been hurried by the traffic, an awkward kiss, a promise to talk soon. She had climbed out of the car, and a moment later she could no longer be sure which among the many rear lights were his. The next day she had discussed the conversation with Lyndsay, who, before Tom, had once gone out with Henry for six weeks and who still regarded herself as an expert on him. Of course he can't remember that far back, she had insisted. He probably saw a TV program about crib deaths and decided it would make a nice addition to his autobiography. At the time Verona had agreed: Henry was dramatizing, as usual.

But gazing at the shadowy ceiling, the conviction swept over her that he had been telling the truth: their mother, nervous, shrill, alternating between periods of furious activity and profound lethargy, had at least once, perhaps often, tried to kill him. Maybe, she thought, that was when it all started: the belief that his ends justified almost any means.

She struggled to recall whether he had said anything else. She pictured his hands motionless on the table, his ears still flushed, the fairy-tale boat disappearing down the river toward Gravesend, but no more words came to mind. What if those ambiguous tail-lights were the last she saw of him? Don't be absurd, she told herself. Just because he had gone away without telling her or Toby, there was no reason to presume disaster. She couldn't count the number of times she had left a phone message, only to have him ring back three or four days later with the news that he had been, or sometimes still was, abroad. Why shouldn't he be in Normandy, as the receptionist claimed? Several friends had houses there. All I need to do, she thought, is find out where he is and tell him that two men are threatening Toby and me, and life can return to normal. On that optimistic note, sleep once more overtook her.

She was awoken, this time unmistakably, by the ringing of the phone. She reached the study as the fax machine disgorged its sheet of paper.

Verona,

For reasons I can't explain now I've made you a reservation at the Heathrow Hilton. Go there asap and I'll join you. Sorry to be so cloak-and-dagger.

XXO Toby

In the midst of her confusion one clear thought surfaced: she must leave before Zeke returned. He must not be implicated in this mess. She bathed, dressed, carried her suitcases downstairs, and, standing in the kitchen, forced herself to eat a slice of toast and drink a cup of tea. The minicab company promised to have a car there in fifteen minutes.

At the kitchen table she tried to compose a letter to Zeke, but everything that came to mind seemed either too much or too little. Finally she wrote *Thursday, 7 A.M. Thanks for everything. I'll be in touch soon.* She glared at the paltry words, thought to amend them, thought to score them out. Instead she seized a hammer and nails from the toolbox in the living room. Upstairs, she rolled up the rug at the foot of the bed. Then she spread out the coveralls she had worn the day before and and nailed them at the collar, the sleeves, the ankles. No way he could think that this gesture was an accident, part of her careless housekeeping. And perhaps he would understand what she was trying to tell him: that what had happened here was as important as the events at any crime scene.

Zeke

10

This account of my life is for my granddaughter, Verona MacIntyre.

I was born in the town of Kendal in the Lake District in 1898. After several pregnancies that ended badly—one small stone in the churchyard, others too brief even for that—my mother was threatened with dire repercussions for any further attempt. She persisted, for which, I suppose, I ought to be grateful. In the heat of argument she would sometimes remind me of the act of heroism to which I owed my existence; of course it might equally be attributed to another kind of act on my father's part. I was christened Edmund Alfred MacIntyre and, for reasons that remain obscure, known as Jigger.

My father, Henry, was the first incumbent of a small parish a few miles north of Kendal. Until his marriage, he had been the bishop's golden boy, destined to rise to dizzy heights in the diocese. But the day before he was due to walk down the aisle, a deacon took him aside and intimated that advancement was now unlikely. As my mother, Susannah, said, "Those prigs." She had wanted to be an actress, and well into middle age she retained the appearance and mannerisms associated with such ambition. She chain-smoked, she wore a swirling blue velvet cloak, and she was seldom seen without her hairpiece, a hank of vivid orange hair that clipped on behind her own fringe to form an unconvincing bun. Sometimes, when I was poorly, she let me play with it.

Almost every day, hail or shine, my mother went out visiting in the parish and talked to whoever she met, old and young, well-to-do and hard up, asking after them and their families and making extravagant claims and promises. I will die if we do not go to Blackpool this Easter. Nothing could be better than haddock for lunch. I detest Jane Austen. Everyone in the parish made fun of her, and everyone adored her. My father stood happily in her shadow, the pergola to her honeysuckle; marriage was his one great adventure. He was a scholarly man, who read both Greek and Latin for pleasure, and he supplemented the meagre living by preparing boys for school or university. In conversation he was witty and droll, but his sermons were uniformly dull. As I got older, I would urge him to liven things up. On the few occasions when he tried, the congregation coughed and fidgeted, vexed at the unexpected interruption of their Sunday nap.

Both the church and the vicarage had been built by the parishioners. To compensate for the pitiful salary, they had chosen a beautiful situation on top of a small hill with a view thirty miles down the valley; to the north the bare hills rose toward the Scottish border. During my childhood I explored most of this wild countryside, as far as I could walk in a day, often in the company of one of my father's private pupils. The most memorable of these was a Tibetan prince whom we called Tiger. How Tiger made his way from a palace in Lhasa to the Lake District, I never understood. He had skin the colour of our local honey and eyelashes so long that my mother claimed to envy them; he wore scarlet robes. I taught him to swim, to tie knots, and to recognise birds. In exchange he taught me the courtesies of his language, how to start a fire without matches, how to walk through a flock of sheep so quietly they didn't pause in their grazing. He lived with us for nearly two years. A year after he returned to Tibet a letter brought the news that his throat had been cut in a palace uprising.

I had never seen my mother so upset. "I don't understand," she kept saying. "A boy who wouldn't hurt a fly. Why would anyone want to kill him?"

The part about the flies was literal. I shared a room with Tiger, and all summer long he ushered the bluebottles out of the open window rather than letting me swat them. As for my mother's question, we were all about to start asking variations of that.

I attended the local grammar school and in 1916 did what most boys my age were doing: enlisted. That was my real education, the war and the men in my company. Many of them could barely read or write, and I became their scribe. You can imagine these soldiers in their twenties, a few in their thirties, writing to their wives and sweethearts and mothers, courtesy of an eighteen-year-old brat. There was one corporal, Ralph, whose letters were so dull I couldn't stand it. *Dear Eliza,* he would dictate. *How are you? I hope your cold is better. I am still all right. Thank you for the socks. Love, Ralph.*

After the first few, I gave him the advice I'd given my father. He squirmed and said he was rotten at that kind of thing but if I had suggestions, go ahead. So I cut loose, wrote about the countryside, the food, the Romanesque churches. We weren't allowed to comment on the war. The next letter from Eliza had a postscript. *Forgive me for remarking, but the last letter didn't sound like Ralph. Keep up the good work.* It was signed *JS*.

Of course, Eliza too was using an intermediary. From then on, JS and I continued to embellish the letters and to include postscripts to each other. After a couple of months I asked if I could write to her separately. The reply contained an extra page: *Dear Jigger, I'd be glad to correspond. I live down the street from Eliza and I'm going to be eighteen this summer, so if the war keeps up, I'll be joining you in France soon.*

I was too embarrassed to admit that I'd been seeking female

company. Odd what the imagination can do. I'd turned JS into a lovely young woman who shared my interests in nature and books. All those things were true, except the gender. When I asked Ralph if I could check something in one of the letters (he kept them under his pillow) and reread them, I realised that there had never been a hint of femininity. I had invented everything, out of loneliness.

But embarrassment had its rewards. Next time I was home on leave, JS took the train from Streatham into Charing Cross and we met at a tearoom. I have no feelings that way, but he was one of the most beautiful boys I've ever laid eyes on, slender, upright with a bright, open face. In the street, both women and men turned to look at him. At first our conversation was awkward and stilted. He asked about my journey; I mentioned a concert I'd attended; he said something about a novel. Then he asked about France. "I can't imagine"—his voice fell to a whisper—"killing a man. Maybe in the dark, maybe with my eyes closed, but if I can see a man's face—"

I drank my tea and thought of the scenes I'd witnessed, and of some I'd taken part in. I couldn't imagine them either. After the first month in France I had decided not to keep count of anything. "You could become a conscientious objector," I told him.

His face reddened as if I'd slapped him. "I don't have the guts," he said. "When you see how they're treated. . . . And my parents, they dread me going, I'm an only child, but my staying would shame them past bearing. Everyone on our street has gone."

I wanted to protest—they'd rather see you dead or maimed than have the neighbours gossip?—but my parents would have failed the same test. Winter after winter my mother cautioned me to dress warmly and not to venture onto the frozen lakes; in summer similar rules applied to swimming and the farmer's old mare. But when I came home to announce that I'd enlisted, she flourished a pair of needles and said she was already knitting me a scarf to take to France. "What about driving an ambulance?" I suggested.

JS's face brightened and he said he'd investigate. Then he reached into his satchel and shyly handed me a brown paper parcel: Housman's *A Shropshire Lad*. On the flyleaf he had written: *For Jigger, with admiration and affection. In the hope of many years of friendship.*

"I hope you like it," he said, smiling earnestly.

For an odd moment I felt like crying.

Now here's the funny part of the story. JS did join an ambulance team and came to France. Our paths crossed several times, and each time he was more altered. No one could have survived over there the way he was, quivering like a blade of grass with every passing word, but JS changed out of all recognition. My recommendation had been meant to spare him; I had had no idea of the terrible choices he would face. Once when we met, he'd just lost a dozen wounded men because the pipe they'd led from the exhaust through the van to heat it had leaked. "But if we hadn't done that," he said, "ninety percent of them would have died of cold and shock. Hobson's choice."

I told him about Albert, a man in my company who had shot himself in the foot. "Cleaning my gun, sir," he had said, when I asked how it happened. His eyes were blue as the sky above Lake Windermere. "Bad luck," I said. The official line on self-inflicted injuries, Blighty wounds as they were called, was severe. Unofficially I couldn't help admire a man who would hurt himself in order to get sent home. Several hours later, I watched the stretcher bearers carry Albert away down the trench, the first stage of his long journey.

"And then last week," I said to JS, "a letter came from his widow." The foot had turned septic and he had died in the local hospital. She was beside herself. He had been determined to go home not out of cowardice but because he'd got it into his head that she was carrying on with a local blacksmith. *I never looked at another man,* she wrote, *but nothing I said made a difference. Something or someone had poisoned his thoughts about me.*

A year earlier, even six months, JS would have cried out against the waste, the irony. Now he drummed his fingers on the table. "At least she can get cracking with the blacksmith," he said.

"Why do you stay?" I asked.

"Because (a) I'm not about to shoot myself in the foot and (b) what would I do at home? Read the obituaries in *The Times*? Dig for victory?" Then he looked me full in the face, which was something he hadn't done in months. "Why didn't you tell me?" he said.

"Tell you what?" I said, though I'd been waiting for the question ever since he came over.

"What it was like here. What *we* were like here."

Our combined ages—he was eighteen, I was nearly twenty—were less than half my present age. We were talking by candle-light in my dugout while the rain fell outside, and our talk was treason, or close to it. The rather good merlot in our glasses had been given to JS by a farmer in exchange for splinting his son's wrist. I started to stammer out an apology, and he laughed.

"Don't," he said. "You couldn't have told me, even if you'd tried. You know it's two years, almost to the day, since Edith Cavell was shot. One of the men in my corps worked in her hospital in Brussels."

He raised his glass. "To Edith, who didn't change." He tipped his head back and drank until the glass was empty. "Did I mention the farmer's daughter," he said, "as sweet a piece of crumpet as ever I squeezed? She made such a racket, I had to put my hand over her mouth." He winked, and I turned away.

Two years later I was in my room at Clare College, Cambridge, struggling with a translation of Pliny, when the porter brought a rather grubby envelope to my door. Ralph, bless his heart, had found someone to write to me. Three days earlier, JS's body had washed up at low tide in the Thames. "His dad says he slipped, but down the pub the word is he jumped from the Battersea Bridge. His pockets were full of stones."

After the war the two of us had grown even farther apart. I was living the snug life of an undergraduate—one of my father's parishioners, who had lost a son at Ypres, was paying for my studies—and JS was drifting round London, trying his hand at journalism. Our occasional meetings, usually in a drab pub near his current digs, were a disappointment, I think, to both of us. Eventually, as he moved from one rented room to another, we fell out of touch.

But those wretched evenings in some smoky room, those weren't what I thought of when I read Ralph's letter. Instead, I recalled the tender openhearted boy who had bought me a book of poetry and begged me to save him. And then I remembered his remark about the farmer's daughter. Perhaps, unbeknown to himself, JS had left behind a son or daughter with the same bright, curious gaze.

The week after Armistice I met a man who changed my life. The regiment had a couple of days' leave in Paris while they organised transport. The weather was seasonal, cold and damp, and there wasn't much to do except go to cafés and try to keep warm. One drizzly afternoon a friend and I found ourselves sitting at a table with two men from another regiment. My pal and the older of the two discovered a liking for dominoes; I fell into conversation with the other. "Charles Howatson," he said. He proffered a bottle of Calvados and began to talk about how he'd been trying to find someone to rent him a bicycle so he could visit Versailles. "It seems daft to be this close and not see the Hall of Mirrors."

A few minutes earlier, when I first laid eyes on Charles's pudgy red face, I had thought, now here's a dim bulb. For years afterward, I was to have the pleasure of watching other people make the same mistake. Sometimes Charles encouraged them; he was canny about the advantage his unprepossessing looks gave him. He kept talking about how the war had changed everything, how people wouldn't be content any longer to work and die in their own little villages. "They know the world is larger," he claimed. "They want to see it."

"Not me," I said. "I've had enough travel to last a lifetime."

"That'll pass," he told me, and we wrangled, amicably, back and forth. Shortly before dark he said, "Come on. There's something you have to see."

Outside, dusk was falling and streetlights were sparse, but Charles led the way confidently from one square to the next until we reached an imposing set of stairs. At the top he pushed open a huge door. In the vast gloom I gradually distinguished the trains lined up at the platforms, like slumbering behemoths. Charles had brought me to the Gare de Lyon. On the far side a single engine let out a sonorous whistle; a burst of steam floated up to the vaulted ceiling. He led us over to the engine and called up, asking permission to climb aboard. I can still remember stepping into that cabin. For years I had been living with mud and cold, smells I couldn't or wouldn't identify. Suddenly I was warm and dry and the air smelled of nothing more sinister than the stoker's coffee and engine oil. My French was still absurdly bad but Charles was fluent. As a boy, he'd spent holidays in Brittany. While he pelted the men with questions, the driver kindly gave me his seat. I rested my hands on the wheel, pretending to drive.

The next thing I knew, someone was tugging my sleeve. *Monsieur, monsieur. Il faut partir.*

Still half asleep, I stood on the platform watching the engine pull out of the station. Even in my dazed state I could feel Charles beside me, observing every detail of the train's departure. These iron maidens were the love of his life. On the steps of the station, looking out into the misty streets, he rocked back on his heels and said, "What are you going to do when you get home?"

"I'm going to Cambridge to study mathematics." I had a piercing vision of a future in which I would sit in lectures, carry a clean handkerchief, wear a gown at dinner. My biggest fear would be missing the curfew.

Charles didn't seem to hear my answer. "You know what I think we should do? Take over my pater's railway."

"I have forty-one pounds in my bank account," I said, exaggerating only slightly.

But Charles, it turned out, had a little more, or his father did, and he absolutely meant that offhand remark uttered at dusk on the steps of the Gare de Lyon. I won't go into the financial details, but after we'd graduated from university we ended up owning a hundred and fifty miles of track and half a dozen stations. We survived the general strike, the stock market crash, and the Second World War, and lost everything when railways were nationalised by the Labour Government, for which we both voted, in 1945.

Seven years after I came down from Cambridge, I married a fair-haired Welshwoman called Irene Talbott. Mutual friends introduced us at a matinee of *The Importance of Being Earnest*. At dinner afterward she did a very passable imitation of Lady Bracknell, and later, when the bill came, she attempted to pay her share. Her parents were both dead, she told me; she lived in lodgings and worked in a dress shop. I was intrigued by her wit and her independence. Eight months after the matinee, I proposed, and four months after that we got married. For reasons that made perfect sense at the time, I did not take her to meet my parents until the eve of the wedding, when we caught the train to Kendal. A taxi dropped us off at the vicarage shortly before dinner. I hadn't been home since Christmas, and the roses by the door were in bloom.

"What a lovely spot," said Irene.

Inside was roast duck and trifle and my mother in top form. She stood at the head of the table, pretending to teach Sunday school. "Now, children, who can tell me why the servant with the single talent was punished? That's right, Tabitha. Darned if I know."

Over the port she sang the music hall song that, before she met my father, she had planned to use at auditions. "I gave up everything for him," she said, producing a handkerchief and dabbing at her eyes. "I never could resist a man in a dog collar."

"Nor I a woman of the stage," said my father. The three of us laughed beneath Irene's watchful gaze.

We retired shortly afterward with remarks about the big day ahead, but upstairs in my old room I felt too restless for sleep. I sat by the window, having a last cigarette, and thought about the afternoon Tiger and I had climbed the hill curiously known as the High Street. We were almost at the summit when he beckoned me over. A few yards away, balanced on a ledge, was an untidy bundle of sticks containing three good-sized chicks. As we crouched behind a rock watching them, a whirring came from overhead. A peregrine falcon was hovering so close that its wingbeats lifted our hair. We froze, not knowing if the chicks were progeny or prey. The answer came a second later when the bird swooped down and bent to feed them.

As we crept away, I saw that Tiger's cheeks were wet with tears. I knew better than to ask the cause. He led us up the final pitch, an almost sheer rock face, at breakneck speed. I had noticed before that, when he forgot my limitations, Tiger climbed as if he weren't subject to gravity.

Left to my own devices, I would probably have begun next to think about JS. All my ghosts were out that night, crying stop, wait, don't do it. But just as I was finishing my cigarette there was a knock at my door. I went to open it, expecting Irene. "Edmund," said my mother, slipping past me, "I have to talk to you." She had not used my baptismal name in over a decade.

Standing there in her white nightdress, her hands clasped before her, she made her speech. "You think Irene's like me, all jokes and silliness. The thing is, Jig, I'm not really like that. I knew that marrying me would ruin Henry's career and that we'd have to scramble to make ends meet. There hasn't been an hour since I walked down the aisle when making him happy and running a pleasant household hasn't been my main preoccupation. But Irene is different. Underneath the giggling, she's shell-shocked. There's some bad history there: maybe a dead fiancé or two. She'll be fine for a while. Then she'll go to pieces, mark my words."

Her earlier joking gone, she was utterly serious. As for me, I would have given almost anything not to be getting married. But such is the contrariness of human nature that, as soon as my mother began to speak, I knew I couldn't back out. "Mother," I whispered—we were both aware of Irene in the next room—"I don't have a clue what you're talking about. You've barely met Irene. Of course you make her nervous. There's no way I'm going to jilt her at the altar, just because you have a bee in your bonnet."

I turned back to the window. I could argue with my mother until the cows came home, but I could not contradict her. A couple of months ago I had begun to notice how reticent Irene was about her past. I'd been talking about the Christmas before I met her, when I'd gone skiing with Charles and his wife. "What did you do?" I asked.

"Oh, I can't remember," she said. "Did you get us a reservation at Cox's?"

We must, during our courtship, have had hundreds of similar exchanges, but for some reason this one irked me. "It's only a year and a half ago," I said. "Surely you know what you were doing."

"Well, I don't," she said, "but I could guess. I went to a service at St. Paul's and had dinner with my landlady. She made the goose and I was in charge of the vegetables: Brussels sprouts with chestnuts and braised parsnips. Afterwards we played canasta. Will that do?" She turned to smile at me. "Oh, Jig. Truly, everything from the time before I met you is a blur. I worked, I slept, I tried to get by."

We were walking through St. James's Park—it was nearly dusk but the pelicans were still drifting around on the lake—and

I reached for her arm and said how lovely she looked. But later that week when I ran into the friends who had introduced us, I asked, casually I hope, how they knew Irene and learned that they had met her only a few weeks before the matinee; Irene had deftly managed to suggest a long friendship. I had been so charmed by her gaiety, and moved by the loss of her parents, that I hadn't stopped to ask certain questions. Still, my doubts might have dissipated—Irene was excellent company—if in the course of procuring the marriage license, I hadn't discovered she was twenty-nine, six years older than I'd thought.

Now, while my mother made one last attempt, I lit a second cigarette and struggled not to tell her everything. "Please, Jig," she said. "I'll pretend to be ill tomorrow, to save face. If you still feel the same about her in a year, I promise I'll dance my shoes off at your wedding."

She was looking at me beseechingly, and just for a moment I thought of Albert, the man who had shot himself. Then she did something inexpressibly touching. In her haste to talk to me she had not stopped even to remove her hairpiece which, although the artifice grew yearly more obvious, she still insisted on wearing. People wouldn't know me without my falsie, she said, when my father or I suggested she leave it off. Now she raised her arms and began, one by one, to take out the pins that secured it. Sometimes, as a boy, she had let me do this for her.

But I was a successful businessman. I kept my doubts to myself and sent my mother away, carrying her switch of false hair. Next morning she was a model of good humour as she carried up a breakfast tray to Irene and acted as her lady's maid. Irene had bought the dress from her shop and altered it herself. Henry performed the ceremony. The church was packed with parishioners and old friends, mostly mine.

We went to Paris for our honeymoon. I took Irene to the Gare de Lyon and we tried to find the café where Charles and I had met. For a while we wandered from square to square while I said maybe that's it, or I think it was on a corner. At last we simply chose one. Over a glass of Calvados, Irene made me repeat the whole story. We came back to London and settled into a modest house she had found in Clapham. For almost two years our lives ran smoothly. Business was flourishing. We went to plays and dinners with friends and entertained in turn; there were holidays in Europe, riding and walking on the Downs. But soon after our son was born, in 1931, something happened; Irene became subject to bouts of melancholy. Or perhaps she no longer cared to conceal them. A nursemaid took care of Dennis, and Irene moved into the spare room. Increasingly, I stayed late at the office and dined alone.

The war cheered her up, perhaps in part because it allowed her to have a job again. To my surprise she refused to leave London or to let Dennis leave. He would go to school, per usual, and hide under his desk when the bombs fell. The Germans must be beaten and it was up to every man, woman, and child to do their part, whether it was piloting a Spitfire or saying multiplication tables. She herself drove a supply lorry and went for long walks around the city, heedless of the raids.

On March 12, 1941, the two of us, as seldom happened on a weekday, were both at home. I spent the morning in my study and emerged for a lunch of braised kidneys, boiled potatoes, carrots. We talked about whether to try to get a plumber to fix the leaky tap in the bathroom and what we should give Charles for his birthday. Afterward, Irene went out to the kitchen to make tea. The housekeeper had given notice in 1939 and it would have been unpatriotic, if not impossible, to replace her. I was reading the newspaper when her cry came.

"Oh, Jig, Jig, come quickly. Something dreadful has happened. I've taken poison."

I called the doctor, I stuck my finger down her throat, I made her drink glass after glass of water and walk back and forth. Why, I kept asking. Why take poison? Why take it now?

She didn't answer. Within an hour she was insensible. The doctor came and said there was nothing to be done. When Dennis arrived home from school, I told him, perhaps unwisely, what was happening and sent him to his room. She died shortly before midnight, making a noise like a door creaking on its hinges.

I don't know how my mother guessed, but Irene had lost not one but two fiancés. The first, the great love, I learned when I searched her desk, was named Dennis; he and I had fought on the same stretch of the front for a few months. Fiancé number two, a less well-documented figure, had worked in catering before he died of polio in 1923. If I could have spoken with complete frankness, I would have claimed that I no longer cared about Irene, that I stayed with her out of loyalty and propriety, but as I sat at her desk, with its neat pigeonholes spilling their secrets, I felt as if my world had once again turned upside down. All the little attentions she had paid me during our courtship, the ardor with which she gave herself to me on our wedding night, even her deceits—which I had interpreted as signs of affection—were, I now realised, evidence of experience and desperation.

The worst was yet to come. I had urged my parents not to attend the funeral; the journey took almost a day and I was not sure that, in their presence, I could maintain my composure. Charles and other old friends kept me company. By unspoken agreement we all just wandered off after the ceremony; there was no pretence of a drink or a meal. I was standing at the gate of the cemetery when an elderly couple, painstakingly smart, whom I had assumed were connected with the shop where Irene used to work, approached. "How do you do," said the man; he had an English accent. "We're Mr. and Mrs. Talbott."

"How do you do," I said.

"We're Mr. and Mrs. Talbott," he repeated. "Irene's parents."

I made a terrible fool of myself but I managed to stop just short of telling these pleasant upright people that they were dead. "I thought you were Welsh," I said stupidly. It was the only safe comment that came to mind.

"On my father's side," said my father-in-law, with a sad smile. He handed me a card with their address.

I spent the night walking around London. Shortly after dawn I ended up by St. James's Park. It was closed to the public, but walking along the Mall I could see the rows of vegetables and the stands of searchlights and antiaircraft guns. There was no sign of the pelicans. I was forty-three years old and a widower.

Two months after Irene's death, my father decided, one pleasant May afternoon, to tackle a task that my mother nagged him about every spring: rolling the vicarage lawn in readiness for her croquet parties. The lawn was large and the roller was heavy. He pushed it back and forth for a couple of hours. Afterward he went to his study to work on his sermon and there my mother found him—his head resting on the desk—when she brought him his six o'clock sherry. Later she told me that the words of the sermon were smudged across his cheek. At the funeral the church was overflowing, every pew filled and latecomers lining the walls. A stranger was in the pulpit; his excellent eulogy only underscored my father's absence.

My mother put aside her hairpiece and her cloak. Her vitality and humour failed her and she fell into self-pity. Three years later, after a trying month in hospital, she followed Henry. That was the word she used when I visited her the week before—I can't wait to follow Henry—and even to me, whose faith had been worn threadbare in France, it seemed true. Now I am over eighty I wish I believed I was following someone.

Or that someone was following me in the right way. Dennis cannot know how eagerly both his mother and I awaited his arrival. How, at the sight of him, my eyes watered. How I rang Charles babbling and sent the most expensive telegram of my life to my parents. But Irene, as I've said, changed after his birth and my efforts to play with Dennis were often foiled by the nursemaid. When we did spend time together, I felt inept. I took him to the Natural History Museum, to see the Albert Memorial, to the zoo, but he had no interest in the things that I had enjoyed as a boy: birds, rocks, trees, swimming. And like his mother he had little sense of humour.

Then came Irene's death and the subsequent revelations. I could not stop thinking about the day she killed herself and the day before she killed herself and the day before that. Had there been clues I missed? Was there something I could have done? I went through every piece of paper she left, every book and every garment, without finding an answer. Finally, a few weeks after my father's funeral, I sent a note to her parents, asking if I might call on them. It was a crystalline summer's day, and I kept thinking as I walked the half mile to their house how often Irene must have passed this way. How she too must have noticed the glorious red roses at number 41, the tall chimney pots across the road, the fox terrier with crooked ears at the house beside the pub.

Mr. Talbott opened the door before I could knock. The room into which he showed me was furnished with the same kind of heavy dark furniture we had at the vicarage. Mrs. Talbott brought in tea, and I realised that of course I should have brought my ration. I started to apologise but she said not to worry; they had extra that month. "Though not what you're used to. It's just from the corner shop."

I assured her it was delicious. We talked about the weather and Mr. Talbott's tomatoes. My first thought had been that Irene resembled neither of them, but as our conversation continued I saw she had her father's colouring, her mother's nose and chin. Presently I couldn't stand it any longer. "I came to talk about Irene," I said. "Why did she never introduce us?" Even in the depths of my self-absorption, I understood it would be too cruel to mention her lie.

Mrs. Talbott's face twisted. "But how could she when she'd told you we were dead?"

"You knew?" In my amazement I turned from wife to husband. They nodded.

"Oh, yes," said Mrs. Talbott. "Irene told us when she broke the news of her engagement. She didn't know what to do. She'd blurted out the lie when she first met you and she couldn't think of a way to take it back. We weren't happy about it, not at all, but Jim and I didn't know what to do either. It did seem the sort of thing that might make you have second thoughts. She made us promise not to call or telephone, but she was very good about visiting."

"But why on earth would she tell such a lie in the first place?"

Mr. and Mrs. Talbott exchanged glances. His must have given permission for she continued. "Irene was always a fanciful girl. For a whole term she wouldn't go to school because one of the other girls said she had a short neck. She fainted when we tried to make her. Then there was a period when she got it into her head that she was adopted. I know children sometimes think that, but Irene grew quite desperate. She kept demanding to be taken back to her real family. In the end I had to get the midwife, who delivered her, to have a word."

As she spoke, I noticed she had Irene's habit of wrinkling the bridge of her nose, though of course it was the other way round. When we were courting, I had teased her about it. "You try doing it," she had said. Amid much laughter, I had found I couldn't.

Mr. Talbott spoke up to say that Irene's two sisters both lived nearby; they had three children apiece. "But even as a toddler, Irene was different. And then after the war—"

"I know she was engaged before we met," I said quickly. "I just want to understand what happened." What I really wanted to ask was did she love me? had she ever? The ambivalence I had felt throughout our marriage had vanished as I walked her round and round the living room.

Together, her parents described Dennis. He lived in the next street and the two of them had met in primary school. He was a nice boy, a gifted musician and mimic, and the only one who could talk sense to Irene. They had wanted to get married before he went to France, but both sets of parents thought they were too young. "When he was killed," said Mrs. Talbott, "she felt she'd been left with nothing, not even widowhood. Then she started seeing that woman."

That woman was a medium who claimed to be in contact with Dennis. They had done everything they could to dissuade her. The doctor had talked to her, and the vicar, but she didn't listen. "She might look like a slip of a girl," said Mr. Talbott, "but she had a will like Napoleon's. That's why she moved into lodgings, because she thought we were interfering."

"And is that why she killed herself?" I said. "Because of Dennis?"

"Heavens, no." Mrs. Talbott shook her head for emphasis. "She had everything to live for: you, her son, a lovely home. Once or twice," she added shyly, "when we knew you were away, we walked past."

Suddenly I was saying, much too loudly, "She pretended you were dead. She bought poison. She took it when I was in the next room."

The Talbotts couldn't have been nicer. They brought me more tea, a sip of precious brandy. Mr. Talbott walked home with me. A week later a letter came. "Ever since your visit we've been thinking about Irene. I wish we could give you a clear answer—she'd learned she was ill, or she was worried about her sanity—but the only thing we can come up with is that, after the terrible shock, we weren't surprised and her sisters weren't either. Irene was never on easy terms with life. When you got married, we thought she'd put the past behind her. But having a baby seemed to set her nerves off again. And of course the war. Sometimes she used to walk over here in the middle of a raid. Perhaps she was hoping a bomb would settle the matter."

I should have stopped then but I didn't. I tried to find the medium Irene had gone to and when she turned out to have died (even mediums apparently do die), I went to another one, a widow who lived in Peckham. Mrs. Langham was stout and gray-haired and wore a gold watch pinned to her bosom, all of which gave me confidence. This was no hysterical waif of a girl, starving herself into fits and fantasies. I became a regular at the weekly meetings in her parlour. Oddly, they reminded me of nothing so much as the war. The dark room, smelling of candle snuff and incense with the bodies crowded around the table, was reminiscent of my dugout. And of course we had lived in a welter of superstition. If you see the enemy lighting a cigarette then you're safe. If you break both shoelaces, you're doomed.

Irene didn't appear immediately, but Mrs. Langham started to get messages. "Soon, she says, soon," she would report, which seemed typical of Irene, unreliable even in death. Then she began to visit. She talked about Dennis (it wasn't always clear which one) and about her parents. She said she loved me. Whenever I asked about the arsenic, she sobbed that I'd never understood her.

I say *she* and *her* as if I believed that I was talking to Irene, and for a while I did. Then one day, we were trying to contact the brother of a young woman named Louise—he had died of TB two years before—and suddenly I grasped that I was holding the damp hand of a hysterical girl and the rather dry, calloused one of an accountant (Vernon, who'd lost his mother), and I could see that the whole racket was driven by us, by our grief and longing. Mrs. Langham was a good listener and clever at picking up hints about the deceased, but she was not a conduit to some vigorously peopled afterlife. I dropped Louise and Vernon's hands and left the room. The next day was Sunday, and for the first time in several years I went to church. Thank God my parents were not alive to see how low I'd fallen, though if they had been, if I had been able to draw on my father's robust intelligence, my mother's sympathy and humour, I like to think I never would have entered Mrs. Langham's dining room.

The war ended, the railways were nationalised, and I retired to the Lake District. Even without my parents, the familiar landscape was the only thing I could think of that might make me feel less melancholy. I was convinced that my life was over in every

way that mattered. One day, walking in the hills, I met a boy carrying a bird. He had found the kestrel lying under a gorse bush
with a broken wing. When he said his father would probably
make him wring its neck, I offered to take it home. Boadicea recovered, and that was the beginning of the second part of my life.
I took up falconry. The birds brought me friends; I renewed relations with some of my father's parishioners. For many years I
kept company with one of my neighbours, a strong, intelligent
woman whom I know my mother would have liked. On the half
dozen occasions when I proposed, she said it would be absurd
from the point of view of our taxes.

And what about Dennis? Sadly, he and I have never had the
closeness I enjoyed with my father. In several respects he did not
get the best start in life, but other people have had worse starts
and managed better. After Irene's death the two of us rattled
around with a housekeeper, the aptly named Mrs. Quick, who
made Dennis do his homework and both of us eat our carrots.
Presently Charles took me aside and suggested that, if I weren't
going to remarry, I should send the boy to boarding school. So I
did. Week after week, I received a dutiful letter. Once I laid out
ten of them, side by side; barring differences in weather and food,
they were almost identical. I knew he wasn't happy. He was poor
at games and a mediocre student. My only hope was that he was
too much of a nonentity to be bullied. He followed in my footsteps to Clare College and studied history.

Up until the age of twenty, Dennis was the boy no one remembered. Had he played on the house football team? Was he the
third courtier in *Hamlet*, or the fourth? He slipped through life
well-nigh invisible. And then, the summer before he finished at
Cambridge, he came to visit me in the Lake District. From the
moment he stepped off the train and loped down the platform
calling "Dad," I knew he had changed. He was accompanied by
two equally loud young men. He told me he'd taken up golf and

might get a blue; his companions were also keen golfers. That night after dinner when Lucy, the maid, served coffee, I saw her dodge his wandering hands. He and his friends spent the week either on the golf course or making a nuisance of themselves at the pub. When he graduated, without the blue, Dennis got a job managing a golf course near York. Once again he followed my dubious example and married a shopgirl.

Poor Millicent. She was high-strung and socially ambitious, and I have no idea what she saw in Dennis other than a meal ticket. When I finally met her on the eve of their wedding, I realised what my mother had gone through. Don't do it, I wanted to tell him. The heavy breathing won't last. But it seems to, or something has. He and Millicent are still married, and he has managed to keep the family afloat with his teaching. I wish he'd continued to run the golf course. My father was a scholar and I have an old-fashioned objection to a man who knows nothing passing on his ignorance, but that's neither here nor there. At least it enabled Dennis to take care of you and Henry. The choice of the latter's name was one of the few occasions on which my son truly surprised me. Forgive me. This is no way to talk about your parents.

Do you remember when you were eight or nine and came to stay with me? I was glad to see that you resembled neither your mother nor your grandmother but your great-grandmother. One morning I took you up the hill at the back of the house to fly Percy, my peregrine falcon. He killed a rabbit and I didn't get him back soon enough. By the time we reached him, a circle of grass was visible through the rabbit's body. Percy had eaten the heart. I worried you might be upset but you turned to me, cool as a cucumber, and asked if you could hold Percy.

"Are you sure?" I said.

You nodded, and I helped you pull one of my leather gloves halfway up your arm and set the bird on your wrist with my own hand underneath.

Henry is a different story. I hope you are not aware of the fact that when he was sixteen he phoned out of the blue and announced that he was visiting a friend nearby. Could he break his journey by staying with me the following night? I confess I was pleased at the prospect. I drove into town and bought lamb chops and new potatoes and a good piece of Stilton. It seemed possible that he was of an age when we might have a conversation. At the station the next evening, I met an unusually graceful boy with my hair and Irene's eyes.

"Hello, Grandfather," he said, offering his hand. "What shall I call you?"

"Jigger."

"Jigger, thank you for coming to meet me."

He went on in this vein, chatty, polite, just this side of unctuous, as I drove us back to the house and took him down to the aviary. He was not really interested in the birds, not like you, but he was not afraid of them as some people are and he made the right noises. Inside the house he commented enthusiastically on the furniture; I pointed out the desk and some other pieces that had come from the vicarage. To my surprise he had brought a bottle of burgundy, and over dinner he plied me with wine and questions: my early life, my family, the railway. He told me that he was hoping to do something similar himself. "Not run a railway"—he smiled modestly—"but to do with property. I've got a good eye for commercial space. All I need is some capital."

"I was lucky in that regard," I told him, trying not to smile at a boy his age using phrases like commercial space, and explained about Charles.

Over the Stilton, he brought up the subject of wills. "Dad made his last month," he said.

I had drunk most of the wine but I knew at once he was lying. Dennis would never be so thoughtful. "Good for him," I said. "Everyone over twenty-five ought to have a will."

"So I've got nine years," said Henry. "But Dad is your heir, isn't he? What would happen if he died before you?"

He looked at me with his clear brown eyes, and it dawned on

me what he was asking. I was seventy-nine years old; we were alone in the house. "Solicitors think of these contingencies," I told him. "That's what we pay them for."

"So, would Verona and I be next in line? Dad claims that we're your only relatives."

"Not everyone leaves their money to relatives. There are friends, charities. How about some coffee? I'd be glad of a hand with the washing-up."

For an alarming moment I thought he was going to persist, but he let it go and loaded the dishwasher. That might have been the end of the matter but for the wine. I had to get up several times in the night, and on the second occasion I noticed a light on downstairs. Even as an old man I remembered the skills Tiger had taught me. I padded down the stairs without a creak. In the living room Henry was bent over the desk he had admired earlier that evening, going through my papers. "What are you doing?" I said.

He turned to me wide-eyed. "Where am I?" he quavered. "Oh, it's you, Grandfather. I must have been sleepwalking. I'm sorry, this hasn't happened in ages."

I told him to get a glass of water and go back to bed.

Next day, after I dropped him off at the station, I sat down and wrote a new will. He was right; I had done the traditional thing and made him one of my heirs. Now I changed it to leave you the bulk of my estate and only five thousand pounds to Henry. This record is for you, if you care to read it, so that you will know something about me and why I chose to leave you my money. I also want to warn you about your brother. Whatever is worst in our family has converged in Henry.

11

Gently Zeke closed the book and laid it beside his smallest clock. As he stood up, he discovered again that his shoulders ached from working in the shop, and his mouth felt stiff from the innocuous phrases—just over a pound, just under, that will be seventy-three pence—but he could no more go to bed than walk on the ceiling. He let himself out of the flat, down the stairs, and into the street. There the night was waiting for him, misty and reassuring. As he set off along the sidewalk, his clothes released the odors of the day. Rounding the corner, he caught a whiff of brassica; passing a bus stop he inhaled the tang of citrus mingled with the earthy aroma of root vegetables.

He counted nothing, not lights, not trees, not dustbins, not even the occasional sets of lovers so entwined he wouldn't have known whether to identify them as one or two, until he crossed the road into the park. In the playground the swings hung motionless; the seesaw tilted at half mast. A few steps farther and he spotted a dark circle on the grass which marked the site of last year's Guy Fawkes bonfire. He had come that evening with Phil and surprised himself by the pleasure he had taken in the explosions of sound and color that celebrated, as Phil pointed out, the failed attempt of a Catholic revolutionary to bring down the government and his subsequent excruciating death. In the finale, a dozen rockets burst into clusters of white and golden stars that fell and fell and never came to earth.

Gazing up now at the starless sky, Zeke recalled that Verona had spoken of her grandfather, how he'd enlisted at seventeen and ended up running a railway. He thought of the soldiers he saw on television: young men barely old enough to drive, wearing those blotchy uniforms meant to suggest a muddy field and carrying weapons any one of which could destroy a small town. At school, when his class made a trip to the Imperial War Museum, he had tried to beg off—two of his most hated words over one roof—but there was no provision for pupils to stay behind. The first sight of the building, with the cannons in front aimed at the road, had confirmed his worst fears. Inside, however, he had discovered a display of wartime fashions and spent the afternoon studying how to fake a stocking seam and make lipstick rather than experiencing the reenactment of the blitz or, as he learned later from his classmates, watching the grainy, flickering films of Auschwitz and Birkenau.

Somewhere nearby a clock chimed the hour, followed immediately by another, more distant. One day, he thought, I'll get permission to synchronize all the clocks of London. But if every clock struck in unison might the noise be too deafening, rocking even the Tower, even Canary Wharf? As the last notes faded, a white cat dashed across the street and disappeared beneath a parked car. Sometimes he found his own behavior as baffling as that of other people. For a week it hadn't occurred to him to look at the notebook, but as soon as Emmanuel left he had fetched it from beneath his pillow and read it from beginning to end. He had had her name all along.

Walking through the soft darkness he understood, as he had not while he was turning the pages, that Jigger's story was organized around three deaths. He pictured Tiger in his scarlet robes, walking in the walled garden of some palace high in the snowy mountains. He sat under a fig tree reading a poem; he threw a ball for a small dog; no one mentioned the unrest in the town below. If only he and JS could have changed places. But perhaps JS did not really want to die either. Maybe he was simply out walking one night, a night much like this one, when he found himself alone near the Thames and succumbed to a fleeting impulse of despair.

In that respect, Irene's death was the most troubling of all. Her life was so full of falsehood that even taking the poison seemed a lie. Zeke had tried, over and over, to talk to the doctors about mendacity. If lungs, larynx, lips can produce the words "I am eating an orange," when the teeth are closing around a stick of celery, then everything about human existence is called into question. Still, almost in spite of herself, Irene had committed certain facts: she had borne a son, she had lived with Jigger for more than a decade, she had cooked their last lunch.

He was walking along the edge of the park, the leafless plane trees on his left, an eighteenth-century terrace on the right. Most of the houses were dark or dimly lit, but on the middle floor of a tall white house an uncurtained window shone and in the window sat a woman. As Zeke watched, she raised her arms and began to braid her long brown hair. A few feet away, with his back to her, stood a man. He too raised his arms and pulled a sweater over his head; he shrugged off a shirt. From a far corner of the room, a woman in a red dress appeared and reached for the first woman's hair. As the braid grew, the man ducked down to remove his trousers and turned, like the women, to face the park. Across sixty feet of misty air Zeke saw his lips move.

Footfalls roused him to his own behavior. Beneath the plane trees a burly woman was approaching. For a moment he entertained the notion of stopping her and explaining that this was how he felt about his life most of the time, as if he were viewing even the people he knew best through a pane of glass, but she passed without a second glance. Reluctantly he fell in behind her. Who was whose lover, he wondered. The woman with the braid and the man? The woman in the red dress and the man? The two women?

These speculations led him to another. Was it possible that his father, in spite of Gwen's deceptions, had found out about Maurice? What if his attack had been triggered by the news? Heart attacks, Zeke had heard, were often preceded by some kind of shock.

At the top of the high street the burly woman disappeared into a block of flats. Zeke paused in front of a shop displaying baths and basins so radiant they seemed to have nothing to do with human functions. Center stage a perpetual stream of water poured into a scalloped basin. He eyed the glistening column, thinking he should tell the chef about this place; the fixtures might appeal to his tastes. And if his speculations were correct, then his father, discovering Gwen's infidelity, had reacted by doing the one thing he most dreaded and had spent his life trying to avoid, which was also the only thing guaranteed to stop her from leaving.

Continuing down the high street, he recalled the final pages of Jigger's notebook. What had happened, he wondered, when Henry discovered that his grandfather had outwitted him? Unpleasant scenes, Zeke was sure. A night bus roared by. In its wake he imagined, fleetingly, inappropriately, a large dimpled ostrich egg leaking sulfurous fumes. Verona's brother was a bad egg. Whatever was driving her to leave home, he thought, and flee from one place to another, had something to do with Henry.

Even as he opened the gate to his parents' abbreviated front garden, the strident hubbub of television was audible. He rang, knocked, counted the blooms on the forsythia, and finally, setting down the bag of birdseed he had purchased from the local garden center, let himself in with the key he tried to use as seldom as possible.

"People get ill all the time, every day, people who are younger, fitter, nicer than you. It doesn't mean you have the right to turn into a—"

"Don't you think I bloody well know that? I shouldn't have to bring up my heart if you'd behave with common decency. For thirty years I've been watching you go google-eyed at everything in trousers that comes into the shop. I'm not even sure—"

"As if you don't lather it on too." Gwen's voice deepened. "'That's a very becoming top, Mrs. Fletcher. I hope your husband knows what a lucky man he is.' 'Oh, I like your hair, Polly. The new color really suits you.'"

Zeke hesitated beside the coatrack, trying to avoid both the sound of his parents' quarrel and the sight of himself in the mirror. You're the opposite of Narcissus, one girlfriend had told him. At first it's refreshing, she added; then it's weird. At the mention of the shop, he had understood that the drama he was listening to emanated not from a machine but from his parents. For some reason his mother was home early and the two of them were embroiled in an argument that seemed to cover the whole history of their marriage, from Agincourt to D-Day.

He was backing down the hall, planning to step into the street and use his mobile phone to interrupt, when the living room door flung wide and a woman in a white pullover and dark trousers appeared. Her cheeks were flushed and her eyes had a metallic gleam as if they could rearrange iron filings across a room.

"You," she exclaimed, "what the hell are you doing, tiptoeing around like a burglar?"

"I knocked, I rang, I slammed the door. I told you yesterday I'd be round to see Dad this afternoon."

"Take a good look at him." She waved her arm toward the living room. "There he is, feeling as sorry for himself as it's possible for a person to be."

"Mum, what are you doing home?" As a small boy in Brighton, he still remembered the time he'd gone to play at Frank's house. Only after several hours did Zeke grasp that the tall, calm woman who kept bringing them juice and biscuits and saying well done and lovely, darling was in the same relation to Frank as Gwen was to him.

"Kevin's minding the shop," she said. "I'm going to change."

She swept past him and up the stairs, leaving him with a trio of unappetizing choices: departure, immobility, his father. Reluctantly he made his way past the mirror. In the living room, a man wearing a blue fleece and jeans was sitting on the sofa, his head buried in his hands. Trying not to disturb him, and doing his best to ignore the bust of Beethoven, Zeke stepped over to the cage by the window. He opened the metal door and held out a handful of birdseed. The parrot stared at him, unblinkingly. With no warning, it gave a piercing scream. Zeke jumped back, startled both by the noise and by how much the bird sounded like Gwen.

The scream roused his father. When Don raised his head and lowered his hands, Zeke saw that his cheeks were damp. Not rain, not water, unless Gwen had thrown some at him, not sweat unless he had suddenly developed a fever; no, those little smudges must be tears, though what had caused them was impossible to say. Silently Zeke approached, once again offering the birdseed. His father peered inside the bag and began to utter a series of harsh cries. His version of an anti-laugh, Zeke thought. He stood waiting patiently for a suitable moment to proffer his other two gifts, tickets for *The Lion King*—didn't all the problem pages recommend a good night out?—and his willingness to work in the shop. Now that he knew who Verona was and that she would phone him, he had no excuse for not helping his parents.

"Tell us," said his father, when he could at last speak, "tell us one respect in which you and I are similar."

"We're both good at mental arithmetic. We both read newspapers neatly. We both hate okra and don't mind the bother of artichokes. We both always signal at intersections."

"Okra," said Don, with a crack in his voice.

"Listen, Dad, the birdseed was a joke. The main thing I want to say is that I hope you're feeling better and the minute I've finished my current job, this kitchen in West Hampstead, I'll work in the shop whenever you need me. You've helped me lots of times, lots. And this"—he held out the envelope—"is a get-well present."

His father made no move to take the envelope or to reply. A feeling of hopelessness came over Zeke. How would he ever find his way around the world when, even in the case of his own family, he so often got things wrong? Now, for example, when he had expected some sign of satisfaction, some acknowledgment that here was the compliance his father had been seeking, the opposite occurred: Don seemed as irate as ever. Before Zeke could sort all this out, the parrot gave another scream and his mother swept in, wearing a long skirt, a low-cut top, and so much perfume he had to clear his throat.

"You might be interested to know," she said, coming to rest beside the coffee table, "that your father has got it into his head that there's some question about your paternity."

Here at least was a problem with a solution. "Don't worry, Dad, there are tests nowadays. I'm happy to have one if you want, but I don't see what difference it would make. We'd still be stuck with each other." He took in the faces of his parents, briefly united by their open mouths. "Funny," he added, because the thought struck him, "I'm afraid of a million things but not needles."

"Bloody hell," said Don, and he and Gwen started to laugh: real, exuberant laughs. The parrot, anxious not to be left out, squawked. Zeke looked on, pleased but bewildered. What had he said that was so amusing?

When the merriment subsided and Gwen, still shaking her head, had once again retreated upstairs, his father turned toward him. "You caught your mother and me at a tricky time. It's not good for either of us, me being a lump on the sofa. When will you have this kitchen finished?"

Recognizing his father's version of an apology, Zeke explained what still remained to be done at the chef's house and re-presented the *Lion King* tickets. He would watch the shop so they could make an evening of it. That sounds great, his father said, and suggested a cup of tea. They were sitting at the kitchen table, companionably sharing the newspaper, when Gwen reappeared.

"I'm going into town," she said, hovering in the doorway, "to do some shopping."

"Shopping?" said Don. "You already have enough stuff in your wardrobe to clothe half of London."

Oh, please, Dad, thought Zeke. Simultaneously he understood that his mother's fancy clothes meant she was on her way to see Maurice and that his speculations of the night before were just that. His father had no notion of Gwen's secret life, though if he had lowered the newspaper at just that moment, he would have seen her lips curl in a way that surely would have made him suspect. Turning to Zeke, she said, "You'll stay and go for a walk with your dad, won't you?"

He nodded, speechless. As the door closed behind her, he moved toward the sink. He scrubbed a plate and another, hoping they would carry him to safety, but each soap bubble seemed to ask *Should I tell him?* without yielding the answer. By the time he finished, he felt farther out at sea than ever in a small, rudderless boat. Meanwhile, his father had discarded the paper and was standing in the middle of the kitchen, stretching his arms first up to the ceiling, then down to the floor.

"Ready?" he asked, twisting from side to side as if doing some primitive dance.

Zeke dried his hands and seized his jacket. In the street Don strode out as if determined to prove his vigor. Passing the corner shop, he began to talk about Gwen again, how hard his illness had been on her, how, when the doctor gave the okay, he'd like to take her somewhere. Maybe back to Malta, where they'd had a brilliant holiday a few years ago. "She's been working like a dog, and I haven't helped with my g and d. Gloom and doom," he translated. "My cardiologist says the prognosis is good, actually very good, but I'm such a superstitious bastard I can't stop behaving as if I'm about to kick the bucket."

His parents' local park, unlike Zeke's own, was fenced all the way round. As they stepped through the gate, a flock of black birds launched themselves a few feet into the air, then returned to earth, claws outstretched, wings wide. They bumped along the sodden grass, touching down two or three times, before finally coming to rest.

"Dad."

"You could manage the shop for a fortnight, couldn't you? We'd make sure you had help."

Stiff light-green leaves, the first daffodils, pierced the faded brown grass along the edge of the path. "Dad," he said again. The sentence about Maurice was perfectly formed in his brain; still he hesitated. It was one of those sentences that, when released, would change everything. Although he had thought that before and been proved wrong.

Two women in purple jogging suits approached, talking loudly. Then a voice shouted, "On your left," and while Zeke was still trying to sort out who had spoken an electric wheelchair whizzed by, bearing a middle-aged man. As he gazed after the man's wispy ponytail, he understood that his longing for Verona had carried him to a new place, still at sea but with a rock to cling to. The rock was this: if he had known she was going to disappear, he never would have left the Barrows' that night. He would have hidden under the desk or slept in his van, anything to prevent her vanishing. Next to that rock was another. One day soon his father would come downstairs to find Gwen gone because no one, meaning Zeke, had warned him.

"Dad," he said again, and when his father broke off his holiday plans he pushed the words out into the chilly air.

"Seeing someone?" Don came to an abrupt halt. "How do you mean seeing someone?"

Zeke faltered. "You ought to talk to her yourself."

"Please." Don swayed slightly. "Tell me what you know."

Zeke stepped around a pile of litter and—it took him a moment to be sure—overtook a woman who was walking a brown rabbit in a harness. He had been braced for accusations, shouts, but this was harder. Whether it was the sight of the rabbit hopping along or his father sounding so old and sad, he had suddenly had enough. He had betrayed his mother's confidences, he had warned Don, he could not deal with one more question or demand. He turned and began to run toward the gate of the park.

12

Whenever a passing lorry shook the flat, whenever his neighbors came and went, whenever someone at the house being renovated down the street used a power tool, Zeke assumed that his parents, separately or together, were about to break down his door, seize him by the part of him that had betrayed them—the throat—and shake him until his teeth chattered. But no one rang his bell or pounded on his door. No arrows of outrage leaped from the phone, which, for once, he was answering in the hope of hearing from Verona. When the doorbell did ring the following morning, just as he was leaving for the chef's house, he discovered not her, not his parents, but a small angular figure, fidgeting from foot to foot: one of the schoolgirls he passed at the bus stop on the way to work? The daughter of friends?

"Zeke," she said, holding out a wad of dark fabric, "I found your jacket."

"My jacket?" Still he could not place her.

"Remember you thought you left it at our house? Well, you did. Gerald hung it up by mistake."

Now he recognized her: Mrs. Barrow, Ariel, her hair neatly brushed and even, if he wasn't mistaken, a little mascara. Her black jacket and dark-green skirt also showed signs of effort, though the lapel of the jacket was marked by several milky smudges. At one of his clinics he had met a woman who spilled almost everything she touched and had only to walk by a table of food for some of it to end up on her clothes. Perhaps Ariel suffered from the same condition. "Thanks," he said, taking the jacket out of her hands. "It's very kind of you to bring it round."

"Can I come in for a moment?"

Zeke tried a trick he had learned from Emmanuel. He stuck out his left wrist and stared in the direction of his watch. "I'm on quite a tight schedule—"

"Excuse me, mate."

One of the boys from downstairs was standing in the hall, holding his bicycle. Ariel stepped back into the street and Zeke was forced to follow. It was, he noted with surprise, a remarkably pleasant morning. The windows of the houses opposite glittered in the sunshine and the air was crisp and smelled faintly of moss.

Ariel perched in the middle of a paving stone, and gazed up at him. "If you're driving I could come with you. That way you wouldn't waste any time."

The boy, who was standing behind Ariel, putting on his bicycle clips, turned to regard her. After a few seconds he raised a hand, thumb down.

"Really," said Zeke, "passengers make me nervous and I'm already late. What do you want?" Why was he being so stern with this woman he scarcely knew, especially after she had done him the kindness of returning the jacket he had left, deliberately, in her house? As she lowered her head, he guessed the answer.

"Come on," he said. "I'm parked this way."

Whatever spurt of energy or optimism had brought Ariel to him seemed to wither in the face of his reluctant generosity. "I'm sorry," she said, as he unlocked the passenger door, "this was a dreadful idea. It was the only time of day I thought I could be sure of finding you at home."

He went round to his side of the van. Up to Ariel if she chose to get in or not. She was still standing there as he jiggled the ignition key into the lock; ever since Emmanuel borrowed the van last spring it had had a slight kink. The engine caught and she scrambled in, pulling herself up using the dashboard and barely managing to close the door before he drove away. For the first mile she said nothing, and save for a sweet fragrance—shampoo? hand cream?—he was almost able to forget her presence. On the radio a dietician with a Liverpool accent discussed obesity in America. Americans were large and growing larger. They ate ten times as much fat as the average Japanese.

He was accelerating away from a traffic light when Ariel spoke. "I was fat as a child."

"You were?"

"I had an operation when I was nine, to fix my eyes. Afterward I had to stay indoors for six weeks, and my mother kept bringing me meals. By the time I went back to school I was huge. The other girls teased me horribly, so of course I kept eating."

If these were her eyes after an operation, he hated to imagine them before. "And what happened? You're the opposite of fat now."

"Careful!"

In turning to look at her he had come within inches of a small blue car. "I did warn you that passengers make me nervous."

"I thought that was just an excuse to get rid of me. What saved me was our gym teacher. She took me aside one day and told me I had the perfect build for a gymnast. I burst out that I was too fat, the first person I'd ever said this to other than my mother. But Miss Christie said she was sure I'd soon lose the extra pounds. Within four months I was thin again and I could walk on my hands. I still can."

"I'd like to see that," said Zeke. "I used to have a friend who could do perfect cartwheels. I don't know how to make excuses. It's one of my major faults, much worse than my driving."

"Wasn't your jacket, I mean leaving it at our house, an excuse?"

Ariel's tone was one of interrogation rather than accusation, but Zeke felt his palms grow slippery against the steering wheel. Looking around, he saw that they were passing the library near the chef's house. He turned into a side street and stopped in the first available space. "You're right," he said. "I did leave the jacket on purpose. I wanted to be able to ask you about Verona, the woman I met at your house."

"I thought you didn't know her name."

"I didn't then. She turned out to be a friend of a friend: Verona MacIntyre." As always, he enjoyed hearing the syllables enter the air.

"What a coincidence," said Ariel. "There's a Verona MacIntyre who hosts a radio show every morning on Mars Radio. Have you heard her? She has an unusually deep voice. But she wouldn't be roaming around London with a suitcase."

Was there any difference between the feeling one had when one recognized a true fact and when one leaped to a false conclusion? On the slenderest of evidence, Zeke was convinced that this was his Verona MacIntyre. And hadn't Emmanuel, he now recalled, said something about radio? At once, so many things made sense: her talent for questions, her gift for listening, her reluctance to talk about herself. He gazed into Ariel's leafy eyes. To think he had done his best to send her away. "Thank you," he said. And then, because he felt he owed her an explanation, he added, "I'm in love with her."

"I guessed. Or to be more precise, I changed the sheets on the spare-room bed. The reason I brought your jacket over is that I keep thinking you can help me sort things out with Gerald." She made a jerky motion with her head, neither a nod nor a shake but something more birdlike. "It's ridiculous. I have a degree in economics and I edit business books, but for some reason I've got it into my head that you'll know what I ought to do."

This *was* ridiculous, thought Zeke; romance was his worst subject but he was in Ariel's debt. In an effort to repay her, he folded his arms, tucked in his chin, and did his best to sound authoritative. "Does he have a girlfriend?"

"I think so. He's often late home and sometimes people call the house and hang up when I answer."

"Still you went to Latvia together. The first time I came round about the painting, he seemed very keen for you to go with him."

He could not have named the states that Ariel was passing through, but he had no trouble seeing that her whole manner changed as if he had offered her an exquisite rose. When she wasn't in the grip of some dismal obsession, he realized, she could be an attractive woman, her strangeness alluring rather than re-pelling. She began to babble about how wonderful Riga had been, how hospitable Gerald's colleagues were, how they had skated by firelight and eaten trout so fresh it tasted of wild strawberries.

"Maybe I'm being presumptuous," he said, "but I wonder if you're right about Gerald? Sometimes it's easier to attribute diffi-culties to a third person rather than confront them directly. In any long relationship there are going to be ups and downs." He had read this advice on numerous occasions, but Ariel listened as if an oracle were speaking. When he fell silent, she undid her seat belt, leaned over, and kissed him on both cheeks.

"Good luck with Verona," she said, reaching for the door han-dle. "I hope she knows how lucky she is."

Zeke longed to detain her—she had become one of the small group who in some sense knew Verona—but even as he searched for the words Ariel had slipped from the van and was hurrying down the street.

At the chef's house, to his relief, no one was home. He carried in lengths of skirting board and molding, maneuvering them through the kitchen and out into the back garden, where the beautiful day once again accosted him. A bird with a speckled chest was perched in the apple tree, chirping, and the same stiff leaves he had seen in the park were coming up all over the gar-den. Back indoors he filled the kettle. As the water began to boil, a low musical humming entered his consciousness. Cautiously he crossed the hall and opened the living room door. Every spare inch was crowded with provisions and dishes from the kitchen, but the hum grew instantly louder. A few steps inside, he saw the chef seated on the floor, cross-legged, in front of the ficus tree. Hastily, hoping to escape notice, Zeke tiptoed out of the room.

Perhaps it was only his imagination, but recently his employer seemed to be showing a marked tendency to prolong any conversation. So long as Zeke was doing something mechanical—grouting tiles, for example—and the chef was satisfied by his *hmms,* Zeke hadn't minded too much. His counselor, Arnold, had taught him to make the sound. When you listen in total silence, Arnold had explained, people worry you aren't paying attention.

But I'm here, Zeke said. They're talking. What else would I be doing?

Planning your summer holidays? Thinking about your next meal? You have to understand—one of Arnold's eyelids closed and opened—most people aren't as confident as they pretend to be. He had shown Zeke how to make the appropriate noise, keeping his lips together and allowing his palate to vibrate. They discussed frequency.

Every twenty seconds, Zeke suggested.

No, no, it can't be to a timetable. They'll think you're making fun of them.

So Zeke had pressed grout between the tiles and *hmm*ed at irregular intervals, more or less following the Fibonacci sequence. But this initial docility had only brought more conversations, each longer than its predecessor. Even as he worked ten-hour days, trying to finish the job for the sake of his parents and Verona, it had become increasingly hard to get any but the simplest tasks done when the chef was around.

Forgetting the kettle, he returned to the garden and began to measure the skirting boards, checking and rechecking the measurements. He was sawing the first length, still finding the rhythm that would make the little metal teeth gobble up the wood, when the chef appeared in the back doorway wearing baggy brown trousers and a bright red T-shirt. His feet were bare.

"Hi," he said. "I hope I didn't seem rude just now." He pointed over his shoulder, locating the *now*. "I try to meditate for fifteen minutes each morning. It ruins the whole thing if I jump up every time the door goes."

Zeke paused, holding the saw steady. "Have you heard of someone on the radio called Verona MacIntyre? She does a show every morning on Mars Radio."

"No, I'm a Radio Four man, but it's morning. Let's try to find her." In the kitchen the chef twirled radio dials resourcefully until he found the station; then he offered to make breakfast on the camp stove he had borrowed.

What a day I'm having, thought Zeke. "I've already eaten," he said gently. "Besides, I need to get these boards cut. It'll be easier for you to make breakfast once I'm out of your kitchen."

The chef raised his eyebrows, which in turn made his hairline ripple. He uttered his own *hmm* sound before retreating to the living room. Soon the odor of bacon wafted into the garden. Zeke balanced the radio on his toolbox and continued sawing. Nothing at nine, nothing at nine-thirty but at ten, after several minutes of advertising, the announcer said, "And now the ten o'clock show with Verona MacIntyre." Then another voice explained that Verona was taking a brief leave. "My name is Casey Lawson, and I'll be doing my best to make the next two hours as lively and indispensable as Verona always does."

Zeke listened spellbound to this woman who was sitting in Verona's chair, speaking into her microphone, discussing property values in London and whether trade unions were still relevant. These airwaves, these frequencies, had within recent memory carried Verona's voice. Surely, like him, they missed her. Only after the show ended as he began to fit the skirting boards into place—miraculously, he had cut them all true—did the import of this new information strike him. He had already understood that trouble must have brought Verona to the Barrows'; now, knowing the kind of job she had, he glimpsed the magnitude of that trouble. He put down his hammer and touched his forehead to the floor.

That night when he got home he arranged five clementines in front of the answering machine, a reminder of the five lightbulbs, and sat down beside them. Verona, he thought, wherever you are, please telephone me. He focused every brain cell on reaching her; he begged the molecules of air to carry his request to her; he promised not to move, not to eat until she rang; he vowed to do a good deed a day for the rest of his life; he promised to learn to ride a bicycle, to tell jokes.

Nothing. Silence. More silence.

Finally, reluctantly, at eleven-thirty, he gave up his vigil and went to bed. Half an hour later he was on the edge of sleep when the phone rang.

"Did something happen yesterday?"

"Yesterday?" He was still trying to recover from the disappointment of hearing the wrong voice.

"Did something happen after I went shopping?" Gwen hissed. "Did you drop a hint to Don?"

"Mum," he said weakly.

"Wake up, Zeke," she said, with such intensity that it was as if she had shouted, although, uncharacteristically, she was whispering. His father must be nearby. In an effort to get his bearings, he climbed out of bed and took the phone over to the window. When he last looked a crescent moon had hung over the rooftops. Now the sky was filled with white clouds lit by the reflection of a million street lamps. For a moment, caught up in the beauty of the spectacle, he almost forgot why he was standing there.

"Ever since your visit, Don has been acting peculiar. Yesterday he even had supper waiting when I got home. I keep asking what's up and he says nothing. He knows how hard I'm working. He's just trying to be helpful."

"I told him."

What happened next was hard to describe. Little fragments of speech—furious, obscene, incoherent—began to spray in all directions, some into the receiver, some not. He put down the phone and went to take a shower. At this time of night, Gwen could be here in fifteen minutes. Washed, dressed, the outside door open, the kettle boiled, he sat at the kitchen table.

It was odd, he thought, given his feelings about the sea, that he liked the sky. The coming and going of clouds was like the traffic on the London streets. He could count them, if he chose. And by night he appreciated the orderliness of the moon's waxing and waning, the rotation of the constellations. He even welcomed the disruptions: shooting stars, satellites, airplanes with their concomitant jet trails. Not that he had ever actually been in a plane. Thousands, millions of people, including almost everyone he knew, entered these metal capsules as a matter of course, but he had never been able to get his mind around the improbable, terrifying prospect of leaving the earth.

The one time he had been to Europe, the summer after his breakdown, he had taken the ferry and survived by dint of wearing his own life jacket and playing game after game of draughts with his father. Several years later, the sight of the black and white checkers could still make him queasy. They were traveling to Naples, where Don's family came from; his parents had moved to London as newlyweds shortly before the Second World War and started an ice-cream shop. On the ferry, as they moved the counters back and forth, he had told Zeke about his first job as an apprentice to a dice maker.

We boys were responsible for unloading the marble chips off the barges. The sacks weighed a hundredweight apiece, and we lugged them ashore across this narrow wooden gangplank. One wrong step and you were in the river. Wouldn't be allowed nowadays. You should have seen the shoulders I had on me when I was sixteen.

And did you make the dice? said Zeke. He kept his eyes fixed on the board, where his father was in the lead.

I ran the polisher for a while—the dust was unbelievable—and then I had a stint on the machine that did the fours. You'd think it was easy, making a little cube with dots, but it's hard to make a die that isn't biased. The foreman would walk up and down exhorting us: "The fate of honest men and women lies in your hands. A single crooked die can ruin a man for life."

As he spoke, Don delved in various pockets until he found what he was looking for in his breast pocket. I made these on my last day at the factory. The foreman gave them to me as a souvenir.

They're beautiful, said Zeke, raising his eyes from the board. The black paint marking the dots on the dice was almost gone, and the stone had a yellowish tinge.

I don't know about that, but they're true. They favor no man, not even their maker. Gwen used to tease me about that. You ought to have made a die that would help you, Donnie, she used to say.

Only later, as they marched through the streets of Naples searching in vain for the addresses Don had written down nearly twenty years earlier when his father was dying, did Zeke wonder why it was that he had never heard about the dice making before. At the time he had thought it was just one of those odd things that you periodically learned about your parents. Phil, however, to whom he'd repeated the story, had a different hypothesis. I bet your dad didn't want you to know that he hadn't gone into the family business. Zeke had forgotten all about the dice until he'd seen his father throwing them the day he came home from the hospital.

"What the hell were you thinking?" said Gwen, slamming the door behind her.

Not true to say he hadn't heard her approach. He had simply allowed himself to have that final image of his father slumped in his armchair, looking like someone let out of the cemetery on bail, rolling the dice over and over as if the two small cubes had the power to decide whether he would live or die.

13

They talked for hours in lacerating circles, and there was nothing to do but give himself up to the words, rushing by like the winter wind. Yet, in spite of all these words, no meeting point was reached, no truce brokered. His behavior was unforgivable, incomprehensible, vicious, outrageous, and nothing he said could convince Gwen otherwise.

"I understand," she said, her hair swirling as if she were both source and subject of the wind, "that you have your precious phobias and fears, but you're not stupid. You do know what you're doing. Who the hell gave you permission to poke your nose into my affairs? For the first time in years, I'm happy. I wake up thinking about something other than whether to put the peaches on special or did I order too much lettuce. Can you imagine what that's like? And you try to ruin it. If I hadn't seen you come out from between my legs, I'd swear you were a changeling."

The final sentence, delivered at full volume, was underscored by a volley of thuds from above. Almost simultaneously, as if in answer, came a series of knocks from the floor: the toga boys banging on their ceiling. Next comes the phone call, thought

Zeke. The police. Although he kept his own eyes safely on his knees, he could feel Gwen glaring at him.

He worried that her response to the protests might be to raise her voice still more, but when she spoke again it was almost in a whisper. "The thing I don't understand is why you would want to hurt me. Not to mention your father."

"I didn't do it to hurt you," he said hopelessly. His mouth had a cottony feel, and his tongue kept colliding with his teeth as if, in a matter of hours, it had outgrown its rightful home. He had apologized, he had tried to explain, he had groveled. The truth was that he had not, at the moment he spoke to Don, been thinking of Gwen, but she had greeted that information with a high-pitched shriek so terrifying that he lost all desire to explain about Verona and his reasoning and thought only of hiding behind the sofa. Now, feebly, he attempted to change the subject. "Would you like some breakfast?"

"If I leave, you'll be the one stuck with everything: the shop, him"—she pointed—"yourself."

Then something at the window, perhaps the lamp-lit clouds, caught her attention. Her eyes retreated and her hair fell around her face. Since she burst into the flat, she had been in constant motion; now, at last, she took the chair he offered. "One thing I've always envied you," she said, "is that you don't seem to know what it's like to want two contrary things at once. Maybe that's the positive side of your condition. I love your father. Of course I don't want to leave him. At the same time, I'm desperate for something new. We've been married for nearly thirty years. I've been working in the shop for nearly a quarter of a century. I can finish his sentences four times out of five."

He barely heard her enumerations. Surely Gwen understood that wanting things that pulled him in opposite directions was at the heart of his condition. Not only did he not know his parents— witness his mistake in talking to his father—but they, after twenty-nine years, were equally ignorant about him. Which confirmed his belief that knowing another person could not be measured in normal solar time. After less than twenty-four hours he knew Verona better than anyone.

Now that Gwen had taken a seat it seemed safe for him to leave his. Without asking again, he measured water and oats into a saucepan. Soon the porridge was bubbling with comforting fierceness. He laid the table, warmed milk, set out honey and sugar, and ladled the porridge into two blue china bowls that he had bought years ago on a day trip to Oxford. He ate in quick, greedy spoonfuls, the first food he'd had, he now realized, since lunch the day before. Gwen did the same. When her bowl was empty she sat back in her seat. "That was just what I needed," she said. "Look at me."

He raised his eyes across the expanse of her pullover, up the tendons of her neck, over her firm chin, her lips, slightly chapped with traces of lipstick still lingering in the corners, her nostrils, shiny and pink as if she had a cold and then—the last inch took an extreme effort—her dark eyelashes still clotted with mascara, the whites of her eyes, her blue irises, and her pupils in which he glimpsed his tiny self.

"I wonder if I can ever forgive you," she said, sounding as if she were commenting on his choice of shirt or asking if he wanted more tea.

She stood up and pulled on her jacket. "If your father asks questions, wants to know persons and positions, whatever you do don't tell him anything. And if he asks what made you think I was seeing someone, be as vague as possible. You can be vague, can't you?" She tugged at the lowest button on her jacket. It was already loose, dangling by an inch of thread. He had noticed that before, how people slammed a loose cupboard door, poked at a hole in their shoe, making sure that what was already fragile fell apart. Under normal circumstances he would have offered to sew the button back on; he liked the feel of a needle slithering through cloth. "You could say a joke someone made at the shop. All right? Even if he threatens to break your neck, I don't want you interfering in my affairs again. Whatever happens next is up to me and"—the button came off in her hand—"Maurice."

He sat there in front of his empty porridge bowl, moving his head up and down in a way that was meant to signal yes, yes, yes. Anything to get her out of his flat. The pressure in the room was once again becoming unbearable. When he had heard how divers, working at low depths, sometimes got the bends, he had understood at once that there was a landlocked equivalent; his mother's presence in a room could cause the same hallucinatory ache in every joint. Perhaps Gwen sensed this, even relished it, for she remained standing with one hand on the doorframe. And then—he was still nodding—she was gone.

He hit the first nail so hard that the hammer left a saucer-shaped dent in the molding. The second, the same. A fortnight ago, even last week, he would have removed the wood, cut a fresh strip, and started over. Making his work as good as possible was one of the cornerstones of his life. Now he looked at the two small hollows surrounding the nails, evaluated the position of the molding—in an alcove destined to house the fridge—and realized that what Emmanuel had been telling him for years was true. No one besides himself would notice. As he drove home the rest of the nails, the thought came to him that he had, unwittingly, accomplished his father's curse; he had made himself an orphan. But how to apologize when all he had done was tell the truth? The very word—*or-phan*—seemed to embody his alternative status.

He was still murmuring *orphan* when the chef, on his way to work, stopped to ask if something was wrong. Yes, said Zeke, and laid aside the plastic wood to describe the recent tumult. His mother hadn't said anything about talking to other people. The chef leaned in the doorway, flexing his eyebrows in the way that made his hairline ripple. When Zeke finished, he volunteered that his parents had separated when he was sixteen. "It's one of the major regrets of my life that I didn't try to stop them. All they really needed was to go to the Loire and eat good food. So I take my hat off to you"—he touched his forehead—"for trying to help. If your mother was dead set on divorce, she'd be gone by now." He announced that he'd left a panini for Zeke in the fridge and let himself out.

So I'm not the only one who reads the problem pages, Zeke thought. Still, he felt comforted. It was true if Gwen wanted to bolt, he had given her the perfect opportunity. That must mean something. But as he fitted the next strip of molding, what came into his head was the question Gwen had asked so stridently, the chef more subtly: was he taking into account the welfare of both parents? I'm happy, his mother had shouted, as if that word could outweigh any amount of pain. Was it possible, Zeke wondered, that her feelings for Maurice resembled his for Verona? No, he corrected himself, not in any respect whatsoever.

He was rinsing the polyurethane off his brush, swishing it back and forth in the turpentine, when his mobile rang. For several seconds after he flipped open the lid, he heard only the fizzing of electrical space.

"Hello, Zeke. It's me, Verona."

She had never known that he had not known her name.

Lacking a table to climb beneath, a chair to hide behind, he slid to the floor, pressing each vertebra in turn against the door of the cupboard. Speak, he told himself. Push air out of your lungs, up your windpipe, across your larynx into this piece of plastic. Speak.

"Verona. Verona MacIntyre.

"I'm sorry I had to leave so suddenly," she said. "I was worried about my brother. There were things I needed to sort out, and I couldn't involve you."

"Why not? Are you all right?"

"Yes." The pause this time was hers, not the airwaves. "I'm fine, but everything with Henry is a mess. I'm in America, in Boston."

"America?" He held the phone at arm's length as if the machine itself had made this far-fetched claim. She said something he didn't catch and he quickly brought it back to his ear. "I don't understand," he said. "How can you be in America?"

"I came because Henry is here. It's too complicated to explain on the phone. I miss you."

Later he couldn't recall whether, in the thrill of hearing her say this, he had managed to articulate his own missing. "Is there anything I can do. Can I help?"

"You could come here, to Boston. I know," she added, "it's a lot to ask."

"But I can't fly."

"Actually it's quite easy these days to get last-minute tickets. Emmanuel could help you, I'm sure he's good at that kind of thing. Please, will you come?"

He started to explain again about his inability to fly, but even as he shaped the words he had a vision of climbing the stairs at the Barrows' only to discover her gone. By his refusal to stay the night he had jeopardized everything; now he had a second chance. If he turned away who knew if he would have a third. "Yes," he said.

"I—" she said, but what verb she meant to utter he never discovered. The silence expanded and expanded until it was clear that she was gone.

He finished the dishes. He carried his tools and equipment out to the van. He piled the remaining skirting boards neatly on one side of the kitchen and wrote the chef a note containing the phrase *family emergency* and giving him Emmanuel's number. Only when he was in the van, driving toward home, did he grasp the magnitude of his promise. He was going to get into a plane and stay there for however many hours it took to cross the huge body of water that presently lay between him and Verona. For five seconds, perhaps six, he was tempted to turn around, drive back to the chef's house, pick up his hammer, and resume work.

Then, as he braked at a zebra crossing for a boy on a skateboard, his apprehensions vanished. She phoned, he thought, she cares for me. During the days of waiting and searching, he had never allowed himself to doubt her affections. Still, that was not the same as knowing that his image was still firmly lodged behind her high forehead.

Everything fell into place. Verona had already called Emmanuel, and after the requisite amount of joking he bought Zeke a ticket for the following day and agreed to take over at the chef's house. Zeke packed a small green suitcase, the same one he had taken to Naples, with two of everything plus extra socks and underwear. Emmanuel said it might be cold, so he added a scarf, gloves, and a hat. He went to the bank machine and took out as much money as it would permit. How many fried-egg sandwiches would three hundred pounds buy in America? A lot, said Emmanuel, and you can use your credit cards there.

Then, with all his preparations made, he faced an obstacle nearly as vast as the ocean: telling his parents. A large number of well-organized forceful brain cells massed in the main hallway of his brain, urging him to say nothing, to just go. But a persistent contingent lurking in the kitchen, occupying the stairs, argued that this was the coward's way out, that his parents would never forgive him, and moreover that such duplicity would taint his relationship with Verona. How could he be worthy of her if he wasn't pure of heart?

His father answered the phone, sounding like his old robust self. "Zeke, how are you? How's the kitchen going? I was watching the weather. We're in for rain."

"Dad, I'm going to America tomorrow."

"America? What the hell are you talking about?"

"You know, America, the country across the Atlantic. I'm going there tomorrow on a plane. I have a ticket. I'm sorry to let you down about the shop."

"Let me get your mother." And then they were both on the phone—which even at the best of times he found trying—united in their rage.

"I have to go," he kept saying. "Verona needs me."

"Verona? Who the hell's Verona?" said Gwen.

"After all this shilly-shallying," said his father, "you finally agree to help at the shop, like Moses coming down from the bloody mountain, and now you announce you're buggering off to America and we can sink or——"

Silently, Zeke replaced the receiver. He did not attempt to sleep that night. Instead, he sat at his kitchen table taking apart his eight-day clock, laying out the springs and coils in careful sequence and putting them back together.

He had persuaded Emmanuel to accompany him to Heathrow by offering his hourly rate and agreeing to take the fast train from Paddington. They met at the station. Emmanuel bought tickets and marched them onto the train. As soon as he stepped into the compartment, Zeke was filled with dread. It was so sleek and clean and filled with TVs. He sat facing rigidly forward, doing his best to follow the summary of the news. The key to surviving the hours ahead lay, he knew, in paying attention to other people's dramas and ignoring his own. They got off the train and took the lift to the terminal. An overwhelming number of people were carrying suitcases back and forth. Alone Zeke would have come to a standstill but Emmanuel led them briskly to the correct queue.

"Listen," he said, "this is how you answer the security questions. Yes, you packed your bags yourself and they've been with you at all times. Yes, you've had all electrical appliances for more than a year. No, no one has given you anything to take on the plane."

The woman behind the desk did indeed ask these questions and accepted his answers as appropriate. He put his suitcase on a scale which in flashing red numbers registered seventeen kilograms and then the case was gone, trundling away on a conveyor belt to who knows where.

"Aisle or window?" the woman asked.

"Aisle," said Emmanuel. "So you can get up if you need to."

The woman handed back his passport and a piece of flimsy

cardboard and Emmanuel was leading him up a flight of stairs, past rows of predictable shops, and over to a sign marked DEPARTURES, where more long queues snaked back and forth. "I can't go any farther," said Emmanuel. He explained the security procedures. "Once you're through you need to look at the monitors to see what gate your plane leaves from."

"Gate?"

"Like the platform for a train. The number of your flight is on your boarding pass and you match that with the number of the gate. Follow the signs—sometimes the gate is ten or fifteen minutes' walk away—and the airline people will tell you what to do next. You'll be fine, mate. Give my love to Ms. MacIntyre." And he was gone, absorbed into the crowd, a free man fleeing the galley slaves.

Zeke stood clutching his newspaper and the bottle of water Emmanuel had made him buy, staring at the silvery hair of the man in front. Beneath his black jacket the man wore a flowing white robe. Several middle-aged women stood in front of him, all wearing robes with jackets over them. Collectively they emitted a comforting smell, like cedar. One robe, two robes, three robes . . . He survived the next thirty-five minutes by counting whatever there was to be counted. When at last he reached the metal detector, a woman, almost as small as Ariel, ushered him through in total silence.

Sitting at the gate, gazing out of the window, he realized he had never seen a plane up close before. In the sky they often seemed no larger than birds; now he saw how big they really were. Even the wheels were taller than the humans who scurried back and forth on the tarmac. And the wing, the one he could see, was nearly thirty feet long. How was it possible that this huge piece of metal could remain airborne, let alone transport him and so many other people? He was still looking around for someone who might be able to answer this question when, in response to a loudspeaker announcement, everyone was on their feet, streaming toward the door, and he was too. It was like nothing so much as being swallowed by a whale. He passed down through the gullet. The metal door stood open before him. He stopped abruptly.

It still wasn't too late to turn around, to take a boat, to find some alternative.

But Verona needed him, needed him now, and a boat would take too long and cost too much. Behind him someone was already saying excuse me and behind that person waited a hundred others, all willing him forward. He moved one foot, then the other. In his seat, 22B, Zeke bowed his head. There was nothing left to count, and he tried not to think about what would happen next. A woman in uniform bent over him and fastened two strips of fabric around his lap. A few minutes later the door closed, and a few minutes after that the plane began to move, first slowly and lumberingly, soon with increasing speed and noise until—Zeke clutched his armrests—they were suddenly, unmistakably, no longer keeping company with the earth.

Verona

14

She had, she thought, borne up pretty well so far, but in the back of yet another fusty minicab, the seat sagging painfully beneath her, the air smelling of something perturbingly sweet which at once suggested something much less sweet, the driver listening to abrasive music as they jolted through the still dark streets, Verona began to cry. How had it happened that one day she was living comfortably in her modest flat, doing her job, seeing her friends, enjoying the last weeks of her old childless life and the next she was racing around the city, a fugitive, with all her immediate possessions in two suitcases, unable to go to work, unable to return to her flat, unable to see Zeke? This has to stop, she thought. I haven't cried since I was twenty-four. Henry is not worth this.

The cab braked, swerved, and leaped forward, all for reasons invisible to Verona but sufficient to jolt her out of her tears. She blew her nose and tried to think what to do next. Instead she pictured Zeke, sitting opposite her the night before, watching her across the card table. She had never felt so fully apprehended by another person. She tried to remind herself that he knew nothing about her. He didn't know that she hated strawberries, he didn't know what she did for a living, or about Henry, or that she seldom crossed the Thames without reciting the opening lines of Wordsworth's "Upon Westminster Bridge." The list was endless, and yet she viewed the many entries with pleasure rather than dismay, things that might or might not be divulged and which meanwhile, in no way, contradicted her conviction that Zeke already knew everything that mattered.

They passed the Holloway prison, the trees in front so severely pruned as to appear mutilated. For some reason, her normal defenses refused to organize themselves around this man. What if he had other attachments, other commitments, a wife, children even? Her last serious lover, a businessman she had met while doing a program on Canary Wharf, had turned out to have both, and neither were so easily dispensed with as he had at first intimated. After a few months of mutual pleasure—her odd working hours, early rising, early bed, had suited Jeffrey perfectly—they had entered into that distressing dance of supplication and denial, wishful thinking and hypocrisy. One day, walking across Hyde Park to the Victoria and Albert Museum, Verona had suggested that perhaps she should break the news to his wife. Even as Jeffrey's mouth opened—was this a joke? a threat?—she had registered the shocking nature of her proposal. Why is it, she'd wondered aloud, that almost everyone would forgive her for having an affair, and him for lying about it, but almost no one would forgive her for telling his wife?

Maybe you could do a program, Jeffrey had said. Get the Archbishop of Canterbury to comment on the idiosyncrasies of modern morality. He fingered the little blue spot on his throat, a relic of the chemotherapy he had had years ago when he was diagnosed with Hodgkin's disease. I know it doesn't seem like it, he said, but I think about this all the time, trying to figure out what to do.

An expression of such boyish anguish had passed over his face that she had relented and spent the remainder of the walk describing the film she had seen the previous evening. In the special photography collection, Jeffrey had filled out request forms for several of his favorite photographs. Each arrived in its own separate box. Gently he lifted off the lids to reveal a series of muted sepia landscapes: a lake with swans, a group of Edwardian picnickers, a vineyard beneath distant hills. Beautiful, he said, his face glowing. Don't you think so?

Verona didn't, exactly, but she allowed herself to be carried along. Enthusiasm for both art and life was part of Jeffrey's great charm. They talked about the exotic places they wanted to visit—Delphi at dawn, the pyramids, the Great Wall of China, Giverny, the Etruscan tombs at Orvieto—and avoided talking about the many ordinary activities they failed to share: spending the night together, having dinner with friends, attending his son's school play, buying a pound of apples, having a baby. He doesn't love his wife, Verona would repeat to herself; he doesn't sleep with his wife, his children are almost grown, his friends don't get on with his wife, he does love me, he does sleep with me, his friends would like me. The answer to her calculations seemed utterly straightforward. What was there to figure out? But of course it wasn't that kind of sum.

She lived for a year on daily phone calls, fleeting visits, a trip to Budapest, and a wonderful weekend at St. Ives before she tipped over a table in a restaurant—he had been talking about his wife's dog—and walked out to a satisfying hush. Three weeks later she had rewarded herself with a holiday in Thailand, which was she thought at least partly responsible for her present situation.

For a few seconds she conjured up the endless blue horizon. Then all possibility of blueness was obliterated by the reality that lay outside the windows of the cab: the sky stalled at a sullen gray, somewhere between pewter and silver, the interminable rows of grim houses. The cab, which had raced along the narrow streets, was now, on the motorway, revealed to have a top speed of forty. When occasionally, going downhill, it reached forty-one, the entire vehicle vibrated as if every nut and bolt were about to shake loose. "Please," she called to the driver above the music, "be careful."

"What?" Lowering the volume, he turned, disconcertingly, to look at her.

She repeated her request and, smiling, he assured her that all was well, he was an excellent driver and fully in command of this excellent vehicle, but he did slow down, or at least the vibrations lessened. She closed her eyes and rested her head against the prickly seat. Why was she thinking of Jeffrey now when a month could pass without his entering her brain? The answer was immediately available. The temptation for her in the garden of love was not knowledge of good and evil, but doubt.

A few weeks ago she had gone to the pub with some people from the radio station and ended up talking to the senior engineer, a darkly rabbinical young man named Gary. He had tried, as people did now that her pregnancy was advanced, to find out about the father; she had retaliated by asking why he wasn't married. Gary set down his pint, neatly fitting it into the previous circle left by the glass. Because, he said, my best friend met the love of his life at his own wedding. She came as the guest of his uncle, and as soon as James laid eyes on her—he was walking down the aisle—he knew she was the one.

How can you think that about a person you've never met, Verona had said. That's ridiculous.

Inconvenient, certainly. James said I do, six years later he got a divorce, a year after that he married his uncle's guest. So that's why I don't get married. The idea of being completely wrong about my own deepest emotions strikes terror in my heart. He raised his glass. Not to put too fine a point on it.

Jeffrey, she had wanted to shout, her own example of the condition Gary dreaded. For months she had believed him to be her Platonic other half, yet sitting in that raucous pub she could find no trace of the emotion that had made her want to walk hand in hand with him across the desert to the pyramids. What if her psyche was playing the same trick with Zeke, acting out of some ancient song of need? As the cab wobbled along, she entertained the traditional fears. She didn't really care for him; she had been misled by his good looks and by his apparent interest in her. He didn't really care for her; he had been curious about what it was like to sleep with someone seven months pregnant.

A thunderous noise made her eyes spring open. Her first thought was that the car was finally disintegrating. Then through the grimy window she saw, passing overhead like a giant bird, briefly blotting out the sky, its wings and belly flashing with lights, an airplane. I must have faith, she thought.

"Where are you going?" the driver asked, pulling into the hotel car park. "Somewhere with a bit of sunshine, I hope."

"I'm not going anywhere," she said flatly. "Your car shakes a lot."

"My car," he said, abandoning his earlier self-promotion, "is a piece of crap. I'm hoping to buy a new one at Easter. Until then we're riding on a prayer and the coat hanger that my dad used to fix the exhaust."

He parked between two buses, each spewing dark clouds. Verona maneuvered herself out of the backseat, handed him twenty-five pounds and, suitcases in tow, made her way over to the hotel. Even at this early hour, the lobby was so crowded that for a moment she simply stood there, baffled. It was as if she had never been to a hotel before, had forgotten the purpose and the procedures. "Excuse me, ma'am," said a voice, and she found herself surrounded by a family of Americans: three dark-haired boys and both parents, the mother bovine, the father gaunt, all wearing plaid shirts and jeans.

Oh, bugger off, she thought, glaring at the five of them, but they had reminded her of what to do next. She joined the queue at the front desk. In the taxi she had imagined herself eating one of those substantial hotel breakfasts. Now as she edged forward, following a man in a camel coat, nothing seemed more delicious than the prospect of climbing into a warm clean bed and giving herself back to sleep.

She held out a credit card, and the woman behind the desk took it without raising her eyes. "Good morning, Miss MacIntyre. Did you have a good flight?"

"I didn't. . . . Yes, thank you. Do you have a room for me?"

The woman was already processing her card and assuring her that she had the perfect room, on the fifth floor, nice and quiet. "One night?" she asked.

"One night. What about the planes?"

"The planes?" Finally the woman raised her eyes to examine this odd customer.

"Is the noise bothersome?"

"You hear them, of course, but there are so many of them and we have such thick windows. It's more of a dull background roar, like the sea." She slid the key across the counter. "Some of our visitors say they find it relaxing."

"I'll keep that in mind," said Verona, picturing a beach lapped, absurdly, by runways. This might make a good program, she thought, this peculiar hotel, everyone coming and going. She fell in behind the stocky young man who had been summoned to carry her luggage; he barely came up to her chin.

"So," said Toby, "where was I faxing you? And what's with the fax, anyway?"

"I was staying with a friend." She moved away from the door to draw the curtains. "Not exactly with him. At a house he's paint-ing." Oh, there was no way to explain this. "As for the faxes, I read somewhere that they're harder to intercept than phone calls."

Outside while she slept nothing had changed. Earth and air still seemed to be composed of the same dirty-gray fabric. Turning back to the room, she found Toby seated on the bed, taking off his shoes. He had always been dexterous, the person one asked to fas-ten a necklace or open a bottle of wine. Now as he fumbled with his laces, she saw what his elegant clothes, a purple cashmere pullover and black trousers, had initially concealed, how pale he was and haggard.

"What's happening?" she asked. "Why are we here? This room is insanely expensive, not to mention inconvenient."

"Unless"—he nodded toward the window—"you're flying."

"Am I flying?" She felt her voice grow small and cold. Already she was twenty-five miles from Zeke, as far as she could walk in a day; now Toby was suggesting that she go still farther.

"I know it's only noon," he said, at last discarding his shoes, "but I'm starving. Can we get some lunch?"

She asked again what was happening and, when he insisted on eating first, gave in and rang room service. While she ordered, he checked his messages. The mundane task seemed to calm him. His boss, he announced, had approved the catalog for their next show. She too felt revived by the brisk assumption of the man who answered the phone that two chicken sandwiches were a perfectly reasonable request.

Still seated on the bed, Toby gave a delicate yawn; his teeth, either by nature or artifice, were perfect. "On the way here, I was thinking that these last few days remind me of when my father was ill and all I did was go to the hospital. I feel as if I'll never have a normal life again."

"That was awful." She had accompanied him one afternoon to the intensive care unit and watched in horror as his father moaned and thrashed among the machines and Toby tried in vain to quiet him.

While they waited for the sandwiches, he brought her up-to-date on his mother, a surprisingly merry widow, and her latest escapade. A knock came at the door and a stout red-haired man stepped in. Looking neither to right nor left—indeed, somehow managing not even to look straight ahead—he crossed the small room and set the tray on the table by the window. Verona signed the bill. He bowed and departed.

"So," she said, pulling out a chair and seizing a sandwich, "tell me why we're here."

Toby, who had picked up his own sandwich, set it down again. "The men came to see me. The same as with you. They were sitting in the dark when I got home. I didn't even realize they were there." He looked at her, making sure she understood, and she nodded. "They wanted to know where you were. They're convinced you've gone to join Henry. I kept saying that was impossible, that neither of us knew where he was. As you can imagine, they weren't very happy about all this ignorance, but it was obvious that if I had known anything I would have told them." He grimaced. "So much for courage and loyalty."

"It was the same for me," she said. "I'd always fancied myself as someone who would heroically resist torture, never betray her comrades. The instant I saw Nigel and George—they didn't even lay a finger on me—I was beyond all that. This is good," she added, indicating her sandwich.

At last he began to eat. "So, we're a couple of lily-livered scum. I did ask what Henry had done. They just repeated what they told you: he's run out on a debt."

"That sounds like Henry." She ate an olive, almost tasteless. "Although surprisingly stupid. After five minutes with Nigel and George, you know they'd never let you get away with anything. I still don't understand why we're eating sandwiches in this absurd hotel."

Between mouthfuls, Toby explained. He had taken refuge with his friends Doug and Simon. When Doug, who designed Web pages, heard what was going on, he had had the same idea as Verona: to trace Henry electronically. He and Toby had gone to the Internet café on the high street. Forty minutes on two terminals had produced a list of the recent transactions on Henry's credit card. To make a brief story briefer, Henry had flown to Boston last Sunday and was staying there in a hotel.

"But why all the drama? I thought something terrible had happened." She tried to keep her voice level. She had abandoned Zeke just to discover that her brother was in America.

Toby piled his crusts on one side of his plate. "This is going to sound mad. I had a dream about you and the baby, that the two of you were in danger. I woke up at five with my heart pounding. So I made you a reservation here and sent the fax."

For a moment she could scarcely contain herself. Then she remembered Nigel standing beside her with the glass of water, his odd cinnamon smell, and how, as he and George closed the door, the glass had slipped from her hand. "I'm sorry," she said, not even knowing what she was apologizing for: her silent fury? the whole impossible situation? "Do you often get warnings in dreams?"

"Once or twice. And if you're going to ask whether they've proved accurate, the answer is I don't know because I always obey them. If a dream tells me not to go to the Tower of London, I don't go. Who knows what would happen if I did?"

With his last words the hotel phone began to ring. Verona started. Across the table, Toby did the same. "Does anyone know you're here?" he whispered.

"Only you."

The ringing stopped. He stood up, put the chain on the door, and tiptoed over to the phone. "They left a message," he said.

15

She woke to the pilot's voice announcing that they were beginning their descent into Boston. They would be on the ground in thirty minutes. The cabin, quiet when she fell asleep, was bustling with people putting away books or headsets, filling out customs forms, adjusting their clothes. Verona climbed out of her seat, luxuriously she had two together, and went to the bathroom. Back in her seat, she gazed down at the fast-approaching clouds and tried to sort out the events of the last twenty-four hours.

When they had played the message, a familiar voice greeted them, Verona, Toby, Nigel here. Listen, we're not playing cops and robbers. All we want is Henry back in Britain. The sooner you get him here, the better. We're losing patience.

So am I, she had said to Toby, after they both listened twice. It's only ten in the morning in Boston. We'll phone Henry right now.

She had dialed the number and spoken first to the hotel switchboard, then reception. Finally the phone was ringing its strange single note, presumably in Henry's room. After four rings a robotic female voice invited the caller to leave a message. She did so, telling him about the men and asking him to phone as soon as possible. She hung up with a sense of relief. They would talk to

Henry, he would talk to Nigel and George, and everything would be resolved. For an hour, nearly ninety minutes, she and Toby had watched television. Then it had dawned on both of them that Henry might not call back.

By suppertime—seven-thirty in London, two-thirty in Boston—they had left five fruitless messages and Toby insisted they go downstairs to eat. Their mobile phones sat mute on the table throughout the meal. When they returned to the room a couple of hours later, the message light on the phone was again flashing. Verona seized the receiver only to hear a woman announce that a packet was waiting for her at the front desk. Toby went downstairs and came back with a manila envelope bearing her name. Inside was her passport with a yellow square of paper affixed. *Happy travels,* it said, in elegant copperplate.

She had vigorously resisted the suggestion. Why should she fly several thousand miles to talk to Henry face-to-face when he did not want to talk to her at any distance? As soon as he learned to walk, she told Toby, I stopped having any influence on him. If either of us is going, it should be you. But Toby had argued, with surprising determination, that she had a huge influence on Henry; besides, he himself was needed at the gallery while she already had leave from her job. Of course, he added, they would share the costs.

They had fallen asleep on opposite sides of the double bed, still undecided, and when they woke to another gray morning and the faint continual vibration of the planes, somehow it was settled: Verona was going to Boston. While Toby organized the ticket, she repacked her suitcases. In the queue at the airline desk he had cheerfully listed things he would like from America—a new suit, maple syrup, CDs—but as they neared the moment of departure, he grew increasingly silent. By the entrance to security he drew her over to the wall. I don't mean to be melodramatic, he said, but there's something I need to ask you.

He reached for her hands. Who is the mystery father?

After months of silence and prevarication finally, this afternoon at terminal three, she had to admit her vanity and failure. There's really no mystery, she said. I went to a sperm bank. Given my age and situation, it seemed the only dignified solution. I couldn't imagine saying to one of my male friends, lend me your semen and I swear you won't have any obligation to the outcome. Or maybe I could imagine that, but I couldn't imagine telling my child, this man agreed to be your father on condition that he could ignore you. It just seemed too, too.... Well, lots of people—she glanced toward the steady stream of travelers—do it, but I couldn't.

What a dark horse you are, Toby had said, swinging their hands. If you knew how many hours Henry and I have spent speculating about your love life. We thought it must be your old beau, the businessman. Do you have any information about the previous owner of your sperm?

He's a six-foot-two nineteen-year-old Welsh medical student who plays the piano for pleasure and enjoys squash. She tried to explain the increments by which paternity had become a secret, first waiting for the amniocentesis, then enjoying the sly remarks about her glamorous affair. Truth to tell, Toby said, if you didn't have a wild fling, I'm glad you went to a sperm bank. I'd feel a little jealous if I wasn't the first person you turned to to fill your turkey baster. He had kissed her warmly on both cheeks. When you come back, he had said, we must have dinner.

She had used the same trite phrase, she realized now, looking down at the brown, hilly landscape mottled with snow, when she phoned Emmanuel from the gate to get Zeke's number. Any time, he had replied, in skeptical tones. She saw houses, a frozen pond, a large factorylike building, and a road crammed with cars.

Fifteen minutes later they were lurching along the runway between occasional mounds of snow. She lined up to leave the plane, answered questions from unsmiling officials, retrieved her luggage, dodged an Alsatian sniffing for drugs, and answered more questions, trying to sound like any other traveler over for a brief holiday. Only when she stepped outside did she fully grasp that she was in America. She had last been to Boston to comment on a presidential campaign, and each step of the journey had been scheduled and accompanied. Now, standing with her suitcases in the biting wind, she felt a sudden longing to be taken care of. She was only here for a couple of days—four, according to her ticket—but every minute away from the one person who could do that seemed a waste.

She was in the back of a taxi, almost as grubby as the one that had taken her to Heathrow, when it occurred to her that Henry might have bolted. At once she felt certain that this was the case. Toby had left a message saying she was on her way, but what on earth had made them think Henry would sit still and wait for a conversation he didn't want to have? "Stupid, stupid, stupid," she muttered.

"You talking to me?" the driver asked, squinting at her in the rearview mirror. He reminded her of an older, darker version of Emmanuel.

"I wish," she said. "Myself."

"Well, whatever happens in the next fifteen minutes isn't your fault."

During her previous visit, she had spent a day interviewing politicians and academics, but all she could remember of the city was a tall glass tower and a red sign beside the river, advertising petrol. As the cab lurched past seemingly endless construction sites, she struggled to control her impatience. We don't know for certain, the midwife had told her, but we believe stress has an adverse affect on the fetus. To which Verona had offered her usual argument about how stress was connected with many positive aspects of our lives and the trick was to learn to embrace it, not avoid it. Now, feeling her heart smashing against her ribs, she was acutely aware that she wasn't making life easy for her cohabitant. I'm going to jump out of my skin, she thought, if we don't get there soon.

At just that moment the taxi pulled over. A shabby red carpet with a canopy above stretched from the curb to a large glass door.

She paid the driver and, ignoring his offer of help, seized a suit-case in either hand and swept into the hotel, almost colliding with a slender Asian woman who was cradling what at first glance she took to be a baby and on second identified as a small white dog with butterfly-shaped ears. At the desk a young man with olive skin and hair gelled into oddly unbecoming spikes began to welcome her to the hotel. "I'm here to see Henry MacIntyre," she interrupted and, pandering to the vernacular, added, "one of your guests."

He turned to his computer and asked how the name was spelled. "M-a-c-I," said Verona. If he's here, she vowed, promising the hardest thing she could think of, whatever happens I won't lose my temper. Then the man was raising his dark eyes to hers, the whites were visible all the way round the pupils, and for an absurd moment all she could think of was Zeke's blue-eyed gaze. "Use the house phone." He pointed. "I'll connect you."

The phone began to ring and still she did not allow herself to hope. Even as she slept her way across the Atlantic, he would have paid for his room and moved to another hotel, another city. The ringing stopped.

"Hi," said a girlish American voice.

She let the phone fall, or at least it disappeared from her hand. She tried to hold on to the desk, to blink away the darkness. This isn't good for the baby, she thought. The room began a slow tilt as she renegotiated her relationship with the floor.

A hand was stroking her forehead; another, or the same, gently held her wrist. Henry, she thought, he's here after all. But when she opened her eyes, the person bending over her was a stranger. Close up, Verona saw the woman in fragments: a blue smock, dark hair curling over a pale forehead, slightly crooked teeth. "I'm fine," she said, struggling to sit up.

"Lie back. What year is it? Do you know who the president is?"

"Yes. I'm sorry. I'll be fine once I've had a cup of tea."

On her other side the spiky-haired young man was also bending over her. "Are you Verona MacIntyre?" he said. "I have a letter for you."

"In a minute," said the woman. "Let me ask her a few questions. Do you have a doctor? Have you had a checkup recently?"

She spoke just a little more loudly than was necessary, as if Verona's hearing had also been affected by her faint. "I do and I have," said Verona. She took a deep breath and sat up, carefully pressing her palms against the cool floor. For a moment the room threatened to tilt again. She focused on the woman's smock until it grew steady. "Really," she insisted, "I'm perfectly all right."

The woman sat back on her heels and eyed her appraisingly. "Have you fainted before?"

What was the right answer: yes, no, occasionally? She offered the last and added that she hadn't had much to eat today. "If I don't feel tip-top tomorrow," she said, "I'll get a checkup."

"All right, but remember, go to your doctor at the first sign of dizziness or blurred vision or anything out of the ordinary. In your condition you don't want to take any chances. How about we get you into a chair?" She stood up, motioning to the clerk, who had been hovering throughout, and a few seconds later Verona was seated in a wing-backed chair.

"Get her some tea and toast," ordered the nurse, and announced that she'd be on her way. She had just stepped into the hotel to make a phone call.

As she drank her tea, ate two slices of toast, registered, and was taken up to her room, Verona never once let go of Henry's letter. Alone at last, lying on top of the spacious bed, she opened it.

Dear Verona,

If you're reading this, you must be furious. Sorry not to be here to welcome you. Please don't wreck the hotel. I got your messages, all your messages, and several from Nigel and George too, so I have a rough idea of what's been going on since I left town. I'm checking out some possibilities. Can't say more, for obvious reasons, but I'll be in touch v. soon. Enjoy Boston until I get back.

Love, Henry

PS My company gets a discount at this hotel.

Perhaps it was the aftereffects of her brief spell of unconsciousness, perhaps the cumulative effect of the last five days, but what she felt was not the familiar surge of anger but a peculiar numbness. She had heard of this phenomenon, people in the face of disaster experiencing a lack of emotion rather than an excess, but had never understood it. What's happening to me, she thought. Why aren't I pounding on the television, smashing the mirror?

She left the letter lying on the bed and, longing for some vestige of normality, ran a tepid bath. As she lay back, watching her belly crest the surface, she recalled the story she had told Toby about Henry and the English teacher. Mr. Sayers, with his bulbous nose and oddly shaped head, had been her favorite teacher. She had often stayed late after class to consult with him about a poem or essay, but that day, as soon as he asked her to stay behind, she had known something was amiss.

Verona, he had said, gazing out of the window towards the rose garden, how old are you?

Thirteen.

And Henry?

Nearly nine.

It never occurred to her that Mr. Sayers might be ill at ease. As far as she was concerned, he suffered from none of the complex emotions he attributed to the characters in novels and plays. Some days he was in a better mood than others. Some days the school cook served charlotte russe.

I am going to burden you with some information, he said. He described how he had found Henry searching the girls' raincoats and how, even when Mr. Sayers said he knew he was lying, Henry had stuck to his story that one of the big girls had asked him to fetch a whistle from her coat pocket.

I put him on detention for a month. And I told your father.

I heard Linda Harris ask him to fetch her whistle, Verona burst out. He must have got confused.

Mr. Sayers turned to look at her and went on as if she hadn't spoken. I decided, he said, that you too ought to be told. Usually older children lead the younger into bad behavior. My own brother did a splendid job of teaching me to steal apples and play tricks on the church organist. In this case, it may be the other way round. Henry, I fear, was born without a conscience, and you will have to be the one to say, and keep saying, lying is wrong, stealing is wrong, hurting other people is wrong. Do you understand?

She had nodded, red-cheeked, and as soon as he dismissed her she ran out of the room and all the way home. Later, though, her anger had been tinged with relief. For several years she had been trying to pretend to herself and everyone else that Henry was normal. Now, sitting in the cooling water in the small white room, she wondered if she and Mr. Sayers had given up too easily. Was there a time when Henry could have been saved? She pictured him slipping his small hand into the girls' raincoats, stealing Toby's money, doing whatever he had done to Nigel and George, and she could not think of a single occasion when her brother had seemed either capable of remorse or susceptible to punishment.

16

Outside it was still dark and the broad sidewalk was empty save for a couple of muffled figures walking dogs. Verona clutched her coat against the icy wind and set off to find the coffee shop the clerk had mentioned. After three blocks, just as she was giving up hope, she spotted a glowing sign. Inside the steamy establishment, she gave her order to the waitress and was rewarded with a brimming plate of eggs, home fries, toast, and pancakes. It was almost worth the trip, she thought, seizing her knife and fork, to have the American version of the Heart Attack Special.

By the time she walked back to the hotel the sun was coming up—leaving London, crossing the ocean to Boston—and the streets were busy with people hurrying to work. In her room she phoned Toby at the gallery. When she told him that Henry had fled, leaving only a note, he said quietly, "I was afraid of that."

"So why did I get on a plane? Why didn't we sit tight and wait for him to pick up the phone in his own sweet time? I'm going to check the flights. With luck I can come back standby this evening. That way I won't even have jet lag."

"Please." Toby lowered his voice. "What did he say in his note?"

She read it, enunciating every word as if she were reading the news on the radio.

"So," Toby said, "he *is* coming back."

"How do we know? He doesn't exactly promise, and, even if he did, so what?"

"He says, *Enjoy Boston until I get back*. And he does promise to be in touch. I'm sorry, I have a customer. I'll call this evening. Please don't do anything rash until we talk."

"What could be more rash than coming here?" she demanded and hung up.

In the desk drawer she found a telephone directory and punched her way stubbornly through the airline menu—international flights, she had a preexisting reservation—until a woman, with the kind of southern accent that English people parody, introduced herself as Tiffany. "What can I do for you today?" she said.

Verona explained her situation. A series of faint clicks emanated from the phone and Tiffany announced there was no problem getting a reservation on the evening flight to London. And yes, there was an aisle seat near the front: 24B. Verona was already calculating the hours until she stepped off the plane and saw Zeke, when Tiffany asked for the code on her ticket. She read out the letters and numbers.

"Thank you, ma'am." Tiffany paused, clicked. "That will be eight hundred and twenty-six dollars. Which credit card will you be using?"

"But that's almost twice what I paid for the round-trip."

"Yes, ma'am." Tiffany's inflection did not change an iota. "The basis for your fare was that you stay over a Saturday night. If you want to fly back this evening, you automatically move to a higher fare bracket."

"What if it's an emergency?"

"If it's an emergency, ma'am, you need to produce documentation—a doctor's certificate, notice of a death. Is there anything else I can help you with today?"

"Let me speak to a supervisor."

"I'll have to put you on hold."

After two minutes of listening to the swelling Wagnerian music, Verona replaced the receiver. There was some tiny satisfaction in picturing the supervisor being disturbed for nothing.

After an hour of useless fulminating, she retrieved her outdoor things and went downstairs. If she had to be in Boston she might as well see the city. At the advice of the concierge she took a train to the Museum of Fine Arts and strolled through their Asian collection, paying particular attention to the Buddhas and the gnarled rocks called philosopher's stones. Perhaps some of the peace and wisdom would rub off on her. She was newly back, still wearing her coat and the hat she had bought from a street vendor, when Henry called. As soon as she heard his voice, she was yelling into the phone, not caring if he hung up. "How could you behave this way? Do you never think of anyone. . . . ?" Even as she heard herself ranting in a way that her midwife would surely deplore, some other part of her was exulting in the return of her hot-tempered self. And for once Henry neither interrupted nor contradicted.

"I know I've been a bastard," he said, when she at last paused, "and, even worse, a stupid bastard."

"Where are you?"

"The West Coast," he said, and quickly added, "Don't ask. In this case ignorance is bliss. Suffice to say there's someone here who I hope can help."

"Let's hope they feel the same."

"Let's," he said lightly.

"So there's no reason for me to stay in Boston." She would call Tiffany back and take the next flight that was less than stratospheric.

"I'd rather"—he cleared his throat—"you did." He began to explain how he was glad to have her comparatively nearby, how he expected to have the situation resolved within twenty-four hours, and then, when she protested that she didn't see what sort of help she could be, given that they were on opposite coasts, he added that he was just a little bit worried about how it would look if she returned to England without either him or the money. "Nigel and George might get out of hand."

"That's crazy."

"Yes, but so is everything else. I used to read about this kind of thing in the newspaper. It never dawned on me that it could actually happen. Please, Verona, now that you're here, it only makes sense for you to stay. We can fly home together."

Grumpily, reluctantly, she promised to stay through tomorrow, on the condition that he phone her. They talked for a few minutes about the weather, bitter in Boston, mild on the West Coast, and about what she had seen at the museum. Henry too, it turned out, had whiled away the day visiting galleries. "We'll have to report to Toby," he said. "Bring him up-to-date on the American art scene."

Alone again, she took off her coat and walked over to the window. Immediately below was a church, the roof white with snow, the steeple bare. Opposite was a brightly lit office building crowded with cubicles and computers. As she watched the people come and go, the spooky thought came to her, as it had so often during childhood, that no one knew she was here.

At school one year there had been a craze for those kinds of questions. What was your most embarrassing moment? Whom do you fancy? What are you afraid of? She had gone home and repeated them to Henry. What's fancy, he'd asked. Do you mean like the little cakes? No, idiot, said Verona, whose own ideas on the subject centered upon a boy named Vaughan. It's when a boy likes a girl or she likes him. She half expected Henry to say that that was stupid, but he had offered the astonishing suggestion that this must be why grown-ups got married. Verona felt her stomach somersault. Even as she argued fiercely against the shameful idea that she and their parents had anything in common, the conviction crept over her that Henry was right. What else could explain their mother and father's improbable union?

With embarrassment, Henry had no problem: his friend Nick's birthday party when he had been exuberantly sick in the middle of Pass the Parcel.

And what are you afraid of, Verona had insisted.

If I tell, will you?

Yes.

I'm afraid of turning into Mum and Dad. And of losing you.

He was eight, his knees knobbly, and his neck so long it looked as if he could swivel his head, owl-like, front to back. What are you afraid of? he said, his eyes fixed upon her.

Nothing. Not a single blooming thing. And Henry, not doubting her for an instant, had nodded. At school, she added, I had to say something so I pretended I was scared of being buried alive. You know, like Edgar Allan Poe having a bell in his coffin.

He didn't know, but he'd nodded again, and they had both begun to speculate what that would be like. Would you end up eating worms and could you hear people talking aboveground? Worms might be okay, Henry had said, but I don't like things over my face.

In the street below, a woman with a fuchsia umbrella passed by. I was wrong, Verona thought, to doubt his story about the pillow. And several people know I'm here, four to be exact: Henry, Toby, Nigel, and George.

Every day she forced herself to visit a major tourist attraction and investigate it as if she were planning to do a program; every day Henry would phone and talk optimistically about his prospects on the West Coast. After she spoke to him she would call Toby, who continued to counsel patience. And every day, every hour, she planned to call Zeke and failed to do so. She wanted to wait until she had definite news, but by the time she realized that nothing had changed, around six or seven in the evening, it was too late to call. Tomorrow, she would think, this will get sorted out and I will fly home. Periodically she checked her answering machine in London. Her new greeting claimed she'd be in and out for the next week, and only the most intrepid friends left messages. Her mobile phone, it turned out, did not work in America. When it grew dark she either went to the nearby cinema—it had six screens—or ate in her room and watched television. One night she went to the launderette.

The baby, judging by its frequent twists and turns, seemed to enjoy her enforced leisure. Her reasons for concealing its origins were not entirely those she had confessed to Toby. True, she had wanted the romance, but she had also needed the privacy. After having an abortion in her twenties and a miscarriage in her early thirties, each with fairly minimal regrets, she had been taken aback to find herself, at the age of thirty-five, longing for a child, first with Jeffrey, later without him. Her parents were dead, her brother unreliable, but it was possible that she might still have her own small family.

For several months, nearly a year, she had resisted the idea, worrying that she lacked the resources to be a good parent. Then in Thailand, on a halcyon afternoon, she had rescued one of her fellow guests from drowning, and something about that narrow escape had made her decide to go to a sperm bank as soon as she got home. She had cautioned herself not to get her hopes up—after all, she was thirty-seven—and she had been both thrilled and disconcerted to get pregnant after a single visit. For most of the next six months she had oscillated between various fears: the baby would have problems, she would be a terrible mother, the baby would hate her for not providing a father, she would feel trapped. And then, only a few weeks ago, shortly before her last meeting with Henry, she had begun to feel a sense of calm happiness, almost as if the baby itself were pumping reassurance into her veins, and this happiness had persisted in spite of all the recent vicissitudes. In part that was why, day after day, she agreed to wait for Henry.

Shortly after 8 A.M. on her seventh morning in Boston, her waiting was rewarded. Someone knocked at her door, and when she answered, there, standing in the brightly lit beige corridor, wearing a dramatic long black coat and a red scarf, holding a suitcase, was her elusive brother, not quite smiling.

"Verona, sorry to be late. Traffic was dreadful." He moved to embrace her and then—she was still holding the door—kissed her cheek. She smelled his stale breath and some combination of coffee and fried food. "Can I come in?" he said, and she stepped back.

Inside, he took off his coat and laid it on the end of the unmade bed. While he surveyed her room, she studied him. His periwinkle blue pullover should have emphasized his good looks but merely drew attention to his bloodshot eyes and stubbled cheeks. His hair was newly cut. "You have a nicer painting than I did," he said, nodding towards the Eakins print. "Otherwise this is identical to my old room. Can I use your shower? It's still too early to check in."

Alone, Verona found herself examining the contents of his suitcase. Henry had set it on the bed to choose clean clothes and left it there with the lid open. She stared down at the folded shirts, the trousers, the sweaters, wondering when he'd learned to pack so neatly. As the steady drumming of the shower continued, she lifted out a shirt and shook it, lifted out another; she unrolled the socks, she checked the pockets of his trousers. She could not have said what she was searching for—a map showing buried treasure? an IOU from Henry to Nigel and George?—but she examined every garment. By the time Henry reappeared she was sitting on the bed, the case more or less restored to its original state. If he noticed that his possessions were a little disheveled, he didn't say; he placed the clothes he'd been wearing on top and closed the lid. "That feels better," he said.

Over pancakes in the hotel restaurant, he kept up a steady flow of inconsequential conversation about Seattle, where it emerged he had spent the last week. Verona ate and listened; the prospect of her own imminent departure lent her patience. When he had phoned the previous evening to say he was taking an overnight flight to Boston, she had known at once from his breezy tone that his schemes had failed and once again phoned the airline. After breakfast, they collected their coats and went for a walk. Outside, the day was cold and windless; the clouds barely skimmed the tops of the tallest buildings. According to Henry, snow was forecast. They headed east. She caught several people, mostly women but one or two men, turning to look at him. Don't, she wanted to say. Every admiring glance only helped to buoy him up. As they passed shops and restaurants, he speculated as to what would be the London equivalent of this street. "Regent Street? Or maybe somewhere in Knightsbridge?"

"I booked a flight for this evening, seven P.M."

Henry stopped so suddenly that he rocked forward on his toes. "This evening? But we need to talk."

"Agreed." The first flake of snow drifted down between them. "And you're simply babbling about the scenery. I've been waiting for a week. I'm not going to wait any longer."

"Okay, okay. So I'm procrastinating. Please say you'll stay, just until tomorrow. I promise I'll tell you everything if only you'll stay."

While the pedestrians parted around them, she returned Henry's gaze. His almond eyes, clearer than when he first arrived, were so dark that she could not distinguish a single glint of green; for the first time she noticed faint lines around them. "All right," she said. "One more day."

"Thank you." Another flake drifted past as he suggested that they take the subway to Cambridge and discuss their troubles in a café there. They walked across a park and along a street lined with antiques shops to the station. As the train crossed over the Charles River, Verona saw in the distance the two sights she'd remembered from her earlier visit: the blue glass tower and the red sign; she pointed them out to Henry and he identified the Prudential Center and the Citgo sign. At Harvard Square station she once again called the airline to reschedule. By the time they came above ground, the snow was falling steadily. Momentarily she forgot their difficulties and stared in pleasure. How long since she had seen proper snow? Maybe two or three years, given London's feeble winters. Mysteriously, when she looked closely, almost as many flakes seemed to be rising as falling. She followed Henry across the street, ignoring a tea shop and a café. Beside the latter an elderly man with hollow cheeks held a sign: SAVING FOR A SET OF DENTURES. PLEASE.

They made their way across another street to a two-story wooden building, the steep roof fringed with icicles. Inside, the walls were painted deep reds and light blues. The customers were either reading or consulting their laptops. She squeezed past apologetically as she followed Henry to an octagonal table next to the window. A waitress took their order for a cappuccino and a mint tea. "Do you want milk with the tea?" she asked eagerly.

"No, thank you," said Verona and, as the girl's smile faded, added, "thanks for asking."

"See," said Henry, "that's one of the few things they know about British people—we take milk in our tea."

While they waited, he again fell back on tourism—his visits to the Christian Science Mapparium, the USS *Constitution*, Faneuil Hall—but Verona could tell from the set of his shoulders that he knew there were no more hiding places. When he paused, she contributed her own visit to the Isabella Stewart Gardner Museum; an easel marked the spot where a Vermeer had hung before it was stolen. "I can't imagine what kind of person steals a painting they can never show to anyone. Is it because they fall in love with that particular painting? Or they like the idea of owning a masterpiece?"

"Maybe for some people," Henry suggested, "a Vermeer is beautiful but a stolen Vermeer is exquisite."

On the word *exquisite*, the waitress set down their drinks. Henry thanked her. As soon as she was out of earshot, he said, "Do you remember our grandfather?"

"Jigger? Of course," said Verona, taken aback. "I inherited his nose. That's what I used to tell myself when the girls teased me at school. You have some notebook of his, don't you?"

"How do you know that?" Now it was his turn to be startled.

"When Toby and I went to your house it was obvious that the men had searched it, so we followed their example. Toby found this leather-bound book. It was addressed to me so I kept it. I've only read the first half." Her face grew warm as she recalled where she had left the book. As soon as she got back to London, she would ask Zeke to retrieve it from the Barrows'. Then she imagined him caught in the web of her lies. Perhaps she could persuade Emmanuel to go instead.

Henry nodded. "I swiped it after he died," he said. "He wrote something rather incriminating about me."

"What on earth could he say that was incriminating? He didn't even know you." This had nothing to do with why she had traveled three thousand miles; nonetheless, she succumbed.

"More than you think. I went to stay with him once. I told Mum and Dad I was visiting you. I knew they'd never check."

This was even more surprising. "Why would you go and see Jigger? I mean, I can understand you wanting to get away from home, but to visit your grandfather? What about girls and wild parties?"

Henry grimaced. "I wasn't thinking love; I was thinking money. Dad was always saying that Jigger was rich, and I was worried he'd leave everything to some stupid charity. I wanted to propose myself as his heir."

"His heir? You were how old?"

"Sixteen, but I already knew that money was what mattered and I didn't want to be hopeless about it, like the rest of you."

In the street outside, a police car drove slowly by in the snow. "So what happened?" she said, ignoring the insult. "How do you go about telling someone that you want them to hurry up and die and leave you all their money?"

"That turned out to be a problem. In my imagination Jigger saw what a fine young man I was and announced that he was going to make me his heir. Unfortunately, that didn't occur." He described how he had phoned, pretending to be visiting the Lake

District and asking if Jigger could put him up for the night. At first everything went swimmingly. Jigger had seemed pleased to see him. He made dinner and Henry plied him with the wine he'd brought, but his hints fell on deaf ears. "And then, in the middle of the night, he caught me searching his desk."

"Christ, what did he say?"

Henry laughed. "I played the oldest trick in the book and pretended to be sleepwalking. I don't think he believed me for a second, but it saved us from having a major row."

"You did used to sleepwalk, though. I remember finding you a couple of times. Once you were sitting by the fire, stroking the rug as if it were a cat." She stroked the table to demonstrate. "I still don't get it. What did happen to Jigger's money? Dad got some, but not nearly as much as he'd hoped."

"He left it to you." He spoke absently; he was looking at the next table where a young woman with waist-length hair was frowning over a notebook.

"No," she corrected. "He left me five thousand pounds, which you teased me about mercilessly, calling me the heiress. The money allowed me to move to London and work for a pittance for the BBC. It was hardly life-changing. Didn't he leave the rest to a Lake District trust?"

He leaned forward. His ears were scarlet. "He left it to you," he repeated.

Her brain was shuddering, struggling to grasp this new information. In the center of the table a bronze circle was embedded in the wood; she ran her finger round the circumference. "I don't understand. If he left me the money, why didn't I get it?"

"I changed his will."

I am going to open my mouth, thought Verona, and let out a scream so loud that the roof will fly off this restaurant and the walls will fall to the ground and everyone sitting here will be deaf for as long as they live.

17

The hollow-cheeked man was still standing outside the café as she stormed by. She did not need to turn around to know that Henry was trailing behind her in halfhearted pursuit. During their childhood she had often run off with the luxury of knowing he would come after her. He was her loyal follower, and she in return had protected him against all comers. She had believed herself to be the sole exception to his bad behavior. Now a little red car fueled by fury and lost illusions hurtled round and round her brain. Heedless of shops and pedestrians, she strode up a broad one-way street. A man tried to waylay her with a petition but she brushed him aside. A girl with a pram darted out of her way. Then, on the far side of the street, she saw a woman in an orange ski jacket stepping out of an archway in the wall around Harvard University. Verona plunged in among the traffic.

Automatically, as she did when entering the tunnels of London or Paris, she took a deep breath, but it was immediately clear that this tunnel was no refuge for the inebriated and homeless. The brightly lit space was lined with posters for a mime festival, several films, a lesbian night out, the classics club. "This is Harvard's main campus," Henry said behind her. "Oddly, it's called Harvard Yard, as if it were some kind of high-class farm."

They were walking alongside a tall brick building. At the front a massive flight of shallow stone steps led up to a façade of pillars and a pediment engraved with the words HARRY ELKINS WIDENER MEMORIAL LIBRARY. In spite of herself, Verona paused and Henry took the opportunity to explain that Harry Widener had been a passenger on the *Titanic*. He had had a seat on a lifeboat but had run back to his cabin to fetch his book—according to rumor a volume of Bacon's essays—and ended up going down with the ship. His mother had given the library to the university with certain conditions, including, until recently, that every student pass a swimming test. "As if," Henry said, "swimming would have saved Harry among the icebergs."

Too angry to speak, Verona continued walking; he fell in beside her. The snow was falling faster now, and the snowflakes had grown in size. She could feel the damp seeping into her flimsy boots and down the collar of her coat. Around them young people with backpacks hurried back and forth, and an occasional adult with a briefcase. They passed a brick building with the names of famous philosophers around the top, then a modern building, and a bronze statue of a man and a woman seated side by side, their laps filled with snow.

"By my namesake," said Henry.

If she went back to the hotel now, she could go standby on the evening flight; she could be with Zeke tomorrow morning.

"We're very near the Fogg Museum," said Henry. "Why don't we take shelter there? William James, the philosopher, lived on this street. He's the one who wrote about scapegoats."

Trying to hold her coat closed against the wind, she caught fragments of Henry's musings. Not for the first time, she was struck by how his obliviousness was an armor more powerful than all her self-awareness. "It's still the right decision in certain situations." He waved a hand at the snow. "Shoving Oates out of the tent. Not that it did any good."

"Didn't Oates leave of his own accord?" she couldn't help saying as she followed him up the steps of a handsome stone building.

He held open the door. "That's just the rubbish they tell schoolchildren to make them share their lunches. Who would go out in weather thirty times worse than this voluntarily?"

Inside it was warm, dry, windless. She hung up her coat, and shook her head to get rid of the snow. Henry joked with the woman behind the counter about how intrepid they felt. "What would you recommend we see?" he asked.

"It's a small collection. You should have no trouble seeing everything, but if you're pushed for time I recommend the Pre-Raphaelites on the balcony. Though of course"—she gave a little smile—"they come from your part of the world."

"Which means," Henry said, smiling back, "that we've never seen them."

He was about to say more when he caught Verona's glare and seemed to recall that they were in the midst of an argument. Ignoring the proffered admission button, she stepped forward into what, she couldn't help noticing, was a beautiful two-story courtyard surrounded by arches. But the large open space only made the red car faster, louder. She had a vision of herself and Henry shouting at the top of their lungs, terrifying the other visitors. She doubled back to the stairs and, without stopping to look at the statues and paintings, ascended to the balcony.

She circled twice, three times, trying to rein in her fury, before she came to a halt in front of one of the Pre-Raphaelites. A woman stood in front of a window that was mostly obscured by hair so abundant that Verona's neck ached. She had worn her hair long through her teens and early twenties until her friend Marian had persuaded her to get it cut. Your hair is a liability, she had argued. It's too gorgeous for the rest of you. Not a problem for this woman, whose green eyes gravely regarded something to which the viewer was not privy.

"What a poseur," Henry said, joining her.

She couldn't bear to look at him. "I know we've had hundreds of rows," she said, trying to keep her voice steady, "but I always thought we were on the same side when it came to everyone else." Briefly, the red car slowed and she realized it was easier to be furious than to acknowledge what fury concealed.

"We are," he said affably. "The odd thing about this picture is that she seems to be simultaneously indoors and outdoors. Look at the sky behind her. Don't you want to know how I did it? A few months after my visit to Jigger, I was over at my friend Blake's house and he showed me this copy of the Magna Carta he'd made for his dad. He went on and on about how he'd made the paper from old rags and practiced the handwriting because you never got the same effect with tracing."

At the time Henry had been bored rigid but later, walking home, he had had a Eureka moment. "It was one of those misty autumn evenings, and I suddenly thought if Blake could copy the Magna Carta, he could copy Jigger's will. I remember I was opposite the corner shop and I burst out laughing. People must have thought I was drunk. It wasn't even the idea. It was the sense of knowing what I was good at."

"So you stole Jigger's will," she said slowly, "and you and Blake rewrote it."

The sound of footsteps made them both turn. A couple were approaching, the woman wearing a cream-colored pullover, a long brown skirt, and high-heeled boots, the man in a beautiful charcoal suit. They were talking in French, the woman moving her hands, the man smiling. Occasionally one or the other would glance at a picture.

"She's saying," said Henry, "that he's a superb lover and that he has the most beautiful member she's ever seen. He seems to be agreeing. She'd probably go into more detail if they were in France and she thought other people could understand."

He began to walk in the opposite direction from the couple; Verona trailed alongside. Far from sounding penitent, Henry sounded increasingly jubilant as he explained what he and Blake had done. They had only changed one page so they didn't have to forge the signatures. The tricky part was getting hold of the will. It wasn't as if Jigger went to work every day. The other part that had required planning was who the money should go to. He couldn't just replace Verona's name with his. He did some research and used his savings to set up a private company.

"I can't tell you how odd it was, waiting to see if it would work. I went off to university facing two very different futures: one in which I'd have a head start and another in which I'd have to scramble." He paused in front of a Canaletto, the *Piazza San Marco*, so exquisitely detailed, even down to a small dog, that it could have been a photograph.

"Scramble like me and everyone else. How much did Jigger leave to the private company?"

"A hundred and thirty thousand. Not a fortune, but enough to get me started on the property ladder. Then I just kept going."

"And"—she could scarcely get the words out—"what about me?"

He turned to her, smiling his most brilliant smile. "You were fine. I always knew you would be because, unlike me, you have a real talent. But if there'd ever come a time when you needed something—if you'd fallen ill or lost your job—I'd have helped. I regarded myself"—he put a hand on his chest—"as obligated."

It's like the snowflakes, she thought. He doesn't know down from up, wrong from right. "Henry, you stole a hundred and thirty thousand pounds from me."

"Ages ago. Given the statute of limitations, you can't prosecute." He was still speaking in an affable, slightly bemused way. "I'm sorry. I shouldn't have told you."

"But you're not sorry you did it, are you? You'd do it again, given half a chance. Mr. Sayers was right about you. You were born without a conscience."

"No," he said, "I wouldn't say that."

In the first room off the balcony, he stopped before a landscape: a village street in winter. A few feet away Verona stared at a painting of a train standing in a sunlit high-ceilinged station, surrounded by hydrangea-like clouds of steam. Glancing at the label, she saw to her amazement that it was the station in Paris where Jigger had gone with his friend Charles. Suddenly she grasped the other part of what Henry had told her: Jigger had chosen her as his heir. No one else approved of her, but he did. Another thing that she was robbed of. The red car was at a standstill; Henry had tipped sugar into the fuel tank, disconnected the battery. Whatever his more recent crimes, surely nothing could be worse than this youthful betrayal.

From the next room came a voice: "*Tu es fantastique.*" Unthinkingly, Verona stepped back to let the French couple pass and fell in behind them. She could make her feet move as long as she watched theirs. She was back out on the balcony again, once more passing the woman at the window, the *Piazza San Marco*. Where were the stairs? Over there, by the pillar. She was at the top of the stairs and then she was heading down, past the ground floor and on, down, to the door marked LADIES. In the wooden cubicle, she bent over the toilet until every morsel she had eaten that day lay in the white china bowl.

She remained in the bathroom, leaning against the wall, until someone knocked at the door; she opened it to discover that Henry had enlisted the woman from the counter. Beneath her solicitous gaze, Verona felt obligated to go through the motions of recovery. She washed her face and hands in the large marble basin and rinsed her mouth with the lukewarm water. "Are you sick?" the woman kept asking. Behind the counter she had radiated respectability; now she was revealed to be wearing torn black clothes and combat boots. "Do you need a doctor?"

Obviously I was sick, thought Verona, then remembered that Americans used the word to mean ill. "No, I just had a shock, several shocks, and they upset my stomach."

"Oh, I'm the same." The woman patted her studded black leather belt. "I used to think I'd grow out of it but I'm not sure one does grow out of things at thirty-four. Is there anything I can get you? If only"—her eyes darted around the empty room—"we had some ginger ale. Here, why don't you sit down?"

Verona sank into a small metal chair. The relief of being told what to do was profound. The woman was still talking, something about a car, did they have one, was it parked nearby? When Verona said they didn't, she hurried out of the room.

Alone, Verona rested her head on the edge of the basin and surrendered to misery and self-disgust. Why had she ever thought Henry treated her differently? "Traitor," she whispered. In childhood it had been a terrible insult. As an adult, she had seldom used the word, except in a sexual context.

From somewhere in the building came a faint steady beeping. Last spring she had interviewed a woman who, as a teenager, had stopped speaking for two years. Wasn't it awfully frustrating, Verona had said, not being able to ask for what you wanted? No, the woman had said. That was easy. Besides, I did ask: I wrote notes. I pointed. It felt so safe not putting things into words. No one lied to me. And I got so much thinking done. I really came to understand why silence is often part of religious practice.

She did have a nunlike face, long and pale. So why did you stop talking in the first place? Verona asked. Why did you start again?

I don't think I can explain why I stopped. There wasn't some shock. I didn't even make a decision. One morning when my mother asked me a question I didn't answer, and I didn't answer the next one either. As for why I started again, I missed it. Not speech so much but all that goes with it, even the bad parts.

And have you ever wanted to stop talking again?

Oh—the woman smiled wistfully—all the time.

Now, shifting her cheek against the cool porcelain of the basin, Verona thought, I should take a vow of silence. No talk, no lies. And soon she would have company. She was picturing herself and the baby pointing and nodding and frowning together when the woman from the counter knocked at the door again.

"Henry's got a taxi. Can you manage the stairs?"

Henry, thought Verona. Since when did they get so matey? She could imagine exactly her brother's flirtatious manner as he drew this innocent bystander into their affairs. She pushed herself out of the chair and headed for the door. The woman followed, urging her not to rush. Upstairs he was holding her coat. She pulled it on. "Take care," said the woman, wedging open the door with one of her boots. "Drink some ginger ale or Coke."

For a few seconds, as the snow swirled around her, Verona forgot everything. She could have been setting out, across glaciers and crevasses, for a base camp twenty miles away. She let the wind grab her coat and started down the snowy steps. At the bottom a taxi waited, windscreen wipers swishing, engine throbbing. She climbed inside.

"Well," said Henry, when he'd given the driver the name of their hotel, "are you going to keep giving me the cold shoulder, to use a seasonal metaphor?"

She gazed out of the window. At the traffic light a man with a large fluffy dog was waiting to cross the street. The dog had its dark nose lifted into the snow. While Henry continued his barrage, she formulated her resolution. She would talk for the common courtesies: food in restaurants, requests, and directions. But no conversation. No questions or accusations. No arguments or half-truths.

At the hotel she struggled out of the taxi and, without waiting for Henry, tramped through the snow toward the doors. A few weeks ago, even a few days ago, she would have bet good money that he would try to wheedle his way back into her good graces. But this morning she had been forced to understand that, in certain major respects, she did not know her brother. She had touched his fontanel, she had accompanied his first steps, applauded his first words. She had, even now, spent more time in his company than with any other human. Yet he had lied to her at the deepest level and she had had not the slightest inkling.

Upstairs in her room, she double-locked the door and added the chain. Pausing only to remove her outdoor clothes, she climbed into bed. Was there any chance, she wondered, that Henry had been lying about Jigger? The idea of two teenage boys altering a will was preposterous. But it made sense of the way he had always been ahead of his peers, had a better car, a bigger flat, nicer clothes. It wasn't even—why was this so hard to accept?— that he didn't care for her. Her needs, her well-being, as she'd tried to explain to Toby, were simply not a consideration. So much for his fear of losing her.

Staring up at the grainy ceiling, she remembered how hard she and Zeke had worked to smooth the walls at the Barrows'. Soon, she thought, the two of them would be together in a room filled with golden light. She still didn't know how Henry had cheated Nigel and George or what had happened in Seattle, but she no longer cared. In the morning she would write him a note and catch the next plane home. Nigel and George weren't about to make unnecessary trouble for her. And if they did, there would be no more nonsense about protecting Henry. She would go straight to the police. She pictured him reading her note, crumpling it into his pocket, and going on to charm the next waitress or museum custodian, for no better reason than a cat kills birds or a hedgehog eats eggs.

18

An hour later she was in the bath, scooping up handfuls of bubbles and smoothing them over her belly, when she heard a faint scratching sound. She stopped to listen. The small room was full of noises—the popping of the rapidly cooling bubbles, the rush of water in the pipes in the walls, the whir of the heating—but no scratching, and at last, after half a dozen attempts, Henry had stopped phoning. She returned to the foam. If you're a boy, she thought, I'll call you Edmund, after Jigger. If you're a girl, Marian. But perhaps Zeke would have opinions about names. The idea was so delightful, so presumptuous, that at once, superstitiously, she had to pretend it hadn't occurred. The noise this time was different, the unmistakable sound of metal on metal. Someone was doing something to the door of her room. For a moment she felt herself sliding toward blackness. Nigel and George: they were forcing the door. She heaved herself out of the bath, sending a tidal wave over the rim, and seized the hotel bathrobe. She was rushing toward the phone, still tying the belt of the robe, when the door swung open. Mid-scream, she heard Henry.

"Thank you. Verona, it's me. Are you all right? I've been so worried. You didn't answer the phone. I thought something had happened to you. Or the baby."

His voice was perfect, warm, anxious, concerned; his expression the opposite. Behind him stood an all-male chorus: the porter whom she often passed in the lobby, the young man with spiky hair from the front desk who had greeted her on the first day, and two men in coveralls, one holding a toolbox, the other a pair of pliers. Each was staring at her with an expression of mingled relief and disappointment.

"Thank you," Henry said again. "We can manage now. I'll call the front desk if we need anything."

Reluctantly the men straggled away. The last to leave was the clerk. "I hope," he said with a hint of menace, "that the rest of your visit goes smoothly."

During these exchanges, Verona took several deep breaths. She practiced looking at something nearby: the fake tallboy that housed the television and the minibar, and something farther away, the snowflakes beating against the dark window. As soon as the door finally closed, she grabbed Henry by the shoulders and, in spite of her girth, began to shake him.

"For Christ's sake, Verona," he exclaimed, pulling himself free. "What the hell are you doing? I knocked, I rang, you didn't answer. I thought you came here to help me, but all you've done is create scenes."

The unfairness made her clench her fists. She longed to shout—how dare he drag her to America, keep her waiting for days, break into her room, steal her inheritance?—but managed, just barely, to restrain herself. If nothing else, her silence had the satisfying effect of infuriating Henry. She went and sat down on the bed.

"So you've got it into your head that you're not going to talk. And what, precisely, will that accomplish? You came three thousand miles to see me, and now you won't say anything. Great."

While he mined a seemingly inexhaustible vein of sarcasm, Verona, still in the aftermath of terror, allowed her mind to drift.

What was the name of the young man whose mother's home help had embezzled all her money? Brendan? No, Brian. She hadn't been nearly sympathetic enough. The issue wasn't the theft, though that was bad enough, the issue was that this woman, whom Brian regarded as a family member, had deceived him. And that's what Henry's been doing for decades, she thought: deceiving me and almost everyone else.

"You're behaving like I've committed the crime of the century, but really you've no idea what I've done."

By both profession and inclination, she regarded the right question as the vise that could crack open even the hardest shell. Now, as Henry poured words into her silence, she was struck by how much of what passed for normal conversation was wasted on arguments and misunderstandings, and by how much harder it was, lacking those diversions, to avoid the truth.

At last he broke off, saying he needed a drink. She kept her face still as he tugged ineffectually at the door of the fridge. Finally realizing she hadn't bothered to get the key to the minibar, he announced he'd get something from his room. "But if you lock me out again, I'll set off the fire alarms. Okay?"

She didn't even nod. As soon as the door closed, she hurried to the bathroom, emptied the bath, and threw a couple of towels on the water on the floor. Back in the bedroom, she pulled on the clothes she'd been wearing before and, on some barely articulated impulse, retrieved her tape recorder from one of her suitcases. Using a pile of books for camouflage, she set it up on the table by the window. If she could get Henry to sit here, the machine would record most of their conversation. This snowy evening in this strange city might be her only chance to hear his version of events.

He came in, holding in one hand two miniature bottles of whiskey and in the other a glass of ice. From the brightness of his eyes, she surmised a third bottle. She went and sat down at the table, hoping he would follow, and he did. While he fiddled with the top of the first miniature, she pressed the button on the recorder. The top came off with a little rip. He tipped the contents into the glass and raised it, mockingly, in her direction. "Here's to you, O silent one. I can't remember how much I told you the night we had dinner."

The simple version was that he had borrowed money, a short-term high-interest loan, from Nigel and George. He had done a couple of deals with them before and everything had gone swimmingly. They had put up the money for properties that Henry knew on the grapevine could be bought cheaply and resold quickly, at a profit. Last summer he had heard about a village in Lancashire. A ring road was planned and its path lay directly through a housing estate; Henry had talked a dozen people into selling. Then it had emerged, when they did the survey for the ring road, that the estate was built on a Victorian mine, the ground beneath virtually hollow. He owned twelve bungalows that no one wanted to buy or even rent; they might actually be worth a negative amount.

"I blame the whole thing," he said, swirling his glass, "on Betty. Aha, that got your attention, didn't it? She may be mute but she's not deaf. You're wondering who Betty is. I met her at the gym. It's the sort of thing she disapproves of, spending money on unproductive exercise when peasants all over Asia are working their fingers to the bone, but a friend had brought her. We were waiting to use the shoulder press. I made a joke, she laughed, and we started going out together, the usual: films, dinner. One evening she took me to Glyndebourne. Someone at the bank where she was temping had extra tickets. I've always known there was an upper-class idyll. That evening I got to see it up close and it was amazing. We made a picnic, took the train down from Victoria, and sat in the gardens, eating and listening. The music was gorgeous, a full moon rose over the Downs, and as the applause faded this bird began to sing. Betty swore it was a nightingale and I believed her. What other bird is warbling away at 11 P.M.?

"She never said much about her family but I never say much about mine"—he raised an ironic eyebrow—"so it didn't occur to me that she was being secretive. Then one day the two of us were having a drink with Toby and we ran into one of his posh gallery friends who turned out to know Betty. We all chatted for a few minutes. The following week Toby phoned, trying to round up people for an opening. Ask Betty to bring her pals, he said. That wouldn't help, I told him. They're all socialists, living in council flats. Then he broke the news. According to his friend, Betty's family owned a huge estate in Lincolnshire, an island in Scotland, and another in the Bermudas. Toby didn't tell you any of this?"

He asked, she knew, only to rub it in; her expression made clear her ignorance. A little sleuthing had revealed that Toby's friend was not exaggerating. If anything, the reverse. Henry didn't mention his discovery to Betty. Their courtship continued; they spent a month at the house in Lucca he rented every summer. He taught her about wines; she taught him about birds. Finally he bought an antique ring and took her out in a paddle boat on the Serpentine.

Where was I? she wanted to ask. And what does all this have to do with Nigel and George?

"I should tell you," he went on, "that Betty isn't at all like my idea of a Betty. She's small, flat-chested. She likes knitting and hill-walking and wait-for-it bird watching. The only thing she can cook is soup, and she belongs to some crackpot left-wing party. She used to work as a teacher's aide in the East End and she's still involved with the Bengali community. She's dreadfully untidy. In other words, we were incompatible in almost every way. When I asked her to marry me—we were by that little island in the Serpentine—she didn't jump for joy or fling her arms around me. In fact, she was silent for so long that I started pedaling again. At last, we were nearly at the dock, she said okay, let's. It's my life, after all. I didn't dare ask what she meant."

For a few weeks, a month, he said, everything was fine. Each time she came over, she brought more of her clothes and books; they set up the back bedroom as her study. But he couldn't help noticing that whenever he said something about marriage, she changed the subject, and some days she didn't wear his ring. Then one evening she said there was something she had to tell him.

"It was all very labyrinthine. Her only brother had died a few years ago of diabetes, leaving her heir to the family fortune. Ever since, her parents had had strong views about whom she should marry. What do you mean, views, I asked. I was ready to convert to any religion, any political party, but what they wanted was genuine blue blood, someone out of Debrett's. If she married against their wishes, they would disinherit her. My expression must have changed. She began to reassure me that she didn't care about the money, in fact she'd prefer to be disinherited, but she did mind that they'd be upset. I did my best to cheer her up. Said that when her parents met me, they'd come round. Everything seemed fine except that I made a colossal blunder: I pretended not to know they were rich."

He drained his glass and reached for the second miniature. "I could get used to this business of your not talking. It's positively restful. Maybe you can guess what happened next? She ran into Toby. The two of them went for a drink, and our golden boy let the cat out of the bag. Her parents owned a picture he was interested in, an early Hodgkin. That night she didn't come home— she still had a room in her old flat—nor the next.

"She collected her stuff while I was at work. She wouldn't speak to me, she wouldn't listen. She'd become convinced that I was the person her parents had warned her about: the callous fortune hunter. She could just about understand my not mentioning it after Toby broke the news, but she couldn't accept my not saying anything when she told me. I swore up and down that I would love her if she were a penniless orphan, but she didn't believe me. It was like trying to scale a wall of glass. Nothing I said made a difference."

Scale an iceberg, Verona silently corrected.

"I didn't think things like this could still happen: that there were heiresses, that I could meet one and fall for her and have her fall for me." He was staring out of the window at the endless riot of snow. Watching him, she caught herself wondering, just for a moment, if he could possibly be sincere. Did he really love Betty, for richer, for poorer? But even Henry might not know the answer to that question.

So, he continued, he had the idea that if he could make some money, quite a lot of money, Betty and her parents would realize he wasn't a fortune hunter. He had gone out on a limb, borrowing not just from Nigel and George but from other people too. Then the report about the mine appeared and everything fell apart. He'd come to Boston for a long weekend to figure things out and in the hope that one of his American acquaintances might advance him the money. "The day after I arrived, I wandered into the library down the street—the guidebook recommended the murals—and picked up a magazine. There was my old girlfriend Charlotte— you know, the one with different-colored eyes who worked as a programmer. She moved here a decade ago, and according to this article she'd made a killing with a software company in Seattle. I got her phone number from her brother in London, and she was thrilled to hear from me. We had a couple of conversations and she suggested I come for a visit. I thought it was the answer to my prayers. We went skiing, wined and dined. Etc." He pointed toward the bed. "But I must be losing my touch. When I asked about a loan she had a major tantrum and dredged up all this stuff from our past.

"So I have two women furious at me, owe a stupid amount of money, am being pursued by two men who don't know the meaning of restraint, and have a sister who won't speak to me." He picked up the empty miniatures and threw them, one by one, at the window. They bounced off harmlessly and fell to the floor. "I hope your machine got all that."

He stood up, bent to kiss her cheek, picked up his suitcase from where it still lay on the end of the bed, and left the room.

Alone, Verona gazed into the swirling snow and pictured him, trudging through the blizzard, wandering the deserted streets. But even as she was embellishing her imaginings, the snow drifting over Henry's body, covering his black coat, another part of her knew, with a confidence unshaken by recent events, that within a matter of minutes her brother would be seated in some bar or restaurant enjoying the interest and admiration of strangers.

A few months after Marian's death, she had been at the airport in Inverness, waiting for a flight to London, when, across the lounge, a man with high cheekbones and sleek hair caught her eye. He had looked at her steadily as he approached. To what do I owe the honor of that hellacious stare? he had asked, with a mock bow.

I like your coat, she had said stupidly, nodding at his voluminous raincoat.

They had talked until she boarded her plane. Julian was a fashion designer, working on his own line of grunge clothing. He was on his way to Paris to meet with some French houses. Verona told him about her job as a research assistant at the BBC. For the next few months he called at odd intervals. It was like having a boyfriend but not. In his smooth voice Julian suggested going to Antigua, promised to send samples of his clothes. When she phoned him, she invariably got a recording.

Then one day the phone rang and a woman said are you Verona MacIntyre? After nearly two years, Jane had got fed up with supporting Julian. She had threatened to call the police if he didn't move out. Going through his papers, she had come across Verona's name and number. I think he's got you in his sights as his next meal ticket. It's a big plus, your living in London.

But what about his collection, his grunge wear?

Jane gave a bitter laugh. His collection, my Aunt Fanny. He did one term at art school and worked in a pizza restaurant. I assume he met you at the airport?

Yes, he was on his way to Paris.

In his dreams. When I met him there, he claimed to be on his way to Venice.

The following day Julian had phoned. He'd like to visit her next weekend. The only snag was that his wallet had been stolen while he was in a pub in Glasgow. Could she lend him some money, just a couple of hundred, until he got his credit cards sorted?

I talked to Jane, she had said. If you phone again, I'll call the police.

The next time she met a man in a public place she had given a false name, a fabricated occupation. It was surprisingly easy and surprisingly enjoyable. She had done it on and off for a couple of years until one day she was having a drink with a friend, and a voice called, "Laurie." Bearing down on her, smiling, was Bertram, whom she'd met at the Imperial War Museum. What luck, he said. I tried to ring you, but I must have got the number wrong; I kept getting some old guy in Tottenham.

My name isn't Laurie.

He began to protest. Everything was the same: her hair, her height. You're even wearing the same bracelet, he said. She kept shaking her head. Bertram was a tall broad-shouldered man with pleasingly regular features. He had told her he was an accountant but his passion was country dancing. You should come sometime, he had urged, and she had promised she would. Now, in a low voice, he said, I don't know what your game is, but if you keep this up you'll get hurt one of these days. I hope it's sooner, rather than later.

Weird, said her friend, as he walked away. They do say everyone has a double.

So about the program, said Verona, were you thinking the full hour? She had done her best to listen to the answer, but an odd sense of shame was bubbling up inside her. She had told Bertram she worked in a pet shop.

Outside the window the storm roared. The truth was, she and Henry were as alike as two peas in a pod, two snowflakes in a blizzard. He went further but she had the same corrupt moral gene. She pressed a hand to the cold glass and watched the snow eddy through her fingers.

Toby was still saying hello when she said, "Why didn't you tell me about Betty?"

"Verona?"

"Why didn't—"

"I was asleep. Give me a minute here."

After nearly ninety seconds of rustling he was back. "I don't know," he said. "There was a natural moment to tell you, early on, when it was still news. Once that passed, I never found the opportunity."

"What about all the opportunities last week? I thought we were friends, Toby. You sent me over here not knowing something crucial."

"We are friends and I sent you over, if that's how you want to put it, because I was afraid Henry was going to get one of us hurt and because he clearly needs help. Betty's neither here nor there. What we're dealing with are two thugs who don't give a damn about—"

"Listen," she interrupted. "Either one of Henry's wealthy friends can lend him the money, or he can sell his house. But I'm through with trying to help. I'm coming home tomorrow."

He gave a kind of groan. "Do I have to explain everything? Some of the money Henry lost was mine. He said I'd ruined his chances with Betty. He persuaded me to take a second mortgage on my flat."

Of course. So here was Henry's "other people," or at least one of them. No wonder Toby had been reluctant to come to Boston, unable to act as his own advocate. "I can't believe you'd do something so idiotic. You know Henry's hopeless about money. He always thinks the next scheme is the big one." For the first time that day she felt like her old self. Her lecturing Toby about Henry was one of the central tenets of their friendship.

"If something happens to Henry," he said, his voice cracking, "I'll lose the love of my life and probably my flat."

Like her, like Henry, Toby's middle-class life was only one layer deep. There was no family safety net waiting to catch him, rather the reverse. He sent his mother money every month. She pictured Julian crossing the lounge at Inverness Airport, she pictured Bertram pointing to her bracelet, and she ended up promising one more attempt to figure out a solution with Henry. "Though what we're accomplishing stuck in Boston, I have no idea," she said.

"You're safe," he said. "That's the big accomplishment."

Only after she put down the phone did Verona realize she had forgotten to tell him about Jigger's will.

The next morning as soon as she was dressed, she went to her bag, pulled out the notebook in which she had written down the number Emmanuel had given her, and dialed it. She wrote down the number of his mobile and dialed again.

"Hello," he said.

Just those two syllables made her feel as if she were standing beside a grove of azaleas on a warm May morning. She had been prepared to grovel, to plead, but he accepted her apology unquestioningly. And in the happiness of that acceptance she did something she had not known she was going to do; she asked him to come to Boston.

"But," he said, "I can't fly."

At first she thought he was refusing. No, he meant he had no idea how to buy a ticket. She said she would get Emmanuel to help. "I'm sure he's good at that kind of thing. Please, will you come?"

He started to say something she couldn't follow, something about airplanes; then he paused. Out of the machine came the single, firm syllable: "Yes."

Before she could thank him, the connection stuttered and disappeared. When she called back the number was unavailable. Was it possible that she was planning to spend her life with a painter, almost ten years younger than herself, who did not know how to book an airline ticket? But I can book tickets, she thought. Zeke has other talents, like telling the truth. I'll teach him about the world, and he'll teach me how to be simple and truthful and the same with everyone.

Zeke

19

The flight took off seven minutes late and they passed rapidly through the clouds. Zeke did not relinquish his hold on the armrests until the pilot announced that they had reached their cruising altitude, an uncountable number of feet above the Irish Sea. Then slowly, cautiously, he relaxed the fingers of his left hand and, when nothing terrible happened, his right. It was unlikely that his grip contributed to their continued elevation—for years he had watched the planes passing over London with no apparent help from him—but who could tell? Perhaps one passenger was always responsible for keeping the plane aloft. Mavis had told him about a study comparing two groups of cancer patients. Both received identical medical treatment, but a convent of nuns prayed daily for one group while the other was left to the usual secular devices. The recovery rate among those prayed for was significantly higher.

Why, he had asked.

Who knows? Mavis had smiled. The whole point of prayer is that it doesn't make sense. I find it reassuring that there are matters beyond our understanding.

Zeke didn't, perhaps because he had so many more candidates

for incomprehension than did Mavis. Now he considered all that he did not know about flying. If only he'd taken the trouble to go to the library before he boarded the plane. He knew roughly that the fuel was converted into energy which moved the turbines, the turbines displaced air, which, combined with the angle of the wings, drove the plane forward and upward, but this was not a situation in which to leave anything to chance. He craned his neck, listening carefully. As far as he could tell, the engine was grinding away as it had been since they reached their cruising altitude. "I'm praying for you," he whispered to the cogs, wheels, nuts, and bolts on which, presumably, their progress depended.

Above his head was a light, a nozzle that, when twisted, delivered a puff of stale air, and a panel. According to the jaunty film that had appeared on the screen in front of him while the plane was waiting to depart, in case of emergency an oxygen mask would drop down from this panel. "Hold the mask over your nose and mouth and breathe normally," the film instructed, showing calm well-dressed people holding little yellow plastic buckets to their faces. Then a different set of calm well-dressed people put on life jackets, inflated them, and blew whistles. If only, Zeke thought, I'd brought my own life jacket, but it hadn't been on Emmanuel's list.

The important thing, Emmanuel had said as they parted at security, is not to think about the fact that you can't get out. Once, on a flight to Majorca, a woman tried to force the door. It was a mess. Just pretend you're on the Picadilly Line, per usual, and you'll be fine.

Now, leaning forward in his aisle seat, Zeke saw the other side of the clouds, white and surprisingly hard-edged, like the icing they used on Christmas cakes, and then even those were gone. The skies were bright and empty. No birds, no other planes, nothing to count. He remembered hearing a story on the radio about a giant asteroid, far away in outer space, that was heading toward the earth; when it arrived, in approximately nine hundred years, life in its present forms would end. Surely by that time, he thought selfishly, Ms. F and her descendants will have fulfilled their hearts' desires.

Between him and the window sat a courtly dark-skinned man who, even before takeoff, had already fallen asleep. In their few moments of mutual wakefulness he had carefully folded the jacket of his suit, taken off his shoes, wrapped himself in a blanket, pulled a black mask over his eyes, filled his ears with plugs of blue foam, and announced that he was going to catch some z's. "Do me a favor," he had said to Zeke. "Don't let them wake me up for food or drink."

How trusting he was. If there was an emergency, Zeke would have to take care of his oxygen mask as well as his own. Still, he was glad to be protected from the window; it was hard not to worry that the small oval panes might fall out and he would find himself sucked into the brilliant beyond. Another reason to keep his seat belt tightly fastened.

While he was waiting to board, Zeke had watched the planes rolling back and forth across the tarmac and tried to imagine what they were like inside. Now he registered that the cabin, for all that the plane had looked so huge, was really not much larger than two trains spliced together. And, as with the interior of a train, everything in sight was made of plastic or metal or fabric. The people too were much more like regular travelers than he had expected. With the exception of his sleeping neighbor, most of them were dressed as if they were on their way to go shopping. The woman immediately across the aisle from him, for instance, was wearing a long-sleeved turquoise T-shirt with dungarees and a red cardigan. He himself had given considerable thought as to what to wear, the clothes in which he would be admitted to America and once again put his arms around Verona, and had finally chosen a pair of black trousers, polished black shoes, a neatly ironed blue shirt, and a black V-neck pullover. Bloody hell, Emmanuel had said when they met that morning, you look like you're going for a job interview.

Suddenly the woman in the navy blue uniform, who had been

pushing the metal trolley down the aisle, stopped beside his seat, fixed her eyes on him, and spoke. He caught only one word: *something*.

"Excuse me?"

"Would you like something to drink, sir?" She bent toward him, one hand holding a small plastic bag and a white napkin, while the other pulled down a square of gray plastic from the back of the seat in front so that it rested a few inches above his knees.

"What sort of drink?" he said, and quickly, her mouth was already moving again, asked for water.

"Water?" she said, and scooped ice cubes into a plastic glass, filled it with water, and placed it in the circular depression on the right side of the tray.

The plastic bag turned out to hold peanuts, which he ignored, but the water he drank, doing his best to avoid the ice. Still holding the glass, he pushed the tray up—it snapped shut in a satisfying manner—and pulled out the contents of the seat pocket in front of him. His haul included a paper bag bearing the words IN CASE OF MOTION SICKNESS; a magazine, filled with photographs of face cream, perfume, watches, and scotch, so glossy that it almost slipped from his touch; another magazine that listed things to do when you returned to earth—play golf in Arizona, buy glass in Venice, listen to Mozart in Prague—and finally a list of safety instructions, showing emergency exits, how to use the life jacket, the system of inflatable rafts available in case of a water landing.

Holding the last, Zeke cautiously extricated himself from his seat and, following behind the drinks cart, circled the plane, checking on the exits. Most of his fellow passengers had by now drawn plastic shades over their windows in order to watch films, and the dimly lit plane had a shimmering, mysterious quality. Keeping a careful distance, Zeke peered out of the window beside one of the emergency exits—PULL DOWN, read a threatening red lever—and glimpsed far, far below a patch of dark water, the Atlantic Ocean going wave, wave, wave. Turning around, he counted the passengers, fifty-seven unless some children were too small to be visible, and the seats, eighty-two, in his section.

With this information he was able to return to his seat and, while continuing to focus one part of his brain—the chamber at the back—on keeping the plane aloft, enjoy the little tray of food that the stewardess set before him. Even the biscuits and the cheese, he noted with pleasure, were individually wrapped. Someone, somewhere, knew how to count. As he ate, he pictured Verona making this journey a few days ago, the seat belt wedged beneath her belly. She had eaten the same neat food. Perhaps she had even sat in this very seat, 22B; the mere possibility made him happy.

When the meal was gone, dessert washed down with a cup of tea so tepid his mother would have hurled it to the floor, he leaned over to ask the girl across the aisle if she could show him how to watch a film. He had noticed, before the meal came, the way she bent toward the screen, utterly absorbed.

"What would you like to see?" she asked, flipping up one ear-phone but not taking her gaze off the screen.

"Something not too alarming."

"What's your idea of alarming?"

"Violence, talking animals, chase scenes, anything to do with boats or airplanes, too much nature, sports."

She pressed a button and at last turned her wide bespectacled eyes in his direction. In the dim light her skin was opalescent and her nose, beneath the dark framed glasses, was unusually small and straight. "How do you feel about nudity?" she said.

"Nudity is—" he was about to say *fine*, only to be shot through with the realization that until he had seen Verona again he wanted to see no one naked of either gender, any age, even in some stupid film. "Out of the question," he concluded.

"So you want to watch mass entertainment but you're unwilling to countenance the mass preoccupations."

"Countenance?" His anxieties were momentarily lulled by the beauty of the word.

"The verb means give approval, the noun means face."

"I know what it means. It's just not a word one hears very often."

"Most people use only a small part of their vocabulary. My attitude is that, besides the opposable thumb, language is one of the few perks of being human." Her head bobbed emphatically. "Everyone should try to use a new word every day."

"That should be easy in America," Zeke said, and caught a movement at the edge of his gaze. A small girl in pink was staring up at him from the aisle, her eyes and mouth forming three almost perfect circles. He widened his own eyes to match and she continued her unsteady progress. A man with jeans worn almost white at the knee followed. Zeke turned back to the woman across the aisle. "We'll be learning all these new words."

"Like *wow*, and *gee*, and *neat*. Yes, I'm sure my vocabulary will enjoy a huge surge forward in the New World."

"They're not posh, like countenance," said Zeke, "but that doesn't mean they're not words."

"You're right," she conceded. "Basically I'm a snob. I think the English language reached its zenith with the Victorians and has been going downhill ever since. Now let's see about a film for you. This is a challenge. My name is Jill Irving, by the way." She fished a magazine out of her seat pocket, the one about golf and Venice, and studied a page at the back. Zeke watched her. Nothing she said was especially reassuring, but her peppery remarks made him feel calmer. This woman did not seem as if she were about to die, or even as if she were engrossed in fending off the possibility. For several minutes, he realized, he had forgotten his duty to keep the plane aloft, and look—nothing terrible had happened.

Forty-five minutes later he was in the middle of watching the film Jill had chosen for him—about a boy from the Midlands who, in spite of his coal-miner father, wants to be a ballet dancer—when his body, and everyone else's, leaped into the air and thudded back down.

A man's voice, American, came over the speakers. "Ladies and

gentlemen, as you'll have noticed we're encountering a little turbulence. Please return to your seats and keep your seat belts fastened until I turn off the sign. I'm searching for smoother air.
We'll be out of this soon."

Zeke pulled his belt tighter. Please, he thought. Oh, why had he
forgotten for a second to pray? Every molecule of his attention
should have been focused on keeping the turbines going. He
looked over at Jill. Her attention remained, unwaveringly, on the
film. "Excuse me," he said.

She remained intent.

"Excuse me," he repeated and leaned over to tug her sleeve.
"Are we about to crash?"

"Crash?" The plane leaped up and down again. At the same
moment Jill's mouth widened, showing two rows of small regular
teeth. "Have you been on a plane before?"

"This is my first time."

"What we're experiencing is called turbulence. For some reason, and this part I can't explain, the air is disturbed with currents
that are bouncing our plane around, but it isn't dangerous, I
promise." She patted his hand, a sure, warm touch. "No one else
is worried."

Looking around, he discovered she was right. Across the aisle a
stewardess was bent over a couple, talking energetically; Jill's
seatmates were continuing to play cards; the little girl in pink, it
was true, was crying but only because the man with faded jeans
was refusing to let her continue her perambulations. "I'm sorry,"
he said. "This would be a particularly inconvenient time for me to
die."

Jill's head tilted. "I hope you'll feel that way for a long time.
Now if you'll excuse me, this is a particularly intense scene in my
film."

Zeke watched his tiny screen and tried not to think about
Verona; he could not bear to calculate how many separate, indi-
vidual units of breath and thought had to be passed through before he was back in her company. My job at the moment, he told

himself, is to stay airborne. More snacks were served, more drinks; his companion slept on, peacefully, behind his mask. He thought of birds with their hollow bones and huge appetites.

They were over the Maritimes, still several hundred miles from Boston, when a commotion rippled through the plane. Zeke saw it pass down the cabin, people removing their earphones, whispering to each other, sitting up straighter to peer over the seat in front. Jill too was leaning forward. Then she was on her feet, heading toward the front of the plane. She had taken a couple of steps when she stopped and turned back to Zeke. "Don't be alarmed," she said. "I'm a nurse. I think someone needs help, but you're quite safe. The plane is fine."

Gradually he understood, how he couldn't say, that a woman in business class had collapsed. At once he undid his seat belt and followed Jill. I was looking in the wrong direction, he thought again. He remembered the man on the bus last autumn sliding to the floor, his father.

"Sir," said a flight attendant, raising her hand.

He raised his own hand, pointing, to indicate an urgent summons, and she stepped back. He reached the cabin he had passed through when boarding the plane, where the seats were much larger and fewer. A knot of people were gathered in the far aisle and from the knot rose a voice, Jill's, counting: "One, one, two, two, one, one." Somehow his urgency persuaded people to let him through. Jill was bent over, pummeling a woman's chest. Zeke glimpsed flesh, underwear. "Tell me what to do," he said, kneeling beside her. "Don't they have those shock things?"

"They're looking for them," she gasped. "Give me your hands." She grabbed his hands and placed them where hers had been. "Keep pressing," she said. "Keep counting aloud. Press on one, release on two. I'm going to try mouth-to-mouth."

He pressed, he counted, scarcely conscious that what he touched was a woman. Only a few hours ago she had made her way to Heathrow; perhaps he and Emmanuel had sat next to her on the train from Paddington or he had stood behind her in line, watching her possessions pass through the X-ray tunnel. Beside him Jill's motions were the opposite of his: when he pressed down she raised her head; when he rocked back she bent to force air into the woman's mouth.

The crowd parted and a man in uniform was bending over them with a red case. He handed two plastic disks attached to wires to Jill. She placed the disks on different parts of the rib cage. Zeke took the woman's warm, limp hand in his. Please, heart, start beating. Please, lungs, start breathing.

A spooky mechanical voice interrupted his litany. "Stand back. Stand back. No one must touch the patient."

Just as Zeke grasped that the machine was issuing instructions, Jill seized his arm and pulled him away. "Go," she said.

Four times the woman's body convulsed in response to the current. Then Jill held up her hand. She put her fingers to the woman's throat and he watched her eyes turn inward—he knew no other way to describe the motion—as she listened to whatever message the flesh was transmitting.

"Her heart's beating," she said quietly, and launched into a flurry of instructions.

The woman was lifted from the floor and laid in a makeshift bed; pillows and blankets were organized; a message was sent ahead to have an ambulance waiting in Boston. The pilot announced that a passenger had collapsed but luckily there was a nurse aboard. Jill sat beside the woman, holding an oxygen mask to her face.

"Why did you come after me?" she said. "Are you trained in first aid?"

"Not really. I did do a course." He pictured the room at the local library, where he had gone last autumn after the man on the bus. In two hours Winifred, the registered nurse, had walked them through what she called the three biggies: choking, drowning, and heart attacks, life-threatening situations in which anyone with a little knowledge could make a difference. They had taken turns practicing CPR and artificial respiration on the dummies, coaching each other while Winifred passed from group to group, correcting and explaining. She had praised Zeke's Heimlich maneuver. You're pushing at just the right angle, she had said.

The woman gave a soft moan; her head rolled from side to side. "My father nearly died of a heart attack last month," he offered.

"Well, thanks," Jill said. "You were a big help. You knew what to do and you weren't afraid to use your strength. That was what was needed."

Zeke stood watching the woman. Her cheeks were mottled with red blotches and her eyelids twitched, as if she were dreaming. Beneath the blanket her chest rose and fell. Tomorrow, he thought, if she looks in the mirror she'll see the bruises on her rib cage where my hands pummeled her and she won't know who made them. "Will she be all right?"

"I don't know. She's not old, she's not overweight, and I couldn't find any medicine in her carry-on luggage, so this is probably her first attack. The best we can say is that she'll have a chance. There are some excellent hospitals in Boston. That's why I'm going there, in fact. I've taken a job at Massachusetts General Hospital."

That was good news, he thought, if anything should happen to Verona. He made a careful note of the information. "What's today's word?"

"Sorry?"

"You said you tried to use a new word every day. What's today's word?"

"You heard it already," she said. "Countenance."

"And tomorrow's?"

"Sufficient unto the day . . ." A little line appeared between her eyebrows. "I can't remember how that ends," she said, shaking her head as if to dislodge the remainder of the quotation. "It'll come to me. The point is, I'll think about tomorrow's word tomorrow. That way it's a response to whatever's going on. Though right now I might not have chosen countenance for today." She stopped again and raised her hand to cover her mouth. "I need to be quiet for a few minutes before we land."

It took Zeke a moment to realize that she was asking him to leave. Can't I stay, he wanted to say. But Jill was looking down, adjusting the blanket around the woman, and he saw that she was even paler than her patient.

The noise of the engine changed and a series of announcements came over the speakers about landing cards, seats in an upright position, seat belts fastened. The man in the next seat removed his mask and earplugs and began to struggle with his shoes. "Smooth flight?" he asked.

Zeke was in the middle of his little *hmm* sound when a grinding noise erupted from the floor of the plane. "What's that?" he said, grabbing the armrests. Oh, Verona, he thought.

"The undercarriage," said the man, looping a thin strip of patterned material round his neck and moving his hands up and down. "Is my tie straight?"

The term *undercarriage* meant nothing to Zeke, but he grasped that the man, like Jill, was in no immediate fear of destruction. Cautiously, he looked over and discovered the blue silk tie listing to the left. "No," he said and, releasing an armrest, motioned the tie down.

Gravity wrestled them back to the other side of grayness. He saw dark sloshing liquid only a hundred feet below. Were they attempting the unlikely eventuality of a water landing? But even as he bent forward, searching for the life jacket under his seat, the runways were stretching out around them with huge white mounds beside them: snow, he guessed. And then they were landing. Like the birds he had watched while walking with his father in the park, they bounced several times before they finally reconnected with the ground. He heard another sound—the flaps on the wings going up—and felt himself being pulled forward in his seat.

"Welcome to Boston," said the pilot cheerfully. "The local time is two thirty-two P.M. Twenty-six degrees Fahrenheit and overcast."

20

A *ding* sounded, not unlike the bell at the shop, and on all sides people rose out of their seats as if they had been forcibly ejected. Zeke slipped on his jacket, picked up his still-unread newspaper and his half-empty bottle of water, and followed his fellow passengers haltingly down the aisle, through the now-empty business cabin, over the threshold of the plane, and up a large plastic tube into a corridor. Unthinkingly he walked behind his dark-suited neighbor until they reached a brightly lit hall, where the passengers separated into several queues, facing a line of glass cubicles, each containing its own uniformed official. After searching the crowd in vain for Jill—for once he felt sure of his ability to recognize a person—Zeke took his place behind the notice labeled VISITORS AND NONRESIDENTS.

For a few seconds, his feet firmly planted on the linoleum, he gave himself over to the pleasure of being earthbound. Then he recalled where that earth was, and his anxieties began to gather. However frightening the journey, his duty, while on the plane, had been clear: to pray and not to pull the red lever except in case of emergency. Now he was thousands of miles from home, much farther than he could walk or drive, even if a continuous landmass were available, and between him and Verona lay a series of people who were likely to be even more perplexing than those he usually encountered.

Following the cardinal rule of any queue, some passengers whisked past the officials and others, for no apparent reason, entered into prolonged discussion. Zeke's arms itched and his hair kept falling over his forehead. The room, he realized, was stiflingly hot; he unbuttoned his jacket and, after a quick survey, decided that removal was permissible. Then he stood, trying not to fidget, and rehearsed his lines. The main thing they want to be sure of, Emmanuel had said, is that you're not planning to stay. Say that you're here on holiday, the purpose of your trip is pleasure. Isn't February an odd time to take a holiday, Zeke had asked. Of course not. You could be going skiing. Or, he added, seeing Zeke's expression, shopping. You're bound to buy something in America.

"Next," came a voice. Zeke stepped over a yellow line and, entering the glass cubicle, found himself facing, across a high counter, his first real American. A plump grublike man, with sandy hair and eyebrows so pale as to be almost indistinguishable from his skin, asked for his documents. Zeke was already offering them but he could not help staring; the man had spoken like a ventriloquist, barely moving his mouth.

"How long are you staying?"

"Five days. I have a return ticket."

What if this being, who could talk without talking, decided that he was not worthy to set foot in America? The man opened Zeke's passport and, with plump fingers, began to turn the empty pages, pausing over each one. He slipped the open passport facedown into a machine and typed. Zeke gazed at the speckled Formica counter, trying simultaneously to imagine what he would do in such an eventuality and to keep it at bay. If you act guilty, he heard his father say, it just sets the buggers off. He had been talking about the health inspectors from the council, but surely the same thing applied to immigration officials. If he won't let me into

the country, Zeke thought, I will cling to the counter and demand
to speak to Verona. In preparation he took firm hold of the edge
and, remembering a lifetime of admonitions, raised his head. But
the officer showed no interest in eye contact. He tapped a few
more keys on the computer, withdrew the passport from the machine, and, flipping open Zeke's ticket, traced the lines of type
with a pudgy finger.

Zeke held on.

After eighteen breaths, the man put the ticket inside the passport along with the customs form and held them out. "Welcome
to America, Mr. Cafarelli. Enjoy your stay in our fair land. And
have a good day."

Downstairs was another large room filled with luggage carousels.
Zeke followed the crowd to one near the end, which was already
circling noisily beneath its burden of mostly black suitcases. Just
as he was thinking how vastly improbable it was that his own
small green case, which he had handed over in London that morning, would have followed him on this huge journey, something
nudged his leg. Startled, he looked down to discover a substantial
brindled dog sniffing its way toward the baggage.

"Excuse me, sir. U.S. Customs dog training."

He couldn't tell if the person who had spoken was male or female. As he watched the squat, uniformed figure move away he
caught sight of a neatly turned ankle. Female, he decided.

"Search, Bruno. Good boy, search." Bruno dutifully pushed his
nose at half a dozen bags and then, in spite of the woman's commands, sat back on his haunches and let his spectacularly long
pink tongue hang out.

A companion in discouragement, Zeke thought. Looking
around, he found many others. Almost everyone was watching the
luggage with expressions he judged to be neither optimistic nor
confident. And as he took this in, he suddenly came to his senses.
What was he doing loitering here when he could already be in a
taxi, heading toward Verona? He could always buy new clothes.
Meanwhile, thank goodness he had dressed carefully for the jour-

ney. He was almost at the exit when some impulse made him cast one last look over his shoulder. There, caught between a battered army duffel bag and a pristine cardboard box, was his green case.

As he lifted it to the floor a voice said, "One moment, sir. Put the case down. Bruno."

The dog thrust its sharp nose against the lid and sniffed along the seam. There's nothing for you to find, Zeke thought, trying to send the message into Bruno's recalcitrant American brain, but innocence did not entirely quell his anxiety. He had read the stories about unsuspecting travelers being used to carry contraband. What if one of those people with red flags at Heathrow had slipped a bag of pills into his case? Then he remembered again the importance of seeming relaxed and began to count the remaining suitcases on the carousel. At fourteen, the dog backed away.

"Thank you for your cooperation," said the woman, sounding in no way thankful.

In customs another expressionless official lifted his case onto a table, clicked the catches, and raised the lid. He wore gloves of the kind used by dentists and doctors; through the milky rubber Zeke could see the dark hairs on the backs of his hands pressed flat. The man studied his alarm clock, squeezed out half an inch of toothpaste, and unrolled a pair of socks. Some principle seemed to forbid him from fully removing any item from the case, and by the end Zeke's clothes were rumpled and storm-tossed. When the man tried to close the lid a gap of two inches remained. He looked at Zeke for the first time. "I'm no great shakes at folding," he said.

After a few seconds, Zeke realized that he was being invited to help repack his possessions. Beneath the man's gaze, he rolled socks, folded shirts, and fitted his spare shoes back together. "I've never seen anyone do that before," the man said, pointing to the socks. "Neat trick."

"My father taught me."

"Family tradition. You Brits are good at that. My dad came from Coventry. Do you know it?"

"I'm afraid not," said Zeke, and the man moved his head from side to side as if yet another Englishman had brought him bad news.

He folded the last of his shirts and took the opportunity to retrieve his hat and scarf. The formula for translating Fahrenheit to Centigrade eluded him, but 26 degrees Fahrenheit, he guessed, was chilly.

He walked through the open door and, instead of the oblivious crowds he had left behind at Heathrow, found himself facing a mass of people holding flowers or shiny balloons or signs saying WELCOME HOME, ABBY. HURRAH, YOU'RE BACK! WE LOVE YOU! For one stupid heartbeat he paused, hoping to see a tall pregnant woman step forward from the crowd, even though she had told Emmanuel that he should come straight to the hotel. But no one approached; indeed, several people turned away.

Outside the air was cold and smelled of exhaust and something that he thought might be snow. He crossed a road and joined yet another queue of people, waiting to climb into a line of dingy white and brown taxis. Emmanuel had warned him that American taxi drivers often barely knew the main streets. Driving a cab is one of the first jobs people do when they get off the boat, he'd said. You should phone the hotel from the airport and get directions. But this advice came back to Zeke only now when there was no pay phone in sight, and he could not bear to delay another second. So long as he had been making his way through the various formalities, he had not allowed himself to fully comprehend what was about to happen. He was about to see Verona again.

A taxi pulled up and the driver, a thin man wearing a faded green anorak and round black glasses, climbed out. As he wedged the suitcase into the already crowded boot, Zeke thought he looked like a giant insect. Carefully enunciating each syllable, he gave the name and address of the hotel. "Do you know where that is?"

"Sure," said the driver. "Ted Williams, okay?"

Zeke moved his chin up and down uncertainly, and the next thing he knew he was leaning as far back as he could in a corner of the taxi, clutching the door handle, as they squeezed between an orange bus and a huge black vehicle. Everything was back to front. The driver was seated on the wrong side of the car and he was driving on the wrong side of the road and cars, mostly much larger, were passing with equal speed on either side. For a few seconds, in his terror, Zeke forgot Verona. The view through the window did little to assuage his fear; on all sides were bulldozers, tractors, makeshift concrete barriers, wire fences, and huge mounds of snow. They stopped beside a booth and the driver rolled down his window and offered several pieces of green paper; money, Zeke thought. TED WILLIAMS TUNNEL a sign proclaimed. A moment later they entered the most beautiful tunnel he had ever seen, the road surface smooth as glass, the lighting bright and hospitable, the walls virginal.

"Excuse me," he said, leaning forward to push his voice through the plastic barrier. "Who is Ted Williams?"

"Who is Ted Williams?" In the mirror the driver's eyebrows rose above his sunglasses. "I guess you don't follow baseball where you come from. Williams was only the greatest hitter of all time. He played for the Red Sox, the local team. Now his son has him frozen."

"Frozen?"

"You know, like cryogenics. Apparently the kid thinks his dad's DNA will be worth something in the future. Not that he's short of cash these days."

"But where does he keep him?" A baffling picture came to mind of a fully clothed man lying in a block of ice on a dining room table or, more plausibly, in a bath.

"There are places," the driver said, "if you pay enough. They have some fancy name but it's just a big deep freeze with backup generators in case of a power cut. You can go there. Say if you're having a bad year, you get yourself iced up, then they thaw you out when you ask and you haven't lost the year. Well, you've lost that year, but you have another one."

They had emerged from the idyllic tunnel and were making their way over bleak, bumpy roads lined with more snow. Between drifts Zeke caught sight of a small metal effigy perched on the edge of the sidewalk, some sort of shrine perhaps. They passed endless car parks, bounded by chain-link fences, as if to prevent the few captive vehicles from making a break for freedom. As for the buildings, they were made haphazardly of brick or stone or concrete, each different from the others. Some were quite modern, others almost in ruins. At one corner he even saw a house made of wood. He had not given much thought to America, the place itself, but he had expected everything to be modern and gleaming.

Meanwhile the driver continued to hold forth. He had been to London a few years ago. "Things pretend to be the same," he said, "but they're different. Like McDonald's. The burgers have the same names but everything's half the size and twice the price. Same with music and clothes."

And what was Zeke doing here?

"A holiday. Funny time of year but it's when you can get away, isn't it? I went over in November. Didn't rain once, in spite of all the jokes. You should come here in the spring. See the lilacs and the cherry blossoms. The Japanese go wild about them."

Zeke did his best to listen courteously, but all he could think of was Verona. What if he didn't recognize her or didn't know what to say? They had reached a more prosperous part of the city, the buildings taller and closer together, the sidewalks clean and popu-lated by well-dressed men and women, picking their way through the snow. But suddenly every light was red, they had to pull over for an ambulance and a minute later for a police car; pedestrians plunged, lemming-like, from the curb; roadworks erupted in their path. Every time Zeke saw a sign saying HOTEL he leaned forward, only to watch it disappear. Once, he was sure, he saw the same sign twice. He was about to question the driver when he pulled over and slammed on the brakes. "Here you go. That'll be twenty-two dollars plus four-fifty for the tolls."

Zeke was already holding his wallet, examining the sheaf of money that Emmanuel had helped him to obtain from a bank at

Heathrow. The notes were all the same size and color and he had to look at them individually to distinguish tens, twenties, and fifties. Only two of those, Emmanuel had said to the cashier; people always think they're fake. In his haste and confusion he was tempted to thrust the whole lot at the driver, but what if he needed to buy Verona supper or a pair of gloves for her chapped hands? He checked the numbers printed in each corner and handed over two twenties. The driver handed back a single note emblazoned with tens. Zeke was almost at the door of the hotel when someone called, "Mister. Hey, mister."

He turned to see the driver, hurrying toward him, holding the green suitcase. "Must be a hot date," said the man, wagging his head.

"Thank you," said Zeke. "Thank you so much." One thing if his luggage had never arrived, quite another to leave it in the boot of a taxi. What an idiot he would have felt, presenting himself to Verona without so much as a change of socks.

He pushed his way through the glass door and stepped into a large space filled with chairs and couches and tables. Carefully he scanned the room, starting with the empty sofa to his left and moving past the fireplace and the groups of chairs and potted plants, hoping that somewhere, among all this furniture, was the one person he wanted to see, but the few occupants, mostly men in suits, were definitely not Verona. Then he spotted a counter; if he followed the shining tile floor that was where it would lead him.

"Good afternoon," said a young man with neatly spiked hair. "Checking in?"

"My name is Zeke Cafarelli. I'm here to see Verona MacIntyre."

"She's a guest? What did you say the name was?"

"Verona MacIntyre," he said happily.

"And your name?"

Less happily he repeated that.

The man turned aside and began to search through a file. Zeke watched his dark hair feathering over his white collar and tried to resist the feeling that all was not going according to plan, that the joyful reunion he had held in his mind ever since he sat on the floor of the chef's kitchen and listened to her deep, warm voice inviting him—no, begging him—to come to Boston was being delayed yet again. She's gone for a walk, he thought, she's taking a nap.

The man turned back to him, holding out a white paper rectangle. "I'm here to see Ms. MacIntyre," Zeke said again, ignoring the envelope.

"Ms. MacIntyre checked out this morning, sir, but she made a reservation for you—a nonsmoking room on the eighth floor."

The man's lips continued to move but Zeke heard only a buzzing sound, like a bluebottle trapped in a lampshade. Was there any possibility that *checked out* meant something else in American? Looking down, he saw a dark sweater, leading to dark trousers and two brightly polished black shoes, each planted in the middle of a sandy-colored marble square. Those were his legs, his feet in the shoes that he had polished over the kitchen sink in London only the night before, flicking the brush back and forth in the way his father had taught him. This, he thought, is more than I can bear.

"Jeez," said a voice, "we're having an epidemic."

Opening his eyes, Zeke saw an olive-skinned face hanging over him. The back of his head, his shoulders, and the rest of his body were resting on something cold and hard. "Sir, sir, are you all right?" the face was saying.

"Where's the letter?"

"Would you like a glass of water? Do you want to see a doctor?"

"The letter," he said again, and this time heard the word as a plea: Let her. Let her be here. Let her come to me.

"Why don't we get you into a chair, sir?"

With the help of two men in gray uniforms, Zeke was transported to a wing-backed armchair. Something small and orange danced at the edge of his vision: the suspiciously regular flames of a gas fire. The olive-skinned man brought a glass of water and the precious envelope. Another man appeared, wearing black garments of such fitted sleekness as to resemble a wet suit. "Mr. Cafarelli, I'm the manager. How are you feeling?"

"Heartbroken."

"Do you need to see a doctor?"

"Not for this."

The man was looking at him so intently that for a moment Zeke wondered if they'd met before. But he knew only one person within several thousand miles and she was gone, leaving instead of her gorgeous person a piece of paper. "Don't worry," he said. "I just had a terrible disappointment. I do know that this is a hotel, not a hospital."

"Very well, sir, but might I recommend that you use room service for the rest of the day. We'll be happy to take care of it."

Zeke moved his head up and down, with no idea what the man was talking about. Why would he want his room serviced? Then a wheelchair was produced and, although he could easily have walked, he sat in it docilely and allowed himself, his suitcase, and the letter to be transported into a lift, down a corridor, and into a pink room with the biggest bed he had ever seen. How on earth would he ever sleep here? The three men turned on the bedside light, drew the curtains, adjusted the heat, asked if he wanted to watch TV; one sounded like Americans on television, one sounded Spanish, one sounded as if he had swallowed English sentences whole and was now regurgitating them. Finally, they left him alone. Making sure to stay well away from the edge, he lay down on the bed and opened the letter.

At first all he saw was her handwriting, much less neat than her grandfather's but still with each letter distinct and martialed into groups. He gazed at them hopelessly, seeing not phrases and sentences but, over and over, the declaration of her absence. I got on a plane, he thought, I came all this way, and you're not here. He wanted to count the hairs on his forearm, climb into a cupboard, take apart the world's largest clock.

A knock came at the door. "Room service."

That mysterious phrase again. The door opened and one of those men in gray uniforms came in, the Spanish-sounding older one. "The manager thought you might like some tea, sir. Where shall I put the tray?"

Zeke patted the counterpane. The man marched around two sides of the bed and halfway along the third, deposited the tray and slid it in Zeke's direction. "I hope you feel better," he said, and left as quietly as he had come.

In the midst of his despair Zeke eyed the white china teapot appreciatively. At least they had teapots in America. But when he reached to pour, the liquid that emerged from the spout was clear. Had he, yet again, misunderstood? Then he spotted a container of different colored tea bags: they expected him to make his own tea. Tears came into his eyes. In every evanescent cell of his body he understood how far he was from home, from knowing how many dustbins there were on the street, which church bell struck the hour first. He opened a little paper envelope—there seemed to be only one of each kind—and slipped the tea bag into the pot. After three minutes he poured himself a cup of not terribly strong, not terribly hot tea. He set it on the bedside table and, turning back to the page, watched the rows of letters coalesce.

Dear, dear Zeke,

I am so sorry not to be here to greet you. I did try to phone you in London, to explain, but you must have already left for Heathrow. I just discovered this morning, less than an hour ago, that I have to go to New York. It all has to do with Henry and his horrendous problems. I don't think I'll be able to get back this evening but I should be back later tomorrow. I'll phone to let you know.

Meanwhile, I hope you can have a nice time exploring Boston. If I hadn't been in a terrible mood I think I'd have enjoyed the Fogg Museum, and I did like the Isabella Stewart Gardner. One day soon I hope I can make all this up to you.

My love, Verona

PS 1 Please don't worry about money. I know this has been terrifically expensive: the plane, not working, etc. We'll sort it out.

PS 2 I hope you understand that I don't approve of Henry's behavior but I still have to help him.

PS 3 You probably know by now, from Emmanuel, that I have no connection to the Barrows. I'm sorry I lied to you about being their niece, but not sorry, not at all, about the rest.

Oh, no, thought Zeke, not New York. He pictured tall buildings, endless pushing and shoving, a park where people killed each other, where everyone had either too much money or not enough. Why was Verona going to such a dangerous place? How could Henry possibly deserve this kind of devotion? Parents and children he understood, but brothers and sisters were a mystery. Two adults did something that they wanted to do anyway, and had a baby. Then they did the same thing again and the result was siblings: two people who didn't necessarily have anything in common besides their parents. Although, he had to admit as he sipped his tea, a sibling might have been a help with the shop. The one time he had asked his mother why he was an only child she had said—kindly or cruelly, he couldn't tell—you were enough. He hadn't given the matter another thought until the night she'd made him dinner and explained how his father's fears about his heart had kept them from having a larger family.

He poured a second cup of tea, stronger but even cooler than the first, and reread the letter. It was astonishing how little information she managed to give. Once again, he thought, my task is to wait, and waiting is one of my least favorite activities. He folded the pages neatly back into the envelope, set it on the bedside table, and closed his eyes. If only he could be frozen until all this was over.

21

The man at the desk didn't seem to know what Zeke was talking about. "Fog?" he kept repeating. "I don't think so. They're saying a thirty percent chance of snow later." And then he did something Zeke had heard about but seldom witnessed: he rolled his eyes. His pupils moved from one corner of the eye to the other as if someone had twirled them on a stick. Was he being rude, Zeke wondered, or was it like the waitress in the coffee shop who had found his request for water incomprehensible until he pointed to another customer's glass of clear liquid. Now, as the man kept quoting the weather forecast, Zeke doggedly refused to move. He wanted to go to this place where Verona had been, to take comfort in sharing a few molecules of air with her. He reached for the notepad and pen lying on the desk and carefully printed: I WANT TO GO TO THE FOGG MUSEUM. HOW DO I GET THERE? Then he drew himself up to his full height. It seems like a small thing, Gwen used to say, but when you stand up straight people are convinced that you're a person to be reckoned with. Napoleon, she went on, had excellent posture. So did Tina Turner. Neither was an immediately useful role model, but in the middle of the lobby Zeke did his best to signal that, in spite of being an inept hotel guest, he was not going to be intimidated. He stared resolutely at an armchair while the man carried his message over to the main desk and, after a lengthy consultation, came back with another piece of paper that he unfolded with a flourish.

Zeke was pleased to see a mass of black, brown, and green lines. He liked maps, the way they made order out of chaos and the peculiar fact that you could point to one and say, I am here. When his English teacher had been explaining metaphor—how it links two things we normally regard as separate—Zeke had been bewildered until he pictured a map. On the plane he was delighted to find a sheet of paper pinned on the wall by one of the lavatories, showing their flight path. There was their journey, neatly drawn from London, across Ireland, the Atlantic, and Nova Scotia to Boston.

"The hotel is here." The man's nails had clear, shapely half moons. "And you want to go here, to the Fogg Museum in Cambridge, across the Charles River." He indicated a meandering blue line. "Either you can take a taxi or the T."

"What's the T?"

"The subway. In London you call it the tube." He continued to explain the system, the nearest stop to the hotel, the nearest stop to the museum, where to change. Zeke wrote down the crucial information. The idea of traveling underground was at once appealing. Surely, down below, Boston could not be so different.

"Thank you," he said, slipping the map into his pocket. He had almost crossed the shiny expanse of marble that lay between him and the door when the man called after him. "You might want to wait awhile. They don't open until nine."

Zeke stopped, midstride, and checked his watch. It was only seven-thirty. Of course he had heard of jet lag, that phenomenon whereby one part of your body remained in the old place while the rest arrived in the new; still, it felt weird to be so alert before dawn. He took the lift again and got out at the eighth floor. The corridor stretched as far as the eye could see in both directions, every door the same flat beige, with only the gold numerals fastened above each little fish eye to distinguish them, though four now had trays sitting outside. Earlier, when he left his room, he had walked the length of the corridor and located three exit signs and an ice machine, improbably full of perfect ice cubes.

Back in his room, he set his own tray from the night before outside the door, made the bed, and tidied the bathroom. After being up for nearly twenty-four hours, he had, in spite of his strange surroundings, fallen asleep soon after drinking his tea and slept remarkably well. Now he lay on the enormous bed, holding a copy of the magazine about Boston he'd picked up in the lobby, and stared up at the ceiling. It looked as if the builder had mixed sand into the plaster, the American equivalent of wood-chip paper, he guessed, a way to conceal flaws. The little red light he had spied in the night turned out to be a smoke detector, and the metal nozzle beside it—he stood on the bed to check—seemed to be a water sprinkler.

He lay back down. All I want, he thought, is to live in a safe place with Verona and Ms. F. In their company he could imagine learning the skills he had failed to grasp the first time round: how to ride a bicycle, how to tell lies and recognize people, maybe even how to enjoy the seaside. But, whatever happened next, a stormy period lay ahead. Back in London, debts must be paid, to Emmanuel and to his relentless parents. And where exactly, now the Barrows were home, would he and Verona be together? At the prospect that he might have to leave his flat where he had lived for six years and where, on even the darkest night, he could find his toothbrush or his pepper grinder by touch alone, he began to count the threads in the counterpane as fast as he could. Just for a moment he glimpsed the terrible possibility that his affections might not be inexhaustible. Overhead the sprinkler glittered.

He jumped up and seized his jacket and hat. He could always pace the street outside the museum until it opened, which was, after all, a predictable event. Almost any other waiting was preferable to the nebulous, painful kind that Verona imposed on him, over and over again.

—

Soon after he changed to the Red Line the train came aboveground. A mechanical voice announced Charles Street station and a hospital with, amazingly, the name Jill had mentioned. Before he could identify the buildings, the train was pulling out of the station and they were crossing a river, the blue line on his map now a frozen gray. Then they were once more down below, among the pipes and moles. Zeke would gladly have spent the day going back and forth between the mysterious Alewife and the equally mysterious, although somehow symmetrical, Braintree. But a sense of loyalty to Verona made him get out at Harvard Square. He followed two boys, each with an armful of books, to the exit marked Church Street.

Aboveground he discovered again the bitterly cold day and half a dozen boxes containing newspapers, some for sale, some free. A small flock of telephones clustered together amid the snow. As he studied them, he heard a roaring noise and, looking up, saw two planes flying overhead, the only familiar part of the landscape. Everything else was different: the brick sidewalks, the low muddled buildings, the cars on the wrong side of the road, even the shapes of the leafless trees. No, not everything. Right behind him was a shop selling soap and shampoo that had branches all over London.

He crossed Church Street, passed an ocher-colored church, and came to a snowy expanse surrounded by black railings. A park, he was thinking, when he noticed several dark slate stones punctuating the snow and recognized a graveyard. The railings led him to another church, this one made of wood, painted light gray, with beautiful clear windows. Standing on the front step, he took out the map and located Harvard Square. All he had to do to find the museum was retrace his steps, walk up a street called Massachusetts Avenue, and turn left on Quincy Street.

He was outside a bookshop when he spotted a metal effigy like the one he had seen from the taxi the day before. He bent down to examine the silver body and faded orange helmet with its snout and two stocky arms; even on closer inspection it seemed to have no obvious use. He stopped a passing boy and asked what it was.

"It's a fire hydrant. If there were a fire the firemen could connect their hoses to this"—the boy pointed at the snout—"and get water at high pressure."

"Is fire a particular problem in Boston?"

"Got me." The boy whistled. "We do have some wooden buildings, but you see fire hydrants all over the country. I bet there was a blaze somewhere, New York or Chicago, and somebody invented some paranoid law. That's how a lot of stuff happens here."

"Thank you."

"You're welcome."

Welcome to what, Zeke wondered, but it seemed to be the expression Americans used to conclude conversations instead of *no problem*, or *right*, or *take care*, or *cheers*. He turned the corner. There was the museum, a handsome stone building, just where the map said it should be and it was open. Inside a sign requested six dollars. He was muddling over his wallet when a voice said, "Excuse me." A woman, dressed in black, reached over the counter, deftly extracted two pieces of green paper, and in exchange handed Zeke a metal button. "Wear this in view," she instructed.

In the two-story courtyard, he closed his eyes, trying to summon Verona. Maybe he should ask the woman behind the counter if she remembered a tall pregnant Englishwoman visiting the museum recently? But when he glanced back she was talking on the phone, one hand shielding the receiver as if whatever she was saying was too good to share. The courtyard itself was pleasingly symmetrical, with a row of arches, like upside-down U's, on the ground floor, and a row of double arches, like M's, above. On one side was a shop, closed, but selling, he guessed, postcards and souvenirs. He headed for the stairs, passing a wooden statue, a saint, clearly very old. On the poorly lit landing he paused in front of a picture of another saint, the gloomy-looking St.

Dominic, holding a large book. The accompanying label claimed that the painting had originally been done around 1246, but within a few years it had been altered twice in pursuit of greater verisimilitude. An earlier version of the left ear was apparently still visible in the middle of the face but not, in the dim light, to Zeke. If at first you don't succeed, he thought, and made a little bow to Dominic.

Upstairs, there seemed to be no one else around. Unable to focus on any single painting he began to circle the balcony, and with each revolution his thoughts grew more agitated. Where was Verona? What was he doing in this strange country? Why did only one of the five churches he'd passed between the hotel and the museum have a clock? When he put his fingers to his forehead, he could feel the questions beating against his skull. He had suggested trepanning to one of his doctors, a little hole to let out the bad ideas. No, no, she had insisted, all you need is to take the right medicine and go to your group.

"Are you all right, sir?" Navy blue trousers, a navy jacket barred his path.

"Not really. I was trying to get away from my thoughts."

"Perhaps," the guard said, "you might look at the paintings. Whatever your tastes, just look at a couple. You'll feel better. I guarantee it."

Zeke said he would try. In a room off the balcony he stopped in front of a roiling sea and moved quickly on to a mountain range. For him these scenes had all the disadvantages of nature in real life, an uncountable mass of vegetation. The only painting in the room that offered some relief was a picture of a train with red fenders, standing in a station surrounded by feathery clouds of steam. The next room contained portraits. This was better, he thought, regarding a ruddy-cheeked man wearing a neat white wig. How much easier life would be if people remained fixed in a single posture. He gazed appreciatively at a woman and a small child. Finally he reached a room full of the kind of paintings he most enjoyed, ones that didn't pretend to be a person or a thing but were simply themselves. He stood in front of a small oil composed of crisscrossing lines for several minutes.

By lunchtime, however, the consolations of art were long gone. He felt so desolate that he would happily have returned to the graveyard, made himself a pillow of snow, and lain down among the stones. Instead, he ate a tuna sandwich at a large factorylike bakery and then stepped into the first men's clothing shop he came to and bought a down jacket. Wearing his new purchase, he returned to the subway and caught a train headed toward Braintree. At Charles Street station, he got out and followed the signs to the hospital.

"Zeke, what are you doing here? You're not ill, are you?"

A person stood before him, a woman, slender, pale-skinned, eyes caught behind black-framed glasses. Her brown hair was secured with two metal clips and she was wearing the light-blue trousers and top he had already seen on several dozen women as he waited to consult, and then gave up on, the man at the information desk. He stared at her uncertainly. The small nose was the same but the lips seemed too pale and the shoulders sloped differently. Then, as her hand moved toward him, he caught sight of a black leather watch strap encircling a blue-veined wrist and remembered noticing both the day before, across the aisle. "Jill, I was looking for you. The man at the desk said they can only find patients, not nurses. I didn't know what to do next."

"Your timing couldn't be better. I'm just coming off duty. Do you want to get some tea?"

"Here?"

Even in Jill's company, the thought of spending more time in this place where every other person was in a wheelchair was daunting. But already she was pulling on her coat and leading the way toward the door; there were some nice cafés, she'd heard, across from the subway station. As they walked, she talked about how different everything was, even the names of the medicines, and sentence by sentence she grew more familiar. "The doctors are very big on patient responsibility. God knows what that means, given that half of them are barely conscious. I couldn't say a word without someone going into paroxysms over my accent."

"Have you seen the woman from the plane?" he asked.

"The woman? Oh, you mean the one who collapsed. No, I'm afraid I didn't think to look for her, though you're right. They might have brought her here."

Together, both first looking in the wrong direction, they crossed into a smaller road lined with brick buildings, many of which housed either restaurants or antiques shops, and stopped at a café with several people sitting in the window. Inside, Jill asked for two cups of tea.

"Hot tea?" said the woman behind the counter.

"As opposed to?"

"Well, iced tea is very popular, though not," the woman admitted, "at this time of year."

They were handed Styrofoam cups of boiling water and tea bags. Jill asked for milk, and they seated themselves at a table near the window.

"Why do you think Americans won't put in the tea bag for you?" Zeke said, tearing open the little paper envelope and lowering the bag into the water.

"Laziness? Fear of being sued if it steeps too long?" Her mouth stretched wide. "Sorry. It's not you. I'm just shattered. And the flat they've given me is a tip."

Oh. She was yawning. "A tip how?"

"Everything." Her voice suddenly had a rusty sound. "The walls are a mess. There are fluorescent lights. The floors are filthy. The taps leak." Behind her glasses, her eyelids started to wrinkle. A drop of water spilled from one eye. Then a drop from the other. She covered her face with her hands.

Zeke pulled out his tea bag and, after a moment's deliberation—she could always replace it—hers. He looked at Jill, her neat hands, so different from Verona's, spread across her face, her shoulders trembling as she uttered small, squeaky noises. She had been sent to rescue him. "I can help," he said. "That's what I do in London. I paint people's houses. Let's drink our tea and you can show me the flat."

"You can't spend your holiday"—she hiccupped—"painting."

"I'm not here on holiday. I came to find someone, but she's in New York. All I can do is wait, and I'd rather wait helping you than traipsing around like I did today. Though maybe, when you're not working, we can go to the Isabella-something museum. I would like to see that."

Jill lowered her hands. "Stewart Gardner," she said.

The block of flats resembled several he had seen that day, a tall brick building, probably dating from the twenties. In the hall Zeke saw that the ceilings were a graceful ten feet, two more than his hotel room, and dark wainscoting lined the walls. Once, not so long ago, this had been an elegant building. Now the walls and floors bore the evidence of much casually moved furniture. He followed Jill up the worn stairs.

"It's odd how they count floors differently, isn't it?" she said.

"Like the hotel," he agreed.

Also like the hotel was the anonymous corridor into which they emerged. They passed half a dozen doors. Jill stopped at the last one on the left, opened it, and motioned him to go ahead. Stepping into a narrow hallway, his first sensations were of dry ferocious heat and cold, buzzing light. The latter came from a circular fluorescent tube mounted on the ceiling. As Jill closed the door, he unzipped his new jacket and slung it over a chair. He had expected the flat to be empty, but in the living room was a beige sofa with two matching armchairs, a dining room table, and four chairs. Cushions would help, he thought; a colorful tablecloth. Some of Jill's despair, he understood, came from loneliness.

"It's ghastly, isn't it? I signed a year's lease because everyone told me how hard it was to find housing here." Her voice had that rusty quality again.

Quickly he said, "It's not so bad. Places always need redecorating between tenants. A coat of paint will make a big difference. Maybe your landlord will pay for it. If you can stand the aggravation, you could ask him to refinish the floors. If not, get a couple of rugs. And some lamps. Have you by any chance noticed a paint shop nearby?"

Jill began to make a strange noise. He looked at her, checking for more tears, but as she bent forward, hugging her arms around her body, he recognized laughter. The cause eluded him but he was so glad to see her cheerful that he joined in, and as he laughed he realized that what the doctor opposed to trepanning had claimed was true: feeling did, sometimes, follow behavior.

When she could speak again, Jill said she hadn't noticed a paint shop. Between them, using the telephone directory and the map he'd been given that morning, they located one a few streets away. While she took a shower, Zeke, once again relishing the connection between a sheet of paper and the city, went to investigate. He found the shop on his first attempt and inside was engulfed by the familiar odors of wood and paint. He wandered up and down the aisles, examining the color charts and tools. At last he pulled himself together and bought spackle, sandpaper, a brush, a roller and tray, a drop cloth, and a gallon of paint. As he stepped out of the shop, he saw a woman walking down the sidewalk toward him, her belly advancing before her like a prow. She passed him without a second glance, but Zeke halted as if she had yelled *stop*. What was he doing, wandering around buying paint, when Verona had said she would call today? He might as well be in London if she couldn't reach him. He set off toward Jill's, walking at top speed, the tin of paint banging against his thigh, counting the parked cars. At one hundred and twelve, he switched to counting blue cars, then red ones.

"What's wrong?" Jill said, as soon as she opened the door.

"Verona," he said. "She might be trying to phone me."

"Come in. Let's call your hotel. That's where she'd phone, isn't it? They can tell you if there are any messages. You can always take a taxi back."

In the presence of her immediate understanding, he was able to step into the flat. Jill dialed the number and handed him the phone. "No messages, sir," said a voice suspiciously like that of the man who'd been so obtuse about the museum that morning.

"Have you checked?"

"No messages."

Zeke put down the receiver. His heart had slowed and his breathing steadied, signs, he knew, that he was calmer. Also acutely disappointed. But at least this time he didn't faint: a pity in a way, given that Jill would have known exactly what to do.

It was only five-thirty but they both admitted to being ravenous. Jill suggested they go to an Indian restaurant a few streets away. "I do notice restaurants," she said. Like the paint shop, the Star of Goa had a familiar fragrance, in this case the comingling of cloves, garlic, coriander, cumin, and turmeric, and the waiter who led them to their table could have stepped straight off a London bus. They ordered a chicken biryani, a vegetable korma, raita, aloo nan, and sag paneer. "I'll have a beer," Jill added, and gave the name of a bird.

"So," she said, when the waiter had brought a sleek brown bottle and poured half the contents into a glass, "I don't mean to pry, but would you like to talk about it? Why you're here, why Verona isn't?"

"What's today's word?" He raised his glass of water and, finding it full of ice cubes, set it down again.

"Disequilibrium. Obviously it means loss of balance, which is part of what I wanted when I took a job here, but I hadn't bargained on quite so much."

The nearest customers, two bearded men at the next table, were also discussing words. "I hate to sound like a grad student," Zeke overheard the one in a checked shirt say, "but I do think the word *seminal* applies to his later films." Seminal, thought Zeke, I'll use that tomorrow. He felt an odd reluctance to talk about Verona, to expose their intimacy to any kind of judgment that might brand him a fool, her something worse. But as he reached for a pappadum, everything came tumbling out. While Jill sipped her beer, he told her about Verona's sudden appearance in his life, her abrupt flight, her silence, and her summons.

"So you arrived at the hotel and she was gone?"

"She'd booked me a room and left a letter, saying she had to go to New York and would be in touch soon."

Jill made a growling noise, which he suspected indicated disapproval, but to his relief she didn't voice it. "It sounds like she's in trouble," she said, tearing off a piece of nan. "Or her brother is. She's lucky you came to help."

"How am I helping by wandering around museums?"

She moved her shoulders in the way people did when they didn't know the answer. "I came here for love too, the other kind." Meaning what, he was wondering, when she added, "Unrequited."

"I'm sorry."

"So am I. We'd been living together for four years and I didn't think everything was perfect—I wasn't that stupid—but I thought we had problems like everyone else. We'd negotiate, we'd compromise, we'd go to Crete and drink ouzo."

"And?"

"Leslie said we'd tried all those things and I was too set in my ways and it was time to move on. She made me feel like a bus stop." She gave a little anti-laugh. "When people spoke about being heartbroken, I used to think it was a feeble figure of speech. I've seen a heart beating in the chest cavity. I know it doesn't break like a china plate. But since Leslie left my chest aches all the time. On the plane yesterday, just for a moment"—her face screwed up—"I envied that woman."

The men at the next table were pulling on jackets and hats. The door opened and half a dozen girls came in, carrying brightly colored shopping bags.

"Oh, hell," said Jill. "I'm sorry. I promised I wasn't going to talk about it to anyone on this side of the Atlantic. I can't stand to hear myself whining."

"I'm not really on this side of the Atlantic." He braved his water glass; the ice cubes were mostly gone. "Mightn't she change her mind? I mean, if she knows how much you love her, won't she want to"—he groped for the expression—"try again?"

"No. What she wants is to break up with me and not feel like a bad person." She was clutching her knife and fork, holding them upright on either side of her plate. It was against the order of things, the way two followed one, the combining of hydrogen and oxygen, that so much feeling should go unanswered, yet such, she was telling him, was the case. "I'm sorry," she went on, in a lower voice, "I've spent sixteen months thinking thoughts like that. *Amor vincit omnia*. But it isn't true. Love conquers fuck-all. Leslie doesn't give a toss about my feelings. As for me"—she lowered her silverware—"I think of Mithradates getting used to poison by eating a little every day. I eat dishfuls and it doesn't seem to help. So if you feel strongly about Verona and there's even a small chance that she reciprocates, don't give up."

The waiters, who had been loitering nearby, now advanced as a group. One took their plates, another the metal curry dishes, a third removed the trio of chutneys.

When they were once more alone, Zeke said, "Can I ask you a question?"

"You already have." She cocked her head. "Sorry, primary school humor."

"Do you think that there's life after death?"

Behind her glasses her eyes widened. "I don't know. Maybe for some people, maybe for a while. One of the rabbis who used to visit the hospital claimed that the spirit lingers near the body for eight days, and that's why it's important to keep the dead company. Myself, I think we're conscious and then we're not and that it doesn't matter very much, except to a few close friends. What do you think?"

He fingered a few grains of rice that had escaped the waiters. "I've had a lot of time recently to wonder why we fall for one person rather than another. I know hardly anything about Verona: she has big hands, she can stop clocks, she had a friend who died. So I've been thinking that perhaps there's some secret part of ourselves that recognizes the secret part of another person. Maybe that's what we mean by the soul."

"I want some tea." Jill waved toward one of the waiters. "You think you're philosophizing, but this is the kind of nonsense you talk when you're in love. When you fall out of love, you'll realize it was just your cunt talking. Pardon me, prick."

His face felt hot and something odd was happening in his chest, not an ache, more like an explosion. He focused on the objects still on the table, including Jill's hands, and the pictures he could see on the wall behind her. When the heat began to recede, he thought, I'm angry because Jill is suggesting that I don't really love Verona. But he had made Jill angry too by going on about this feeling she was trying to forget.

"I'm sorry," he said. "I shouldn't have said anything."

"I'm good on fear of flying, poor on love. Let's drink our tea and talk about something else."

Perhaps it was her mention of Mithradates, but he found himself telling the story of Verona's grandfather, how he'd fought in the war, started a railway, married Irene, and how, after more than a decade, for no apparent reason, she'd taken poison. And then her deceased parents had appeared at the funeral.

"Amazing," said Jill. "She pretended they were dead and they went along with it? My parents would shout the house down. It's one of my deep fears: that a friend or lover will turn out to be utterly different than I'd thought." She tilted her head. "Has that ever happened to you?"

Zeke buried his face in his cup of tea. "Not yet," he said.

22

Zeke was filling holes in the walls of Jill's living room, taking pleasure in every aspect of the familiar activity—judging the size of the hole and the amount of spackle needed, pushing it into place, smoothing it with the palette knife—when he heard a knock at the door. Before he could decide to answer, a key was turning in the lock.

"Hello. Anyone home?"

As the heavy footsteps approached, Zeke stood there uncertainly, palette knife poised, wondering whether to declare his presence. The footsteps carried into the room a substantial person wearing workman's boots made of leather the color of custard and a dark blue jacket, like the one he had bought. From his size and stance, Zeke guessed the interloper to be a man though his face was hidden by the hood of his jacket. Inside the living room door he stopped to fumble a large ring of keys back into a pocket and sniff once, modestly. At no point did the hood turn toward the corner where Zeke stood. He thinks he's alone, Zeke thought, knowing the man would be angry when he found he wasn't. At just that moment the man pushed back his hood. Everything about him that had been moving stopped.

"Who the fuck are you? I have the tenant down as Ms. Jill Irving."

"She's at the hospital. I could ask you the same question."

"You could, and the difference would be I'd answer. I'm Chance Donaghue. I work for Mr. Wolfberg."

"Chance?" said Zeke. "Wolf?"

"Wolf*berg*. He owns the building. Ms. Irving phoned yesterday and had a fit about the state of her apartment so I came to check it out. I've told them before it's a mistake to rent to foreigners. They have unrealistic expectations." The man reached again into a pocket of his jacket, not the one in which he had deposited the keys, and Zeke wondered if he was going to produce a gun, like people did in American films. If he does, he thought, I'll throw a chair at him and shout *Fire!* The man's hand reappeared, holding nothing more sinister than a spiral notebook. He put the book on a chair and removed his jacket. The person who picked up the notebook again was significantly smaller.

Zeke set the spackle down and approached. "How do you do," he said. "I'm Zeke Cafarelli, a friend of Ms. Irving's. I'm giving her a hand. Was your father a gambler?"

"A gambler? Oh, you mean my name. No, my mother said it as a joke when the nurses at the hospital kept pestering her about what to put on my wristband. As she points out, at least she didn't say *mistake*. So"—he consulted the notebook—"there's painting the living room, the taps, some problem with the showerhead and the grout in the bathroom, the floors. And it says fluorescent lights—allergic." He looked up from the book, his brown eyebrows raised beneath his brown fringe. "That's a new one on me, but I suppose it's possible. I'm allergic to sunlight. Even when I was only four or five I got terrible headaches in summer. I would lie in bed longing for rain. How does she manage with shopping?"

"Shopping?"

"Most stores have fluorescent lights. It seems like it would be quite restrictive."

"I think," said Zeke carefully—this was not his area of expertise—"she may have been speaking metaphorically."

"Oh." Chance's whole body rocked back and forth. "I get it. She hates the lights, and she thinks if she pretends it's medical, we'll fix them. I don't see why not. Do you mind if I check out the bathroom?"

As he turned to leave the room, Zeke saw that his hair hung halfway down his back in a neat braid. Two pools of water marked the place where he had stood; a trail of smaller damp patches led toward the door. Zeke went back to filling a row of holes at eye level where something, a shelf probably, had been removed. Six holes later, Chance returned and announced that he would arrange for a plumber and an electrician to come as soon as possible. "And you're painting the living room?"

"Yes." Then he remembered that assurance was not his to offer. Verona might summon him at any moment. Once again he felt resentment at the uncertainty that now governed his life. "That is, I plan to but it's possible that I'll be called away."

"Called away? Are you sick? religious?"

"Not that I know of, but I'm only in America for a few days."

"Lucky you." Again Chance's whole body moved up and down in what Zeke understood to be approval. "I'll put in a work order to have the living room painted, and Ms. Irving can always cancel it." He scribbled a couple of lines in the notebook and returned it to his pocket. He pulled on the jacket, becoming once again his burlier self, and approached Zeke, hand outstretched. "Nice to meet you, Mr. Cafarelli. If you ever need a job in the U.S., give Mr. Wolfberg a ring. We can always use a good painter. Have a nice day."

Reluctantly, Zeke took his hand. He would have liked Chance to unzip his jacket again, sit down, and talk about what it was like to be allergic to sunshine and how long it took to grow his braid. As they were shaking hands, he remembered one of the few jokes he understood. "When a person says that to my friend Emmanuel, he says, don't fucking tell me what kind of day to have."

Chance's lips parted revealing two rows of completely white teeth, his hands came together in a clapping motion, and his heavy cheeks shook. Oh, thought Zeke, American laughter.

By the time Jill returned, all four walls were covered with two coats of magnolia paint and he was standing on a chair, working on the ceiling. But while he applied the paint some comparable process seemed to have occurred inside his head; all his hopes about Verona, which he had carried so carefully around London, across the Atlantic, and through the highways and byways of Boston, had been obliterated by a single question: why hadn't she phoned? He remembered the story she'd told that first afternoon about getting rid of people by writing their names on the wall and painting over them. As he ran the roller back and forth, he could not imagine that he would ever find her in this strange place, that they would ever be reunited, and even if both of these were to oc- cur he could not believe that anything good would come of it. What on earth was he doing here, inconveniencing himself, his parents, and his customers?

"This is fantastic," said Jill. "It looks so much better." She stood in the middle of the room, her glasses shining with droplets of water.

"I'm going home."

"You must be tired after doing all this. Do you want to get some supper? I could walk part of the way with you."

"Walk?"

"To the hotel. I looked at a map today and it's not that far. We don't need to keep taking taxis."

"I mean to London." Even his only friend in America no longer understood him. Beneath his feet the chair creaked, and drops of paint sprayed from the roller. Later, he could neither re- member nor repeat the speech he had made as he struggled to ex- plain how useless his presence here was: how he couldn't sense Verona in any shape or form, not in the Fogg Museum, which he knew she had visited, and not in the hotel, where he knew she had stayed; how his parents needed help. "I made a mistake," he said. "I thought she cared for me."

"Can I see her letter?"

"Her letter?"

"You told me when you got to the hotel she'd left a letter for you. I don't mean to be nosy, but if you were willing to let me read it. . . ." She spread her hands, and he caught a whiff of disinfectant. "Maybe I could tell you how it strikes me." Her normally pale face was flushed. Was that just the effect of coming into the warmth? No, she was saying something else now, about how when she'd gone back and reread Leslie's letters it had been obvious that she was being given the brush-off; she simply hadn't wanted to acknowledge what any stranger would have grasped in a nanosecond.

"Nanosecond?"

"A very short period of time. When I asked one of the nurses on the orthopedic ward where they kept the splints, she said, 'I'll be with you in a nanosecond.' She was ten minutes, but that's not what it means."

"It's at the hotel." He climbed down from the chair and bent to wipe up the spots of paint. "I'd like that."

While Jill went to change her clothes and he rinsed the roller, a few shards of his feelings for Verona emerged. He remembered his Uncle Stephen, the one who had dropped dead of a heart attack, pointing to the smallest patch of blue sky and saying look, enough blue sky to make a pair of sailor's trousers. He and Jill would go to the hotel; he would produce the letter, which he had folded into his last clean shirt; she would read it and pronounce, irrespective of his longings. He could still recall his first glimpse of the astonishing truth that his thoughts and feelings made no difference to other people. His third-form teacher, Miss McCallum, had written on the blackboard the sentence, *Douglas ate his porridge*.

What does *porridge* do in this sentence, she asked, head swiveling like a periscope above the pond of pupils.

Don't let her pick me, thought Zeke. He stared at his desk, shaping the five words so that even busy Miss McCallum would understand them. Then he wondered if *pick* was ambiguous. Don't let her ask me, he thought. He tried to make his thoughts like the Viking shield he'd seen in his history book, strong and invincible. Don't let—

Zeke?

On the faces of his fellow pupils he saw an expression that over the course of the next decade he had ample opportunity to learn to recognize as a mixture of glee and relief. Miss McCallum had ignored his sturdy well-formed sentence and was staring at him with her colorless eyes while he scrambled, undefended, around the empty rooms of his brain. In one of the rooms he stumbled upon a saying of his father's: Nothing like a bowl of porridge to stick to your ribs. Porridge, he said, sticks to Douglas's ribs.

The class shrieked.

Quiet, girls and boys. Zeke, don't be cheeky. I'll ask you one more time. Given that *Douglas* is the subject and *ate* is the verb, what is *porridge*? We studied this last week.

Trying not to move or breathe, he stared at the top of his desk, waiting for the storm to pass. He did not bother to think anything at all. What was the point if no one paid attention? Miss McCallum had sent him to the punishment desk, the wooden desk in the corner with so much chewing gum stuck underneath that sometimes, revoltingly, a wad brushed his thigh. And then Caroline Power, whose eyes had a glassy look that had made him believe she was thinking a sentence similar to his own, volunteered that porridge was the object. How could something so formless be an object?

Only years later, after university, after his breakdown, did he grasp that even at their most vivid, their most neatly organized, his thoughts were invisible, not only to teachers and tyrants but to everyone from the most perceptive doctor to the driver of the 73 bus.

While Jill waited in the lobby, he went to his room to retrieve the letter. The first thing he saw was that the bed had been remade with the pillows under the counterpane. Then he noticed the red light on the phone, blinking. Almost on tiptoe, he approached. He raised the receiver and heard only the usual high-pitched note.

Downstairs Jill was nowhere to be seen. For a moment, as he scanned the crowded lobby, he was afraid she had left. But no, she wouldn't do that. He forced himself to walk slowly around the perimeter, looking at the different people: a group of men holding briefcases and phones, two women in fur coats, a couple with several children. At last, in one of the armchairs near the fire, he saw a familiar pair of legs emerging from beneath a newspaper.

"Jill." He tugged at the front page. "The light is flashing, in my room."

"What light?" She lowered the paper and, at the sight of him, dropped it. "Let me come up and take a look."

In his room she picked up the receiver, pushed a button, which he now saw was labeled MESSAGES, and held it out to him. "You have one message," said a mechanical American female. "I will now play your message." With the first syllable, the first fraction of sound, he knew that the caller was not Verona. He sank down on the bed, so disappointed that he didn't care who or what was coming next. "Hello, Zeke? It's Gwen, your mother. I got this number from Emmanuel. I can't believe you're in a hotel in Boston. But they put me through so I suppose you must be. Anyway, I need to talk to you. Call me on my mobile."

The American voice returned with instructions about repeating, saving, or deleting. He put the receiver back on its cradle. "My mother wants me to call," he said.

"Oh," said Jill, clasping her hands. "Is everything all right?"

"She didn't say. She seldom does." And it was true: Gwen's

messages were almost always commands—call me, come round—with neither reason nor explanation. "What time is it in London?"

Jill looked at her wrist. "Ten to ten. I can wait downstairs."

"I'd rather you stayed."

"I'll go over by the window and practice my yoga. May I use one of your towels?"

Then he had to ask her how to telephone London and she wrote out sixteen numbers. I don't want to do this, he thought. Jill emerged from the bathroom with a towel and lowered herself to the floor on the far side of the bed. He heard a *huh* sound and her legs in their black leggings appeared above the edge of the bed, toes pointed toward the ceiling. He picked up the receiver and dialed, twice fumbling a digit and having to begin again.

"Took you long enough," said Gwen. "What if your father had had a relapse?" She was off, like a greyhound after a rabbit. When finally he could get a word in, he begged her to slow down. Maurice had delivered an ultimatum; meanwhile Don, thanks to Zeke's warning, was being nice as pie. "Why couldn't he have been like this all along?" she said. "Cooking meals, taking me to the cinema." And then, the day Zeke left, she had found something while checking her breasts.

"Something?"

"A lump, a lump that wasn't there before. I don't know what to do."

"Go to your doctor."

"I meant about Maurice. I worry he'll do a bunk. It seems too much to ask. I'm married, I'm forty-five, I've kept him waiting all these months, I have a husband who's ill, and now this. Though I won't really know anything until they do a biopsy. The doctor did say most of these things turn out to be benign."

Even over three thousand miles, he could feel her longing that this should apply to her. From the floor came a series of *huh*s; the black legs dipped out of sight. And in the midst of his despair he had a moment of illumination. His condition, which sometimes made him feel so different from other people, was only one bend on a winding road along which many other people wandered. "I'll be back soon," he said.

"What use is that?"

"Well, you phoned me. You seem to want my opinion or something. So I'm asking, can you wait for a few days? Tell Maurice you don't want to do anything that might upset Dad while I'm away."

"How long is a few days?"

By the weekend, he promised, and said he had to go. For several seconds he luxuriated in the silence. Then he crawled across the bed until he was looking over the edge. Jill was lying on her stomach with her head and feet raised, bowlike. He could hear her rhythmic breathing. Presently she lowered her head onto her folded arms.

"Did you finish?" she said. Slowly she rolled over so that she was looking up at him from a distance of a couple of feet. Her eyes were large and dark, like those of some nocturnal animal.

"I had an idea while I was on the phone," he said. "I wanted to tell you."

"Go ahead. I am, as they say, all ears. Which is just as well given that, without my glasses, you're a blur."

"I'm not sure if I can put it into words." He told her about Gwen and the lump and how he had problems recognizing people, especially people he knew well, and that while Gwen was talking, he had had the thought that maybe he wasn't so different from other people. They might behave as if they could walk through all the rooms of their brains and everything was in plain view, like the fruit and vegetables in the shop, but in fact lots of things were hidden from them: lumps, feelings, ideas. "So I'm not the only one," he concluded, "who sometimes mistakes A for B."

Jill blinked, twice. "Of course not. I hope you can remember that." She sat up, stretched her arms above her head, and yawned. "Has your mother seen a doctor?"

"Yes. She's having a biopsy. It's funny, first my dad getting ill, now her."

"You'd be surprised how often I've seen these kinds of coincidences in hospital." Her face was so close he could feel her breath on his cheek. "You meeting Verona, your dad having a heart attack, your mum having a scare."

"My meeting Verona is quite different." He moved away, swinging his legs to the floor.

"Still, it's an upheaval. Do you want me to read her letter?"

In the confusion of Gwen's news he had forgotten their original plan. His first thought now was to refuse. Jill no longer seemed the ideal, sympathetic friend; besides, he didn't want to betray Verona by showing her private letter to someone else.

"You don't have to," she added. "I'm only trying to help."

She too turned away and, rising to her feet, bent to retrieve the towel. She *is* trying to help, he thought, as she returned it to the bathroom. He could not recall a single occasion when she had been less than encouraging about Verona. "What's today's word?" he said.

She clapped a hand to her mouth. "I'd forgotten all about it. So much for improving my vocabulary. We could choose one together."

"Let's, over supper." He stood up, fetched the letter from its hiding place, and handed it to her.

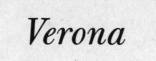

Verona

23

Verona stood at the front of the ferry from La Guardia Airport into Manhattan and held on to the throbbing handrail. Beyond the windows the water—fresh or salt, she didn't know—shone darkly, and along the shore tall feathery rushes bent in the wind. The air smelled of diesel oil and bitter coffee and, just occasionally, the expensive perfume of the woman standing next to her; all the other passengers were either talking on the phone or reading. Verona couldn't see her face, the woman was several inches shorter, but from her posture and the way she watched the shoreline, she had the impression that her companion might be on the verge of tears. A lost lover? a lost job? a deviant child? All tragedies, Verona suddenly understood, that might befall *her* at any moment. My hostages to fortune have tripled, she thought, and was amazed at how swiftly her life had changed.

A plane, coming in to land, passed overhead. As she followed its journey, Verona pictured Zeke perhaps even now flying toward her. What would he do when he found her gone, leaving only an awkward letter to welcome him? But how could she explain the complexities of the situation with Henry when she barely understood them herself? Turning back to the water, she saw a wooden crate floating toward the boat. She braced herself for the collision but, at the last second, it disappeared without a sound. I'll see him tomorrow, she thought, trying to raise her own spirits and, through some miracle of telepathy, Zeke's. In the anonymous hotel room she would tell him everything: Henry's crimes and misdemeanors, Nigel and George's relentless pursuit, her own disheveled romantic history, which had made her so stupidly reluctant to pick up the phone. She was still pondering the list when, off to their right, beyond the rushes, a throng of tall glittering buildings came into view.

"Magnificent," said the woman beside her. "I love being reminded that Manhattan is an island." She raised her face, and Verona saw dark eyes made darker by the careful use of makeup, a small pert nose. "Forgive me asking, but are you all right?"

"I'm fine," said Verona, and nearly added that she had been wondering the same thing about her interlocutor. "I didn't expect the city to look like an illustration for *Pilgrim's Progress*."

"I'd say Kafka's Castle, the place always in view that you can never reach."

"Well, I hope we'll be an exception. I'm just over from London for a few days."

The woman remarked that she looked quite far along to be traveling abroad. And then—perhaps she made some gesture of encouragement—Verona began to pour out a muddled version of what she had imagined telling Zeke: Henry, debts, ruthless creditors, lies.

The woman listened, wide-eyed and silent.

"You know," she said, when Verona paused, "you can only do so much. Your brother isn't your responsibility. If he's an adult, if he's clinically sane, it's up to him how he lives his life. Your responsibility is to yourself and your baby."

It was exactly what Verona had been thinking, but as soon as she heard the words spoken aloud she disagreed. "Actually," she burst out, "I hate all that putting-yourself-first American nonsense. I think the main reason we're here is to take care of each other."

But her rudeness was lost in the sound of the loudspeakers announcing the first stop. The woman reached into her handbag. "This is where I get off. If you need any help while you're in New York," she said, holding out a card, "pick up the phone. Unlike almost everyone else in the city, my husband and I have two spare rooms since the kids left home."

And that too, thought Verona, was so American, the openhanded generosity. When they were once again sailing along she read the card: *Marcia Hirsch, psychotherapist: individuals, couples, and family counseling. Children welcome.* She tore it into twelve tiny pieces and dropped them in the rubbish bin.

Yesterday, in Boston, after she had telephoned Zeke, she had spent the remainder of the afternoon going for a long walk through the snowy city and avoiding Henry. She was fully aware of her promise to Toby to make one more attempt, but first she needed to recover from the quarrels and revelations of the last twenty-four hours. This morning she had woken to clear skies and the conviction that today everything would be resolved. She had gone downstairs, hoping to find Henry in the hotel restaurant, but there was no sign of him. After a leisurely breakfast she had finally broken down and called his room at 9:45, 10:02, and 10:13 and each time reached the voice mail, which could, she reminded herself, mean he was talking on the phone. At 10:20 she had walked down the corridor. The door of his room was open. Inside, two women in striped uniforms were making the bed. Where's the man who stays here, she asked.

The older woman smiled and nodded. No English, she said.

For a moment Verona was sure she'd mistaken the room number. Then other excuses leaped in. He was doing an errand. They'd missed each other coming and going to breakfast. There was his shirt draped over the chair; there were his papers on the desk. But the swath of white material turned out to be a towel; the pile of papers, restaurant menus. She stepped farther into the room—the woman uttered some sort of protest—and pushed open the bathroom door.

Empty, gone.

She raced down the corridor. When the lift came it was already full, but she pushed blindly forward. At the ground floor she was out and striding across the lobby while her fellow passengers were still reconstituting themselves. Ignoring the queue at the front desk, she went straight to the clerk and asked if he had any messages for her. At least this time she didn't faint when he held out the envelope, but for a few seconds she could not bring herself to take it. Whatever its contents, its existence once again signaled Henry's absence. Please, she thought. Within the last forty-eight hours, he had demolished most of her ideas about him and about herself, so why did she feel as if she still had so much to lose?

Dear Verona,

Do you remember Adrian Lepage? He was at university with us, or at least with me. Now he's a businessman in Manhattan. I called him a couple of hours ago, and I'm catching the first train tomorrow to New York. It would be excellent if you could follow.

Why, you may ask? Because I need help.

What sort of help? Strategizing on how best to present unappealing facts. (Do you use bullet points in radio?)

Please, V, you've come all this way. Why not a little farther?

And why the rush? Let's just say that I'm desperate to leave for the same reason you came, difficult visitors. Capisce?

I will be staying with Adrian on the Upper East Side of Manhattan. He's expecting you too. Please phone 212-555-5125 when you get in.

Love, Henry

PS I plan to check out by phone after I get to New York so I won't get any messages this morning. Be sure they give you my company discount on your bill.

At the phrase *difficult visitors* she had stopped reading to search the lobby. Useless to pretend she was calm when she could feel sweat prickling her face and chest. She had gone upstairs and crammed everything back into her suitcases; only then had she thought to phone Zeke. She dialed three numbers, both of his and Emmanuel's, and listened to three recordings. He must be on his way to the airport, perhaps already waiting in those interminable lines. Just in case, she left a message on his home phone: Something came up and I have to go to New York for the day. I'll be back in Boston this evening or first thing tomorrow. She and Zeke could spend the day in one of the enormous hotel beds, and fly back to London together. Meanwhile, every noise she heard made her start.

Downstairs she checked out and reserved a room for Zeke. She told the clerk she'd be in the lobby for the next half hour. If anyone rang, could he call her to the phone? Sitting at a table so small that it barely accommodated a sheet of hotel stationery, she had at first been unable to write a single word beyond *Dear Zeke*. She tried her customary trick of silently mouthing sentences. Think before you speak, Mr. Sayers used to say, unable to grasp that for her speech was thought. Now her lips remained frozen. I should kiss his shoes, she thought. I should spread my coat over the snow for him to walk on. What use were a few paltry excuses in the face of her abominable departure?

At last she stammered out a note that did little more than repeat her phone message. Then she had taken yet another taxi and caught yet another plane. At La Guardia she had seen signs for the ferry and decided, on a whim, to take this more romantic form of transport.

The last stop was announced and she disembarked with the remaining passengers. A young man wearing a jacket covered with badges insisted on carrying her suitcases and hailing her a taxi. As it trundled north, she studied the crowded sidewalks with relief. Here, surely, she could be anonymous; here, she and Henry could talk in safety. She had phoned the number he'd given her from the airport and got only an answering machine. Now she asked the driver to drop her near a coffee shop. She dialed Adrian's number from a pay phone and left another message.

She had been sipping mint tea and skimming *The New York Times* for almost half an hour when a pair of hands covered her eyes. She uttered a small scream and wrenched them away. "Christ, Henry. We're not five years old anymore."

He stepped into view, smiling, palms raised as if to show he had no further tricks up his sleeve. He was dressed like an American, with a blue shirt over a black polo neck and pleated black trousers. "Sit down," she said. "What the hell's going on?"

"Let me get some coffee. Do you want anything?"

Several answers sprang to mind, but she shook her head. She watched him approach the counter. He must have made a comment or asked a question because the young man behind the espresso machine laughed. He reached under the counter and held out something that Henry leaned forward to study. As he smiled and talked, Verona had to struggle not to rush over and drag him back to the table. None of this—Nigel and George's threats, his own dire situation, her pursuit—had made the slightest impression on him.

"You'll never guess," said Henry, setting down his cappuccino. "That boy used to work at my friend's restaurant in Notting Hill. I thought he looked familiar."

Too angry to speak, she glared.

"Oh, God." He took a sip of cappuccino and licked the foam from his upper lip. "Are you back on your Trappist kick?"

"Henry, I came all this way because you're in trouble. I'm not going to pretend that everything's fine and we're here for a nice holiday." Even in the midst of her fuming she managed not to mention Zeke; she wanted to protect him from Henry for as long as possible. "If you're not interested in sorting this out, I'll get the next plane to London."

"And conveniently, you're already packed. I'm sorry, I'm an idiot. I do appreciate your efforts. I just can't stare into the abyss

twenty-four/seven, as Neal"——he motioned toward the counter——
"so aptly phrased it."

She had chosen a table by the window, happy to find one free.
Now, in the street, two men strolled by so close their jackets almost grazed the glass. Was that——? Before she could formulate the
question, they had disappeared into the crowd. Across the table
Henry too was staring after the men. Beneath the smooth mask of
charm, she glimpsed the jagged edges of his anxiety. He set down
his cappuccino and began to explain what had transpired since
he threw the miniature whiskey bottles at the window and left her
room. He had spent the day after the blizzard dealing with business matters in London. In the evening he had gone downstairs to
the bar. He was talking to two women from Santa Fe, in Boston to
promote their jewelry, when the bartender asked if he was Henry
MacIntyre and held out the phone. The next thing he knew, Nigel
was yelling at him.

"The last straw," he said, snapping a wooden coffee stirrer in
half, "was that just before he hung up he said hadn't I better buy
my lady friends a drink; they were looking at the bottom of their
glasses. When you told me about coming home to find Nigel and
George, I didn't understand." He shredded an empty sugar
packet. "After all, they didn't hurt you. But it isn't what they actually do that's so frightening. It's the feeling that they could do
whatever they please."

She let his words hang there for four seconds. "So why are we
here?" she said.

"I'm hoping I can persuade Adrian to lend me the money as an
investment."

"Which means you'll still have a huge debt."

"But he won't come after me with a blunt instrument. I'm fairly
sure I can pay him back in eighteen months." He drummed the
table. "Two years tops."

"Why don't you sell your house?"

"That house is my only asset." His voice rose so that even the
boy at the next table, who was listening audibly to heavy metal on

his Walkman, glanced over. "If I lose it, I'll be starting at the bottom, the very bottom."

The place you've never actually been, she thought, but didn't say. Henry was holding forth about London house prices, how the market was out of control, how everyone had to keep moving up not to lose their place, and with every phrase he seemed more like his usual buoyant self, which in turn, she supposed, made him seem more like a man to whom you'd want to lend half a million pounds. "So what are the chances of Adrian saying yes?" she asked.

"I don't know. But I thought you could help me to ask him."

"Ask him what? Make that a soy milk latte, Nigel."

In her imagination, George had loomed large in all possible ways. Now her first thought was how much smaller he was than she remembered, five foot eight, perhaps on tiptoe five nine. He was standing beside their table wearing black jeans, a red shirt, and a gray cardigan, the last obviously hand knitted and a size too large. In one hand he held a briefcase; in the other a leather jacket. "Do you mind if we join you?" he said.

At George's first syllable, Henry had pushed back his chair and half risen. His ears, Verona saw, were scarlet but she was oddly calm. The terror she had felt when Henry had persuaded the manager of the hotel to break into her room, when she had read his letter and known that Nigel and George were in Boston, failed to appear. Her heartbeat remained steady, her skin cool. Of course many people had been injured, even killed, in public places, especially here in the States, but now that she was once again in their presence, she had faith in Nigel and George's self-interest. They wanted money, not carnage.

"Henry," she said warningly. And then to George, "Not at all. Can you find some chairs?"

First, like a finicky waiter, he cleared away their dirty cups and stirrers and napkins and empty sugar packets; then he moved her suitcases closer to the wall; finally he begged a couple of chairs from nearby tables. Verona pushed her chair back from the small table to make room and then, as Henry sat there, eyes downcast, told him to do the same. By the time George had everything organized, Nigel arrived, carrying their drinks, his crooked pinky sticking out in a parody of politeness.

"Hiya," he said brightly. "Henry, Verona. Long time no see." He raised a mug with a mound of whipped cream on top. "Cheers."

"Hello," she said. She caught again the faint smell of cinnamon, but perhaps this time it came from his drink. His green shirt was the exact same velvety shade as the foliage in the pre-Raphaelite painting at the museum. Unlike George, Nigel had remained constant. He was as plump as she remembered, but no more so.

"Dreadful weather," he went on. "I always forget that about America. It's bloody freezing in winter, at least in this part of the country." In the bright light of the café she could see the faint creases of his lower eyelids.

"You must be wondering why we're here," said George, his red lips moving in that exaggerated way she'd noticed before. "We're fed up playing games. You owe us money, Henry. If you can't get it from Betty or some other pal, you can borrow it on your house and put up a FOR SALE sign."

Henry started to speak, stopped, cleared his throat.

"Yes?" said Nigel, patting his mouth with a napkin.

"What we did was illegal," Henry said. "No court would acknowledge your debt."

"You used the crucial pronoun," said George. "*We*. Any court would acknowledge your part in some rather dubious transactions. You'd certainly lose your job and your reputation. Not as valuable as in Shakespeare's day but still worth something." He turned to Verona, and she noted that his head, like her own, was unusually large. "I'm sorry," he said, "if we alarmed you. We don't usually go in for strong-arm tactics, but your brother promised us he had the situation in hand. Then he vamoosed."

"Still"—at the next table the heavy-metal boy got up to leave—"that didn't mean you had to break into my flat."

George nodded. "Nigel used to be a locksmith, and we got a bit carried away. We had the idea that you could bring pressure to bear on yours truly." He had been looking at her as he spoke; suddenly his eyes slid over her shoulder. Following his gaze, Verona discovered that he was watching the departing boy. Oh, she thought. Everything that had happened fell into a new pattern. George too, she understood, had been a victim of Henry's omnivorous charms. Some of the present mess was probably the result of his being a little too obliging, going a little further than he would otherwise have done. The boy, having wound his scarf twice round his long neck and buttoned his jacket, headed for the door. "So," said George, returning his attention to their conversation, "would it be too much to ask what we're doing on the Upper East Side of Manhattan, not exactly my neck of the woods?"

He looked at Verona again, then at Nigel. It was as if the three of them were the adults at the table and Henry was the badly behaved child whose problems they were trying to solve. She felt him squirming beside her and was glad. "Henry has an old friend here," she said, "a businessman, who he thinks might be able to help."

George and Nigel exchanged raised eyebrows. "That didn't seem to work out too well in Seattle," said Nigel. "What's the setup this time?"

There was a pause of several seconds; she nudged Henry's foot, meaning, answer, stick up for yourself. He cleared his throat again. "Adrian went to university with me, and he's always liked England. I'm hoping the bungalows will strike him as a good investment, his very own piece of the old country. Or he could be a shareholder in my company. He's made a killing in cable television."

George took a sip of his latte. "I'm not keen on the bungalow idea," he said. As he listed his reservations—the delays, the strong possibility of the survey report coming to light—Nigel kept saying "Right, right," and even Henry made an involuntary gesture of assent. They might, Verona thought, have been any four English visitors to Manhattan, talking business.

"So," said Nigel, leaning forward with his elbows on the table, "either you're offering him a legitimate investment—in which case you need convincing documents—or you're making this sound like a mercy loan with your house as security, and if this guy has any sense he'll get you to put that in writing. Suing someone transatlantically is a nightmare."

At the counter, the espresso machine let out a burst of steam. "The thing I don't quite get," said George, "is why not go to the bank? If I had the choice of buttering up my bank manager or going cap in hand to an old friend, I know which I'd choose. But none of our beeswax. As long as you pay us, we don't care how."

Two patches of color had appeared below Henry's cheekbones. "Things are a little complicated," he said.

"That's where the personal element comes in," interjected Verona. Her triumph in Henry's discomfort had turned back into the old desire to protect him. "If Adrian knows it's a crisis, he'll understand why Henry can't wait for the bank bureaucracy." She felt as she did sometimes at work when an interview unexpectedly took off, both excited and calm.

"And what sort of crisis takes this much money?"

She hesitated, looking at Henry where he sat low in his chair, arms tightly folded as if even his own embrace was better than nothing. "It's a gamble," she said, "but maybe he should tell a version of the truth."

"Well, it's up to you"—George spread his hands—"but right now we need some security."

"So what we were thinking," said Nigel, "is that we'd hold on to your passport."

"No." She was on her feet, her chair falling backward, the table rocking. "This has nothing to do with me. What if I have an emergency, what if—"

Nigel was standing beside her. He grabbed her arm with his

crooked hand and, just as she opened her mouth to scream, let go. "Sit down," he said quietly. "We don't mean yours. Henry's will be enough."

George righted her chair and she sat down again. Slowly, still giddy from the shock, she resumed her seat. The baby, who had been quiet since she got off the plane, kicked fiercely, as if protesting these sudden antics.

"You can't make me hand over my passport in a public place," said Henry.

"We can't," agreed Nigel. "But we can phone your boss and tell him what's been going on."

As he flipped open his mobile phone and recited a London number, Henry reached into his breast pocket. "What do I have to do to get it back?" he said.

A flurry of negotiations followed. Henry would try to talk to Adrian today. He would suggest a notarized agreement that he could show to Nigel and George. Optimistically, the money could be wired to his bank account within the week.

"One piece of advice," said Nigel. "Don't let him go too long thinking this is a friendly visit."

"Got you," said Henry. "Do you think there's any way to use Verona?"

Now the allegiance had shifted. She was the outsider, and the three men turned to study her. "Wait a moment," she said, clasping her belly.

"Maybe nothing too explicit," said George. "Just suggest that she's worried sick about you. I hope, by the way, you've got medical insurance. You two don't need any more debts."

"Absolutely," said Henry. "As soon as we've spoken to Adrian, we'll be on the next plane."

"All things being equal," said Nigel, holding up the passport.

Perhaps it was the aftermath of the morning's exertions or the sense that a solution was in sight, but as Verona watched them put on their jackets, she remembered her exchange with Henry about the stolen Vermeer. "Do either of you know anyone who's stolen a famous painting?" she asked.

George glanced up from buttoning his jacket. "Art theft? Not our line. I do have a pal who's been involved in a couple of switches— you know, when they nick the real painting and leave a forgery."

"So some of the famous paintings we're looking at in museums are fakes?"

"Almost certainly." He eyed her more closely. "Did you have something in mind?"

Any moment he would be making a note of her request: Renaissance masterpiece, plenty of scarlet and gold leaf, no St. Jeromes please. "I do this radio program," she said, feeling foolish. "I thought it might be an interesting topic."

George inclined his massive head. "Well, we've all got work to do. Phone us as soon as there's news."

One behind the other, he and Nigel deposited their dirty mugs in the dishpan and threaded their way between the tables and through the glass door. Only when they disappeared into the mass of pedestrians did Verona turn back to Henry. "How did they find—" she started to say, but he was already in full voice.

"You idiot. 'I do this program,'" he simpered. "When will you get it into your head that not everything is about you?"

He was sitting bolt upright, his cheeks still flushed, his eyes wide and furious. She stared back with a quick kindling fury that matched his own. Wasn't a resolution finally in view? Hadn't she done well with Nigel and George when Henry was at his most pathetic? But as he continued to rant, she was distracted, first by a feeling, then a thought. The feeling consisted of a stabbing pain in her throat. The thought was that there were absolutely no guarantees that Adrian would agree to the loan. Tentatively she swallowed. Her throat felt as if a fork had been dragged up and down the inside for several days. It must be the central heating, all the changes of temperature. "I'm not feeling very well," she interrupted. "Could we go to Adrian's flat?"

She slept for the remainder of the day and much of the next, and for once the baby, normally at its most energetic when she lay down, moved gently. She woke to drink and go to the bathroom and read a few pages of the book she found by the bed, a thriller set in New Orleans, before slipping back into antic dreams. People came and went—Henry, Adrian, his wife, Suzie, who looked a little like the therapist on the ferry—asking if she wanted anything but she didn't, except more hours of darkness, more sleep. Toward the end of the second day a man appeared at her bedside, a doctor friend of Suzie's, who took her temperature and listened to her chest. "She doesn't have a fever," he said. "All she needs is rest and plenty of fluids."

And somewhere in the midst of this, Henry bent over her to whisper that Adrian had agreed.

On the fourth day she woke at dawn and knew herself recovered. Her elbows and knees, ankles and neck still ached, but her mind was fresh and lucid, like the countryside after a storm. In this landscape one feature stood out, obdurate as Everest. She must talk to Zeke. When she had bathed, dressed, and tried to stay out of Suzie and Adrian's way as they hurried to work, she was at last able to commandeer a phone.

Sitting on the edge of the bed, she noticed for the first time the presence of a large television. The screen gave back her ghostly reflection. All morning she had been longing to hear Zeke's voice; now that she was poised to do so, her palms were slippery and her heart drummed in her ears. She spoke to the hotel switchboard, listened to Pachelbel's canon, spoke to another operator, and at last heard the phone ringing. "The guest you are calling is not available. Please wait for the tone and leave a message." The tone came, insistent and uninviting, and then, even more uninviting, that buzzing silence into which her words were meant to fall. She hung up.

Oh, why wasn't he there, she thought. She needed to talk to him.

So how had Zeke felt, demanded her reflection, when day after day she had left him in silence with no way to reach her?

Whatever scrim had obscured these facts had vanished during her illness. She was acutely, vividly aware of how her behavior must seem from Zeke's point of view. She had tricked him into letting her stay at the Barrows', disappeared with no explanation, invited him to Boston and disappeared again, promised to call and failed to do so. How could any of this make sense to someone who didn't know about Henry? Or how could it make any but the worst kind of sense? And now she and Henry were returning to London. As soon as she emerged from her room, he had taken her aside to ask if she was well enough to travel that evening.

None of this, though, would have stopped her from hurrying to Boston and begging Zeke's forgiveness. What gave her pause was the dream. It had come to her that first evening at Adrian's and several times since. She was at the airport, waiting to board a beautiful white plane. Her row of seats was called; she walked toward the door. But as she reached the threshold of the plane, her water broke and before she could cry out she was surrounded by Americans—Adrian, Suzie, the therapist on the ferry, the men from the hotel—all holding her down, all insisting that she give birth in America. She had woken up, clutching her belly. It was just her subconscious, she thought, processing George's gibe about medical insurance. But every time the baby moved, she was afraid.

In the end she left a message so flat and faltering that as soon as she hung up she wanted to reach into the machine and retrieve it. And she'd forgotten to tell him she'd been ill. If he didn't know that, then she must seem like the most heartless person alive.

Before she could call him back, Henry came in to say that their sandwiches had been delivered. He was in a boisterous mood. "The limousine will be here at three so you can pack after lunch. Come on," he added. "Time to be charming. Let's make Adrian feel that lending me money is the best thing he's done in years."

If she hadn't still been tired, still under the spell of her dream, still at the mercy of these unfamiliar surroundings, surely she would have stood firm and excused herself for five minutes to make the call. As it was she rose and followed Henry docilely out of the room. She would phone from the airport.

Zeke

24

Two or three times an hour, once four, the girl in the seat beside him uttered a series of high-pitched coughs, sounding so much like a small animal that, on the first couple of occasions, Zeke bent down to search the aisle for a stowaway. Save for these periodic eruptions, she sat remarkably still. Perhaps, he thought, she was meditating. Meanwhile, he noticed with surprise that his dread of flying had lessened. Once they were airborne and he had examined each of his fears—being sucked out of the window, landing in water, a turbine bursting into flames, a wing falling off, the pilot having a seizure or deciding, for his own obscure reasons, to head for the Sahara—he was able to settle down to anticipating the nicely partitioned meals and choosing a film. First, though, he got out of his seat and went to the back of the plane to see if he could find the triangular rip in the upholstery he had noticed four days earlier above the toilet door. But the light was poor, and before he could complete his search a flight attendant pointed out that the toilet was free and he felt obliged to go inside.

Apart from the black miasma filling every corner of his skull, leaving America had turned out to be much easier than entering. No plump ventriloquist had questioned him as to why he wanted

to go to London, no dog drooled over his suitcase, no man wearing obscene rubber gloves fumbled through his possessions. Zeke
almost wished they had; a little aggravation might have dispelled
the dreamlike quality of his departure. As it was, only the flecks of
magnolia paint rimming his nails testified to the bizarre events of
the last few days. He had got on a plane, he had stayed in a hotel,
he had explored Boston, and now he was sitting on another plane,
all without seeing Verona.

The day after the conversation with his mother, he had finished
painting Jill's living room and returned to the hotel to find the
message light on the phone once again blinking. Cautiously he
followed the steps Jill had shown him and was rewarded, at last,
with Verona's voice, but not her voice as he remembered it, warm
and inviting. She sounded hoarse and hesitant; she was in New
York, she sent her love, she hoped he was out doing something
nice. Then came a noise like his own *hmm* sound.

"I don't know how to tell you this, but Henry's finally got
things organized and we're flying back to London tonight. I'm so
sorry, but every time I sneeze I'm afraid the baby will come early.
I need to get on a plane while they'll still let me."

He had played the message eight times, each time thinking that
he might hear something different, might hear her saying *I'm in
the lobby*, *meet me at the Fogg Museum*, and feeling more incredu-
lous than the time before when the message ended, "See you in
London; I can't wait." He had always understood the expression
uprooted as a metaphor. Now he avoided looking down for fear
that he would be able to discern the forking white roots that he had
torn so painfully, at such inconvenience and expense, out of the
shallow soil of his life. As he listened, he understood that every
minute since he landed, even those when he claimed to be full of
doubt, he had believed that Verona was about to appear; he would
round a corner, turn over in bed, step into a restaurant, and there
she would be, her lovely, large, specific self.

He had taken refuge in the cupboard with the ironing board,
leaving the door ajar so that he could count the coat hangers lining

the rail and the nails in the molding. Why, he had wondered, for perhaps the four-thousandth time, did he want to be with this woman? She was not beautiful, like Mavis, nor did she seem to need him, like Cecily. But Mavis was taken several times over. As for Cecily, who had been nominally his girlfriend for the last two years of university, he had had the uneasy feeling that compassion played a larger part in their relations than affection; she had shown him the scars on her wrists on their second date, described what a stomach pump felt like on the third. Her vague angst was initially compelling, then terrifying, and finally dull. When he told her that no, he didn't want to meet her parents, no, he didn't want to stay the night, she had wailed like a siren, tried to jump in front of a bus. Sometimes he thought his own breakdown had been partly a way to avoid her, in which case it had been entirely successful. Since his recovery, a series of other women had rung his doorbell or his phone, but an acute sense of his own limitations, and of how quickly both misunderstandings and agreements arose, made him wary. And then, with Verona, something about the way she listened, the stories she told, her dead friend, her sweeping belly, her personal electricity, had made him forget all his sensible doubts and reservations.

When he had counted every hanger and nail hole, he had emerged from the cupboard and phoned Jill to tell her he was leaving as soon as possible. Christ, she had said, you're like a toy on a string. Whatever Verona says, you—

I only came to America, he interrupted, because of her. Why would I stay when she's gone? Apart from anything else, I can't afford it.

Oh, she said, I thought. . . . Then he heard a little gulp, as if she were taking a deep breath, several deep breaths. When she continued her voice had that rusty quality it had had when she was upset about her flat. Forget it. I can't thank you enough for helping me these last few days.

You know my mother isn't well, he had said, and was both pleased and ashamed when, sounding more like her old self, Jill said of course and that if he ever wanted to consult her about medical matters he shouldn't hesitate to pick up the phone. He thanked her and urged her to get in touch when she came back to London. They exchanged addresses.

Only after he hung up did Zeke realize he had forgotten to say anything about her, how he hoped she found true love or whatever she was searching for, but she was on duty at 7 A.M. and he didn't want to disturb her again. Later, in the middle of the night, the phone had rung. Still half asleep, he had picked up the receiver. Hello, he had said. Verona? No one spoke, but as he lay with the phone pressed to his ear, looking up at the tiny light of the smoke detector, he was almost sure he heard another of those gulps.

Now, as he began to eat the omelet the flight attendant had set before him, he calculated that his late-night caller couldn't have been Verona; she was already flying. While the sky outside the oval window lightened and darkened, he watched a romantic comedy and tried not to look at his watch too often. He couldn't wait to be home with his clocks and his neatly organized drawers and well-known street. They were over Ireland, the pilot announced, then the Bristol Channel. Soon he saw a spreading mass of orange lights on the ground below and recognized the city where he lived.

Inside, the terminal was different from America but not immediately like London. He and his fellow passengers walked along endless corridors lined with advertisements to passport control. The woman at the desk barely glanced at his passport, and a few minutes later he retrieved his suitcase. Without Emmanuel, he ignored the sleek expensive train and headed for the underground. As soon as he got on the train and saw the rows of upholstered seats, the abandoned newspapers, the grotty wooden floor, he had the reassuring sense of being close to home.

The plane had landed at five past eight. Soon after ten he turned the corner into his street. The wind ruffled his hair. It was a cold night for London, but still much warmer than Boston. A magnificent stand of white clouds rose up to the south; at the far end of the street, the church steeple stood out like a witch's hat. For a few seconds, looking at his dark house, Zeke entertained the notion that his keys would no longer work. Or that if they did, the flat they admitted him to would be utterly different from the one he had left a few days ago. A flowery three-piece suite would dominate the living room; his bedroom would be lined with huge televisions like the one in his hotel room. Nonsense, he thought, everything will be just where I left it.

But before he went inside, he must check the street. He set his suitcase down in the doorway. In the gloom he made out the two dustbins to the right of his front door. Next door his neighbors' three bins were tucked neatly against the privet hedge. He moved down the street, making an inventory of every house until he reached the corner. He crossed over and did the same on the far side until he was again facing his own unlit house. Suddenly he saw that his imaginings of catastrophic change had been correct, though not their details. The ash tree, two doors down, was gone.

He raced across the road. Perhaps he was misremembering; the tree was farther away than he recalled, four houses down, say, instead of two. But no, here was a stump, calf high, the diameter of a large dinner plate. He bent down to feel the rough grain of the wood beneath his palm. It had been one of the few trees he genuinely liked. Once, during a dodgy period, he had counted the number of larger branches every day: forty-six. Now in a matter of days, a matter of hours, all those years of patient growth had been annihilated. Surely this wouldn't have happened if he had remained at his post. He added it to the list of all he had neglected in his life because of Verona: his father, his mother, his customers, his clocks.

25

He woke, bewildered, to discover it was nearly noon. How had he slept so late? Picturing his hotel room in America, he knew the answer. Some part of him had failed to board the plane, was still loitering in the cupboard with the ironing board or staring at the gloomy thrice-painted St. Dominic. He went through his refrain, begun in boyhood, later adapted: My name is Zeke Antony Cafarelli. I have two arms and two legs. I am a member of *Homo sapiens*, a species of placental mammal that lives on the planet Earth. I live in the metropolis of London at 35b Chester Street, and there are twenty-two white tiles above my kitchen sink.

He bathed, dressed, and, finding that the milk in the fridge was still good, had a cup of tea and a bowl of cereal. Then he forced himself to go into the living room and approach his answering machine. Eleven messages. As he fetched a notebook and pen, he suddenly noticed the silence. For the first time in several years no clock was ticking. Verona, without even touching them, had brought them to a standstill. Four prospective customers had called; Gwen twice; Emmanuel said he'd finished the chef's house; Phil said Mavis was home. His credit card company wanted to confirm his new vigorous usage. The first and last calls were from Verona.

He listened to all the messages once, then a second time, writing down the customers' phone numbers. How often, in the days before his departure, he had hurried home, praying that hers might be among the voices trapped inside the machine. Now it was, and he listened closely as she said she was back in London. "I don't expect you to understand, but could we talk? Please. My number—"

He wrote down the number after those of his would-be customers. His hand moved toward the phone. Then it stopped and moved away. He couldn't have said exactly what his feelings were, but he knew he was not yet ready for more turmoil. Or at least not this kind of turmoil. What mattered now were his parents. He decided to walk to the shop, a journey of half an hour, forty-five minutes at most, that would allow him to become reacquainted with the fire hydrantless streets of his native city.

Even from a distance he could see that the display outside the shop was sparse, but when he stepped inside, the bins of produce were once again full and appetizing. There was no one around; his mother must be in the bathroom or getting something from the cooler. As he stood waiting, he began to pile the bananas into a neat pyramid.

"Can I help you?"

Startled he turned and caught sight of a fair-haired woman, kneeling beside a crate of lemons. The next thing he knew, she had her arms around him and was hugging him so hard his ribs clicked. "You're back," she said.

"Yes," he said obviously, and was glad to hear the shop bell ring.

For the remainder of the afternoon, he left Gwen to charm the customers and worked in the storage rooms, taking out the rubbish, breaking up empty boxes, unpacking full ones, filing delivery notes. Here at last were tasks he knew how to perform, and many of them. By closing time he had the rooms more or less tidy. He pulled down the grill, locked the door, and while Gwen sorted the money went to work on the floor.

As the black and white tiles emerged, gleaming, he sensed something else, less harmonious, also emerging. Once at university, one of the women he shared a house with had come home from a Chinese herbal shop with a piece of mushroom in a jam jar. It's alive, she had told Zeke. All I have to do is keep it in the fridge with fresh water, and it will grow. But why would you want it to? he had said. It's a medicine, Astrid explained. Just a small piece will cure rheumatism or conjunctivitis. He had refrained from pointing out that she was not, as far as he knew, suffering from either. For the first few days she had changed the water regularly, but soon he was the one watching over the mushroom, checking on it daily, sometimes hourly, aware even while he sat in lectures and tutorials of this presence growing larger and blacker and slimier in the fridge. Now, as he scrubbed the entrance to the shop, he thought his mother was like that mushroom; her feelings grew in secret ways he didn't understand. At Christmas, Astrid, still oblivious, had gone home for the holidays. After several days alone in the empty house, Zeke had finally wrapped the dark mass in paper towels and carried it home in the largest plastic container he could muster. The next day he came down to find his parents' fridge empty. His father had thrown it away.

He finished the floor and set the brush and mop to dry beside the cooler. Gwen was at her desk, pressing buttons on the calculator, and for the first time he was able to study her freely. As far as he could judge, she did not look ill, though her nail polish was ragged and her hair separated into little clumps. Maybe he had merely imagined some new feeling pervading the shop.

"Almost done," she said, tapping away. "Do you have time for supper?"

"Yes. Where's Kevin?"

"It's his day off. I got Emmanuel to come and help unload stuff this morning. Have you seen him since his makeover? He's a real fashion plate."

He stared at her, perplexed. Where were the insults and the shouting? As she tapped out a few more numbers, he had a sudden hopeful thought: perhaps her illness had brought about a reconciliation with his father.

The walls of the restaurant, even the ceiling, were a shade of red so close to that of fresh meat that it was like stepping inside a large animal. Not surprisingly, Zeke thought, only one table was occupied. Two bearded men in white shirts were seated in a corner near the kitchen, reading newspapers and drinking out of small tumblers. The waiter, after Gwen had refused a table by the window, seated them beside a wall hung with many small dark pictures, which at least obscured some of the red. "Would you like something to drink?" he said.

Gwen asked for a glass of merlot. "Just water," said Zeke. He rested his eyes on the nearest picture, a church with several spires, conscious that across the table his mother was examining him, her expression not dissimilar from that with which she scrutinized the beetroot or the cress. Only when the wine came did she break her silence. "Well," she said, tilting the glass in his direction, "you've certainly surprised me this time. I'll never complain again about your being stuck in a rut."

"How are you? How's Dad?"

"Don is like I told you on the phone. Butter, if he were allowed it, wouldn't melt in his mouth." She began to speak in an oddly deep voice. "Ooh, you look lovely today. That blouse is so becoming. What a good idea it was to start selling fennel again." She drank some more wine. "He's driving me mad. First he makes it hard to stay with him and now he's making it hard to leave."

"He loves you," Zeke said. Before he could elaborate, the waiter was back, pen poised. Turning to the menu, Zeke discovered that it was handwritten with many impenetrable flourishes and words beginning *ts*. Why had his mother insisted on coming to this lurid restaurant that served something called Georgian food? "Do you have a suggestion?" he asked.

The waiter did. The lamb was very nice, the smoked fish moist, the tripe delicious, the liver tasty, the mutton stew hearty.

"I'll have the lamb," said Zeke, "with vegetables." Gwen said they would each have a bowl of borscht and asked for the special. The waiter scribbled and departed. During the next five minutes he brought bread, water, and bowls of fragrant deep-pink soup at intervals that made conversation difficult. At last they were alone again.

Gwen released her wineglass and reached for a spoon. "I want you to meet Maurice," she said.

So much for his hope that her health scare might yield one good outcome. He blinked several times, trying to hold back his disappointment. "You know I'm bad at meeting people. As you've pointed out four hundred times, I lack the social graces. And what about Dad?" Tentatively he tasted the soup; it was delicious. He took another spoonful and another. He tore off a piece of the dark bread.

The porcelain of the bowl was shining through the last of his soup when Gwen finally answered. "Actually," she said, "in a funny way, because you miss most of the games people play, you're quite a good judge of character. I know"—she must have guessed his amazement—"I've said other things, but at the shop I could see why you put up with Emmanuel. Once he stops messing around, he's a good worker. This soup is nice, isn't it? While you were washing the floor, I phoned Maurice. He'll be here any minute."

So that was what he had sensed in the shop and why she hadn't wanted to sit in the window, normally her preferred location in any restaurant. He turned toward the door, dreading even as he did so that it would open to reveal the notorious Maurice. "I wish you hadn't done that. I'll feel weird with Dad."

"I'm sorry," she said and—another surprise—sounded as if she meant it. "Tell me what's happening with Veronica?"

"Verona," he corrected. He gave the shortest possible version: he liked her; he thought she liked him; it didn't work out.

"But you went to America together?" The corners of her mouth rose. "It seemed so romantic, the two of you flying across the ocean. Especially you, with your phobias."

Why did nothing stay still these days? Even his mother's disapproval was unreliable. "On the phone you said you'd never forgive me. That you and Dad would be in the poorhouse because I'd deserted you."

Gwen ran her fingers through her hair. "Do I look okay? I didn't have time to take a shower this morning. You couldn't have chosen a worse week to bugger off, but of course I'm glad you like someone. You're nearly thirty. You should be settling down."

"Your hair needs combing. And your nose is shiny."

"Thanks." She pushed back her chair. "Now remember, not a word about my little scare."

He watched as she zigzagged between the other tables, several of which, he now saw, were occupied, and then turned to counting the pictures.

"Excuse me, are you Zeke?"

A man wearing a bulky jacket was standing beside the table. Nothing about him looked familiar, but Zeke felt even less trustworthy than usual. "Yes," he said cautiously.

The man held out his right hand. "How do you do? I'm Maurice Shaeffer."

Zeke stood up. The feeling inside his head reminded him of those wretched few minutes when the plane had thudded up and down. Keeping his eyes fixed on the table, he offered his own hand, and as they stood there, palm to palm, a thought alighted amid the chaos: This man has a perfect handshake. He let go, stepped over to the nearest empty table, retrieved a chair, and set it on the third side of their table.

"Thank you," said Maurice. "Are you sure I'm not intruding?"

And then he didn't do what people normally did when they asked such a question, which was to presume the answer they wanted, but stood there, waiting for Zeke to speak.

"We were expecting you. My mother is in the bathroom."

Maurice unzipped his jacket and slipped it over the back of the chair. Beneath he wore a navy blue fisherman's sweater. "I already ate," he said, "but I might have a glass of wine." He glanced around the restaurant, searching for a waiter, Zeke thought, but the men in white shirts had disappeared. His father would have grumbled, perhaps pounded the table, but Maurice simply twitched a shoulder and asked how Zeke's travels had gone.

"Not great. It was very cold and I found America"—he paused, searching for a word that summed up, even partially, his experiences—"confusing."

"I know what you mean. I went to Miami a few years ago, just for a week, but there were two drive-by shootings and the couple in the next room were mugged going to the beach. Gwen's glad you're back."

"Yes. I was at the shop," he said, inanely. From the next table came the clink of cutlery; a stout woman and two small boys were spooning up borscht.

"I tried to help a couple of times," Maurice said, "but I can barely tell a carrot from a cucumber."

How could that be, Zeke wondered. Unlike people, vegetables were easy to identify. "What do you do?"

"I work in a carpet shop—wools, berbers, vinyl, some nice Indian rugs, the so-called Persians. I stumbled into it, a part-time job after school, but I enjoy it. There's a lot to learn about rugs, a lot of history. That's how your mother and I met. She came in to look at carpets, and we started talking about her dream room."

"Her dream room?" He imagined a space like the walk-in cooler where Gwen's dreams were inventoried floor to ceiling, nightmare to pastoral, gothic to romantic.

"Her perfect room, the room where she felt she'd be most herself."

"Which is not a restaurant toilet. I'm glad you found each other." Gwen bent to kiss Maurice.

In a matter of minutes she had transformed herself as surely as Daphne into a laurel. Her face seemed lit from within, her hair gleamed, even her clothes looked newly pressed. Was it really possible that she was in any way ill? As she took her seat, the waiter appeared with their food. He set down the plates and greeted Maurice with a clap on the back. "How are you? We haven't seen you in weeks."

"I'm fine, Leo. Busy, though I suppose that's good. Am I in the way here? How's your sister?"

"The same. I go every Sunday and read her the newspaper. Not very cheerful, but the nurses say I should talk to her and I can't think what to say." Beneath his bristling eyebrows, Zeke saw, the man had small, pleasant eyes.

"She'll come round," said Maurice. "Her body just needs to get over the shock. These are my friends. Gwen, Zeke, my old compatriot, Leo."

The three of them said hello and Maurice asked for a glass of whatever Gwen was drinking. While Leo fetched the wine, he explained that Leo's sister had been in a car accident the day before Christmas and was still in a coma. "Eat," he admonished and, as if to release them from the demands of conversation, began to talk about Russia; two years ago he'd gone to Moscow and St. Petersburg for his holidays. "I went to visit Lenin's tomb in Red Square. That was an odd experience, queuing up to see a dead man. People were chatting away as if they were waiting for a ride at the funfair. And when you finally get to the body—they only let you see it for a moment—it's bathed in this peculiar red light. He reminded me of my father."

"How?" said Zeke. His ravenous hunger had been appeased.

Maurice moved his head up and down. His light gray eyes—it took Zeke several minutes of surreptitious study to figure this out—were set a little farther apart than most people's. In the middle of his chin was a dimple. Zeke pictured him at school, pressing the point of his pencil there, hour after hour.

"I wonder that myself," Maurice said. "I suppose the main thing was that you never knew what my dad was thinking. My sisters and I counted on our mother to translate. Of course"—he drank some wine—"it's not fair to judge a man by his eighty-year-old corpse. Did you ever see the dead chap at the British Museum?"

"What chap?" said Gwen. "You do ramble on." But the three little lines that often appeared between her eyebrows to emphasize such remarks remained in hiding.

"They have him upstairs, near the Portland vase. He was found in a bog in Norfolk, and when they examined the body they discovered he'd been garroted. They think he was a sacrificial victim." He looked back and forth between Gwen and Zeke. "Sorry, history is one of my hobbies. As your mother says, I do tend to go on. Especially when I'm nervous."

Why would he be nervous, thought Zeke, and, seeing the way his mother smiled at Maurice, understood. "If I'd been given a choice," he said carefully, "I'd have tried to get out of meeting you, but I'm glad I wasn't. You're not at all like I'd imagined."

"I'm not like most people imagine," said Maurice. "You don't expect someone with a French name to have ancestors who farmed the steppes, but my mother adored Maurice Chevalier. It could have been worse. She was mad about Bob Hope too."

"In Boston I met a man called Chance. His mother was joking with the nurses at the hospital, and they wrote it down on his birth certificate."

The waiter came over to see if everything was all right. Maurice ordered more wine; Gwen and Zeke said they were fine. Then Maurice asked how things had gone at the shop. He and Gwen talked about a film they wanted to see, and he said that tomorrow he was measuring the function rooms of a hotel near King's Cross. "Years ago, when I was first starting in carpets, I botched the measurements of a ballroom. What a disaster. You must have things like that in your work."

Now that Zeke had started to look at Maurice, he couldn't stop.

The dimple moved as he spoke and so did the rest of his face, as if all his features were participating in the conversation. So entranced was Zeke that it wasn't until his mother said, "Tell him about that kitchen," that he understood that Maurice's last remark had been addressed to him. Under her prompting, he described the time he'd fitted new kitchen cupboards so high that the owner of the house couldn't reach the bottom shelf. On another occasion he'd tiled an entire bathroom in white rather than blue, but the owner had welcomed the change. Maurice asked who bore the cost. Then he finished his wine and announced that he must be on his way.

"I'm glad we got to meet at last," he said to Zeke. "I've heard so much about you." And for once the familiar comment sounded appreciative rather than sinister. He stood up, put a ten-pound note on the table, kissed Gwen, shook Zeke's hand again, and turned to leave. On his way out he stopped to chat at a couple of tables. Neither Zeke nor Gwen spoke until the door closed behind him.

"Well?" she said.

"I like his dimple."

"His dimple?" Gwen's eyebrows flew upward.

He pointed to his own smooth chin. And quite suddenly his mother, like Jill when he asked if she'd noticed a paint shop, was laughing. "Oh, Zeke, you're priceless. Seriously." She leaned closer. "Did you like him?"

"Yes, I did." The answer leaped out as if it had nothing to do with him. "And I could see why you liked him. He paid attention, and he told good stories."

Gwen sank back in her seat. "I shouldn't have sprung him on you, but I was sure if I asked you'd refuse. You know, he and I have the same birthday. We only have one horoscope between us."

A sharp pain stabbed his chest as if someone had slipped a stiletto between his ribs. When was Verona's birthday? He had no idea. Bugger off, he thought, meaning the pain, Verona, the whole mess. "But what about the doctor, Mum? You never answered my question."

She clutched her glass. "They're doing a biopsy on Monday. I'm scared, Zeke. You know how long it usually takes to get an appointment. It makes me think I must be at death's door and I don't even feel ill. I'm only forty-five. I don't deserve this."

Whatever transformation she had accomplished in the bathroom had worn off. Almost from one minute to the next, the lines around her eyes were deeper, her cheeks thinner. This was what she would look like in ten years' time. "Illness isn't something we deserve," he said, quoting he couldn't remember whom. "It's a part of life. We do our best to stay healthy, and it comes along anyway. Like me, like Dad." He reached across the table and touched her hand. "Would you like me to go with you to the hospital?"

"I'm not at death's door." She patted his hand. "Don will come with me. What I really need you to do is mind the shop. We could close for the day, but we've got all the produce rotting away if we don't shift it."

"You'll leave the money in the usual place?"

"Of course," she said, and made a scribbling motion to the waiter.

Zeke had been feeling deeply sorry for himself, but as he walked home through the lamp-lit streets he spared a moment of sympathy for his mother, worried about her own health, burdened by his father's, struggling to choose between old loyalties and new affections. Imagine, he thought, being with a man who would take you to visit the embalmed body of a dictator. He passed a pub, still loud with conversation, and paused to examine the display outside a late-night shop. The cauliflowers looked surprisingly fresh, but the bananas were almost black and the peppers limp and shriveled. Zeke resisted the impulse to pick them out and throw them away. Inside, half a dozen men were standing around the counter, holding cans of beer and watching television. For some reason, he thought of Jill. What was her word for today, he wondered.

26

In his parents' modest front garden, Zeke raised his hand to ring the bell. One of his doctors had explained the way people greet each other—*hello, how are you?*—by saying it was like ringing a doorbell to see if the other person was home. So why can't I just ignore them, Zeke had said. Like Mum and Dad do when it's someone collecting for charity, or Mrs. Gillespie from across the street. The trouble is, said the doctor, clicking his pen, they can see that in a certain sense you *are* home, and so not answering seems rude. It's as if your mother and father were sitting in the window when Mrs. Gillespie rang the bell. Zeke had protested that it wasn't fair for people to always assume he was home. I'm sorry, the doctor had said, I don't make the rules. I'm simply explaining the prevailing customs. During this century, in the West, we expect a certain consonance between body and person. When the former is present, we assume the latter is too, except in cases of sleepwalking or mental illness. So *hello, how are you?* isn't really like ringing a doorbell, said Zeke. Right, said the doctor. Maybe forget the bell.

Now Zeke lowered his hand and studied the forsythia. The last time he had been here, before he left for Boston, he had been in love with Verona and there had been one hundred and eleven flowers in bloom. Today he wasn't sure how to describe his feelings. There had been another message from her on the machine, but once again he had left the house without phoning her; as for the flowers, bobbing in the wind, they foamed in all directions, too many to count. He was searching for some other source of numerical comfort when the door opened to reveal a ruddy-cheeked man wearing a blue fleece.

"Zeke," he said. "You're back."

Just before the man's arms closed around him, Zeke glimpsed to the left of his windpipe a livid scar, the faint dots of the stitches on either side still visible. "Dad," he said, trying not to make it sound like a question. He counted the blooms on the nearest spray of forsythia—thirteen—and did his best to relax. As the arms slackened and the man stepped back, Zeke pieced together the limbs and features of his father, whom he had known for twenty-nine years: the broad lopsided shoulders, the eyebrows beginning to bristle, the prominent wrist bones and broad hands.

"I phoned you a few minutes ago," Don said. "You must have already been on your way. I was about to go for my walk. Come and say hello to Long John Silver, and then you can tell me all about your travels."

Not all, thought Zeke, following his father to the living room. How could he explain that he had flown three thousand five hundred and thirty-eight miles to meet a woman and failed even to lay eyes on her? Carefully ignoring the piano and the bust of Beethoven, he crossed the room to view the parrot. It was hanging upside down from its perch. "Say hello," said his father. "He's got a vocabulary of eighteen words so far."

The parrot eyed Zeke, swung himself upright, and said, "Hello," in a voice exactly like Don's.

"Good boy," said his father, offering a seed between the bars. "Best present I ever had. Thanks."

Zeke repeated the words he had heard so often in America. "You're welcome."

Outside, they both commented on the wind. Zeke remarked how well his father was looking. Don agreed. "I turned a kind of corner," he said, as they literally did the same. "When I was in hospital I couldn't stop raging about why this terrible thing had happened to me. Suddenly I understood that I had it back to front. What I should be asking is why am I one of the lucky buggers who are saved? I had an attack but I'm not pushing up the daisies. According to the doctor, I could have another twenty or thirty good years if I keep exercising and stay off the fish and chips."

On the other side of the street a tall slender woman was walking a swaybacked dog.

"Now of course," his father continued in lower tones, "there's this business about your mother."

Zeke placed each foot carefully in the middle of a paving stone. His father's eyes were fastened on him. Three stones. At school he had asked several of his teachers why he could feel people looking at him, almost as if their eyes were reaching out and touching him; none of them had offered a convincing explanation. Eleven stones.

"She did tell you?"

He moved his head up and down, hoping to loosen his father's gaze. Fifteen. Sixteen.

"I'm sure she's going to be fine. Ninety percent of these lumps turn out to be harmless. They just need to be sure."

They reached the intersection and, to Zeke's surprise, came to a halt. His father had always used to plunge into the road, as if daring the cars to run him down. Now he waited patiently until there was a gap in the traffic. Inside the park he strode out, arms swinging. Zeke loped beside him. In the middle of the grass, half a dozen of the usual black birds were standing around on their sooty legs. They weren't making any sound he could hear, but he had the impression from the way they cocked their heads that they were sending messages back and forth about which bench offered the tastiest sandwich crusts and where to find nesting materials. Oh, Verona, he thought. He said the first thing that came into his head. "When the plane came down in Boston, it bounced like those birds do when they land."

"How was the flight? I must say your mother and I were gobsmacked. After all these years of saying you couldn't fly, you get on a plane for seven hours."

"It was okay. Once we were in the air I could see that no one else was afraid. A woman across the aisle helped me to watch a film. Then we had to rescue—" He broke off, realizing it might be tactless to mention the heart attack and the spooky-voiced defibrillator.

"What?" His father walked even faster. "So, it didn't work out with this woman?"

Again he felt Don's eyes upon him and again he did his best to avoid them, falling several yards behind. What was the answer to that question? He thought he had found a person who understood his shortcomings without sharing them, who could make sense of the world, who knew that the heart of Robert the Bruce was the ultimate weapon. And maybe—he wanted to be fair—all those things were true, but the same person also urged him to get on a plane one day and forgot all about him the next. He recalled how Verona had described her parents, her talkative father, her mendacious mother, and claimed that she took after both of them. She had warned him but he hadn't listened. A clattering noise interrupted his thoughts. An empty beer can was blowing along the path. With one stride, he caught it underfoot and flattened it.

His father stopped and waited. "You'll find someone soon," he said. "A good-looking hard-working boy like you isn't going to get left on the shelf."

I don't want someone, Zeke almost shouted, I want Verona. And at once added, no, I don't. What I want is to have my brain back, my normal predictable life. He thought of the Romans tilling salt into the fields of their enemies. Was there some mental equivalent that would eradicate these longings? A child—a boy, he decided—was pedaling toward them on his tricycle. He and his father separated, giving him a wide berth.

"How do you think matters stand with your mother?" Don swung his arms out before him. "Other than her health?"

Zeke turned his attention to the birds. If they felt his eyes, they didn't show it. There were seven now. Had he miscounted before, or had a new one arrived? It was like the ash tree. Things changed when he wasn't watching.

"I won't bite your head off," his father was saying. "I'm actually glad you told me. I was so stuck in my own misery I didn't see I was driving her away."

Seven beaks, fourteen wings, fourteen feet.

"Careful."

He looked down in time to avoid a pile of dog turds.

"People with dogs," said his father. "Christ."

"I wonder if we'll see the rabbit today."

"The rabbit?"

"Last time we were here a woman was walking a rabbit on a lead. Brown with floppy ears."

"Zeke." Don grabbed his arm. "I need your help. I know your mother and I have had our differences—we're both too stubborn for our own good—but I don't want to lose her."

Zeke stared down at his father's hand, the nails slightly ridged, pale with pressure. He pictured Maurice, his dimple waxing and waning, as he talked about Lenin's tomb. He pictured his mother, standing in the doorway of his kitchen, admonishing him, whatever happened, to say nothing more to his father. "Dad, I'm sorry I can't help. This is between you and Mum. Ask her your questions."

The fingers grew paler. "You son of a—"

Zeke kept himself, every bone and muscle, absolutely still.

His father let go, his hands falling by his sides. "Please," he said, as if he were carrying a huge trunk up a narrow staircase. "I need to know whether she's still planning to leave me."

Zeke watched three of the birds rise in clumsy circles toward the leafless treetops. And just like the last time he had gone for a walk with his father, he followed them, fleeing down the path toward the gate, heedless of Don's cries.

⌒

So long as his legs were moving his head remained empty, but—as he turned into his street and his pace slowed—the familiar thoughts began to show up. As he fitted his key in the front door, there she was quoting *Steppenwolf* and dropping her boots. Climbing the stairs, he recalled her descending in her crumpled green dress to press her lips to his. Be gone, he admonished. But what was he left with? For a few seconds he could not think of a single thing he had ever done besides pursue Verona. Nonsense, he had all kinds of hobbies: having nervous breakdowns, fixing clocks, seeing his friends, disappointing his parents.

It took every molecule of willpower to go and sit in the kitchen without looking at the answering machine. "I have to be very careful," he said aloud.

And even as he said the word *careful* he was on his feet and, as if some huge magnet had pulled him there, standing beside the machine. It was flashing the number 4.

Mavis, whom he recognized at once, answered the door, wearing a kimono the color of the sea in a Japanese painting and holding Brenda. "Zeke," she exclaimed. "What a surprise." She kissed him on the cheek and said how glad she and Brenda were to see him. This last seemed quite untrue. The baby's arms and legs were pumping furiously, as if she were swimming in the deep water of her mother's robe, and when he bent to kiss her she gave a little yelp.

In the kitchen, Mavis set Brenda on a blanket on the floor and offered him tea and, if he'd stay for supper, macaroni and cheese. Then she asked if there was any news about Gwen. As he explained that the biopsy was tomorrow, she moved around the kitchen, kimono swishing, getting things out of the cupboards and the fridge.

"Your mother is so brave," she said, handing him a wedge of cheese and a grater. "Do you mind?"

She bent down to ask Brenda which she'd prefer for supper: pureed carrots or potatoes and peas. How Brenda announced her choice he couldn't tell, but within a few minutes she was seated in her high chair, the agitated owner of a bowl of green mush. While Mavis coaxed her to eat, Zeke made tea for both of them, grated the entire block of cheese, drained the noodles, and made the sauce. When the casserole was in the oven and Brenda was absorbed in banging her stuffed elephant with a wooden spoon, he at last asked after Phil and learned that he was out on his rounds, tuning pianos. "He fell terribly behind while I was away," Mavis added.

Away, he knew, meant sleeping with the market gardener—or was it a Portuguese sailor?—but Mavis showed no sign of remorse. Instead she asked how he was after the big trip. "Forgive my saying so," she said, "but you seem a little glum."

"Verona doesn't care for me."

"Oh." Mavis wrinkled her nose. "How do you know?"

He described the utter failure, at every stage, of his journey to Boston. "Well," Mavis said, as he fell silent, "I have to say it sounds as if you've broken up without ever getting together."

Zeke clutched the edge of the table and stared at his knees. Why did he feel as if she had raised a saucepan and brought it down, hard, on his head? In spite of everything, it seemed he had been hoping that Mavis, an expert on unorthodox romance, would find a way to contradict him. He was in the midst of once again expelling Verona from some niche or alcove when Phil arrived home.

To his own surprise, but not apparently theirs, Zeke accepted Phil and Mavis's invitation to spend the night. Lying on the sofa, staring up at the glow of the streetlights seeping through the blinds, he pictured his answering machine blinking away: 4, 4, 4. Or perhaps now some other number: 5 or 6 or 7. Was her voice one of those inside the machine? Almost certainly. Now, when he didn't know what to do with her messages, she called all the time. From the room above came Mavis's rather heavy tread and lilting tones, followed by Phil's saying a single unmistakable word: Yes. Yes to what, he wondered. Yes, the macaroni and cheese was good? Yes, you can run away with an underground engineer? Yes, let's have another baby?

Zeke was struck again by the unknowable nature of other people. Other things, when you got close, revealed themselves — clocks, doorbells, trains, wallpaper steamers—but humans only grew more puzzling with proximity. Look at Phil, who for ten years he had believed hated untidiness and who was now thriving amid disorder. Had Zeke been wrong about him? Or had Phil been wrong about himself? Once again he recalled the story of Verona's grandparents. He imagined the two of them, having lunch together that damp March day, talking about the plumber and the war. And afterward Jigger sitting reading the paper, until Irene shouted from the kitchen, "I've taken poison, Jigger. I've taken poison."

Throughout a decade of marriage, she had concealed from her husband the most important facts about herself: her living parents, her dead lovers, her despair. Now his own parents, after more than quarter of a century, were growing increasingly estranged. His conviction that he and Verona knew each other in some special way was mere vanity; by his best reckoning they had spent seventeen hours in each other's company. If she had been waiting in America and they had gone on to live together, he would have had to endure the knowledge that at any hour, of any day, she might set fire to the house, come home with twenty dogs, sail naked down the Thames.

In the shadowy darkness there was nothing tangible to count. I'll count forms, he thought. He pictured the three kinds of triangles: scalene, isosceles, equilateral; then a pyramid, a circle, a sphere, a square, a cube, a rectangle, a parallelogram, a trapezoid, a spiral. Arnold, the counselor who had taught him the *hmm* sound, claimed that was how he should visualize his return to health. I don't feel better, Zeke had been insisting. After all these months I'm still afraid I might suddenly be unable to leave the house or that the paving stones will swallow me up. Arnold made that sucking sound which, Zeke had learned, indicated exasperation. You don't feel better, he said, but take my word for it, you are. This isn't like taking the train from London to Brighton, a few delays but basically a straight journey in one direction. You'll feel better, then worse, then better, but the better periods will get longer, and eventually you'll be sure that they'll return. No one feels good all the time. Not even you, said Zeke. Not even me, said Arnold firmly.

By the next morning, the cold wind of the previous day had brought rain. As Zeke drove through the choked streets toward the shop, he wondered if maybe he could avoid the answering machine forever. Move to another flat, buy whatever he needed at the Oxfam shop, change his name. Or perhaps he could give away the machine and change his phone number. She'd call for a few days, a week at most. What she was suffering from, he guessed, was not love but guilt: the feeling you had when you'd done something irreversible and wished you hadn't. But soon he would disappear from her brain as surely as the Chinese mushroom had disappeared from his flatmate's. When Astrid returned after the Christmas holidays, he had been braced to explain how he'd been doing his best to protect it, but his father had thrown it out before he could stop him. She had never once inquired about the former occupant of their fridge.

As he pulled up at the rear of the shop, he saw a white rectangle hanging limply from a nail in the middle of the back door. For a nanosecond he thought that Verona had made her way here, through rain and wind, to leave him another letter, but as soon as he was close enough to read his own name—*Zeek*—he guessed that Kevin was making his excuses for the day. Which was fine by him. He didn't care for his mother's swaggering shop boy with his endless chat about football and nightclubs.

Despite the rain the shop was busy, and for once Zeke was grateful for the events that normally rattled him: greeting the customers, watching them pinch and pummel the produce, answering questions about whether he would have pineapples or mangoes or star fruit anytime soon, fussing with bags and change. At six-thirty, while he was offering Ray, from the fishmonger's next door, half price on a bunch of spinach and a pound of tomatoes, the door swung open and his father was suddenly in the middle of the shop.

"She's going to be okay. It was benign. There's nothing to worry about. She's fine. Fine!"

Zeke understood instantly. His mother might be hit by a car tomorrow, but for today she was saved. While his father reeled around the shop, embracing first Ray and then him, making a clumsy attempt to juggle three lemons, he felt the muscles of his face forcing his eyes open, pulling at the corners of his mouth. Like his father, he was beaming uncontrollably.

"Come and have a drink," Don said. "We're celebrating."

"Dad, I have to close the shop. Why don't you and Ray go? I'll come round as soon as I'm done."

"Close the shop," said his father, "or leave it wide open. Let everyone help themselves. Not often you get two lucky breaks in the same family. I know this sounds like one of your daft ideas"—he hefted a cabbage like a bowling ball and looked over at Zeke—"but I kept worrying that Gwen was going to pay for my good fortune."

Gently Zeke set down Ray's spinach and tomatoes. Why, he thought, was he so absurdly slow to comprehend even the most obvious things? Of course you didn't get good fortune for nothing. And if Don didn't pay and Gwen didn't pay, then the account was still due and, in his small family, that left him. No wonder

Verona kept abandoning him. In the cosmic economy she had had no choice but to punish him. And now, he surmised, he was punishing her, to settle her brother's account.

So many things were different that in the pub, when his father asked what he was having, Zeke said a pint of bitter. Then—several neighbors and friends had gathered and people kept jumping up to buy rounds—he had two more. He had a lengthy conversation about foxhunting with Ray and, more plausibly, he discussed new bus routes with his aunt. As he walked home through the lingering drizzle, he finally understood why people drank. Nothing had changed, but he didn't mind as much. Inside his flat, he wasn't even tempted to go into the living room. He brushed his teeth, drank a glass of water, and climbed into bed. He was about to fall asleep when it occurred to him—he'd listened to people talk about drinking for years—that he should set the alarm clock. He sat up, pressed the buttons, and let sleep roll over him.

The next morning as he drove toward Emmanuel's house, he experienced a new respect for his old friend. If this was how he felt most days, it was astonishing that he even got out of bed, let alone came to work and wielded paintbrushes and power tools. The mysterious word *hangover* now made perfect sense. Someone seemed to have walked through his brain and hung heavy dark curtains across doorways and windows. He turned into Emmanuel's street and there was his friend, leaning against the wall in front of the house, smoking a cigarette. For nearly three years, morning after morning, Zeke had double-parked, jumped out to ring the doorbell, and sat behind the wheel, hoping that the flashing of his indicator conveyed his apologies to other motorists as they squeezed past.

"Where have you been?" Emmanuel said, as he clambered in. "I thought you must have had an accident."

"I didn't think you'd worry. You're often late."

"But you're always on time. Your being ten minutes late is like me being ten hours late. How was America?"

Zeke moved his shoulders up and down. No sentence, not even many of them piled together, would convey what he had been through since Emmanuel bade him farewell at Heathrow. On the phone when he had called to make arrangements about their new job—painting an empty flat for a letting agent—Emmanuel had asked the same question and he'd changed the subject.

"What do you mean?" Out of the corner of his eye he saw Emmanuel wriggling his shoulders in imitation. "Did you like Boston? What happened with Verona?"

"It was cold. Nothing happened."

"Nothing? How could nothing happen when you were in a hotel together?"

Bleakly Zeke sketched the main events of his journey. "Can we talk about something else? I got drunk last night."

As he had hoped, that distracted Emmanuel. Then there was buying the paint and having breakfast. By nine o'clock, drop cloths spread, radio playing, they were filling the walls and masking the woodwork. The flat was a soulless, modern conversion. No wonder, Zeke thought, that the future tenant had requested tangerine paint for one wall in the living room and a mixture of blues and greens for the kitchen and bathroom. He got through the day by counting cups of tea, glasses of water, aspirin, how often the radio played certain songs, how often Emmanuel went outside to smoke, but no amount of counting could stave off five o'clock. As they made their way downstairs, Emmanuel suggested they wait out rush hour at the pub.

"I can't," said Zeke. "It made me feel—"

"I don't care what you drink, lemonade, water, but we need to talk."

He was still stammering out objections when Emmanuel seized his arm, as his father had done a couple of days before, and led him down the street. At the main road there were two pubs on opposite corners. They chose the one named after a British prime minister.

"So let me get this straight," said Emmanuel, when they were settled at a corner table with a pint of beer and a glass of water. "Verona went to Boston because of some kind of crisis with her brother. She asked you to join her. At the hotel there was a letter saying she'd gone to New York, again because of the brother, but would be back soon. Then you got a phone call saying she was flying back to London."

"Yes."

"Weird." He shook his head. "I've known chicks to do some crazy things, but this wins the prize. Especially when she's big as a house. Although maybe that has something to do with it. You know, hormones." He sat back in his chair and stared across the table. Zeke did his best not to look away. There was something in the middle of Emmanuel's forehead, in the place where Indian women wore their bindi; presently he recognized it as a smudge of tangerine paint.

"With anyone else," said Emmanuel, "I'd say run while the going is good. Who needs this level of aggravation? But I've known you for three years, and I've never seen you interested in anyone before. I don't get why Verona clicks with you, but maybe you should try to find out what's going on. Give her a chance to explain."

"I don't believe in explanations." It was something one of his doctors had said.

"Oh, crap. Who told you that? Some effing doctor."

For nearly an hour they wrangled back and forth, Emmanuel stubbornly insisting that Zeke should give Verona a second chance. "It wouldn't be the second," said Zeke. "It would be the third, the tenth." He was surprised to hear his own voice sounding so firm and definite.

"Who's counting? When you were in a bad way people gave you a hundred chances."

But Zeke continued to cling to the few facts he could articulate. He had done whatever she asked, deserted his parents, turned his world upside down, and in exchange she had given him nothing but loneliness, expense, boredom, heartache. "I didn't decide not to talk to her," he told Emmanuel, "any more than I decided to fall for her. Every time I go to phone her I can't make myself do it. My feelings have changed."

"So," Emmanuel said, getting to his feet, "they can change back. The course of true love never did run smooth."

He headed for the Gents, leaving Zeke to ponder this claim. Was it true that his feelings could change, again and again: that one day he would drink his coffee white, one sugar, the next prefer it black with three? How could he navigate the world if everything, including himself, was in flux? Maybe other people—his parents, Emmanuel—could manage these twists and turns, but he couldn't. When I get home, he vowed, I'll listen to the answering machine and erase her messages and that will be that. He was about to explain all this to Emmanuel, but his friend was hurrying toward the table, brow furrowed, shoulders stiff.

"I forgot I promised Gina to buy the groceries," he said, reaching for his jacket. "Can you give me a lift to the tube?"

He listened to her messages, one by one by one, trying not to hear the words—the pleading, the requests, the explanations and supplications—trying to simply let her voice wash over him. He had heard of people who turned sound into color. Now he lay down on the floor, closed his eyes, and tried to let the colors of her voice wash over him. He caught flashes of scarlet and gold and a deep earthy brown he had seen in a tapestry at the Victoria and Albert Museum. It had belonged to some queen—Anne? Victoria? Mary?—he couldn't recall. But at times, when her voice broke or strained, he glimpsed something else, a timorous yellow, a fearful mauve, the faintest edge of violent blue. Sometimes she sounded like Cecily at her most desperate, like the other women who had pursued him with such unnerving disregard for his inclinations.

He didn't know how long he lay there listening, pressing RE-PEAT over and over. His clocks chimed quarter hours, half hours, and finally twelve distinct strokes. Midnight, he thought, the witching hour. He listened to her words one more time and pressed ERASE. Then silence. Did silence have a color? He stood up and restored the machine to its position on the table. If only there were a button he could press in himself. He had asked one of his doctors about this, the one who had compared greeting people to ringing a doorbell, why certain thoughts came up over and over again, even when he didn't want them to. That's a very interesting question, the doctor had said. Everyone experiences this to some degree. The only thing I can suggest, as soon as you notice it happening, is try to interrupt. Music can help. Some people find a powerful smell—mint, lavender—works for them. Or a brisk walk. In your case it's especially important to break the cycle before it takes over.

Too late for music, he thought, it would disturb his neighbors, and mint would only remind him of the shop. He walked from room to room, searching vainly in his neat bedroom, his immaculate kitchen, for something that would finally, irrevocably banish Verona. At last—he wasn't at all sure it would work—he unplugged the answering machine, put it in a shopping bag, seized the trowel he used to tend his window boxes, and let himself out of the flat.

Almost at once, even passing the stump of the ash tree, he felt fractionally better. The night was cloudy, starless, moonless. Years from now, he thought, perhaps I'll tell someone about my adventures with Verona and the stupid thing I did one night. He made his way through side streets to the local park. He walked across the grass, past the scorched circle marking the Guy Fawkes bonfire, until he reached the row of houses where, late one evening after reading Jigger's notebook, he had watched the man and two women. Tonight all the lights were off and he wasn't sure which house it was. No matter. He paced thirty feet away from the leafless plane trees, knelt down on the damp grass, and began to dig.

The ground was surprisingly hard, and in the dark it was difficult to figure out what he was doing. It must be tricky, he thought groping around with the trowel, for blind people to garden. He did his best to pile the soil in one place. After several attempts he at last had a hole large enough to accommodate the answering machine. He wound the cords tightly around its body and set it down in the earth. "Good-bye, Verona, good-bye, Ms. F," he said. "Fare thee well."

Then he pushed the soil back on top, stamped it down, and covered it with the few ragged pieces of grass he had managed to save. Probably there was some law against this, he thought, burying a machine in a public park. If charged he would explain that it was an emergency. He bowed once to the grave and turned toward home. At the first rubbish bin, he threw away the shopping bag and the trowel. A waste of both, but he wanted no part of her to reenter his home, or his brain.

Verona

27

At every stage of Verona's departure from America, difficulties arose. The limousine, which Adrian had booked to take her and Henry to the airport, arrived late; an accident choked the highway; the airport itself, once they located the correct terminal, was a maelstrom of confusion. Almost no one spoke English. The loudspeaker announcements were incomprehensible. The lines to check in tangled across the concourse; so did the lines to get through security. By the time Verona was free to call Zeke, she and Henry were at the gate and the plane was boarding. At the row of phones she squeezed in between a man in a fake fur coat and a girl in a powder-blue tracksuit and dialed the number of the hotel in Boston. As she listened to the phone ringing, she remembered telling Zeke how she had written the names of everyone she wanted to get rid of on her bedroom wall and painted over them. That was what they would do with America. After a dozen rings the hotel operator answered. She was on hold, waiting for the switchboard, when she felt Henry tugging at her sleeve.

"V, we have to go. You can make all the phone calls you want from London."

Like an echo came an unusually clear announcement: last call for London. Furious with herself, with the tediously slow hotel staff and the punctual flight, Verona relinquished the phone and followed Henry down the jetway. As soon as she entered the no-man's-land of the plane, she knew she had done something irrevocably stupid. Nothing was more important than talking to Zeke. Besides, her suitcases were in the hold; they wouldn't have left without her. She let Henry go ahead and turned back down the aisle. She was almost at the door when a flight attendant stepped in front of her.

"Madam, the door of the plane is closed."

For as long as it took to blink, Verona imagined clutching her belly, complaining of pains. But that would be inviting the dream to come true. She allowed herself to be ushered back to her seat. Slowly, implacably, the plane rolled away from the gate.

"What was that about?" said Henry. "Are you all right?"

"I made a terrible mistake."

"Tell me about it. I'm a master of mistakes and how to survive them."

He was leaning back in his seat, his eyes closed. Studying him at close range, she noticed for the first time in years the tiny scar just below his hairline where, one winter afternoon, he had cut his head on a radiator while they were playing catch. As the plane accelerated down the runway and into the air, she finally confided in Henry. She began with finding Nigel and George in her flat and went on to describe her appeal to Emmanuel, her meeting with Zeke and their day together, Toby's frightening fax, her precipitous departure to America, and how she had invited Zeke to Boston, only to find herself going to New York.

"You mean"—Henry opened his eyes and turned to look at her—"he came all the way to Boston, expecting to see you, and you weren't there."

"Yes."

"And you didn't speak to him just now?"

She gave a small, miserable shake of the head. If Henry was shocked, matters were even worse than she'd imagined. He reached over and patted her knee. "Poor Verona. What a lot of trouble I've caused you. But look on the bright side. You would never have met him if it hadn't been for my bad behavior."

Somehow that twisted fact, and Henry's pride in it, did make her feel slightly better. "Do you think he'll ever forgive me?" she said.

"You *are* in a bad way if you're asking me that." Then, seeing that she was beyond teasing, he went on to explain his theory of lovers' quarrels: the real problem was not forgiveness but coming to terms with lost illusions. "People can forgive each other until the seas run dry, but if you've lost the feeling that the other person is special and amazing then it doesn't help much."

As he spoke, the noise of the plane's engines shifted to a lower note; they had reached their cruising altitude. "So is that what you think about Betty," she said, "that your relationship was based on illusions?"

"Well, certainly on her side. She had the bizarre notion that I was a nice person. As for mine, I wish I'd had the chance to find out. I probably idealized her hopelessly as the rich beautiful socialist."

"Are you going to get in touch with her?"

"I change my mind twenty times an hour. Unless some miracle occurs—she catches me rescuing a drowning child or giving my wallet to a blind man—I don't think much is going to change. She doesn't trust me, and who can blame her?"

"Maybe I could talk to her." As soon as the words were out Verona was struck by her own contrariness. Her brother had betrayed her twenty times over, yet the old habits of loyalty persisted.

"Maybe," he said vaguely. And then, "Yes, if you explained what had happened—how I was tempted and fell but it doesn't mean I'm rotten to the core—perhaps she'd understand. I could talk to Zeke." He was sounding more confident by the syllable. "Tell him it was all my fault you'd abandoned him in Boston."

Would that help, she wondered. She had no idea. As two flight attendants approached with the drinks cart, Henry, still enthusing about this plan, asked for her mobile phone and entered Betty's number in the directory.

"A gin and tonic, please," he said, and then, to her, "If you were drinking, I'd order champagne."

"Bring it to the hospital in six weeks. When I was ill I kept having this dream that the baby was going to be born in America."

"Not exactly a fate worse than death. It would have been nice for our new relative to have joint citizenship. So who's the father?"

His voice was so casual that for a few seconds she nearly told him the truth. "Oh, no, you don't," she said. "It's quite enough that you'll be an uncle. You don't need to know anything more than that."

"After all we've been through." He sighed theatrically and raised his glass.

"After all we've been through, I have two questions for you, or a question and a request."

"Let's do the request first, while I'm still feeling sorry for you."

She had barely uttered Toby's name when he interrupted.

"Yes, I borrowed money from him, and yes, I'll pay it back. I do have some morals, you know. Besides, it would be very inconvenient for me to have my best friend on the street. And the question?"

"Why do you change the topic every time someone suggests you use your house to raise money?" The big advantage of discussing difficult matters on the plane was that there was no escape. The disadvantage was that it was easy for Henry to hide his expression by staring out of the window, leaving her only a glimpse of his profile.

"You know the house in Lucca where I go in the summer? It came on the market, and I took out a second mortgage to buy it. The bungalow scheme had already fallen apart and I knew Nigel and George would have a fit if they found out. I haven't even dared tell Toby, though I'm sure he'll be pleased in the long run."

He had almost beggared his oldest friend to buy a house where he spent barely a month a year. "Why do you do these things, Henry? It causes so much trouble."

"I can't answer that in general," he said, "but the house in Lucca is my favorite place in the world. Nothing makes me happier than to sit on my patio with a glass of the quite average local wine and gaze out across the olive groves and churches. Don't ask me why."

Immediately after dinner, she fell asleep and woke only when Henry shook her shoulder. He was at his affable, efficient best as he guided her through Heathrow, retrieved their luggage, and got them on the train to Paddington. They took a taxi from the station to her flat, and he carried her suitcases upstairs. "Do you need me to get you anything?" he said, setting them down in the hall.

She was standing in the doorway of the kitchen, taking in the dirty dishes, the grimy floor, the solitary slice of toast sticking out of the toaster, the papers on the table weighted down with a jar of damson jam and, for some reason, a candlestick. On the counter were the two bags of groceries she had bought on the afternoon of Nigel and George's visit. She was so dismayed by the squalor that Henry had to repeat his question.

"No, thanks. The two things I need are right here: bath and bed." She went into the bedroom and drew the curtains to hide whatever disorder was lurking there. As she turned back to the newly darkened room, she saw that Henry had followed her. "What is it?"

"I meant what I said on the plane. I'll talk to Zeke, make him understand that you were being a good sister rather than a bad girlfriend."

She was so tired her bones no longer fit together. "Actually," she said, "I'm a wretched girlfriend. I'm cowardly when I ought to be brave, obstreperous when I ought to be conciliatory, quick to anger, slow to forgive, stubborn over the stupidest things." She crossed the room and kissed his cheek. "But if I need you to testify on my behalf, I'll let you know."

She had in the course of her career done hundreds of interviews, filled thousands of awkward pauses, but something about Zeke's answering machine seemed to render her peculiarly inarticulate. She left another unsatisfactory message as soon as she woke up. Then it occurred to her that she could at least make sure he wasn't still in America. She dialed the hotel and was told he had checked out that morning. Optimistically he was on a daytime flight to London, which meant he would land at eight or nine, be home by ten or eleven. He wouldn't call tonight, she thought, he'd be worried about disturbing her, but surely tomorrow. It would do her good to wait, as he had in Boston.

She took refuge in cleaning. She threw out everything that was rotten or mouldy. She unpacked and bought groceries. She did two loads of laundry and made the bed with clean sheets. She got out the vacuum and went through the entire flat. She scrubbed the stove and the fridge and the counters until the place was cleaner than it had been at any time since she moved in, several years ago. Then she walked down the street to the flower stall and bought twenty pounds' worth of spring flowers. Back at the house she gathered seldom-used vases and arranged them in every room save the bathroom. As she set the irises on the mantelpiece, she noticed how dirty the living room windows were; she must find a window cleaner. I'm nesting, she thought, I'm getting ready for someone. She pictured the baby revolving in its private darkness, Zeke flying to London, both coming toward her. Tonight, tomorrow, she would be in his presence. Meanwhile, she realized there was one person already here whom she could bear to talk to, who indeed owed her a conversation.

⁓

When she stepped into the gallery, Toby was standing in front of a large crimson painting talking to a willowy young man. She paused in the doorway, watching as he pointed to one corner, then stepped back, drawing the man with him, to examine the canvas as a whole. "You can see the influence of the colorists," he said, "and his use of organic forms reminds me of van Gogh."

"Or Gauguin," suggested the young man.

"Absolutely," said Toby. "He has a super essay about Gauguin, Cézanne, and Pollock."

"Something for everyone," said Verona.

"Verona," said Toby. In a few strides he was embracing her.

The young man—he was not as pretty as Verona had feared—turned out to be the latest gallery assistant, Lawrence. After a brief exchange of pleasantries he withdrew discreetly, promising to deal with customers. Toby led her to his office with its black leather furniture and bright prints.

"You look magnificent," he said. "Like a galleon under full sail. I bet the Americans loved you. They appreciate size over there. Tell me everything."

"Why don't *you* tell me everything?" She sat down in the most upright of the chairs and regarded him steadily where he stood, leaning against the desk. "I still don't understand why you never mentioned Betty. And the business about you being one of Henry's creditors makes me feel totally manipulated."

His freckles disappeared in a tide of color. "I'm sorry. I was an idiot not to tell you."

"An idiot because I found out anyway?"

"Please," said Toby, and as if summoned, Lawrence appeared, murmuring apologies for intruding, with two cups of tea and a plate of biscuits. "Verona, listen," Toby continued, when they were alone again. "I'm sorry about Betty. It wasn't deliberate. I assumed Henry would have told you. When I realized he hadn't, I didn't want to betray his confidences."

"Crap."

"But what difference would it have made?" His blush was fading. He helped himself to a biscuit, then put it back.

"I wouldn't have gone." At once this seemed true. Toby had flattered her into believing she was the only one who had any influence on Henry, the only one who could sort out his latest shenanigans. From the gallery came the buzz of the door, the sound of greetings.

"Tell me what happened," he said. "Are Nigel and George still about to shove Henry in a ditch?"

She tried to recall his expression when he had caught sight of her a few minutes ago. He had been surprised but not very. "So you haven't talked to Henry?" she said lightly.

For one second, two seconds, five, Toby hesitated. "Well, yes." She set down her teacup.

"Only for a minute," he added. "I knew you were back. That nothing terrible had occurred. I'm not trying to put one over on you, really, Verona."

"Really," she said. I've been a fool, she thought, a complete fool. Of course he and Henry had had a thorough debriefing. To the long list of Henry's crimes she must now add the theft of Toby's friendship. But perhaps all along Toby had courted her only as another way to get to Henry. She was the latecomer, the odd one out. "Tell me," she said, "about your dream."

"My dream?"

"The dream that made you fax me at six in the morning and ask me to meet you at Heathrow. Or was that a lie too? Just a way to get me to go after Henry?"

"More, more," he said, holding up his hands and beckoning. "Bring on your hot coals, your derision. I am a liar, a wastrel, a slut, a dilettante. I deserve all the abuse you can heap on me. No, I did have a dream. Why else would I be up at six in the morning?" He had dreamed that two men, who both were and were not Nigel and George, were chasing the two of them, her and him, through a town much like the one where they had gone to university. Verona was holding the baby.

"What sex was it?"

"A boy, with dark curly hair, maybe eighteen months, like one of those precocious Christ childs. Don't you know what it is? I thought you had that test."

"Someone knows, but not me." A boy, she was thinking. She cupped a hand to her belly and the baby kicked, twice.

Soon, Toby continued, they were trapped in a narrow street ending in a high wall. Nigel and George had caught up with them, seized the baby, and disappeared. "You know how sometimes the most vivid part of a dream is not what you remember but the feeling you're left with? I felt that the two of you were in danger. And"—he risked a small smile—"it does sound like your going to America was a good thing."

"My going made absolutely no difference to Henry—he sorted out his problems in his own inimitable fashion—and it's caused me major disruptions."

"Your young man." His smile grew brighter. Then, as if someone had wiped them clean, his features went blank. "Oh, hell, I suppose I wasn't meant to know about that either."

Through the door she heard Lawrence's muted voice. "Organic," he was saying.

"Let's get this straight," she said. "There's no such thing as telling you or Henry something in confidence?"

"Of course there is. I can be silent as the grave. I didn't tell him about the baby's father. Cross my heart." He looked at her indignantly for several seconds before he shrugged. "The truth is, mostly not. We both love you. We're both terrible gossips."

"How often do you talk?"

"Every day. Well, perhaps not literally but most days."

Absurdly, pathetically, her eyes were pricking with tears. She was the last to know everything. It occurred to her that Toby had probably known for years about Jigger's will. "What about all that stuff you told me about Henry stealing from you at university?"

"I asked him about that today. At first he denied it, then he said it wasn't theft, it was a long-term loan and handed me two twenties." He shook his head, ruefully.

Not just a brief talk on the phone, she thought. "But, Toby, what is all this for? Henry's straight."

"Sort of." He flipped a well-manicured hand back and forth. "Not everything is about fucking. We both have other people for that. There are worse things than knowing who you love."

For a moment they both sat silent, examining that claim. Then she caught sight of his watch. Nearly seven-thirty. In a matter of hours Zeke would be home, the place he never would have left but for Toby. "So," she said, "Henry went to all this trouble to woo Betty even though it was just fucking?"

"Betty's over." Toby stood up from where he leaned against the desk and stepped across the room to a row of three vivid prints. "But I didn't see her as a threat." He fidgeted with the middle print, tilting it left then right. "In some ways I'd rather Henry were settled than running from one girlfriend to the next. It's what he wants these days, what he thinks he wants, the so-called normal thing. If she has some cash, even better."

He looked over at Verona, trying to smile and so obviously failing that she decided not to play her ultimate card: the house in Lucca. "Did you like her?"

"Yes." He nodded. "I did. I may pretend to be a cynic but I like other people to be idealists. Betty actually wants to make the world a better place. And she's gorgeous."

He made one final adjustment to the print and returned to his desk. "Well, it's all water under the bridge now. Tell me about Zeke. When do I get to meet him?"

"When I do," she said.

28

As soon as she gave her name, Emmanuel began to shout. "Where the hell have you been? You've upset Zeke in a major way. How could you do this?"

Verona felt better by the syllable. After two days of leaving unrequited messages, the relief of knowing that Zeke was in London, walking these streets, painting rooms, and drinking cups of tea, and that this person, who was yelling into the phone, had seen and spoken to him, was profound. She wanted to ask a dozen questions: What did he say about Boston? Was he worried about the cost of the trip? Had he mentioned her? Why wouldn't he return her calls? "Is he all right?" she said.

"What do you think?"

"I don't know. That's why I'm calling you. He won't return my messages and he never picks up the phone. Could you give me his address?" She reached for her pad of paper and pen.

"His address?" Emmanuel's voice rose. "He went all the way to America because of you, and you stood him up. That would be anyone's idea of a nightmare, but for Zeke—well, I'm amazed he hasn't had another freak-out. You didn't phone for weeks. Now you phone all the fucking time. . . ."

While he continued to list Zeke's tribulations—his parents had health problems, he was behind with work—she lowered herself into the wicker chair where she had sat during Nigel and George's visit and stared at the daffodils on the coffee table. All but the tardiest buds had opened and the slender green spears she had carried home from the flower shop were now a mass of yellow trumpets. How effortless it seemed for them to be themselves. When at last Emmanuel paused, she said, "I was only trying to help my brother. Tell me where Zeke lives and I'll go and apologize. What else can I do?"

"You've already done quite enough. Just stay away. Do whatever you were doing before you started this niece business. You know he went round to the Barrows'?"

"Oh, God." Of course. "Were they furious?"

"No." Emmanuel snorted. "They were thrilled to have a new relative."

For a moment she was afraid he was going to hang up, but beneath the brusqueness she detected something else: a faint note of pleasure. He was enjoying scolding her. "Do you think he still cares for me?" she said.

"What?"

She couldn't tell if he was astounded at her brazen question or simply hadn't heard. "Do you think he cares for me?"

"Not if he has the brains he was born with. Why are you calling anyway? You're not just about to show up with your suitcases, are you? Because I'm going out."

She asked again for Zeke's address and Emmanuel again began to shout. She was always putting him in these impossible situations. He felt responsible for the whole business. He didn't want Zeke upset anymore. She held the pen very tightly. "Well," she said, "can I come round and talk to you? Or meet you somewhere for a drink?"

"I told you I'm going out."

"How about later, or tomorrow? Please, Emmanuel, give me

half an hour. I truly never meant to hurt Zeke. It's not something I can explain on the phone."

"You know," he said, and worryingly he sounded less bellicose, more reflective, "in Thailand you could barely give me the time of day. You wrote down the wrong phone number. Now, suddenly, when you need something, you're all over me. I'm not stupid. If the tables had been the other way round, if I'd turned up out of the blue, you wouldn't have raised a finger to help."

As he spoke, her mind was racing. Think, she goaded herself, think. She pictured Emmanuel at the bar on the beach, wearing his orange mesh T-shirt, flirting outrageously with Jade and Vicky and Sara. "That first week in Thailand," she said, "I couldn't get near you. You were always surrounded by bikinis. Mr. Popularity. If it hadn't been for the business with Trevor, we wouldn't have exchanged two words."

Her flattery worked. "That was weird, wasn't it?" said Emmanuel. "And the way he and Sara rushed off without so much as a thank-you. He was lucky you spotted he was in trouble. Christ, is that the time?"

And before she could take advantage of his better mood, he was gone.

She sat there, alone with the flowers, feeling as if she'd run up ten flights of stairs and hit a wall. For a few seconds the future stretched before her, utterly empty. Then, setting aside the pad of paper, she stood up and went into the spotless kitchen. The phone book lay open on the table. For the twentieth time, she read down the column of names. At some point during the last forty-eight hours, when it had dawned on her that Zeke was not going to return her calls, she had looked him up and discovered a single listing for Cafarelli, D. and G., his parents she assumed. She had rung directory assistance only to learn that, like her, he had an unlisted number.

Now she thought of calling his parents and appealing for help. I fancy your son. You'd have an instant grandchild. Better still, she could go to their shop. Buy celery and radicchio and slip in the odd question: Where was Zeke these days? Had he said anything about a woman? Or she could pretend to need someone to paint her living room. But they would give her the same useless phone number she already had. She closed the directory and put it firmly back on the shelf. What she must remember was that this wasn't about finding Zeke literally. If that was all she wanted, there were a dozen ways to accomplish it. It was about finding the part of him that cared for her, which somewhere between London and Boston had got mislaid and which she desperately needed to recover. Meanwhile, she phoned her producer and said she would be back at the radio station tomorrow.

For the second time in her life, a taxi dropped Verona at the Barrows' and she rang their doorbell. In the middle of her program that morning she had suddenly remembered her grandfather's book, abandoned in their spare room, and been appalled at yet more evidence of her carelessness. Now, standing on the doorstep, she allowed herself to fantasize that Zeke would answer the blue door. But no, the door was opening and standing before her was the small woman from the many photographs in the bedroom. Her absorbed expression suggested that she was still seeing whatever she had just been looking at through her reading glasses rather than the person standing before her. "Yes?" she said.

"My name is Verona MacIntyre. I wonder if I could talk to you for a minute."

Mrs. Barrow's glasses, dangling from a cord, fell to her chest. "So," she said slowly, "you're the famous Verona. I suppose you'd better come in." She stepped back and, when Verona was inside, led the way to the kitchen. "Forgive my saying this," she said, over her shoulder, "but Zeke didn't mention that you were pregnant."

"I don't know how to begin to apologize."

"Then don't. Have a seat." She motioned to an empty chair and herself sat down behind several piles of pages. "I'm Ariel and I'm afraid we need to watch the clock. My husband will be home soon and I'm worried he might call the police. He's still beside himself about your staying here."

"And you're not?"

"I was when we first found out." Her gray sweater was marked by a constellation of dark stains. "I'm sure you can imagine it was very disturbing to think of a stranger having the run of my house. But when I talked to Zeke and we figured out who you are—you do this radio show, don't you?—I realized it was more complicated than that."

Verona nodded gratefully. "It is complicated. Some men were looking for my brother, and I needed a place to stay where no one could find me." She gestured at the stove and the counters. "Zeke didn't know anything about what was going on."

"Did you just come to say that?" Ariel glanced over at the clock. "Because, if so, please don't worry. We understand he's not to blame, at least I do. The whole thing was so improbable. I'm glad you're back. He seemed upset when you disappeared."

Verona studied the nearest pile of dog-eared pages. "He was, but I spoiled everything. I asked him to come to America, and then I was ill and couldn't see him. Now he won't talk to me. I feel terrible."

"It sounds like you should," said Ariel crisply. She asked again why Verona had come and, when she explained about the book, led the way upstairs.

Every day since she left, Verona had pictured this room. Now here it was in all its ordinary shabbiness, the miscellaneous furniture, the faded curtains, the scuffed floorboards. Had Zeke understood, she wondered, why she'd nailed the coveralls to the floor?

Ariel was already peering beneath the bed. "Lots of dust, a pen, and a Ping-Pong ball," she reported. She stood up, holding the ball. "I just remembered. The first time Zeke came round he talked about a book he wanted to return to you. It must be the same one, don't you think?"

"He found it," Verona exclaimed. "Fantastic." Suddenly it seemed all her problems were solved. She was still expressing thanks and delight as Ariel hurried them down the stairs to the hall. Through the half-open door she glimpsed the living room where she and Zeke had worked together. How pleasant it looked with its immaculate walls and bright rugs. Ariel, turning to usher her out, caught the direction of her gaze. "Gerald likes it," she said with a shrug, "but it still feels a bit formal to me. We always end up in the kitchen."

On the doorstep, she shook Verona's hand and wished her luck.

In the first pub she came to, Verona stopped and ordered a sparkling water. The news that Zeke was in possession of Jigger's book had filled her with elation—he was an honorable person, he would have to give it back—but as she raised her glass she realized how easy it would be to return the book without seeing her, through Emmanuel or the radio station or by leaving it on her doorstep in the middle of the night. And then—a terrible thought—whatever was between them really would be over.

"Are you okay?"

She looked up to see a thin, scruffy boy watching her intently; a V-shaped piece was missing from one earlobe. "I'm fine, just doing my breathing exercises."

"Cool," he said, and moved away.

No, she insisted, overriding both her own doubts and Emmanuel's accusations: Zeke was just catching up with work, recovering from the journey, getting his own back by making her wait. She took several deep breaths. The clock above the bar showed nearly six. She ought to go home and prepare for tomorrow's interviews, but she felt too restless to read her notes attentively. Catching sight of her mobile phone, lying on the table beside a beer mat, she remembered the offer she had made to Henry on the plane. If she couldn't fix her own love life, maybe she could fix his.

Betty said hello in a small, soft voice that got louder and harder as soon as Verona identified herself. "I have nothing to say to Henry," she said. But this was the kind of refusal Verona knew how to deal with. She explained that she had a tape of Henry she wanted Betty to hear, how important it was, and at last, after several more demurrals—she was in the middle of studying, the weather was horrible—Betty agreed to meet her at a pub near the radio station. Then Verona was rushing home to collect the tape and on to the Hamilton Arms. The place, crowded at lunchtime and after work, was at this hour almost empty. She settled herself, with another sparkling water, at a corner table. She was remembering that snowy afternoon in Boston—and how some combination of Henry's passion for Betty, Toby's needs, and her own panic had made her follow him so ill-advisedly to New York when a young woman came through the door.

"Verona?" she said, pulling off a striped woolen hat.

She was at first glance as Henry had described her, small and slender, but in no way did she seem to merit Toby's epithet of *gorgeous*. Beneath her duffel coat she wore an assortment of colorful garments: red jeans, a pink pullover, a blue shirt. It was impossible to guess if the clothes came from a secondhand shop or an expensive boutique. They shook hands.

"Would you like a drink?" Verona asked.

"No, thanks. I don't mean to sound rude but I just want to get this over with. So what's the tape?"

Verona explained that they could listen to it at the radio station, and they headed for the door. Outside, rain was falling. Wishing she too had brought a hat, Verona turned up the collar of her coat. "What are you studying?" she said, as they walked to the zebra crossing.

Betty said that she was applying to teachers' training college, to teach mathematics. "I like that it doesn't matter what background the kids come from, and I like that there are right and wrong answers."

Zeke, Verona recalled, had made a similar comment about accounting. "Last year," she said, "I interviewed a Pakistani businessman who's started an after-school program. He was very evangelical, believed that math was the universal language and everyone should learn it." She did not add that later, when she left the station, his chauffeur had accosted her and led her over to the open window of a long black car. She had bent down, and there was Mr. Mirza reclining on a mass of cushions. Ms. MacIntyre, he had said, patting a cushion, may I have the honor of your company? She had declined politely, claiming she'd lose her job. As she walked to the underground, the car had kept pace in the street beside her.

The windows of the radio station were ablaze; inside, the main evening show, the counterpart to her own morning show, was on. Verona paused to listen to the host reviewing a play. She signed Betty in and led the way down the corridor, searching for an empty studio. In the first two, interviews were in progress; in the third, Gary, the engineer, was bending over a switchboard. The next studio was empty.

Betty took off her hat but the small room was surprisingly chilly and they both kept on their coats. Verona set up the tape player on the table between them. As she slipped the tape into the machine, she found herself strangely nervous. This was not just about Henry; somehow it had become intertwined with her own fate. If she could persuade Betty to give her brother another chance, maybe she could persuade Zeke to do the same.

"So what are we listening to?" said Betty.

"It's a tape I made last week of Henry." She did her best to explain the circumstances: that she'd decided not to speak; that they were in Boston during a blizzard. She expected Betty to ask what had taken them to America, but instead she said, "What was it like, being silent?"

"I didn't do it for very long, but it was interesting. I'm someone who talks all the time. Suddenly I understood that language is a major distraction."

Betty drew her coat closer. "After my brother died, I didn't talk for two months. At first it was because without Robin conversation seemed pointless. Soon I began to like it for its own sake. Everything was simpler and, I don't know, less fussy. Would you mind," she said, "if we started?"

Henry's voice filled the room. Except for the occasional muffled word, perhaps when he had turned toward the window, he was remarkably clear. Betty leaned forward with her elbows on the table. Verona sat back, watching her as closely as she dared while Henry described buying the bungalows. After years of listening to him discuss various deals, she had not given the particulars of this one much thought. Now, seeing Betty's frown, she understood that he had been trying to cheat the villagers. They had, in the end, benefited from his greed, but that had not been his intention.

He moved on to Betty and their courtship, Glyndebourne, their engagement and subsequent rift. Then he returned to his present difficulties. "There was my old girlfriend Charlotte" he said, "you know, the one with different-colored eyes."

Hastily Verona reached for the machine but Betty held up a hand. There it all was, the ruthless pursuit of the ex-girlfriend. Verona listened aghast. She had been so wrapped up in her own longing for Zeke that she had forgotten about Henry's dalliance. "We went skiing," he said, "wined and dined. Etc." Or perhaps, she thought, in some uncharted part of herself, she had wanted revenge. She gripped the arms of her chair until, at last, he fell silent.

"Thank you," said Betty. She gave Verona her first wholehearted smile.

"I'm sorry." All her hopes lay in disarray because of a few inches of tape. "I feel like an idiot. I'd forgotten about—"

"Charlotte," prompted Betty.

"What I remembered was Henry's face as he talked about you and how I'd never seen him look that way before."

"Too bad you didn't have a video." She rubbed her hands together. "Is it this cold when you're working? You can practically see your breath."

She seemed so unruffled that Verona could not help asking, "Why did you agree to see me?"

"Henry was always talking about you. Besides, it's not every day someone offers to play you a tape of your ex-fiancé."

"I never knew Henry talked about me."

Betty, however, did not add any details. She sat fingering the hem of her pink sweater. "I'm sorry," she said, "after you've gone to all this trouble, but it won't work. I need someone I can rely on in certain fundamental ways. I don't think Henry would ever be that person."

"Don't you love him?" She could barely get the words out.

"I do, but I'm hoping it will pass." She was still looking down at her lap, and Verona noticed her eyelids, smooth and translucent. Betty *was* gorgeous. "Did he know you were recording him?" she said. "It seems an odd thing to do."

"It was odd," Verona agreed. "I don't normally go around taping people."

"Did he know?" Betty repeated, raising her eyes.

"No." Then she remembered her resolve to tell the truth. "Well, I tried to hide it but he guessed."

Betty nodded approvingly. She would make a good teacher, thought Verona. She wanted to apologize again but it seemed useless. She had messed up everything: Zeke, Henry, Betty, herself. "There's an engineer here," she said, "we passed him coming in, who refuses to get married because a friend met the love of his life at his own wedding."

"Verona," said Betty gently, "it's hopeless but it's not tragic. My brother going blind and dying was tragic. I'll be fine."

"And Henry?"

Betty stood up and pulled on her brightly colored hat. Then she reached over to the machine and pressed replay; the tape whirred backward. "If he had any sense," she said, as she pressed ERASE, "he'd move in with Toby."

"Toby?" Verona echoed.

"Yes. Toby dotes on him, and it would mean that Henry would

always be the center of attention. No distractions." Betty patted her own flat belly. "No children."

Of course, thought Verona. What better solution to Toby's passion, Henry's selfishness? She pictured Toby mastering the intricate espresso machine, Henry charming the patrons at gallery openings. She was suddenly, overwhelmingly tired. Her clever scheme had done nothing but harm. If it had not been for Betty standing there, she would have curled up on the floor and slept until morning. Slowly she struggled to her feet. Slowly she picked up her bag.

"Did you go to a sperm bank?" Betty asked, moving toward the door. Verona gave the slightest of nods. "I thought you must have," she continued, "when Henry told me you wouldn't say who the baby's father was. If I don't meet someone in two years, that's what I plan to do."

In the street, she helped Verona to flag down a taxi, kissed her on both cheeks, and walked away into the rain.

Back at her flat, Verona set the alarm, got ready for bed, and, once she was there, called Henry. They had not spoken since he brought her home from the airport. Now she heard voices, music. "Hang on," he said. "Let me go somewhere quiet." He was back in forty seconds. "How are you? I heard your show today. The interview with the tiddledywinks champion was a riot."

The baby, tranquil since she finished work, began to twist and turn as she told Henry about her conversation with Toby. "I didn't realize quite how close the two of you are."

"Good old Tobes." He laughed, missing or ignoring the edge in her voice. "My secret sharer. He was scared to death by this business with Nigel and George, especially after they showed up at his flat. That's why he suggested you come to America. And, of course, I thought you'd be an asset, the mother-to-be, making witty conversation with potential investors."

On the chest of drawers at the foot of the bed the white tulips glowed. "What do you mean," she said carefully, "*suggested*? His friend tracked you down on the Internet and then, when you didn't answer our calls, it seemed like one of us had to come and talk to you."

"I'm sure he could have found me on the Internet—Nigel and George did—but he didn't need to. We talk every day."

"So the two of you . . ." She trailed off. Toby had said the same thing, but she'd assumed he meant every day *except* the days when Henry had vanished. All along, while they'd been fretting over Henry's disappearance, Toby had known exactly where he was.

"We were worried about you," Henry was saying. "You started behaving so weirdly, taking leave of your job, rushing around with suitcases. Toby was afraid it wouldn't be good for the baby. But we weren't sure you'd come to Boston if I just asked. It was his idea to make you feel you were rescuing me. Of course, that was before Charlotte entered the picture."

"But"—the baby gave a sharp jab, as if it too were arguing with Henry—"when Toby and I were in the hotel at Heathrow, Nigel and George telephoned. They even dropped off my passport at the front desk."

"Actually, Toby fetched your passport, I lent him your keys, but when Nigel phoned, he decided to pretend they'd left it for you. He said the timing couldn't have been better."

No wonder, she thought, the handwriting on the little note—*Happy travels*—had looked familiar. She lay there holding the phone while Henry described their campaign to get her to America. The Internet search had been a joint idea. "The only fallout," he said, "was your young man. Have the two of you kissed and made up?"

"Absolutely." Whatever resolutions she'd made about telling the truth did not apply to Henry. "What about you and Betty?"

"Oh, it was a nice idea, thinking I'd be a good person and live in a mansion with tons of money, but she was much too high-minded for me. I'm back to slumming it with the bankers and secretaries. Hang on a minute."

He turned away from the phone to say something she couldn't quite hear. He was still laughing as she replaced the receiver.

She slept with the phone on her bedside table, but for the first time since she returned from America she didn't dream, and the next morning, as she rode down the crowded escalator at the underground station, Verona glimpsed a new feeling. Perhaps, just possibly, it was time to accept that Zeke didn't want her. The price of helping Henry in his hour of need had been losing Zeke. No, she corrected herself as she made her way along the crowded platform, she had lost him because of fear and anxiety and stubbornness. If she couldn't understand her own behavior, how could she expect Zeke to? Her task now, she thought, as the train squealed into the station, was to prepare for the baby. She set to work at once by asking a loutish-looking young man if he would mind giving her his seat.

He jumped to his feet with a sweet smile. "Sorry. I was dreaming I'd won the lottery."

Seated, she took out a notebook and began a list of things to buy in the next few weeks: a mockingbird—plus or minus a golden ring—a bottle of burgundy to drink in twenty-one years' time, a slow-growing bonzai tree for company, a plot of land in the Outer Hebrides, a copy of *Steppenwolf*, a paintbrush.

Zeke

Verona

29

Ten days after she spoke to Betty, Verona found herself interviewing an expert in behavior modification. Ms. Taylor turned out to be a large greasy woman with fierce dark eyes and badly crowned teeth; her clothes, a shapeless cardigan and a baggy skirt, looked as if they had been pieced together out of old blankets.

"Welcome, Ms. Taylor, and thank you for being with us today. Could you describe for our listeners what it is you offer parents and children?"

Ms. Taylor leaned into the microphone and asserted that there had been a crisis of confidence among parents. "Mothers and fathers," she said, "no longer see themselves as automatically in charge. They consult children about such major decisions as what kind of car to buy and where to go on holiday. At the same time, they no longer feel able to discipline their children in appropriate ways."

She had a surprisingly pleasant voice, firm, clear, well-modulated. No one listening, thought Verona, would guess at her grotesque appearance. "And how do you help?"

Ms. Taylor explained that she retrained the parents, teaching them to adhere to clear rules and to administer fixed punishments and rewards. They telephoned her nightly for reinforcement.

"So you don't actually meet the children?"

"No, that's not necessary. The parents are the problem. My system, if followed, works for all save the most exceptional cases."

"And how," asked Verona, "did you get into behavior modification? You don't have children yourself and you don't"—she hesitated—"have a degree in psychology or social work."

She had hesitated not because she was worried about upsetting Ms. Taylor but because suddenly, midsentence, it had occurred to her that Zeke might be listening. This was her chance, perhaps her only chance, to send him a different kind of message, one that came without demands or expectations. As Ms. Taylor explained her qualifications, she scribbled a couple of notes.

"What you're saying sounds awfully sensible," she said, as soon as the woman paused, "but surely there has to be room for mistakes and forgiveness, not just punishments and rewards. At some point almost everyone, parent or child, does something they profoundly regret, something that can't be undone." Ignoring Henry's theory of lost illusions, she argued for love and mercy.

Ms. Taylor opened and shut her mouth several times during this speech. "I'm afraid that's all a bit too cerebral for me," she said, when Verona finished. "The kinds of problems I work with have to do with bedtime and homework and chores. You'd be amazed how one child refusing to go to bed can bring a whole family to a standstill. I aim to get the machinery running smoothly again."

They chatted for a few more minutes about her down-to-earth approach, her notions of suitable rewards and punishments; then an assistant led Ms. Taylor away and it was time for Verona to read the news and report on the traffic. Later, as she emerged after the second half of the show, she ran into Gary in the corridor.

"Good interview," he said, "though that Taylor woman seemed a little scary."

"She was a toad. I'm sure she does worthy work, but I couldn't bear her."

"I liked what you said"—his dark ringlets swayed—"about mistakes and mercy. We grow up thinking everything can be fixed, but some stuff there's just no way around except forgiveness."

So there was more to his not getting married, she thought, than his friend's story. One of these days she would have to ask him. Now she nodded and said she had a meeting.

Zeke had the table covered with tiny cogs—his eight-day clock had persisted in running slow since he returned from Boston—when the doorbell rang. His mother was on the doorstep, her face unusually pale but not, he could see at once, from sickness. She was vibrating with excitement, as if she had just sold an entire box of pineapples or successfully exhorted money from several delinquent customers. "I tried to phone," she said, "but as usual you seem to be relying on telepathy."

Upstairs, she sat quietly across from him. No, she didn't want tea or water. She just wanted to talk to him. He picked up the tiny screwdriver and, replacing the loupe—he always wore it in his right eye—began to fit one of the screws.

"There's no easy way to say this," she said. "I've decided to leave your father, and I've told him so."

He finished inserting the screw and turned to look at her. Through the loupe she was large and fuzzy, which seemed oddly appropriate.

"Could you take off that thing?" she said, pointing. "Do you understand what I just said?"

Without the loupe, she at once became smaller and more distinct. "Yes," he said.

"Is that all you're going to say?"

He looked around his brain. He couldn't see anything else he wanted to say. "I think so."

"Do you blame me?" The three little lines had appeared between her eyebrows.

"No. I'm sorry for Dad but I don't blame you."

"I do," she said. "I thought I'd be married to the same person forever, but this is my one life, my one shot. The thing that threw me"—she was clasping her hands together; perhaps she was wringing them?—"was that Don didn't get angry. He actually seemed to understand."

"Isn't that good?"

"Yes, of course, but it made me feel like I'd made a terrible mistake. You know I always wanted more children. I'm even sorrier now that you're on your own." Her cheeks turned pink; briefly she seemed to be holding her breath. He was about to remind her that he had never wanted a sibling when she launched into the practical details: her new address, what was happening at the shop. "I'll be there for the next few weeks, until he finds a manager. You'll keep an eye on Don, won't you?"

"I'll do my best."

She stood up. "I hope—" she began, but she didn't say what. For a few seconds her blue eyes tugged at him. Then she turned to examine the neatly displayed innards of the clock. Zeke stood up and put his arms around her.

Verona was sitting on the sofa, studying one of her baby books, when the phone rang.

"Hi," said a familiar voice that she couldn't quite place. "This is Emmanuel."

"Hello." Her hand tightened around the phone. "How are you?"

"I was wondering, would you like to get together, have a drink?"

Her first instinct was to refuse—she wanted to work on her list for the baby—but after the reprimand of their last conversation, she didn't have the nerve. She would go and apologize and take a proper interest in him and his tumultuous life with—what was her name, Tina? Gina? She wrote down the address of the pub and said she'd be there in an hour.

She had hoped for the slight advantage of arriving early, but as she stepped through the door the first person she saw was Emmanuel with a half-empty pint before him. She walked over, acutely conscious of her bulk. "Sorry if I'm late," she said, bending to kiss his cheek. "Can I get you another?"

"I'm okay. Here, you sit down. What would you like, juice? Lemonade?"

"Orange juice with sparkling water would be great." While he went to the bar, she took off her coat and reminded herself that she was not here to ask a single question about Zeke. She was here to listen and talk about Emmanuel.

He set a glass before her and resumed his seat. "Cheers," he said, tilting his own glass in her direction. "When are you due?"

"Early April. I'm hoping to keep working for another month so I can take all my maternity leave after the baby's here."

"That makes sense. You're mostly sitting down, aren't you? Wouldn't do in my line of work."

"How are things? How's your back?"

"My back?" He sounded startled. "My back is okay, touch wood. I have some exercises the doctor gave me, and they seem to help."

"And what about your girlfriend? Last time I came round you were expecting her."

"The only time," he corrected. "Gina's fine. She keeps me on my toes, which is no bad thing." He took a long drink of beer. "She wants us to do what you're doing."

What I'm doing, she wondered and then, seeing his glance, understood. "You mean have a baby?"

He nodded. "The whole bit: live together, have a kid, maybe two."

"How do you feel about that?"

"I say I'm not ready, but she claims I'll be saying that when I'm eighty. This way the baby and I can grow up together."

"So you think you'll do it?"

The bartender had turned up the television, and around them the voices of the other customers rose in competition. Emmanuel flicked something—a crumb? a piece of lint?—off his sleeve. "Unless she changes her mind," he said, "about being with an idiot she has to drag kicking and screaming every step of the way. How do you feel about it?"

"It's funny," she said, "no one ever asks me that. I suppose it's got beyond the stage when my personal preferences count. I'm meant to be a hundred percent radiant. I'm thrilled but scared. You know: the pain, will I be a good mother, all that stuff."

"Well, best of luck." He drained his glass and, after asking if she wanted anything, went off to the bar. He returned with another pint and two bags of peanuts. "Not very healthy," he said, handing her one, "but better than nothing. I had an idea about you and Zeke."

Before she could tell him it was no longer relevant, he was outlining his plan. He and Zeke were painting an empty flat in Camden. On Monday morning he would phone and say he was under the weather; then Verona could go to the flat. "You can call in sick, can't you? I don't feel comfortable giving you his address, but this way you'd get to talk to him face-to-face."

All her resolutions vanished. Wasn't this what people claimed? You just had to stop struggling and the door would open. If she hadn't felt so unwieldy, she would have jumped up and hugged Emmanuel. "Or better still," she said, "I know this isn't so convenient, but maybe you could go to work with him, and then you could let me in and leave." She looked at him, hoping he wouldn't force her to spell out her fear that Zeke might, quite literally, shut the newly opened door in her face.

"Okay, we'll do it that way. I did try to talk to him about this whole business and he's dead set against seeing you. Gina reckons he's protecting himself." He wrote down the address of the house for her; they agreed on a time.

"I can't thank you enough," said Verona, "but why did you change your mind?"

He smiled sheepishly. "I was in the newsagent's the other day, buying fags, and they had the radio on. I heard what you said about mistakes, you know"—he lowered his voice—"forgiveness. This thing between you and Zeke is beyond me. I don't get why you like each other. I don't get why you stood him up. But I've screwed up plenty of times." He raised his glass. "This may be one more."

She began, once again, to offer her thanks. "If there's ever anything I can do for you—"

"As a matter of fact," said Emmanuel. Haltingly, he explained that Gina had a small business, making cakes. "She has a whole special line for Valentine's Day, stag parties, that kind of thing. And she'll copy any photograph in icing."

Verona listened, bewildered. Should she be asking Gina to bake her a cake? She'd happily order a dozen. Finally he got to the point.

"It would be a big boost for her if she could be on your show."

How distracted she must be to have missed this familiar request. She got out her notebook and wrote down Gina's details. "She sounds perfect," she said. "I'll talk to my producers about her at our next meeting. Just so you know, though, I'm not the only person involved in the decision. I can't promise it will work out."

"So that's two things," said Emmanuel, "we have to keep our fingers crossed for."

On Saturday, after helping Gwen with the morning rush, Zeke went to a couple of rummage sales and returned with two new clocks. The one from the fifties, which he had thought just needed adjusting, proved on closer inspection to be hopeless. But the other, a lovely Edwardian traveling clock, looked as if it could be fixed. He would work on it later. For now he laid out the vegetables he had brought from the shop and set to work, making minestrone soup. This isn't forever, he told himself as he chopped an onion. I'm still on the train, going forward; we've just paused for repairs. Soon we'll be chugging along.

He was glad when Monday came and he could rise purposefully at his normal hour, eat a bowl of cereal, and head off through the morning mist to collect Emmanuel. Here too things were back to normal; there was no sign of his friend. Zeke had to double-park and jump out to ring the bell. After eight minutes Emmanuel appeared. He was uncharacteristically quiet during the drive to the house, a hangover perhaps, and for once Zeke caught every word of the morning news. At the house, they carried up the paint and headed to the nearest café. They both read the newspaper while they ate.

Back at the flat, Emmanuel announced he would start on the bedroom. Zeke wanted to object—it would be more efficient if they finished the living room together and then separated to work on the smaller rooms—but Emmanuel's eyes were so bright, his jaw so taut, he didn't dare. Not a hangover, Zeke thought, perhaps a row with Gina.

He had just started on the edge of the ceiling when Emmanuel called out that he was going for cigarettes. As the door closed behind him, one of his favorite songs came on the radio and for a few seconds Zeke thought of going after him. But it was too much trouble to come down from the ladder. They would play the song again. He finished the section he was working on. As he climbed down to move the ladder, he felt that peculiar prickling sensation: someone's eyes were touching him. He turned around and there, standing in the doorway, wearing a pair of pristine coveralls, was Verona. He recognized her instantly.

Very carefully he set down the paint and fastened his own gaze on the wrinkled drop cloth.

"Emmanuel let me in," she said, and her voice was all the colors he'd imagined. "But it's not his fault. I begged and begged."

Her feet—she was wearing rather dirty tennis shoes—stepped forward and stopped. He pressed his fingers to his forehead. He could feel the thoughts beating against his skull, trying to get out. She was here at last. He was trapped. She was as tall as he remembered. Emmanuel had betrayed him. He was terrified she would beg, or cry, or shout. One clear thought rose above the others: I don't want to feel this way.

"Please," she said. "Let me at least try to explain."

"No," he said, raising both hands. "I don't believe in explanations."

She stopped again. Her voice grew pale and watery. "I've come to take Emmanuel's place for the day. He said to start on the white wall by the window."

He raised his eyes a few inches and discovered Ms. F even more prominent than when they first met; her mother was already holding a paint tray and roller. Without another word she moved toward the corner by the window and began to paint. He didn't know what to do. He could feel the key of the van in his pocket against his thigh but even as his hand reached toward it, he remembered the ceiling, barely begun, and the carpet fitters were due on Wednesday. If she just stays quiet, he thought, I can manage.

She had spent all weekend thinking of what to say, going over and over her apology as if it were the most important script of her life, but as soon as she laid eyes on Zeke in his ragged sweater and jeans, saw the tender hollow between his collarbones, saw the way he pressed his hands to his temples, she knew she must bide her time. He was on the edge of flight. She did the only thing she could think of to keep him there. She kept quiet and painted.

For two minutes and ten seconds he remained rooted to the spot. Then at last, finally, he retrieved the can of paint and climbed back up the ladder. He dipped his brush into the paint. After eleven minutes, during which he had moved the ladder three times, she came to a small hole in the plaster.

"Do you have any spackle?" she said.

"Emmanuel has it in the bedroom. I'll get it for you."

He descended, left the room, and returned with a can. As he started across the room, she could feel him hesitating. She stepped back, well out of his path, and pointed out the hole, to the left of the window. While he stood there, meticulously pressing spackle into the wall, it was all she could do not to fling her arms around him. She stared at his fair hair curling over the neck of his sweater. One thing he didn't do in America, she thought, was get a haircut.

He stepped back, still not looking at her. "I'll put it over here," he said, "in case you find more holes."

"Thank you."

When he was safely back up the ladder and they had both resumed their painting, she said, "Growing up, one of my favorite stories was about a princess who's immune to gravity. If she isn't tied down, she keeps floating away and she finds everything funny. The only time she's like other people is when she goes swimming in the palace lake."

"How can that be?" he said. "Gravity isn't something you can shut out, like weather or light."

"I think it's a metaphor," she said. "Emmanuel told me your parents had both been ill. I'm sorry."

"My father had a heart attack and my mother found a lump in her breast, but they're better, mostly."

She moved to the next stretch of wall and let the silence grow. If she waited, might he say something else? She fetched more paint and took the opportunity to go to the bathroom. He moved his ladder and continued his careful painting. Just as she was losing hope, he said, "A woman on the plane had a heart attack too."

"That must have been awful." She dipped the roller and spread the paint as high as she could reach. "Was she all right?"

"There was a nurse, Jill. We did CPR together; then she used a defibrillator. Everyone had to stand back and you could see the woman's body jump with the electricity, not like anything you could do on your own. But her heart started beating again." He paused to wipe away a smear. "It's what they used to do to people whose brains were out of order. Maybe she woke up feeling completely different. I need to paint the ceiling where you're standing."

She stepped back while he moved the ladder into place; for just a second his blue eyes rested on her face. Oh, please, she thought. He turned back to his brush. "I'm not positive," she said, "but I think the current they use in electric shock treatment is quite a lot less."

"I hope so."

As he was nearing the end of the ceiling, he looked down and saw that her tawny hair was flecked with white paint. He had a sudden piercing memory of what that hair had felt like beneath his hands: warm, thick, alive. Before he could apologize for spattering her, she glanced up. Their eyes—he'd never really understood the expression—met. Then she was saying something about lunch; she had brought sandwiches. Would he like to take a break? To his own amazement he said he would be ready in ten minutes. She went out into the hall and returned with a backpack, from which she proceeded to produce various bags and bottles. I can't sit down with her, he thought, share a meal. She'll get back inside my brain again, take over every room, and it will be just like before when she got inside me. She'll vanish on the outside.

He heard a thud and looked over to see her wrestling with a five-gallon bucket of paint: she was setting up a little dining area with buckets for seats and an empty box for a table. "Don't lift that," he said, and jumped down to help.

She had brought smoked salmon sandwiches, chocolate biscuits, apples, and a bottle of orange juice and a bottle of water for each of them. He positioned his bucket as far away as he politely could.

"According to my pregnancy books," she said, "my appetite ought to have stabilized by this stage but I still feel hungry all the time. Who owns this flat?"

This was the first time, he thought, he'd heard her mention Ms. F. He explained that they were working for a letting agent. She nodded, took another bite of her sandwich, and asked what he planned to do after lunch.

"The kitchen."

Had the last few weeks been a mirage? Had he really endured first her long silence, then her increasingly shrill messages, then again her silence? And now here she was so calm and ample, talking about the differences between farm-raised and wild salmon. It was like his mother in the shop, one moment scolding him and the next praising the parsley. As she set her sandwich down to drink some juice, he saw that her knuckles were still faintly chapped. No wonder, given the cold in Boston. If he had been sitting closer, he would have touched the rough, red skin. Thank God, he wasn't.

They finished eating, she went to the bathroom, and he set up the drop cloths in the kitchen. The small square room reeked of neglect, but two days from now, freshly painted, with a new fridge and stove, it would be transformed. He started her off applying blue paint to the walls and got busy cleaning and masking the skirting boards.

"I'm sorry," he said, kneeling in the corner, his face hidden, "I didn't answer your phone calls. It's not like me. But then going to America wasn't like me."

"I am very sorry," she said so slowly that it was almost as if she were spelling each word. "I'd like to tell you what happened, if you can bear it."

She took a step to the left and ran the roller through the tray. He edged to the right, rinsing the sponge and wiping the next stretch of skirting board. He made his *hmm* sound and she took it for permission.

"It all has to do with my brother," she began.

As they circled the small room, she told a story about deals and debts, her brother and two men called Nigel and George, and how she herself had done some shameful things. "Henry tricked me," she said, "but it isn't all his fault. I behaved badly too." He listened as best he could, but some parts of the story were so bizarre and others eluded him altogether. The more she talked, the more her voice took on the colors he didn't like.

"I did try to stop you from coming to Boston but I was too late. Then I thought I'd be back from New York almost immediately but I had some kind of flu. I couldn't lift my head off the pillow. And I was worried about the baby being born in America. None of this excuses my behavior, but maybe you can understand a little better."

But, but, but, he thought. He focused intently on a brown stain on the skirting board that refused to yield to his scrubbing. It turned out to be a knot in the wood. He moved on to the next stretch.

"Can you ever forgive me?" she said.

Eighty-two seconds elapsed. She rolled the paint up and down, up and down, the same stretch of wall. Finally, without raising his head or ceasing to scrub the skirting board, Zeke spoke.

"My mother is divorcing my father. She's met someone else. I thought the lump in her breast would make her change her mind, but it only seems to have made things worse. She keeps saying she doesn't have a minute to waste. People used to tell me that feelings changed and I was sure they didn't, not mine anyway. It turns out I was wrong.

"I don't really understand what you just said: why you left me, why you didn't phone. I know I have my shortcomings but I wouldn't have done that to you. I never want to feel again what I felt when that man in Boston handed me your letter. So maybe I could forgive you—I'm not even sure what that means—and we could be together, the three of us, for years and years, but I'd always be afraid that one day you'd nail your clothes to the floor and disappear again. Or take poison."

She had been listening intently, hoping for a chink of light. Now—what did he mean about poison?—she prepared herself to answer, to swear she'd never, ever do anything like this again. But before she could speak, he rose to his feet and stood there looking at her across the small room.

"I would die if that happened," he said. "And that's not a metaphor." His eyes shone with unshed tears. "I think you'd better go."

She had been prepared to plead, to promise anything and everything, but as she looked into his face, his eyes almost the same color as the paint she was applying, his high smooth forehead with the delicate veins visible in each temple, words left her. This was not an argument or a debate or even a romantic quarrel. This was another person speaking to her from deep within the country of the self, offering her his painful hard-won knowledge. What use to say that life is change? Her own eyes filled. She set down the roller and turned away.

Outside, unbelievably, the sun was shining. A calico cat lolled on the pavement. People were coming and going in the street, talking and carrying groceries and books and small children. Several of them stared at her, and she could imagine the spectacle she presented, bulging out of her now paint-smeared coveralls, her face red with the effort not to cry. She put her hand on her belly. Only a few more weeks and she would have someone of her own, someone who would never leave her, at least not for a decade or so. She was at the corner of the street, wondering which way to turn— she had come by taxi—when she remembered Jigger's book.

She stopped irresolutely. She could ask Emmanuel to collect it for her. No, she thought, if this was the end, she wanted it to be the end, however bitter, however heartbreaking. She would go back and ask Zeke to drop the book off at the radio station and there would never be anything between them again. They would each continue to live in this large city as if the other did not exist. She walked determinedly up the street. She hadn't, in her despair, bothered to pull the outside door shut. Now she found it still ajar, wedged on a flyer for a new tandoori restaurant.

In the gloom of the hall someone was coming down the stairs.

"Verona," he said.

"I didn't come to bother you anymore," she said, speaking as quickly as she could, not daring to raise her eyes. "I just want my grandfather's book back. Ariel, Mrs. Barrow, said you found it at their house. Could you drop it off at the radio station? Emmanuel knows where it is."

As she spoke, the baby kicked with such urgency that she gasped. She clasped her belly. Not yet, she thought, you're not ready. Please, wait a few more weeks.

Then a hand appeared beside hers, pressing gently against her hard flesh.

"Verona," Zeke said again. "I'll try."

Acknowledgments

I'm grateful to those who talked to me, both professionally and personally, about their experiences with Asperger's syndrome.

The MacDowell Artists' Colony gave me time and space: my gratitude to this splendid institution.

I would like to thank my wonderful editor, Jennifer Barth, for her fierce engagement with this novel and her many indispensable comments. My thanks are also due to her assistant, Sam Douglas, and to the many others at Henry Holt who've supported this novel, among them George Hodgman, Richard Rhorer, Maggie Richards, Annsley Rosner, Kenn Russell, Elizabeth Shreve, and John Sterling.

Once again I want to thank my remarkable agent, Amanda Urban, for her help and guidance.

And happily, as always, I am deeply indebted to Andrea Barrett, who kept me company in every sentence.